Praise for Kerryn Mayne

JOY MOODY IS OUT OF TIME

"This book is incredible! Kerryn Mayne takes us on a roller coaster ride of motherhood in the suburbs. As uplifting as it is dark, *Joy Moody Is Out of Time* will knock your socks off." SALLY HEPWORTH

"Utterly original. An engrossing tale of lies and secrets that will keep you guessing to the very end." AMANDA HAMPSON

"Mayne combines her signature dark humor with insightful observations about what it means to be a mother, to create a page-turning suspense that will have readers guessing to the very last page." LISA IRELAND

"Mayne's skillful storytelling and brilliant characterization will take readers on an unforgettable journey—a must-read for fans of Liane Moriarty and Sally Hepworth." KELLY RIMMER

"Unique and quirky, this is a charming who-done-what mystery with a cast of original characters." SARAH BAILEY

"Highly entertaining and with an incredibly unique premise, Kerryn Mayne has done it again—crafted a witty, gripping read with characters like no other." HOLLY CRAIG

"If you google 'beautifully crafted, enigmatic characters with too many secrets for one person to possibly keep,' Joy Moody will pop up, right next to Lenny Marks. Kerryn's blend of humor, suspense, and an insider's knowledge of crime (as a police officer, not a perpetrator) saw me reading at three o'clock in the morning. This is a gem of a novel." MICHAEL THOMPSON

"Mayne seamlessly navigates the delicate space between humor and tragedy in this riveting family tale meets cracking crime mystery. Clear your afternoon—you won't be able to put it down."
ELIZABETH COLEMAN

"Please read my book: I have lots of kids to support." KERRYN MAYNE

LENNY MARKS GETS AWAY WITH MURDER

"A contagious blend of light-hearted moments and dark action; it's hard to believe this is a debut . . . Kerryn Mayne is just at the start of a long career." *The Weekend Australian*

"Brilliantly imagined . . . it's the characters who make this book, each with a uniquely layered backstory that fits into the plot like a well-oiled machine." *Herald Sun* (five stars)

"Such a brilliant combination of light and dark, charm and suspense. A debut you won't forget!" CANDICE FOX

"Devilishly fun: top marks for Lenny Marks!" BENJAMIN STEVENSON

"Kerryn Mayne makes a very grand entrance into the Australian literary scene. With humor, heart, and characters you come to love, this is a book you will devour and keep thinking about later!"
SALLY HEPWORTH

"An incredible debut, which will have you both laughing and crying."
PETRONELLA McGOVERN

"Both heart-warming and heartbreaking . . . the unforgettable voice of Lenny." *Good Reading*

JOY MOODY

IS OUT

OF TIME

KERRYN MAYNE

ST. MARTIN'S PRESS
NEW YORK

First published in the United States by St. Martin's Press, an imprint of
St. Martin's Publishing Group

JOY MOODY IS OUT OF TIME. Copyright © 2025 by Kerryn Mayne. All rights reserved.
Printed in the United States of America. For information, address
St. Martin's Publishing Group, 120 Broadway, New York, NY 10271.

www.stmartins.com

The Library of Congress Cataloging-in-Publication Data is available upon request.

ISBN 978-1-250-34050-4 (hardcover)
ISBN 978-1-250-34051-1 (ebook)

Our books may be purchased in bulk for promotional, educational, or business use.
Please contact your local bookseller or the Macmillan Corporate and Premium Sales
Department at 1-800-221-7945, extension 5442, or by email at
MacmillanSpecialMarkets@macmillan.com.

Originally published in Australia by Bantam, an imprint of
Penguin Random House Australia

First U.S. Edition: 2025

10 9 8 7 6 5 4 3 2 1

For Gary
It was never about your arms xx

JOY
MOODY
IS OUT
OF TIME

PROLOGUE

JOY

August 1, 2023

4:34 p.m.

There were only five minutes left for Joy Moody and her twin daughters. They were ready, and expecting, to be gone at 4:39 p.m. exactly, and Joy was nothing if not exact. It was the first of August and she had long been preparing Cassie and Andie for this moment: their twenty-first birthday and their return to 2050.

Time seemed to pass in an excruciatingly slow manner, but it was the same slow, steady beat that it had always been, of course. They could rely on something as orderly and consistent as time. Unlike Joy's memory, which was now neither of those things. Her deceit had fused into truth, and she was about to realize what Andie had figured out weeks ago—they were going nowhere. There would be no trip through time; they would remain in the small courtyard, under the peppercorn tree, behind the building that was both their home and livelihood.

Four minutes remaining. The supermoon would rise soon, but not before Joy's agitation launched into overdrive. She had felt re-markably calm as she and the girls sat on the weathered wooden bench as their final minutes in that time and place drew to a close.

Now that calmness was long gone. She bit down hard on her lip to try to retain her composure.

Three minutes left.

4:37 p.m.

4:38 p.m. Donna watched them from the top of the fence, her feline contempt obvious, as if she already knew Joy was a fool.

4:39 p.m.

Joy feared she was at risk of passing out if she didn't remember to breathe. She sucked in huge gulps of air and checked the girls either side of where she sat. Her arms were tightly linked through theirs so there was no risk of one going without the others. The nearness was a comfort, despite her angst.

Cassie had scrunched her eyes closed, leaned against her mother's shoulder, and was coiled in readiness. Andie, however, was staring right back at her, a look on her face similar to the cat's. Andie had been a mess all day, ranting about the impossibility of time travel and a father she was sure she had found in the here and now. She was a stubborn girl when she wanted to be, just like Joy herself. Something Joy could hardly resent her for, given she was probably the reason Andie had learned such an inflexible attitude.

4:40 p.m. Joy checked her watch, scanned the sky, and muttered about unreliability being quite intolerable.

They waited some more, the minutes excruciatingly long.

4:48 p.m.

4:49 p.m.

At 4:50 p.m. Joy stood, leaving a mother-sized gap on the bench between her daughters. As if to really drive home the point that they were nowhere new, Joy caught a waft from their nearby trash can.

"We don't appear to have gone anywhere," Joy said through clenched teeth.

"No shit."

The obnoxiousness of Andie's words roiled Joy so quickly and thoroughly that she turned and slapped her across the face before she could give it a second thought. Cassie gasped, Andie cried out, and Joy pulled her hand back as if it had touched fire.

"I didn't mean that," she said quickly, but the damage was done. It was the first time she'd ever raised a hand to either of the girls. Her eyes blurred, both from tears and the tickle of a headache that was dogged in its pursuit of her. "Something's wrong," Joy insisted, shaking her head, hoping to avoid what she'd just done. "Maybe we're early? What's the time?"

Cassie shook her watch free from under her sweater. Andie kept a close eye on her mother, one hand pressed against the red mark ballooning across her cheek.

"Almost five." Cassie sounded apologetic.

What must the girls think of her? That she was going mad? Or just a downright liar? Joy inhaled deeply, almost painfully, and looked up, hoping to find the all-important supermoon they'd waited so patiently for.

It was nowhere to be seen. A moment of panic; maybe she *was* going mad.

"Where is it? Where's the moon?" she muttered. Neither daughter replied. Andie pulled a packet of Fruit Tingles from her jeans pocket and flicked one into her mouth, crunching down hard and loud, as if she was trying to irritate her mother.

Joy paced the yard, looking skyward. She hurried to the trunk of the hulking peppercorn that was too big for the space, a mistake far too deeply rooted in the ground by the time Joy had moved in. She peered into the spot she'd always used to communicate with the year 2050. A simple but effective system that kept them off the radar of The People. She put her hand in the gap, feeling for an envelope or a rolled piece of paper, but there was nothing. No explanation for the lateness, or rescheduling of plans, which had happened the year before so it was always a possibility.

Joy spun around, an errant branch scraping across her face, feeling like fingernails digging into her skin. She clapped her hand to her cheek and found it wet with blood. There was no time for that now; she could deal with a silly scratch later. The idea of time was suddenly very tenuous; they had so much of it, but simultaneously none at all.

Joy ran her fingers through her hair, scratched hard at her scalp, and looked at her daughters. "Something is not right, not right at all."

"You can say that again." Andie remained defiant, although she looked more sheepish now, and wary of her mother. Joy's fingers were still imprinted on her daughter's face. She felt like a monster.

"It's all right, Mum." That was Cassie, always so sweet, always ready to come to her defense. Joy saw the glance she gave her sister. She could usually read her girls like pages of a book, but this exchange wasn't clear, like it was from a story she'd never read. She'd been *so sure*. Now doubt was clawing at her mind. Was she wrong? *Had* she lied?

"No, no, no, no, no." Joy couldn't stop once she'd started; she tapped at her forehead. "No, no, no." Her headache turned from a niggle to a firecracker. She hated what was happening to her. The fence rattled as Donna leaped off it, down into Monty's yard on the other side. Even the cat was done with them.

Joy moved back to the peppercorn and put her hands on its trunk, wondering at everything this tree had seen in its years. It had seen her girls grow, had watched her kiss the only man she'd been with besides Arthur. It had seen what had happened to Britney.

Oh, good God, Britney! Joy had gone and told the police where to find her, thinking she was doing the right thing. But only because she was supposed to be long gone; the three of them were meant to be twenty-seven years from now and out of reach.

Joy readjusted the bag she had slung across her chest so the strap didn't rub on her neck. It was heavier than she'd expected, her life savings just about the only thing she thought warranted being carted through time. Apart from her girls, of course, but that was a given.

"I'm going to get Monty," Andie said. "He'll know what to do."

Joy ignored her; she was busy trying to work things out. She realized she was actually muttering aloud and wondered if Cassie and Andie had heard her talking about Britney. Would they realize what she meant? She was really making a mess of things. She'd been so careful, for so long, only to drop her bundle at the eleventh hour. If there was an eleventh hour. There was a chance, a sliver of suspicion creeping in, that this wasn't the end. But if it wasn't the end, she had no idea what that meant for her family. She supposed they'd just stay put and keep working in the laundromat and be of no significance. The Daughters of the Future Revolution would just remain her daughters. Nothing more, nothing less. Was that enough? Could Cassie and Andie forgive her? Things were not okay.

"I'll wait here," Cassie said, and Joy heard the back gate creak open as Andie hurried off.

Joy caught sight of the moon then. The illuminated orb usually had a calming influence on her, reminding her of her place, their size in the scheme of things. They were all just specks. Hands pressed firmly on the sturdy trunk, she carried on talking to no one in particular. "The supermoon is here now. We were in time. They need them. Right date. Right time. It was right. I checked it. The moon is up. Now. We are here." And then her voice dropped, so low it was almost imperceptible even to her own ears. "What have I done? *What have I done?*"

There would be no time travel, nor was it ever a possibility. This was one of the things Joy had meant to put right long ago, before she'd forgotten.

However, something she'd told the girls *would* come to fruition. She would be gone by the end of the day, just not in the manner she had expected.

Joy Moody would be dead by midnight.

PART ONE
LIFE IN A LAUNDROMAT

In visions of the dark night
I have dreamed of joy departed.
Edgar Allan Poe, "A Dream"

CHAPTER 1

JOY

July 4, 2023
Four weeks until the twins turn twenty-one

It was always busier in the cold months at Joyful Suds, Bonbeach's premier laundromat. Joy Moody, proud owner and operator, hadn't sat down all morning.

"These will be ready for collection between 3 and 6 p.m.," Joy told Brett Carmichael, a regular. She had never thought much of Brett; he always looked at her like she was an appetizer, and she did not appreciate that. But she would prefer she serve him and his hungry eyes rather than one of her daughters having to. If he found Joy attractive, then he must have been positively gobsmacked at the sight of Cassie and Andie.

Joy had once thought herself somewhat beautiful, but these days she considered herself more utilitarian than eye-catching. While she still maintained her hair and nails, always had her eyebrows and top lip waxed, she didn't make time for make-up or anything she deemed showy. Perhaps that was right up Brett's alley, or maybe he was just not that fussy. She was long and lean and always had been, not shapely like her daughters, who glowed with youthfulness and purpose and in summer tanned in a way she never had. It was obvious to her that they weren't her biological children, although she considered herself their mother in every other conceivable way.

She didn't find Brett's gaze flattering in the least. At fifty-six she was still angry at most men and would happily punch him on the chin. But that was unprofessional, and Joy Moody would do just about anything to avoid being considered unprofessional.

"Have a joyful day." She smiled as Brett took his receipt, giving her a final up-and-down glance before leaving.

Out the front window, a Melbourne-bound train trundled past and Joy watched it go. The tracks ran all the way to the city, like veins shuttling blood back to a heart. The Moodys never went that far afield, nor did they use the train. But the noises—the crossing bells, the trains' horns—were comforting reminders of home. Across the tracks and double-lane highway were more houses and, behind those, the beach. Her beach, as Joy thought of it. They lived close enough to the ocean that on still nights, Joy would lie in bed and hear the waves churning over on themselves.

The only other customer in the shop was Hal, using the free washing machine. Hal had come and gone from the laundromat almost as long as Joy had run it, just over two decades now. Machine number six was exclusively for the use of those between permanent abodes. Hal was a kind-eyed, older gentleman who reminded her of driftwood, in that he was so intricately weathered he was quite striking. He had barely uttered a word to her in all his visits and certainly never looked at her the way Brett Carmichael did. She knew his name because Cassie had told her. Cassie had that way about her; people just wanted to tell her things and she absorbed it all like a Chux dishcloth. Joy had always had to keep extra watch over Cassiopeia.

Today, Joy had made Hal a coffee, which she delivered quietly, along with a muesli bar from the vending machine. She had tried to give him a fiver a few times—she did that quite often with the people using Britney's washer, as she had always privately called machine number six—but Hal had made it clear that was one step too far. He would leave it tucked somewhere at the register for her to find later. He didn't want her money, though he would happily accept the free spin cycle and a cup of coffee.

"Thanks, miss," Hal mumbled, taking the coffee and snack.

Most took Joy's demeanor as brusque, sometimes to the point of dismissive. In the one hundred and fifty-two Google reviews the laundromat had received in its existence, just one wasn't a five-star rating. And that two-star review still bothered Joy. The customer in question had taken her abruptness as outright rudeness and reviewed her accordingly. Later, when he'd unpacked his jumbo bag of washing and realized it had never been cleaner or softer, he'd wanted to take it back. But it was too late. His review was committed to the annals of internet history.

Joy disappeared through the in-between and back to the house. The three Moody women occupied the residence attached to Joyful Suds. It was one of four two-story townhouses in a tidy row, pushed up tight like Lego blocks. They shared a common wall with Monty Doyle, locksmith, who shared one with Linh Tran, tattooist, and she shared one with Ellen Scott, lawyer, who made Joy look like a ray of sunshine. The laundromat had the distinct advantage of its own parking lot, which the neighboring shops argued should be for general use. Joy disagreed entirely and had signage made clearly denoting the lot was for "Joyful Suds Customers Only."

Their home was modest in size and required the twins to share a bedroom on the second floor, but it served them well. Besides, Joy thought the girls would share a room even if they had the chance to sleep separately, not that she'd ever asked. The townhouse was dated now and lacked natural light, but it was paid off in full, an inheritance from Joy's father. He'd been a savvy businessman, but an insecure father, having never recovered after being widowed in his thirties. Joy had been three and her brother, Grant, six when their mum had died. A week after the funeral, a rotund housekeeper, Hazel, arrived. Their father went back to work, his days stretching longer than ever, and they just got on with it. Her mother was relegated to photographs on the wall, becoming less and less like a person who had ever existed in real life and more like a character in a story. Joy had been just a toddler, after all, and could only assume now that any recollections of her mum were really just memories of Hazel.

Cassie and Andie were eating breakfast at the table. Cassie was sketching the box of Cheerios in one of her notebooks and Andie was reading something; she was often nose-deep in a novel. It was probably an Agatha Christie, which Joy didn't mind her reading now that she was twenty. She'd been worried about Andie diving into the crime genre and finding out the terrible things people did to one another, but the general fiction section had become awfully lustful, and murder and mayhem seemed preferable to that. It was easier vetting her daughters' reading material when they were younger, when the books tackled topics Joy felt comfortable having her children read. It was up to her to keep them safe, and that meant both in body and mind. The girls didn't need to be unnecessarily distracted by trivialities.

The laundromat was born out of necessity when she realized her employment choices were limited with twin newborns, no husband, and a lack of official paperwork for the girls. She grew it from an empty shell, painting the walls pink (her favorite color) and laying the checkerboard floor herself, while her daughters slept in rockers in the house behind the shop. She was more than a little proud of herself and what she'd created at 225 Station Street, both a home and a living for her little family.

Joy looked at her girls and smiled to herself. So little time left, she thought, but she couldn't dwell on that. She crossed the room to the kitchen, picked up a black marker, and struck another day off the calendar. Open plan was too generous a term for their living space, but it wasn't entirely inaccurate. The kitchen flowed into the dining area, which also housed her desk and a bookshelf. And then the couch and her armchair formed the lounge nook. The three Moody women together could stand hand in hand and reach from one side of the house to the other. *Home* was what came to mind when Joy looked around.

"Four weeks to go," Joy said, trying to remain upbeat but feeling the gaping hollowness that came every time she considered her world in four weeks and one day, when her girls had left her. They would be gone, twenty-seven years into the future, to the year they were born. She had done the math and knew that she would turn eighty-three in 2050. This was not only a grand old age, but one she couldn't fathom reaching, not without Cassie and Andie beside her. And also on account of the brain tumor she was playing host to, which was no longer allowing her to ignore its presence.

Joy took two Panadol and gulped some water. She didn't want to use the more heavy-duty painkillers that the doctor had prescribed for two main reasons: outright denial and because the twins knew nothing about her condition.

Andie was watching her. Andie always seemed to be watching.

Joy's body ached with tiredness, and it was only 9 a.m.

CHAPTER 2
CASSIE

July 11, 2023
Three weeks remaining

The pace and vigor with which Cassiopeia Moody folded laundry was quite a spectacle. Customers had been known to watch her as they waited for their clothes to finish in the dryer or even stay a few extra minutes after they were done. It didn't hurt that Cassie was rather nice to look at, a vision in her pink Joyful Suds polo shirt, which did nothing to flatter her figure although the color did complement her light olive skin tone. She was the quieter of the twins and often didn't even register the audience, not like she did when she was not folding clothing (or sheets, or towels, or whatever it was that came her way). Then she was painfully aware of any attention, especially from the opposite sex.

She flicked out each garment like a bull whip and folded it quickly, precisely, the way she and Andie had been taught by their mother. It was the only acceptable way—efficient, professional, on time—and could be summed up in two words: Joy's way. Always Joy's way, though Cassie was happy to take instruction.

The door to Joyful Suds swung open, but Cassie was busy making sure the corners of a towel were tucked in neatly and didn't look up.

"The way you do that is like synchronized swimming." It was Shawn, the man who stocked the laundromat's vending machine, wheeling in a cart stacked with boxes. He visited them every three weeks but wasn't due until Monday. Joy wouldn't like that he had come early.

"It's not your usual day." Cassie checked the door behind her in case Joy had noticed Shawn's arrival. It connected the laundromat to their lounge room via a funny little thoroughfare that she and Andie had always called the "in-between." The door—with its "Staff Only" sign—remained closed. That didn't mean her mum wouldn't know, though; Joy often watched the CCTV. Cassie knew she did because she would say things she'd only know if she was keeping an eye on them, like "Julia can't use machine three for her dog bedding" or "Was Frank asking you for a discount again? He's got some cheek."

Cassie wasn't afraid of her mother—she loved her dearly. She just preferred to avoid irritating her. Both she and Andie had noticed how tired and forgetful Joy had been of late, and the last thing they wanted to do was add problems to her problems, whatever they might be.

"I go on holidays next week and I didn't want anyone else to visit my fave customer," Shawn explained.

"Oh, right. That seems really quite reasonable," Cassie replied, thinking that Joy was just as likely to be chagrined by a different person from Vin's Vending showing up on time as she would with the usual one coming early.

"So, how's things?" he asked.

"Fine, all fine," Cassie replied, beaming warmly. The words were her standard response, all part of good customer service, but it was not her standard smile. She liked to smile this way at Shawn, who made her feel wonderfully fizzy.

He returned the grin. He had a dimple in one cheek that was adorably unsymmetrical.

"And what are your holiday plans?" she asked.

"I'm heading to Bali with some mates. Should be pretty sick."

"Indonesia would be lovely."

"Have you been?"

"No. Not yet." And probably not ever, she thought. Cassie knew many things about Indonesia and other places (especially Antarctica—she was incredibly intrigued by all that ice), but the reality was she'd barely left the suburb.

Shawn moved the cart over to the vending machine in the corner. They'd had to remove one of the Speed Queens for it to fit, but it was a good investment; at least that's what Joy said. Cassie wouldn't know a good one from a bad one. The machine did have its perks, though: occasionally Cassie and Andie got to pick something as a treat. Cassie always went with E11: salted chips in a bright blue crinkly foil packet. She loved the way she would catch the taste of salt on her lips after she'd eaten them, sometimes hours later. Andie, on the other hand, was trying to sample every single thing in the machine. For two people who looked the same and had come from the exact same zygote (Cassie didn't love biology like Andie did, but their single-egg beginning fascinated her), they could not have been more different. Almost like they were the exact opposite of each other, rather than two halves of the same being.

Shawn whistled as he tore open a couple of boxes and started pulling out packets.

Cassie opened a washing bag on the table and began neatly stacking the folded garments into it.

"Hey," Shawn said from the open doorway of the machine. "So I was thinking and all, maybe sometime you and I could go out and get a drink or something?"

"Oh, well . . ." Cassie breathed out heavily, making a concentrated effort to fill her lungs.

"No pressure or anything, yeah? I just thought, you know, we get along and stuff. And I'd love to see you when I'm out of this polo shirt." He blushed and quickly clarified, "Not naked, I mean. I don't want you to see me naked . . . unless you were. I mean, ugh . . . I just meant, it could be fun."

His request was so delightfully awkward she couldn't help but smile, even though the thought of being naked with him, or anyone, was terrifying. Cassie wouldn't be going out with anyone, adorable dimple or not. To start with, the Moodys didn't drink—"That's a quick road to calamity," Joy would tell them whenever they passed Gordon's Tavern on their way to Woolworths. And the twins did not date. So there was really nothing she needed to think about. Still, she didn't want to say no to Shawn.

"Can I get back to you on that?" Cassie saw the look that crossed Shawn's face, clearly showing he thought she was just being polite and not saying no outright.

"Yeah, yeah, course." Shawn turned back to the machine.

Cassie started to say something else, wanting to let him know that if she could, she would definitely see him outside work. It just wasn't up to her. She was no ordinary girl in a laundromat waiting for a handsome guy with easy access to salted chips to sweep her off her feet.

In three weeks, Cassie and Andie would be twenty-one and they were set to be collected by their real parents and return with them to 2050 to help fight for the freedom of the world. They had been preparing for this since they were ten years old, and it surprised her how the thought of it still came with an involuntary shudder. She had tried hard to stamp on the doubt she felt about the unknown, but when she pictured the year 2050, she saw a barren wasteland where their home had once been. And in her dreams, which felt more real than she'd like to admit, she imagined reaching for Andie's hand and not being able to find it. A painful lurch of loss hit her every time she thought of this.

Her imaginings didn't align with what Joy had told them about the future. Things were much as they were now, she had assured them, although a different government was in power and their priorities were not for the safety of the citizens, only for global domination. That's where the twins came in and why Joy was so insistent on them excelling in their studies. Their battle would be fought largely with intelligence, not guns and bombs like the wars before them. It still terrified Cassie, though. She was clever—they both were—but what if that wasn't enough? She'd wanted to learn karate, or kung fu, or something that might help; she was sure it would be of use. After the twins had read *The Hunger Games*, Andie had convinced their mother to let them take archery lessons, just like Katniss. They'd barely slept the night before, and the drive four suburbs over felt like a trip to another planet; they never usually traveled so far afield. But it had gone terribly, Joy snatching them away only halfway through their lesson.

Cassie had no idea why; Joy wouldn't speak a word on the drive home. The twins could only assume The People, who were intent on hunting down the girls, had found them there. They'd never gone back, and Joy refused to enter into any further discussion about it. She told them it didn't matter anyway, because there was no physical fighting in the future, and they were better off saving their strength and energy for their homework. Knowledge was power, Joy said often, and she was probably right, but Cassie wanted the feeling of the bow in her hands again and the whoosh of the arrow as it shot past her toward the target.

Cassie quashed the thoughts of the future and the whirlpool in her belly. She was a Daughter of the Future Revolution and that was more important than any one person, or the inconsequentiality of a date.

As Shawn was leaving, he dropped a packet of chips on the table and nodded toward them. "I broke this one open by mistake, so I'll just leave them here. I think you like these ones, right?"

Cassie felt that breath-constricting tightness again as she nodded at Shawn, unable to muster quite the same smile she'd greeted him with. His leaving felt final. It would be one of many goodbyes she would face in the coming weeks, all the while not being able to explain exactly why.

"Well, I'm off. See you in a few weeks, yeah?" As he disappeared with his cart of snack boxes, Cassie felt tears start and tried to blink them back.

Having a secret destiny was sometimes a real drag.

CHAPTER 3

ANDIE

Andie pressed the swab hard against the inside of her cheek and rubbed firmly. She was determined to do this right; she didn't have time to mess it up.

Linh Tran was watching her closely. Andie was very fond of Linh and didn't want her to think she was weird or strange or anything like that. She just wanted Linh to like her back.

They were in the screened-off section of Lotus Tattoos, which had been the Bonnie Mini Mart, owned by a lovely Indian couple, before Linh set up her business there almost two years earlier. While the convenience of the mini mart was missed—it was one of the places Joy actually let the twins go alone, and Andie loved the easy access to Fruit Tingles—Andie was thrilled to have Linh in the neighborhood. It had come as a shock to them all to see a thirty-year-old woman running the newest business in the strip. Joy had prepared them for a burly, tattooed man who would arrive by motorcycle. Linh was nothing of the sort and Andie found herself immediately captivated by the new woman, her artwork literally worn on her sleeves. Every time Andie looked at her, she felt like she noticed something different: a blueish diamond tattooed on the back of Linh's left shoulder, a word swirled and scrolling across her collarbone, cherry blossoms dancing up her arms. Linh had caught her staring on more than one occasion, and while Andie played it off as merely being intrigued by Linh's tattoos, she was well aware it wasn't just the art that was capturing her attention.

Her mum, of course, had a great distrust of the new arrival, although Joy had seemed equally suspicious of Ram and Sangeeta when they'd run the mini mart. Andie knew Joy had very little time for anyone other than her two daughters. This was both lovely and completely suffocating.

"I think that's it." Andie reread the instructions on the History Mystery instruction pamphlet. "Do the swab, seal it, check the details. Return in prepaid envelope."

Linh kicked back in her tattooing chair, mobile phone in hand, and looked at Andie. "And you'll find out in a couple of weeks if you're the descendant of the king of England or something?" Linh's thumbs darted across her phone screen.

Andie did not have a phone and, despite not knowing how to use one, desperately wanted her own. "Exactly." Although it was not at all the reason behind her sudden rush to discover her ancestry.

Months ago, in the back of a magazine someone left in the laundromat, Andie had noticed an advertisement that piqued her interest: "Solve your past fast!" She hadn't spent much time looking at magazines since getting into trouble for harboring a couple of *Cosmopolitan*s as a teenager, but this called to her. It was exactly what she needed: to solve her past. Or possibly her future, if Joy was to be believed, and Andie was becoming increasingly convinced she should not put all her faith in what her mother had to say.

Andie had ripped the page from the magazine and stashed it deep in her pocket until she got the chance to hide it under the loose floorboard in their room. She hadn't dealt with it straightaway, because ordering and paying for something online was beyond her abilities and she hadn't been sure she had the guts to do it. She knew she was prone to a lot of talk and very little action. But Linh had unwittingly given her the motivation to do it—she knew very little of the twins' upbringing and nothing of their supposed future role—but it was during their conversations that Andie realized she was allowed to *ask questions*. Linh showed her it was okay to want something for herself, and Andie had come to believe there was more to life than obeying the word of Joy Moody.

Leaving it very much to the last minute, if Joy's timelines were anything to go by, Andie had ordered a DNA testing pack with Linh's help, and all she could do was hope the express service would get the results back before her twenty-first birthday. She was counting on the "fast" bit of the slogan being accurate and not just a convenient rhyme.

Now Linh picked up the pamphlet and scanned the step-by-step instructions. "It says you need to register your test online to get the results emailed."

"A bit of a problem there." Andie pursed her lips.

"You don't have an email, do you?" Linh did not seem surprised.

"No."

"Want me to make you one?" Linh waggled her phone at Andie.

Andie checked her watch. Joy had left with her handbag and car keys that morning, announcing she'd be back in an hour. Off to another undisclosed appointment, which were becoming more frequent of late. It had always been pretty much just the salon or the supermarket in the past, but now there were more personal errands than ever before, leaving the twins with Joy-free time they had rarely experienced. Andie didn't think it was as simple as their mother trusting them more. She presumed Joy was up to something.

Joy was never flippant about time frames; if she said an hour, she would be back within five minutes either side of that time and so Andie made sure she was too. She didn't want her burgeoning friendship with Linh to be scrutinized by her mother. It didn't matter that she was doing nothing wrong; a lifetime of experience had shown her that Joy would be unimpressed. The Moodys kept to themselves, and the twins certainly didn't do anything without Joy's express approval.

By Andie's count she had eighteen minutes left, thirteen if she wanted to err on the side of caution. "Okay, can you show me how?" she asked.

Linh nodded, slipped off her chair, and dropped down on the couch next to Andie. She was close enough for Andie to notice a subtle yet distracting scent radiating from Linh's skin—more than deodorant, but not as overpowering as a perfume. Was it possible Linh just smelled this way? Nervously, Andie popped a Fruit Tingle in her mouth, enjoying the sherbet zing on her tongue.

"Right, so you need a username. What are you thinking?" Linh asked.

"Username? I don't know."

"What's Andie short for? Andria?"

"Andromeda."

Linh tilted her head and gave an impressed sort of nod. "That's really cool."

Andie felt her cheeks turn crimson at the compliment. Of course, her name was nothing at all to do with her—it was her mum's choice—but it was so pathetically important that Linh liked her. She was the only thing Andie had solely and wholly for herself.

"Make it this." Linh's shoulder leaned into Andie's as she showed her the screen. Warmth seeped from her bare arm. It felt like electricity was passing between the two. "GalaxyGirl. What do you think?"

"Perfect." Andie actually didn't care what it was, just that Linh had picked it.

"Right then. You, my friend, are now the proud owner of an email address." Linh clapped her hands together. "Although how you don't have one already is beyond me. It's like you just arrived from another planet."

You're not far off, Andie thought. "Mum just doesn't like technology all that much," she said, wishing she could elaborate.

"Yeah, fair enough. It'll be the death of the human race, I'm sure. Or at least I think that every time I scroll through my socials." Linh laughed.

"That's pretty much what Mum says," Andie replied. And it was. Joy loved to wax lyrical about the twins' return to the future and the integral part they'd play in the Global Wars. This included all the ways in which technology was humanity's downfall. That life was being taken over by automated systems and that once those advancements fell into the wrong hands, the people were powerless. The government was a superpower and there was no way to stop them once they'd seized control. Humans had over-relied on computers and systems and didn't know a way without them. Joy would point at the stream of people outside, walking up or down the sidewalk with their eyes glued to their devices. "They have no idea," Joy would say, sighing, but now Andie wasn't sure it was the people outside the window with the problem.

She'd wondered over the years at some of the things that happened in their little house, not to mention the probability that two such important people were holed up in a pink laundromat. And now she saw flaws in Joy's stories that she hadn't really dwelled on before.

There was the time when they were thirteen and Joy came home with a mobile phone—necessary for the business and new CCTV, she'd claimed. Joy had told the twins for years that the gamma rays from technology would give away their location, but now she said it wouldn't be a problem if she kept the phone in an empty coffee jar wrapped in foil. Andie should've questioned that further.

Two years later, when she was feeling particularly bold, Andie had sent a letter to the future through the hole in the peppercorn tree, just as her mother said she did. She wanted to see if the postage system to the future worked—it was so rudimentary it beggared belief. For three days she checked each morning only to find the letter in the exact place she'd left it. The fourth day, she mentioned casually to her mum that she was sending mail to her parents in 2050, and the next morning it was gone. She was sure Joy was pulling the strings but just didn't know how to prove it.

Her evidence-gathering stalled after that, and there was no point enlisting her sister's help. Cassie was bound to believe their mum even in the face of incontrovertible proof. Then came their twentieth birthday, the year they were originally meant to return to the future. Since they'd turned ten, and Joy had told them of their significance, they'd worked toward their departure from Joyful Suds. And it was set in stone, or so Andie had been led to believe, that they would leave on their *twentieth* birthday. But when they woke up on that auspicious occasion, Joy announced the plans had changed, blaming a solar eclipse and a miscalculation in time. Were they really meant to believe the future could just be rescheduled?

Joy hadn't raised her children to be fools and so, as her mum and Cassie rejoiced in another year together, Andie was simmering. She wasn't about to keep blindly following her mother; she wanted to make her own decisions about their past and their future. She wanted her freedom and, more than anything, she wanted a way out. Every time Joy mentioned the twins being skyrocketed into 2050, Andie's belly ached with the thought of what awaited them in the future. She hadn't explored enough—or any—of the world she inhabited here and now, and she didn't want to leave it behind for one that sounded far worse, destiny or not.

"Can I look at your phone?" Andie asked.

Linh shrugged and handed it over, then got to her feet. She tinkered with her colorful pots of inks and checked the plug of her tattoo gun.

To Andie the phone felt like a portal to another world. She opened Safari, although she couldn't think of a thing to search for. She had no idea where to start.

"You and your sister intrigue me," Linh said.

"Why?" Andie asked, distracted by the screen.

"Identical twins. There's something very interesting about that."

"That's true, but it's just the way it's always been."

"Do you have a secret language?"

"No."

"Can't speak to each other telepathically?"

"I don't think so."

Linh laughed.

Andie loved that noise. It was on the tip of her tongue to tell her friend everything. She was sure Linh wasn't part of The People; Andie trusted her. She felt the words forming, ready to tell the truth, until the door to Lotus Tattoos swung open, letting in a flurry of cold air and a few deadened leaves, along with two women, giggling and talking a mile a minute.

Linh poked her head around the partition and said she'd be out in a second.

The moment was gone.

"I'll speak to you later." Andie straightened her pink polo shirt as she stood. "Thanks for your help."

Linh looked back at Andie, a silent "sorry" passing between them.

Andie would say nothing now and maybe not at all; the arrival of the two women had reminded her of reality and secrets and Joy's ire. If her mum was to be believed, it wasn't safe anywhere.

CHAPTER 4

JOY

Joy's head almost went through the roof of her car when Monty Doyle knocked on the passenger side window, jolting her awake. Damn him for finding her in the library parking lot, where she'd gone for fifty minutes of shut-eye. What was he even doing there? She'd never known Monty to be a reader.

As if she'd spoken out loud, Monty held up two hardbacks. "Just returning my books," he said.

She could wind down the window or at the very least acknowledge him politely, but she felt caught out and out of sorts and wanted to distance herself immediately.

"You okay?" he asked, his thick ginger eyebrows furrowed. He looked genuinely concerned, even behind the heavy mustache that disguised many of his facial expressions. She'd always found mustaches debonair, largely because of Tom Selleck, but also on account of her ex-husband, Arthur, despising them.

She looked at her still-smiling neighbor, then blinked long and hard against the midmorning sun, which was incredibly pleasant unless you were in your car with the windows wound up. Then it was a little stifling. She checked her watch. It had only been thirty minutes and she'd been in such a deep, restorative sleep, making this interruption all the more annoying.

"Yes, all's well. Thank you, Monty." She spoke loudly instead of opening the window, not wanting to invite any further conversation.

He started to reply, but Joy turned the key and the weathered silver VW jumped to life, humming gently. The car was a faithful old thing, much like she considered herself to be.

Monty still looked a little confused. She supposed she could give him a lift back to their respective shops—he didn't have a car of his own and must have either walked down or caught the train—but she didn't need to be back at the laundromat for twenty-five minutes and thought if she found another quiet spot, she might be able to sleep for at least twenty of those.

As the VW chugged toward the road, Joy checked her rear-view mirror and saw Monty standing with his hands very much in a "What the heck?" position. She hated to be rude, but she really needed the nap and none of the questions.

Anyone who knew anything about Joy—few and far between— were well aware she had an iron constitution and was a workhorse. These qualities were perhaps better suited to describing a cattle dog or a tractor, but Joy prided herself on being reliable and strong. Taking daytime naps was a weakness she didn't care to display, much less explain.

At first the tumor had hardly made a difference. The headaches were manageable; with basic painkillers, she could get on with her day. But in the past few weeks, just as the pamphlet the oncologist had given her suggested, Joy had become tired to the point of needing to sneak out for sleep-breaks. She didn't want the girls to worry about her. And she couldn't genuinely quell their concerns if they suspected their indefatigable mother was slowly grinding down, because, horrible as it was, that was the truth.

Joy, not yet sixty, was running out of steam. Her doctor—a man with wiry hair and wonky glasses—had told her the tumor was likely to be aggressive, making her think of the German shepherd who'd lived next door to her as a kid. He wouldn't talk about time frames, reluctant to commit to anything because it was "just too unpredictable," which angered Joy because she liked things to run on a schedule. As a medical professional, he should have been able to give her accurate, precise information.

After tearing up Thames Promenade, frantically scanning for a good, quiet place, Joy spotted the empty tennis club parking lot and pulled in. This time she gave herself a couple of inches of fresh air through her window, turned the car off, reclined the seat, and attempted sleep. It eluded her, but the headache that started to thrum did not.

It was the side effects and lack of guarantees that had turned her off the prospect of treatment. The more the doctor explained the road ahead, the more it sounded like guesswork. Instead of paying proper attention, Joy had become fixated on one of the oncologist's haphazard nose hairs, but she got the impression that something akin to "Doctor Alfred's Cure-All Snake Oil," peddled by a two-bit hustler, might have done just as good a job as the litany of drugs he suggested. In the end she'd thanked him for his time and bought a bottle of vodka on her way home, the word "glioblastoma" shooting around her mind like a pinball.

It wasn't the first time Joy had stuck her head in the sand about something significant. In fact, it was fair to say that Joy Moody tackled a number of life problems with this particular tactic. It hadn't necessarily worked any better on previous occasions, but she wasn't one to sit and dissect her choices. She generally thought of the future and not the past, unless she was cursing Arthur and his concubine, Nina (who had also been Joy's best friend). Sometimes she did like to sit and wallow in that episode.

Joy kept her eyes closed, failing to drift off but persisting none-
theless until her alarm sounded. The whole exhausting day still lay
before her and she decided maybe today she could be late back. She
could tell Cassie and Andie she'd been stuck in traffic or her appointment ran late. They would be okay for another thirty minutes.
She pressed snooze.

In three weeks, it wouldn't matter so much what happened to
her. By then the twins would be twenty-one and they'd head into
the future, where all her hard work raising them and nurturing
them would save the planet. She'd done so well.

Suddenly Joy's eyes flicked open and she stared at the gray carpet-
like roof of her car.

"No, Joy," she said. "They are not going anywhere. You need to
toughen up and tell them the truth."

The truth.

Joy scanned her brain for the particular snippet of information
she was looking for. She had been finding things more and more
overwhelming since hearing the doctor's big words about the atom
bomb growing in her skull. She forgot things, she mixed them up,
she got angry, and then emotional as well. In February, when she'd
realized the symptoms were persistent, she'd gone to the GP cautious but hopeful, wondering if there was a non-scary explanation
for the anger she didn't realize she was capable of, or the unusual
forgetfulness that had her mixing up customers' names, significant
dates, and where she'd put her keys, watch, phone. He'd sent her
off to the specialist, who confirmed her worst fears. Cancer. Tumor.
Terminal.

She'd gone from almost solving cryptic crosswords in her sleep
to being unable to complete a basic sudoku, forgetting that it was
numbers one to nine that filled the boxes and trying instead to insert
letters. Most of this she'd been able to keep hidden from Cassie and
Andie, but she sensed Andie had noticed things were amiss. Andie

had always been astute like that. It was one of the problems with having raised such remarkable daughters; they'd become smarter than her.

One of the things worrying her most of all was that she knew the stories she'd told Cassie and Andie about the future were just that—stories. Exciting and brilliant, but categorically *not the truth*.

She'd had to mine deeper into her memories than ever before to recall how the stories started and why. She meant to end it years ago, and now she needed to do it quickly while she still knew fact from fiction. She couldn't blame the brain tumor for everything; she had been lacking courage for many years, long before those cells started to turn bad. She could've and should've told them on their twentieth birthday. Instead she'd made up *more* lies to buy herself an extra year. One more year before she had to explain to her precious daughters that it was never meant to go this far. She couldn't have predicted how the year would unfold, that she would start to lose her grip on what was real and what was fantasy. She'd fed the twins the plot from her favorite books and had repeated it so many times, with such candor, that it had become *their* story. Joy was impossibly sorry, but thinking of a way to unpick the mess she'd made was exhausting and seemingly impossible.

The deception had almost come undone on more than one occasion, and sometimes she wished she'd let it. Once, she had taken the twins to a "try-it-out" day for archery when they'd decided they needed to shoot arrows like assassins in the future. Joy had conceded, since it didn't involve interacting with a team, but she hadn't expected her old boss to be there—apparently Leonie had been inspired by Geena Davis.

Leonie had gushed about the twins and fired questions like arrows: "How old are they? What school do they go to? Are you still living in Bonbeach? Should we catch up for a coffee? What's your phone number?" In hindsight, Joy realized they were fairly standard, polite topics of conversation for two people who had been fairly close as work colleagues, but she had panicked, thinking Leonie would blow down her flimsy house of cards. The last time they'd seen each other, Joy hadn't been pregnant and the dates just didn't add up.

Joy had manhandled both girls to the car and driven off, tires spinning in the gravel parking lot. They never went back and when the girls asked why, she told them the thing parents had long said to their kids when faced with too many questions: "Because I said so."

In the tennis parking lot, Joy practiced explanations for her lies. "I made it up to keep you safe." She spoke quietly, worried that someone passing by might hear her or that Monty would spring up again, though she knew his knees wouldn't have allowed him to hightail it to this parking lot in eight minutes.

She licked her lips and tried again. "I lied, girls, but I actually promised your mum I'd keep you safe. So that's what I did."

No, Joy thought, that sounded far too defensive. But she had to tell them something, because they'd be mighty disappointed on their birthday when there was no time travel and no heroes' destiny awaiting them. How would they feel to find out they were simply normal twins wearing matching pink polos in a cruddy bayside laundromat? She corrected herself; Joyful Suds was anything but cruddy.

Cassie and Andie were ten years old when the lie had begun.

"Why can't we go to school too, Mum?" Cassie had been staring out the front window of the laundromat, watching schoolkids drag their school-shoed feet along the train platform. The station was in clear view from the shop and they'd watched hundreds of trains come and go. It wasn't the first time this question had come up.

Andie was right beside her and jumped on the sentiment immediately, almost like she'd set Cassie up to broach the subject. "Yeah, we want to go to *normal* school."

"You can't, I've told you before," Joy said. "The best education is here with me."

"You mean you know more than all the teachers in all the schools?" Andie pointed at one of the clusters of schoolchildren.

Once upon a time Joy had gone down an internet rabbit hole looking for a way to get the girls' birth certificates on the black market so she could enrol them in school, but she'd found nothing of use other than stories about people being taken to court for falsifying documents. Joy just didn't have the sort of network to help her procure such things, and she couldn't risk getting herself arrested.

Aside from telling them the truth—which was just not a possibility then—she had no idea what to say. So she went with something she knew inside out and back to front. The books—a trilogy—that had brought her solace in the darkest of times.

"It's high time I told you where you came from," Joy said. "Come with me. I'll take you back to where it all began."

The twins sprang to their feet, sharing a conspiratorial look and barely containing their excitement as they followed her through the in-between. It was usually such a dull day-to-day existence in the laundromat; hardly anything happened that a ten-year-old would consider thrilling. But this story of babies mailed through rips in the fabric of time and left under peppercorn trees filled her daughters with delight. They drank it in like the first time they'd been allowed Fruit Cup Cordial. What kid, Joy thought, didn't want to be told they were more than just every other kid? She had dreamed about such things when she was younger, imagining that maybe her mum hadn't died at all but was a super-secret spy and had to leave her family to take on a dangerous government mission.

Outside the tennis club, Joy pressed her eyes closed again and felt the warmth of the mild July sun beating through the car windshield, warming her chest.

Her heartbeat began to slow. She fell into a comfortable, if short, sleep.

When her alarm went off, Joy was a million miles away from her plan to right things with the twins. A plan she had made just minutes ago. For now at least, Joy's ailing brain would fail to recognize any distinction between *The Fortis Trilogy* and the lives of her daughters, believing they were one and the same.

This wasn't the first time, nor would it be the last, that fact and fiction became indistinguishable. But this time, Joy had a brainwave. How had she never thought of it before? She would go with them! On the tail of the supermoon, on the first of August 2023, Joy Moody would travel through time with her twenty-one-year-old twins, the Daughters of the Future Revolution. The thought made her tingle with excitement.

Joy started the car and drove back to Joyful Suds, smiling at her own ingenuity. She didn't notice that she passed Monty Doyle walking along the sidewalk on her drive back, but she wouldn't have stopped even if she had.

CHAPTER 5
CASSIE

July 18, 2023
Two weeks remaining

The rain made it impossible for Cassie to take her chicken-loaf-and-lettuce sandwich to her usual spot on the beach, so she made an extra one and headed to Doyle's Locksmiths next door. Monty almost always had time for a round of chess and had never been known to knock back a free lunch.

While, for obvious reasons, it was paramount that the twins kept to themselves, Monty's had long been on the list of Joy-approved places they could go. It therefore went without saying that Monty was someone they could trust. Their neighbor, through chess, had taught her how to be patient and tactical. The game wasn't her mother's or Andie's forte; they both preferred heated bouts of Uno where the pace was rapid and the time commitment far less. But Cassie enjoyed the change of scenery, and more often than not, Monty's cat, Donna, would curl up on her lap, purring contentedly, while they played.

Donna seemed to remember Cassie saving her life; the bedraggled stray had been wedged between the fence and their shed, mewing sadly, her white fur drenched from the rain. The cat had caused innumerable scratches to Cassie's hands and arms as she'd been wrenched from her confines and brought inside to warm up and be wrung out.

Joy had been adamant that the cat could not stay with them and dashed off to the vet to have her returned to her owner. Andie and Cassie were not religious—it wasn't something that Joy included in the Suds high school homeschooling curriculum—but they'd prayed to a higher power to have Donna returned.

It sort of worked, because she came back, eventually, to Monty's, which was good enough for them. How Joy got him to agree to keep a stray cat, they'd never know. The novelty of a new pet wore off fairly quickly for Andie, who found Donna cantankerous at best, but the cat's presence regularly drove Cassie next door. A small wooden chess set was on the table one day and she'd checked it out, asking a number of questions about it. Perhaps that was exactly what Monty had had in mind, smiling as he asked if she wanted to have a go.

At Monty's there was a general sense of calm, plus the cat, chess, and as much instant coffee as she wanted. It didn't taste great, but drinking it made her feel like an adult. He even kept a cup just for her with a large "C" emblazoned on it.

Cassie made the coffees that day, letting Monty finish an order he was working on. She could hear the key duplicator grinding as she boiled the kettle in the house behind his shop. On his kitchen counter lay an array of plant cuttings, each cut end carefully wrapped in a sodden paper towel. Monty seemed to be endlessly propagating his orchids despite his garden already overflowing with them. He treated them as if they were pets. Cassie heard him over the fence, cooing to the plants in his greenhouse, talking to them as if they needed his voice to grow as much as they needed the perfect balance of soil and the right amount of light. Maybe they did.

Doyle's Locksmiths had an in-between just like Joyful Suds

did, although Monty hadn't bothered with a "Staff Only" sign. He clearly didn't have the problem the laundromat had with confused customers, looking for the bathroom. More than once, when Joy or the twins had left the in-between unlocked, someone had wandered through and appeared in their lounge room. It had been a little scary the first couple of times it happened; Cassie's propensity for the dramatic had made her think The People had tracked them down and were going to take one, or both, of them. But over time she'd stopped worrying quite so much, realizing people simply didn't read signs and liked to try door handles.

"I've only put one sugar in," she said now, placing two steaming mugs down next to the sandwiches. Monty's store, unlike the laundromat next door, was as messy as Joyful Suds was neat. The front counter was littered with metal grindings, handwritten receipts, and half-finished orders. Usually an old locking mechanism would be lying around, something Monty was tinkering with, fixing it up or pulling it apart, his can of trusty WD-40 always in reach. He was the one they brought things to when they needed them fixed. Occasionally, he was even put to work maintaining the Speed Queens in the laundromat. He could do many of the repairs for them and Cassie was his enthusiastic apprentice, watching closely, asking endless questions. It was how she'd learned to do some of the basic fixes herself.

Monty sipped from his mug. "I could probably do with the extra one today, if I'm honest."

Cassie considered him properly then. He looked pale, a little sickly. The fluorescent lights didn't help, but he certainly wasn't himself.

"I'll get your stuff," she said. "You don't look the best."

"Can't do much about that, I'm afraid—born that way." He laughed but didn't stop her from dashing back into his kitchen to get his glucose monitoring kit, along with the sugar bowl.

Donna mewed impatiently, as if beseeching Cassie to move faster; the cat was worried about Monty too.

"I'm coming, Don-Don."

Cassie took the little black case back to Monty, Donna at her feet. They hovered patiently while he pricked his finger and did all the usual things. This wasn't an uncommon occurrence during their visits; he was a little lax with his diabetes management and Joy often tutted about his poor diet and lack of exercise, telling Monty off, like he was a recalcitrant teenager. She said she didn't want to find him keeled over on his shop floor one day from his lack of self-control. Despite being quite outspoken, Joy never usually meddled in other people's business, but Monty and her mother had an interesting dynamic. Andie's theory was that they were secret lovers, but Cassie just couldn't see it happening. Their mother was not the romantic sort.

"Well?" Cassie asked, not bothering to look at the numbers on the display. They meant nothing to her; she could never remember what constituted a hyper or a hypo, just that sometimes he needed insulin to get him feeling back to normal.

"It's not so bad," he said and zipped his little kit back up. He pointed at his coffee cup, now with more sugar than coffee in it. "This'll fix me up." He took a long sip. Even when it was way too hot for Cassie, Monty seemed to be able to down his coffee without flinching.

She relaxed then and sat opposite him. Donna wove through her legs, now deeming it acceptable that Cassie touch her, and settled on her shoe, purring happily.

Their chess board was a modest size and had small magnetic pieces that Cassie liked to click together while she was mulling over her next move. The magnets had been handy for the times Donna had interrupted their games by launching herself on the table to ensure she was the center of attention.

Their games always began the same. Monty would play the black side and Cassie the white. Monty always sat facing the door to the shop. Their moves were thoughtful but quick, and they were well aware of one another's weaknesses.

She let Monty sit quietly for a few moments, sipping his sugar-laden coffee and slowly regaining some color. Eventually he nodded at Cassie, giving her the go-ahead. Cassie interwove her fingers, cracked her knuckles, and began. She liked a Scotch game opener and moved her first pawn from E4 to E5.

"How's your mum?" Monty asked a few moves later, his head bent over the chess board.

Cassie looked up at him. "Fine," she said. "Why?"

Monty exhaled audibly. "No reason." He stared intently at one of his pawns.

"Monty? What is it?"

He looked up, caught her eye, and paused a moment too long. It was only a flicker of time, but Cassie saw it for what it was: Monty was worried about her mother.

"Nothing, just haven't seen her all that much of late. She must be busy."

"The usual, I guess." Cassie had always been very protective of her mum, and it wasn't as if she could mention that Joy was likely preoccupied with thoughts of her daughters being sent into the future. But as she said it, Cassie realized that Joy wasn't keeping things as routine as she usually did. On one hand she still ran the laundromat with her inflexible sense of order and woke early for her ocean swims each and every morning. But at the same time, she was away from home more often, her emotions had become as unpredictable as rolling dice, and her memory had faltered on more than one occasion. The day before, Cassie had overheard Joy struggling to remember Kevin's name. Kevin had been a Joyful Suds regular for years, and forgetting who he was was like not knowing which way to flick the light switch, or that trash night was every Tuesday. Cassie had tried not to dwell on it. But it had bothered her at the time, and she would kick herself if she had been too self-centered to notice something important going on with her mother.

Cassie always tried to focus on the positives, although she'd fallen a bit short lately. The thought of leaving Joyful Suds and her mum kept her awake at night. She'd always believed the sacrifice would be worth it—she would be a hero! But that had been when it was years away. Now she was close enough to feel the ragged breath of destiny, and she wished it weren't her and Andie who had to lose everything. She was actually—and secretly—more than happy to stay at 225 Station Street, Bonbeach, with her mum and Andie, and Monty next door and Donna giving her sporadic permission to cuddle her.

It was incredibly cowardly of her to think that way, though. If the Fortis Empire had already been formed (this wouldn't happen until 2041, sparking the '42 Wars), she would be one of the citizens they'd "reprogram" for having hostile views about the Empire. This meant certain death. The Empire monitored everyone's thoughts, or at least everyone who was microchipped, which was a requirement at birth. If parents didn't submit themselves and their children to being chipped, they would be cut off from everything: employment, government payments, holding bank accounts, or even shopping in the supermarkets. They were pushed out, to the edges of civilization. Citizens had taken to hiding rebellious friends in their basements and garages. But when thoughts were monitored, there was no hiding from the Fortis Empire, and the Programmers would make sure the traitor was no longer.

She wished she weren't an incredible bunch of atoms, like their mum always said. She'd prefer to be just an average bunch that got to stay put in Bonbeach, playing occasional games of chess.

The door opened, and Cassie spun around to see who it was.

"How can I help you there, son?" Monty asked the man who entered, his shirt tight across his chest, tie neatly knotted, and belt buckle polished. "Not a hair out of place," Joy would have said.

The man smiled widely with teeth so white they looked fake. "I'm hoping to speak to the owner. Would that be you, sir?"

Monty stood. "Yes, why's that?"

The broad smile broadened farther. "Ivan Kopek from Kopek and Hart Developments. We wanted to speak to you about an opportunity."

"No, thanks." Monty sat down again, looking back to the board. "Your go, Cass."

Cassie felt uncomfortable at the curt dismissal; she wasn't used to this sort of display from Monty. He nodded at her, urging her on. She slid her knight to take Monty's bishop.

"Nice move," Ivan said, and Cassie noticed Monty bristle.

Ivan continued. "We're speaking to all your neighbors. The market around here is going gangbusters. We do all the groundwork, no effort on your part whatsoever. All you have to do is find yourself a lovely new place with the bucket of money you'll get."

Cassie thought of Monty's tired, dark house and considered the lack of customers frequenting Doyle's Locksmiths. He could get himself somewhere brand new to live, with a huge backyard for his orchids. She wanted to tell him to consider it, that it wasn't the worst idea. But the thought of her mum being there alone made her stop. It was bad enough Joy would be saying goodbye to the twins, let alone Monty too.

Monty just sniffed. "There's more to life than money, young man, and one day you'll realize that."

"How about I just leave this here? You can give me a call if you have any questions or want to chat about the future." Ivan produced a business card as if it were a magic trick and dropped it on the counter, scattering some metal shavings.

Monty slid a pawn across the board, compromising one of his rooks. An amateur move, and not one Cassie would expect of Monty, meaning he was more bothered by the man's visit than he wanted to admit. Ivan, meanwhile, chirpily farewelled them both, as if it had been a pleasant visit and they'd all gotten along famously.

The door closed slowly and Monty watched to see where Ivan headed. "That's the third one this month. I feel like there's more developers than customers lately."

What would happen to her mother, Cassie wondered, if Monty wasn't around either?

"You'll keep an eye on her, won't you? After we're . . ." Cassie trailed off. "If for some reason Andie and I go away."

"Planning a trip, are you?" His thick eyebrows rose.

"Well." She scrambled to think of something, then remembered her chat with Shawn. "We are twenty-one in a couple of weeks, and we thought maybe we'd go to Bali."

"Oh, really." He sat back, surprised. "I mean, that's a great idea. I think travel is an excellent thing to do while you're still young." Monty paused. "You'd tell me if something was wrong, wouldn't you?"

"Yep." Cassie studied the chess board. She hated lying to Monty and knew if she met his gaze, she might tell him everything.

"Of course I'll keep an eye out," he said finally, as he tried to defend his remaining knight.

Cassie's shoulders relaxed and she found herself smiling. It made her feel better to think that once Andie and she were gone, Joy would still have someone.

CHAPTER 6

ANDIE

Dinnertime was always 6:30 p.m., always together, always at the table. Tonight Andie had made beef stroganoff and potato mash. She liked cooking more than Cassie did, but it was still a chore they shared between the three of them, as equally as seven days could be divided in thirds. Because of her affinity with cooking, Andie took the extra day, which meant Cassie got an extra day of dishes.

There was generally a rush (more like a steady trickle; laundromats didn't tend to have lines) of people arriving to collect their serviced wash orders between 5 and 6 p.m., but there was a strict 6:30 cutoff at Joyful Suds, so the Moodys could sit down to an uninterrupted family dinner. Even if they heard the counter bell ring, Joy would tut and hold up a hand to stop whichever one of the twins jumped up from their seat. They'd be forced to ignore it, an anomaly in Joy's usual mantra where professionalism and putting the customers first came above all else.

Andie's DNA sample was long gone in the mail, and she stopped by Linh's to check her email every chance she got, disappointed to find an empty mailbox each time. She wished she had sent it off earlier, but she couldn't change that now. She had her suspicions about what it might reveal, anyway. The twins had heard all about Arthur Tennant, Joy's first and only husband. He had done the "unthinkable"—that was Joy's description—which was to have sexual relations with Joy's ex-best friend, Nina. Joy never managed to say Nina's name without adding an insult before or after it, and Andie had always found it curious that Arthur didn't get the same treatment. Sometimes Joy even managed to sound wistful when she mentioned him. Surely it was at least half his fault?

They knew about Arthur and Nina because they came up regularly when Joy spoke on the topic of sexual education. She said it was important the girls knew the anatomical workings and the biological basis of reproduction and sexual intercourse. But Joy went to great lengths to emphasize the torment of entering into a relationship with another person. The anguish, even years after the affair, was still clearly haunting her. She couldn't impress upon them enough that men would follow their penises wherever they took them, making Andie think when she was younger that a penis worked like a magnet and was drawn to vaginas (which she assumed had some sort of magnetic pull) in a manner that the owner of the appendage was unable to control. By this logic, Joy shouldn't have been mad at Arthur or Nina at all; their bodies had just performed their intended functions. Later, through age and maturity, as well as the *Twilight* novels, Andie came to see that there was a bit more to it than what Joy had taught them. She wished she'd known earlier; she had been legitimately terrified of serving male customers for a good couple of months after the magnetic-sex talk.

That aside, Andie had a sneaking suspicion that she and Cassie might very well be Joy and Arthur's children. The timeline fit, and the twins didn't look dissimilar to the photographs they'd seen of Arthur from the wedding. In those, a pleated purple sash hugged his waist, and Joy had explained it was a cummerbund, which was a word that tickled Andie pink for some reason. Why Joy would lie about not being their actual mother was a complete mystery to Andie, but it made sense that Joy wouldn't want Arthur or his new wife to have any part in raising them. It was all part of her mother's tangled web that Andie was determined to untangle.

"Delicious, as always." Joy forked in a mouthful of stroganoff and chewed contentedly. "You're a whiz, Andromeda. What would we do without you?"

What *would* Joy do without her? Or them? Without overstating it, the twins were the anchor to Joy's boat. Andie couldn't imagine sticking around once the truth was out. It was impossible to think they'd still all live side by side as if nothing had happened. Andie was prepared to be vindicated; they weren't from the future and Joy might very well be their birth mother, but that didn't mean she was ready to just smile and get on with it as a happy little family. She was done being held hostage by her mother's every will and whim.

"Do you think I can take my sketchbook with me?" Cassie asked.

"To the future?" Joy clarified.

"Yeah. Do you think I can take it?"

"No, I'm afraid not. Just the absolute minimum."

"I'd give up something else to bring it," Cassie pressed. "Will I be able to get another one, once we get there?"

"I'm not sure. I would think so, don't you?" Joy sounded upbeat.

"If you don't know, how would we?" Andie was purposefully waspish.

Joy thought for a moment, eating her stroganoff and looking toward the ceiling as if a brilliant answer would fall from it. "We should probably decide what to take with us soon, though, shouldn't we?"

Andie noted the shift in the words Joy was using. Future talk had always been aimed at the twins, with the exclusion of Joy. But now she was sounding very much like it was a party-of-three sort of thing. That was unusual.

"Us? Why does it sound like you're including yourself in this?"

Joy smiled, straightened in her chair, and put her fork down. She held out both hands to the girls seated on either side of her at their well-worn dining table. Cassie dropped her cutlery immediately, putting her hand in her mother's. Andie considered her options, not particularly liking any of them, but decided to see where this was heading. She slipped her left hand into her mother's right.

"My girls." Joy's voice burst with possibility. "I've decided I'm coming with you." Joy beamed and Cassie squealed. "We are all going to 2050 together."

CHAPTER 7

JOY

July 19, 2023

Joy drafted agendas and took minutes for the Bonbeach Association of Traders, a grand name for what was really just the four owners of their little cluster of shops on Station Street. They met quarterly, though any of the members could call an extraordinary meeting if the need arose (it never did). They rarely all saw eye to eye, nor did they resolve much. Joy's parking signs were always a hot topic, which said a lot about the gravity of the issues in their pocket of Bonbeach.

Many meetings ago, the idea of a round-robin for roles had been raised: a different chairperson, a rotation of note-takers. But it was quickly dismissed, given Joy was reluctant to relinquish her tasks, believing herself to be the best equipped for them. Likewise, Ellen Scott just didn't seem to have it in her to take a back seat and had, by default, become their chairperson. That meant Monty and Linh could just show up and toss in their two cents as they wished.

Joy knew the accuracy of the minutes was all the better for her doing them. At least they had always been in the past, but when she went to type up the minutes after the previous meeting, she'd found some peculiarities. A shopping list was written under agenda item

four, and while Joy couldn't recall the details of what they'd discussed, she was quite sure it didn't involve bananas, tamari almonds,
English muffins, and AAA batteries. She'd listed Sangeeta, who'd run
the Bonnie Mini Mart with her husband, Ram, under "attendees"
and had to concentrate very hard to come up with the right name
for their current members. Sangeeta had moved out years earlier. It
did make her pause and wonder if she should go back to the doctor.
It was probably too late for that, though. She still struggled with the
idea the tumor was getting the better of her. It simply wasn't in Joy's
nature to admit defeat and she'd thought, with a ridiculous sort of
naivety, that she could ignore her cancer into submission.

This time around she went in to the meeting with a steely resolve to keep her focus sharp. They held the meetings at Ellen's,
because Ellen hadn't—to the best of anyone's knowledge—left her
building for six years. Besides, a laundromat was not the place for
a business meeting, and heaven forbid they should hold one in the
tattoo parlor.

It was the first time Joy had—albeit fleetingly—considered sending her apologies for the meeting, because what difference did it really make now that there were only two weeks to go? But it was the
sort of control Joy just couldn't relinquish. She made up twenty-five
percent of the quorum and was careful to take that responsibility
seriously. What if they voted to take down the "Joyful Suds Customers Only" signs in the parking lot in her absence? She certainly
wouldn't put it past Ellen to jump on that opportunity, and it didn't
matter whether she and the girls had left the neighborhood or not,
it was the principle of the matter.

They'd reached agenda item six: other business. A quick scan of
her notes indicated Joy had managed to stay on track and she quietly congratulated herself.

"I've been approached by a developer this week about selling,"
Linh said.

"Is it GM Enterprises?" Ellen asked.

"Or that shifty Igor chap? He was just far too nice," Monty said through gritted teeth.

"Ivan, was it?" Ellen's lips pursed as if she'd tasted something unpleasant.

"Ah, yes, that's the fellow."

Joy thought back to the last visit she'd had, only a week or so earlier. She tried to recall the name of the company, but it was eluding her.

"I don't know. It's the first one I've spoken to." Linh leaned back in one of Ellen's chairs and rubbed her fingers together. "They offered a lot of moolah."

Linh always managed to look relaxed. She was so cool and calm it was unsettling. The last time Joy remembered being that impassive about things, she'd been seventeen and high as a kite. Maybe that was Linh's secret—perhaps she could hit her up for some. Imagine that, Joy thought, rolling a joint with Linh in the lane behind the shops. What would her daughters think? Their straight-as-a-curtain-rod mother getting stoned. Little did they know that Joy's boyfriend, back when she was a happily experimental teen, had grown weed in the spare room of his share house. Danny used to name the varieties he'd grow after characters from *Star Trek*, which he loved to watch while completely baked. The McCoy wasn't so bad, but she'd had a pretty crazy experience on the Christopher Pike and had sworn off it from then on. It had turned out, once she stopped smoking with Danny, they didn't have much in common, nor did he have much to say, and the relationship quickly petered out. He was never meant to be a keeper anyway.

Arthur—on the other hand—was. Or at least gave the impression he was. In hindsight, Joy should've enjoyed Danny's company much more; he might have been away with the pixies a lot, but he was not shagging her best friend. He was also the one who introduced her to *The Fortis Trilogy* and she still had the copies he'd given her for her eighteenth birthday. She'd been surprised at his thoughtfulness, but later found out it was a set of books he'd been given and had rewrapped quickly when he realized he'd forgotten her birthday. Whatever the reason, she'd now read them more times than she could count.

"We've discussed this at previous meetings," Ellen said, the matter not up for discussion again. "You'll get me out of here in a coffin and not a moment before. Joy doesn't plan on leaving either. So there's not much point you or Monty selling up—they can hardly bulldoze through the middle while we're on either end."

Joy didn't appreciate Ellen answering on her behalf, though the sentiment was true enough.

"Well, I'm sixty-eight and I'm not planning on cutting keys forever. I don't want to see this old building go anywhere, but maybe we're getting to a point where we should think about it, see what they have to offer." Monty looked around the room. "I won't do anything unless we're all on the same page, though."

"You're sixty-seven," Joy said, not looking up from her notes.

He shrugged. "Potato, potahto. What do you think, ladies? I'm sure we could get a nice-sized place in that retirement community they've built where the old RV park was."

"Are you suggesting we'd all move together?" Ellen asked, clearly not a fan.

He shrugged. "If you like your neighbors, why not take them with you?"

Joy held back a smile; it was a lovely sentiment. Monty was wearing one of his endless array of flannelette shirts. Joy used to wonder if she'd recognize her neighbor if he wasn't dressed in one. Years back, she had solved this quandary; he was unmistakable, even without one of the shirts. She wasn't so convinced about the very average depiction of Ned Kelly tattooed on his right shoulder blade, and Monty had never revealed the story behind it. Despite maintaining a publicly surly attitude toward him most of the time, Joy was very fond of Monty.

"I mean, *I'm* not retiring," Linh said, swiveling left and right in her chair like a schoolchild, "but I can move Lotus just about anywhere. Especially for that sort of money. My customer base will come with me—I'll just update it on the socials."

"The socials." Ellen scoffed. "You can sell up when I die, I'll write that into my will. Put that in the minutes, Joy."

Joy put it in the minutes, but not because Ellen directed her to; it was the sort of thing that warranted recording.

"So in the next tornado, if a house falls on Ellen, we can all sell up and be millionaires," Linh deadpanned.

Joy couldn't completely suppress her laugh at that, and she saw Monty's eyes crinkle, the ends of his mustache flicking up in a barely concealed smile.

"Laugh all you like," Ellen replied snippily, "but this is the house my husband lived and died in. That's not something I'd be able to just *update on the socials*."

They all fell silent then, chastised for their lack of compassion. It was eight years ago that Joy had seen the dark-windowed undertaker's van in the back lane with a police car beside it. There had been no sirens, no flashing lights, all very quiet and strange. She remembered thinking with a panic that they'd come for Britney and hadn't breathed again until she saw their focus was Ellen's place. The relief had been palpable, though she felt selfish for having thought only of herself.

It must have been sudden. One day she'd watched Ellen's husband, Wesley, casually plucking the capeweed from the nature strip and then she'd never seen him again. Ellen had grieved privately. Her office didn't reopen for almost six months and Joy worried for her, watching her backyard from the top-floor window for any

signs of life. The mail was collected, the back gate clicked occasionally, and the back garden (Wes had been mad about his veggie patch) remained tended. Ellen herself, though, was like a ghost. Try as she might, Joy just couldn't spot her. As a person who had a robust respect for privacy, Joy didn't seek her out and quietly delivered dinners to Ellen's back door instead. It was no good having her neighbor die of starvation when home-cooked meals were being prepared just doors away, and she didn't want to ever see that little black van return. She'd package up the food in one of her Esky bags and take it to Ellen's back door, knock loudly, and then disappear quickly, only wanting to notify Ellen of the delivery, not to see or speak to her. The dishes would reappear on the bench in her backyard, washed and repacked neatly. They continued in this stealthy, silent dance for quite some time and had never discussed it in person, and Joy knew then that they were both cut from a similar cloth: the shut-up-and-get-on-with-it style.

If Ellen did leave the house, no one ever saw her do it.

"If that's all for 'other business,' then I think we are done," Joy said, breaking the silence, ready for the meeting to wrap up. She harbored the knowledge she wouldn't be at the next meeting, quibbling over petty matters. That thought was tinged with sadness; she would miss them all, even their trivialities.

She waited for Ellen to broach the parking lot signs, but she didn't, maybe in solidarity over the developer issue. Joy not selling up made it easier for Ellen to stand her ground. Of course, Joy couldn't have anyone nosing around in her backyard. She'd kept secrets too long for them to be disturbed just yet. And she wouldn't tell this bunch that it wasn't only the developers who were bothering her of late; her brother had resurfaced. Grant was looking for a way to shake some money out of the property, *her* home. When Grant and Joy had inherited their father's estate, it was to be split evenly, though nothing specific was mentioned in his will regarding who got what. It had been Grant's idea—"It's just common sense," he'd said—to take one property each. Grant chose the newer building in Mulgrave, already occupied by a restaurant that had taken up a five-year lease, and she didn't haggle with him, happy enough to take the empty shop on Station Street. The proximity to the beach was its main drawcard, perhaps its only one. It was hard to rent out in the state it was in, old and unkempt. Cold in winter, hot in summer, drafty all the time, with an overgrown backyard and shuddering pipes. But with Arthur's and Joy's combined income and no mortgage, it didn't matter that it sat empty. And thank goodness it had, or where would she have gone?

Joy used the end of her pen to massage her temple, her headache causing just minor discomfort today. Nothing like the heavy metal concert of last night. She'd succumbed and had an Endone, which had made her feel spaced-out and nauseous. Admittedly, though, it had knocked the top off her headache, and she understood why some people became full-blown drug addicts. She had plenty of the strong drugs; she filled the scripts every time her GP had offered them, even though she wasn't taking many of them. This had created a nice little stockpile, which was handy since she wasn't planning on returning to that GP, and certainly not to her oncologist. She had a sneaking suspicion they had both been infiltrated by The People. They had too many questions about things beyond her medical condition. Did she have help at home? What was her support network like? Would it be helpful to bring her daughters along so they could all be part of a round-table discussion about Joy's treatment and health?

Nice try, Doc, she thought now. He was either luring her away from the girls or getting her to bring them right to his door. Joy Phyllis Moody would not be so easily fooled.

"At the next meeting we will have to discuss the insurance and the guttering along the back—it's rusted right through," Ellen said, bringing Joy's attention back to the present. "We should consider a special levy for it so it doesn't have to be a large lump sum."

"Why would we replace it if they're just gonna tear our block down anyway?" Linh spoke while scrolling through her phone, which summed up Joy's impression of the younger generation. She had come to assume most of them just didn't know better. Her daughters were much better mannered, not that they had phones to bury their noses in anyway.

Ellen grunted, but Monty spoke up, always the peacekeeper. "If Linh decides to sell up, then so be it. Everyone has their price, and you've got to look after yourself. We will all be fine."

"Well, we don't all have the luxury of being nomadic artists." Ellen's tone was caustic.

Linh looked up, narrowing her gaze. It was the least calm Joy had seen her. Linh's past was her own business, and Joy thought it was unnecessary for Ellen to bring it up in this manner. She herself had googled their young neighbor when she'd first arrived, at Ellen's prompting. "Linh Tran, youngest ever recipient of Artemis Prize, disappears." The article detailed that midway through a prestigious luncheon, Linh had stood up and left and not been seen for seven years, before resurfacing as a bayside tattooist. The prize artwork was to be bid on at auction—the starting price was eye-watering—but it had disappeared in a puff of smoke along with its creator. Joy understood the need to keep things private and she allowed Linh the courtesy to do the same. It was unlikely, though, that she and Linh had the same reason for not divulging their pasts.

"Did you get that, Joy?" Ellen asked.

Joy looked at her notes and shook her head. "No, I didn't."

Ellen spoke slowly, patronizingly. "Meeting concluded, 11:15 a.m."

"Right-o then, 'Concluded.'" Joy scribbled the time at the bottom of her page, caring very little about whether she'd be able to decipher it later. She was not planning to type the notes up.

Monty and Linh said their goodbyes and bustled out of the office, the crisp air from outside bursting in to mingle with the stuffiness inside.

Joy gathered her pencil case and closed her notebook. "Have you got a minute, Ellen? I need some advice, if you will?"

"Pun intended?" Ellen asked. "I specialize in wills, after all."

"Oh, yes. I see. Well, it is will-related, I guess. I was wondering what rights someone would have to an inherited property after the estate had been settled."

"How long?"

"Twenty-five years."

Ellen chortled. "Not a snowball's chance in hell."

That alone made Joy feel a bit better. Grant had been adamant that he had a rightful claim to part of the property at 225 Station Street. He'd had to sell up his Mulgrave property to pay out a bad investment a decade earlier. It had been worth a decent amount, but it paled in comparison to what the land Joyful Suds occupied was now worth. Joy knew that Grant must have been in financial dire straits to seek her out. It was the only reason he usually bothered to talk to her. How he'd decided he was entitled to a slice of her inheritance and hard work was beyond her, but she wasn't so silly to think things with Grant would resolve easily.

She'd told him he was being ludicrous but had fretted about it since. What if he did have a lawful claim? Grant had even been so kind as to offer that she could pay him in installments so she didn't have to hand over one lump sum.

"And what sort of claim would that person have if, say, I wasn't here anymore?" Joy was imagining the laundromat standing empty and unclaimed. Of her and the twins in 2050 and Grant sniffing around whatever he could get his grubby mitts on. She knew she shouldn't begrudge her brother in quite such a fashion, but she also knew he'd just fritter the money away, like everything else he'd lost over the years. Two marriages, numerous businesses. He'd filed for bankruptcy years ago and had left a number of investors high and dry. He wasn't only a terrible businessman, he was also unscrupulous. The worst combination.

"Are you in trouble?" Ellen asked.

"Oh, no. Not at all."

"Is it your ex-husband? Has something happened?"

"It's got nothing to do with Arthur." Joy had trouble meeting Ellen's fixed stare.

"You *do* have a will, don't you?" Ellen eyed her carefully.

"Yes, of course."

And she did. It left everything to her daughters, with her brother listed as the next in line because, at the time she wrote it, he was a better option than leaving that section blank. Not that she could have ever predicted a scenario where her children wouldn't be around to receive their rightful inheritance. But given that was now the case, she'd decided to leave everything to Monty. Aside from her girls, he was as close as it came to family.

"Does it include all your wishes, as well as instructions about your estate?" Ellen pressed.

"I made sure it was quite precise." Joy wanted to ask Ellen to draft a new will, but the words were caught behind her teeth and she knew she'd not be able to get them out. She'd have to find another way to get it done. She'd sooner show up at a BAT meeting in her underwear than have Ellen draw up a new will for her. There was no doubt Ellen would do an excellent job of it, but Joy knew she'd feel turned inside out explaining her personal circumstances to someone she knew. And she could only imagine what Ellen would think of her excluding the girls in place of Montgomery Doyle. It wasn't as if Joy could explain their impending departure. Telling Ellen would generate questions Joy was not prepared to answer. And the last thing she wanted was for Monty to have to fight it out with Grant after they were gone; she had no doubt her brother knew enough shifty lawyer types to help pull some strings.

Ellen murmured, "Yes, I suppose you would." The lawyer sat back in her chair. "Is everything okay, Joy?"

Joy clenched her notebook in her hands. Embarrassingly, she felt the urge to cry. She was getting sick of the unpredictability of her emotions. "Fine, thank you."

"Well, you know where I am if you need anything. I am happy to look over your most recent will or amend it so you can include— or preclude—someone from it if that is relevant."

"I appreciate that, but it's not necessary."

The words fell between them in a little swirl. She imagined the conversation they'd have if either of them dropped their defenses for long enough. About the crushing loneliness of losing their respective husbands, albeit in very different ways, or the pressure of always being the decision maker, the one in charge.

Ellen furrowed her brow and thrummed her nails on the desk. "Well, whatever you do, don't use one of those cheap homemade will kits—they're a downright embarrassment to the profession. I am right here, ready and able to help. I can have it drawn up, your instructions as pointed as a saber, in no time."

Ellen couldn't have realized she'd just given Joy the perfect way to appoint a new benefactor while avoiding her scrutiny. Joy would pick up a will kit at the post office the following day; she was quite sure it would do the job just as well as Ellen could, despite her misgivings.

"I better get back," Joy said instead. "Thank you again."

She would miss Ellen. They were so alike in many ways: loyal, dependable, and tough as bloody nails.

CHAPTER 8

CASSIE

July 25, 2023
One week remaining

When lunchtime arrived and there was no rain in sight, Cassie took the opportunity to eat her ham-and-cheese sandwich on the wooden ramp of beach hut number 149. It wasn't the prettiest, or even the neatest, of the little beach huts that lined the foreshore at Bonbeach, but there was something whimsical about the green-and-blue clapboards that drew Cassie to it. It was set just far enough back in the dunes to be a little bit private, and was not one anyone thought to stop and take a picture in front of; there were plenty of brighter options for Insta-perfect backdrops.

Unbeknown to Cassie, this was also the exact spot her birth mother had sought refuge many years ago, when she couldn't return to her own home. A little awning, jutting out from the pitched white roof, had given just enough cover to protect her and her sleeping bag from overnight rain. It was an average place to try to sleep, but a lovely one to sit and watch the waves on a mild winter day.

Mid-sandwich, Cassie became distracted by a dead possum lying in the sand. It still looked perfect, as if it had just dropped dead on a trip to the beach. There was something peaceful about it lying there; she didn't find it disgusting or sad, just another part of life. There was no death without life and no life without death.

She immediately set about sketching the possum, detailing the subtle changes in the color of its fur. The soft scraping noises her pencil made against the paper were always pleasant to her ears.

She had drawn almost everyone she had ever met. Usually from memory, because most people were put off by having her watch them so intently with a pencil in her hand, apart from Andie and Joy, who barely registered her doing it anymore. When she met someone, she would attempt to remember as many things about their face as possible, squirrelling the information away until she was able to purge it onto paper. It had never occurred to her that she was trying to capture every facet of life for any other reason than because she liked drawing. But as the time to leave drew closer, and her stomach wound tighter with the very thought of it, Cassie realized her recall of people, places, and things was almost the only thing that soothed her. Not the assurances of her mother, or the knowledge of a greater purpose. Only pencil on paper made her shoulders unfurl and her tummy settle.

Cassie knew she didn't want to leave home. She also knew the fate of the free world was bigger than one person and that Joy wouldn't tolerate her refusal to go, would tell her it was not befitting one of the Daughters of the Future Revolution. And Joy would be right, of course.

The year before, with just a fortnight to go before their return to the future, Cassie had found herself unable to eat and racked with stomachaches that wouldn't settle. Anxiety had gripped her in its sharp claws until the day arrived—they turned twenty years old—and they were handed a reprieve. Cassie had gulped with relief and happiness and hugged her mother. Later, when she was alone, she had cried her heart out for having walked so close to the edge and, instead of being saved, discovering she had to stay on it, dangling off a cliff for another year.

Now, with only a week to go, the talons of anxiety had taken hold again. She'd developed no superhuman strength or advanced intelligence; she was still just Cassie, the girl from the laundromat. She felt like a fraud and knew they'd all see through her the moment she arrived in 2050.

"Hey." A man waved at Cassie as he powered through the dense sand.

"Hi," Cassie returned politely. She registered his face, scanning its features.

"I know you, don't I?" he asked.

"I don't think so." Cassie looked back to her notebook. "Don't Trust Strangers" was imprinted on her mind. Even before she and Andie were told, age ten, to watch out for The People, Joy had them on high alert for stranger danger. Some people, she'd said, were just *bad,* especially to women.

"Yeah, I do," he continued. His smile was pleasant and his teeth were very white. "You work at the pink laundromat."

"Oh, yes, I do." Her blushing was involuntary.

He seemed pleased with himself for placing her, but she also knew her Joyful Suds polo was visible under her black puffer coat.

"Now, don't tell me." He clicked his fingers. "I'm trying to remember your name."

Cassie waited while he appeared to scan an internal database for information she was quite sure she'd never given him. They didn't wear name tags in the laundromat and only a handful of regular customers knew to call her Cassie. She got called Andie about as frequently, most people not able to pick the subtle differences between them. She was sure she didn't know this man; his face was too striking to have forgotten.

"My brain sometimes. I'm sorry, I can't remember," he said,

defeated as he took a seat next to her on the sandy wooden ramp. Close enough that she caught a whiff of his aftershave and it wasn't awful—sandalwood, she thought—although it was more masculine a scent than any of their laundry powders.

"It's Cassie."

"Ah, that's it," he said. "Cassie. Sassy Cassie."

She was not fond of that rhyme but didn't know how to say that. Politeness had been drilled into them. "Just Cassie."

"Well, Just Cassie, I'm Just Omar."

He was watching her intently, silently. She was never one to need to fill a silence; she had long found her place in the breaks in conversations and was happy to inhabit them quietly.

"I've been working at the train station, doing the upgrade," he said. "Right opposite your shop."

The train station across from Joyful Suds had been overhauled in recent months, works that seemed to last forever and fill the laundromat with dust, making Joy a little frenzied. The workers had petered out lately, only a few arriving here and there now, planting trees, painting parts of the building, hanging signs.

"We probably all look the same from where you are over the road. Loud blokes, causing traffic chaos."

He wasn't wrong, she thought. A blur of fluorescent vests and stop signs, too far away for her to make out individual faces. Omar was dressed in jeans and a tee, no sign that he was working today.

"And a lot of noise," she said. "I'm sorry, I don't recognize you."

"That's okay, Cassie. I noticed you." His eyes bored into her to the point she needed to turn away, looking into the black spiral binding of her sketchpad and hoping she could disappear into it.

"Whatcha doing there?" He pointed to the paper, which she tried to hide from view, closing the cover. She didn't like to show anyone her drawings; they felt too personal.

He reached his hand out and stopped the book from shutting

fully. Cassie wasn't used to this sort of contact and jumped at his touch.

"You drew this?" he asked, and she wondered if he'd noticed how uncomfortable his nearness made her.

"Yes."

"It's so good. Can I see?"

"I'd prefer not," Cassie replied, voice quiet.

"Of course, but what good is art if there is no one to appreciate it? It's like a beautiful woman that no one is around to see." Omar nudged her gently and her skin prickled with goosebumps.

She looked at him. His brown eyes held a tiny sparkle, his smile slightly crooked. It was endearing, this imperfection, and reminded her of Shawn and his cute dimple. If she was to draw Omar, which Cassie immediately knew she would, she imagined shading in the detail of his arms with her raw umber–colored pencil. There was an electric energy about this man, and he'd taken the time to stop and talk to her. It wasn't as if he was luring her off anywhere. She'd learned her lesson long ago about being too trusting too quickly. Schoolkids had invited her down to the beach once, and then let her have a puff of their cigarette. She hadn't wanted to be rude, so she'd done it, even though she knew she shouldn't. It had tasted awful and she'd almost led The People back to her mother and Andie. But this was different; she was older now, wiser.

She checked her watch. It was almost time for her to get back, but a minute or two couldn't hurt. She opened the book again, pushing it toward him, and he looked at the drawing of the possum.

"Is it . . . ?"

"Dead." She pointed to the still animal behind them.

"Gross," he said, laughing, but added quickly, "Not your draw-ing, just the possum, you know. Possum stew."

Maybe it was slightly strange to be drawing a dead animal when there was so much beauty around her. She could have picked a seagull, or a dog walking by, but instead she'd picked a carcass. Omar was right to laugh, she conceded. She still had a lot to learn about the social intricacies of the world, although it was too late to bother now. Knowing how to talk to handsome boys was not important in the scheme of things, not where they were going. And he wasn't really a boy either; if she had to guess, she'd say he was at least twenty-five, maybe even thirty.

She slid the book from Omar's hand and stood quickly, dusting the sand from her pants. "I have to go."

"Can I see you again?"

The comment took her a moment to process. "I'm running late."

He was undeterred. "I'll keep an eye out for you, Sassy Cassie."

She hurried off through the sand, hating the nickname, but feeling a fluttering of excitement that this man had noticed her, specifically *her*. Cassie looked back, paused a moment, and gave Omar a smile and a wave.

CHAPTER 9
ANDIE

Seven days before her twenty-first birthday, Andie was back in Linh's shop, lying on her bench, being inked with a constellation. They'd done this before, Linh drawing something on Andie just to see how it looked. Andie would love to have the courage to get an actual tattoo. She often felt rebellious, but not to that extent. Joy would pop her top. Andie did love her mum; she just didn't like her all the time.

Having Linh this close to her was one of the reasons Andie allowed her skin to be used as a canvas. Sometimes she felt like a boring, cardboard cut-out of a person around the uncontainable Linh Tran. Her friend's very being hummed with life, from the beautiful way she laughed to the lilt of her words, which were far more Australian-accented than Vietnamese ("I grew up in Frankston, you know"), and the sprays of artwork across her body. She was colorful and beautiful and funny, and Andie wondered if this was what it was like to have a crush on someone. She knew how small her life had been in comparison to Linh's and often felt intimidated by her friend's sophistication. Linh was older, wiser, worldlier; Andie had barely left Bonbeach. She understood folding laundry and excelled in biology but had never had to read the train timetable or board a plane. Whereas Linh had trained in the UK with a tattoo master, whatever that was, and had slept in a tent in the Mongolian desert. These sorts of things were beyond Andie's comprehension.

Some things made Linh uncomfortable, though, and she stumbled over her words in a very un-Linh-like way. Andie now avoided questions about when Linh started drawing, how she learned it, or what she did before she was a tattooist. She understood what it was like to not be able to tell an unencumbered truth and just tried to enjoy the present while she could.

The pen and Linh's fingers across her skin gave Andie goosebumps. Linh was drawing on her right side, covering her ribs with something Andie knew she would struggle to wash off later. Not because of what was being drawn but who was wielding the pen.

If she actually knew for sure there were only seven days to go in this world (and not just in her mother's head), she would tell Linh what she really thought of her, because what would it matter? And while she was pretty sure there weren't only seven days to go, she might actually only have one day left, or two, or nine. A cement mixer could careen through the front window of the laundromat and squash her between the truck and the free-to-use washing machine. Or she might choke to death on a cube of cheese, her mother serving Kevin or one of the other regulars and not knowing that one half of the twins she'd lied to forever couldn't breathe. Anything could happen in the next few days, but what wouldn't happen— and of this Andie was quite sure—was that her time-traveling biological parents would arrive and take her and Cassie back to 2050, to aid the fight against the technology that threatened freedom in a place that was once Bonbeach. Or might still be Bonbeach—the details on that were unclear.

Linh's glossy, black hair fell over her shoulder, brushing against Andie. She didn't dare move in case the lovely feeling of it sweeping her forearm went away.

"Do you think you'll ever really get one?" Linh asked.

"Yes," Andie replied confidently, then gave it some thought. "Maybe?"

"What about Cassie—would she do it?"

"Oh no, this is not her sort of thing at all."

"What is her thing?"

Andie thought for a moment. "She draws a lot. Plays chess with Monty. But basically, she's into doing whatever Mum tells her to do."

Linh laughed softly but held her concentration. "Sounds like the daughter my mum wanted."

"Your mum isn't happy with you?"

"Look, I don't think she pinned her hopes and dreams on her only daughter becoming a tattooist, but I think what bothers her more is that I'm thirty, unmarried, and have no kids, nor any immediate interest to pop any out."

"You don't want children?" Andie had always assumed it was a woman's natural desire to want this.

"Not anytime soon. I mean, maybe at some point. But I've got shit to do and babies just aren't really my bag. Who knows, though, what the future will hold?" Linh gently swatted her. "Stop moving."

Andie couldn't see what Linh was doing, but she didn't care; she'd let her draw anything she wanted. "It's funny to hear you talk about the future, like you get to choose. I was never allowed to choose." Andie realized her arms had erupted in goosebumps.

"You're making it sound like you are destined for some sort of arranged marriage."

"Oh, no. Nothing like that."

"I mean, there's nothing wrong with that if you are. I kinda assumed you were really religious, with the homeschooling and no internet and all."

"The Church of Joy Moody, maybe." Andie laughed awkwardly. She wanted Linh to keep asking questions, but her throat felt swollen in sudden panic. What if Joy found out about this conversation? Joy seemed to read minds like the Fortis Empire could. "But no, it's not that."

"Fair enough."

"I've never even been in a church."

Linh didn't speak, just kept drawing, and Andie took it as acceptance. It was bursting out of her, though; she just felt like she needed to share this with someone.

"Do you believe in time travel, Linh?"

"No," Linh answered, unfazed. Her breath was warm on Andie's skin.

"My mother does."

"Oh, yeah? I thought Joy would be more an anti-vaxxer, conspiracy-theorist type."

"She thinks Cassie and I are from the future." Andie paused and Linh stopped what she was doing, resting one hand on Andie's waist while she inspected her work. "And that we were sent to her for safekeeping."

"Really?" Linh's interest seemed piqued, but she was certainly not alarmed, perhaps thinking Andie was pulling her leg.

"Yes, really. But that's what she's had us believe for the last twenty years. Actually," Andie corrected herself, "since we were ten, so just a decade."

"And what are you meant to do when you get to the future?"

"Help the fight for freedom."

"Been in many fights?" Linh asked. "I didn't take you for Daniel-San."

"Who's Daniel Sun?" Andie asked.

"The Karate Kid. I mean, do you know how to fight?"

"No." Andie laughed, knowing how silly she sounded and how red she must've turned. "We're not fighting in the swords-and-guns sort of way. We are there for our . . . it's silly, really."

"No, tell me."

"Our knowledge."

"Oh, like *The Fifth Element*."

"I don't know what that is."

"Multipass?" Linh said in a strange voice. All Andie could do was shake her head.

"Oh that's right, you don't have a TV. Sorry, I forgot. What do you mean, though?"

"It's stupid, really."

"Let me decide for myself."

Andie paused, wondering how best to put it; she'd never had to explain it all before.

Linh gave her something like a tickle and Andie flinched.

"Come on," Linh prompted. "Out with it."

"Cassie has math and physics, and I have biology. We are not prodigies or anything, it's just what we learned. We are supposedly the children of scientists, Joy has always said. Now I think she just picked subjects we were good at and made us focus on them." It was a rabbit warren once she got down it. "We are just a couple of pieces of the puzzle. There were a whole heap of babies sent back through time. All born around twenty-fifty and children of the outliers that opposed the new regime."

"Right."

Andie hurried to clarify what she'd said, feeling stupid. "I know it's not true. It's not something I believe in anymore. I was younger then and just believed whatever Mum told us."

Silence fell over them. Andie heard Linh's pens drop onto the little metal table beside them.

"I've finished."

Andie was too embarrassed to look at her friend, wondering if she could take back this sudden gush of personal information. In all the times she'd imagined telling anyone, she had never dreamed of such a benign reaction.

"So," Linh said a silent minute later, "tell me about the future."

"I don't know about the future, I've never been there. We are meant to go back in seven days."

"On your birthday?"

"Yeah, it's the day our real parents are meant to collect us and take us back. They found a time slip and . . ." Andie sighed, not wanting to finish the sentence.

Linh frowned. "Would you say that you and Cassie are considered Daughters of the Future Revolution, by any chance?"

"What made you say that?" Andie sat up, shocked. "Linh, are you working with The People?"

"No. I work for myself. Wait here." Linh disappeared into her own in-between.

Andie shook her head; suspicion came naturally. The People *didn't* exist, they never had, and she was not time traveling in a week. She knew this.

She got up, went to the mirror, lifted her shirt, and studied her right side. It was a galaxy, swirling stars around a glowing orb in the center, with pinks, blues, yellows cascading out from the middle, giving it shape and life. Linh had made her GalaxyGirl. It was beautiful, and Andie was immediately sad that it wouldn't last forever.

A thought gripped her, like a hand around her throat. What if she was wrong?

She pulled down her top and sat down again, hoping she hadn't been fooled. If that was the case, she'd doomed them all.

Heavy footsteps signaled Linh's return. "Have you ever seen these?" Linh held out a box set of books and Andie felt her shoulders drop. Linh wasn't part of a secret society out to exterminate her and Cassie. No one was. She hated how her mother had burrowed so deep into her consciousness that she was doubting herself, even when Joy wasn't around to do it for her.

Andie slid the books out of their case and took in the cover: *The Fortis Trilogy*. She'd seen them before. "Mum loves these books."

"Do you know what they're about?"

"I've never read them. Mum said maybe when we're older, but that they weren't appropriate yet."

Linh walked over to the couch and dropped down beside Andie, close enough that they touched. The hairs on Andie's arms sprang to attention at the proximity.

Linh tapped the cover of the top book, which was in a far better condition than Joy's set. A serious-looking girl's face stared out at them, half-covered by a shadow as if it were eclipsed. "I have a feeling I know why she wanted to keep you away from them."

"Why?"

"Stop me if any of this sounds familiar." Linh flicked through the pages of the first book quickly, inhaling the scent. "I may be a bit rusty on the deets—I haven't read them for a while. So here it is. In 2042 a war broke out. Three powerful countries united forces in an attempt at global domination. They were relentless. Any country that thought they were safe or protected soon found out they didn't have a patch on this new Empire. Right?" Linh licked her lips and kept going. "People were going missing and the government brought in new laws about everyone needing to be tracked, so that if they did go missing, they would be able to find them. What it meant was constant surveillance and most of the population were microchipped. *1984*-type shit, you know?"

Andie had read George Orwell and was pleased to finally get one of Linh's references, but she didn't have a chance to revel in this. Instead, she felt her skin heating up and her back teeth involuntarily grinding down hard. What Linh was telling her was more than just eerily familiar; it was the same story Joy had told them again and again.

"It all backfired when this mega country reprogrammed these chips and weaponized the civilians. Cities fell within days. They didn't care to take prisoners. And what's more, the government didn't even have to *do* anything. By reprogramming the chips, they got people to kill each other, or themselves."

Andie wanted to stop Linh—it was all too much—but she stayed silent, listening as Linh went on.

"The only people not affected were the ones who were considered lawbreakers. But they weren't actually doing anything wrong— they were scientists and former leaders and people who could smell a big fat rat." Linh jiggled her eyebrows. "They sent their children back in time to be looked after until they were old enough to join the fight. But through that same time slip or rip, or whatever you want to call it, a group of soldiers from the Empire got through. They formed The Society and managed to find and eradicate all the boy children from twenty-fifty."

"Which is why they're the *Daughters* of the Future Revolution," Andie said flatly.

"Yeah."

Andie felt sweat lining her palms and underarms, and her ears were ringing like something had exploded next to them. It was one thing to suspect Joy was lying and another to be holding incontrovertible proof that their lives were built on bullshit.

"What if she really believes this?" Andie was desperate for a sensible answer, but if she didn't have one, she couldn't expect her friend to either.

"I'm sure she meant well. Parents tell their kids all sorts of stuff, right?" Linh said. "Santa, the Tooth Fairy . . . parents flat-out lie. Do you think she just wanted you to think you're special?"

"It's like she really believes it. I don't think she's quite right. Lately, she's been . . . not herself."

"She might just really love the stories and got so caught up in it . . ." Linh couldn't even finish her sentence.

"That she believes we *time traveled* to her?"

"Well . . ." Linh sighed. "Oh, is this why you wanted to do the DNA thingy?"

Andie nodded. That seemed so long ago now.

"Do you think she's hiding from someone? Like an abusive ex-husband or something?"

"Maybe, but it's more like she's hiding *us* from someone."

"Who from?"

Andie gulped. It was a really good question.

The shop door swung open, the silver bell above it dinging chirpily. Linh's appointment had arrived. Andie had to get out of there; everything felt stifling hot and scratchy all of a sudden. She collected the books and charged out, past the customer and onto the sidewalk.

Andie had some reading to do.

CHAPTER 10

JOY

Joy slid out her iPad from between two of her sweaters. A pang of guilt always smacked her when she used it. The twins were not allowed television, and yet she indulged in it almost nightly. Joy pulled her headphones from her bedside table drawer and unraveled them, plugging them in and popping them into her ears. She quickly navigated her way onto Netflix. Reality TV had become something of an obsession; it was like a warm blanket over cold limbs. Despite being absolutely exhausted, she needed to see if Chrishell and Jason stayed together on *Selling Sunset*.

It had been hard raising Andie and Cassie on her own. Worth every ounce of lost sleep and every iota of stress, but also the hardest thing she'd ever done. When they were little, the days had seemed interminably long. On top of the usual trials of parenting, Joy was always waiting for someone to try to take the girls. It had only happened once, with disastrous consequences. The babies had been so little that she knew they wouldn't remember, but it didn't make Joy feel any less agitated; if they'd found her once, they'd find her again. She knew not to let anyone get too close, even if they seemed innocent enough. And Britney had—Joy had considered her a friend at one time.

When the twins were about seven, Joy had been making dinner when she saw Britney's face appear on the TV—they had one back then. Britney was one of many lost souls listed in a missing persons television special. It was probably a little irrational, but Joy decided the TV had to go at that point. The twins never would have recognized Britney, but it felt very dangerous, having that sort of technology in the house. That night, Joy cut the power cord with scissors, then tipped water into the back of the screen. She didn't want a chance to change her mind. The TV sat there in the lounge room, its blank screen staring at them all, until they got rid of it in the next hard trash collection. It was for the best, Joy reasoned. Besides, she loved the way the twins' imaginations bloomed when they had no choice but to make up games they wanted to play.

Some days, at the park by the beach, Joy would let the twins play until their legs were almost too tired to get them home. Joy would spread out the picnic blanket and they'd lie side by side by side, watching the white puffs of cloud pass by. It was Cassie who started one of their favorite traditions. They'd been lying down, letting their bodies be warmed by the sun and squinting against the glare, when Cassie pointed up and said in her sweet little voice, "I see a horse jumping a log."

Joy didn't see anything of the sort in the mess of clouds above them, but Andie must have, because she pointed in a slightly different direction. "Granny Smith apple with three bites." And as they kept pointing, they became more and more ridiculously specific about what they could see (or not see) in the clouds. Joy tried one out—"bicycle tire with one broken spoke"—and the girls giggled. She was part of the game and she loved it, a dimension to being a mother she hadn't known she needed. It wasn't enough to just do all the things that needed to be done for life to go on, they needed to accept her in the role. And they did.

They played that game many times over the years, always trying to one-up each other with the things they pretended to spot. "Cordless drill with Phillips-head screwdriver attachment." "Hippopotamus eating watermelon." And on the game went, and so did the years, until Joy realized they were too old to play it anymore.

At the age the girls were now, Joy had already been dating Arthur and had no time to stop and look for imaginary objects floating through the air. She'd been so busy being a girlfriend he could take seriously, trying to laugh at all the appropriate moments, impress him with her easygoing nature (not like the other girlfriends, who seemed so uptight), and be physically attractive to him at all times. She was not herself around Arthur, but that was the Joy he'd fallen for, so it was a character she had to maintain. The effort seemed worthwhile because the handsome, lovely, affable Arthur wanted to be her beau, and then her husband. The version he loved was the better Joy, and she had to maintain the facade.

This had almost made it worse when he didn't want her in the end, even when she'd painstakingly crafted herself into the wife she thought he wanted. She hated that he'd left her, she hated that Nina-the-backstabbing-moll had done what she did, and most of all, she hated herself for pretending to be someone else in order to have a man love her.

The American-accented voice of Christine Quinn in her ears snapped Joy back to her show. She used her finger to drag the episode back to the beginning. No point missing out. Her guess was she wouldn't have the opportunity to watch much reality TV, if any, in 2050. She had important things to do. It was also her hope, although she didn't dare say it out loud, that she might be revered as a bit of a hero. She had, after all, kept the twins safe for twenty-one years. It was weird, though; she kept getting all muddled up about the twins' birthday and the supermoon rising and what exactly they had to do once they returned to the future. Almost as if she had misunderstood something along the way. It niggled at her, like wondering if she'd left the iron on when she left the house. And yet whenever she did double-check it, she had always turned it off. She needed to trust her instincts more.

It made her realize she hadn't updated Andie and Cassie's future-parents about the plans. They needed to know, she presumed, that she was coming along for the ride so they could figure her into their plans; it would be rude to show up unannounced. She could ask them about advances in medicine when she got there; she didn't want to make it sound like she was going to be a liability.

Joy picked up a pen and pad from her bedside table, pressed pause on a fight between real estate agents, and wrote a note to place in the peppercorn tree before her swim in the morning. That would give them plenty of time to plan. She reread her note, worried she was downplaying the importance of her joining them. If she stayed put, the brain tumor would almost certainly be the death of her. Maybe that was as clear as she needed to be. Joy added a "P.S." to the note. Satisfied with the addition, she folded it neatly and placed it back on her bedside table, ready to take down to the tree in the morning.

Joy started the program again, snuggled down under her duvet, and watched Christine show a magnificent property that had a price tag with as many zeroes as Joy had washing machines.

CHAPTER 11

CASSIE

July 31, 2023
One day remaining

Each day since meeting Omar, Cassie had hoped to see him again. It wasn't unusual that she would go to her favorite spot, sit and draw, enjoy the waning winter sunshine. But it was unusual that she'd spend extra time doing her hair and making sure she put a slick of Vaseline across her lips so they looked glossy. She had gone so far as to undo all three buttons at the neck of her Joyful Suds polo shirt, something they were not allowed to do in the shop. One button was all Mum allowed. Cassie also ensured that her sketching consisted of things much more appropriate than a dead marsupial. Today she had chosen to draw a woman in a red bathing suit, whom she watched wade into the churning ocean as if it wasn't shockingly cold. The woman made her think of her mother.

It was like Mum needed the water and salt, that her DNA called her to it each and every morning. There was hardly a day Cassie could recall when Joy hadn't been to the beach before opening the laundromat in the morning. She went on Christmas and even when she'd been up all night with the girls and their various illnesses over the years. She was always back before the girls climbed out of bed. It hadn't occurred to Cassie to think their mother irresponsible for leaving them alone while she scratched this itch. The act was as necessary to Joy as breathing, washing, eating.

Cassie hadn't told her mum or Andie about Omar and had no intention to. She wouldn't be able to stand it if they quashed her enthusiasm, which was more than likely. Joy's teachings rang firmly in her ears; Cassie knew what all men were after, and that they shouldn't be trusted, but now there was just the one day to go, she longed for that feeling again, that warmth in her belly when Omar told her how he'd noticed her. *Her.* Cassiopeia Moody and not Andromeda. For once, she was one whole person and not half of something.

It had been with heavy feet that she dragged herself home after her lunch break each day that week, not seeing Omar or any sign at the train station of the hard-hatted workers with their bright vests and utility trucks. It was as if she'd imagined him. She hoped that wasn't the case.

The woman in the surf floated on her back in the lapping waves. Cassie's pencil flew over the page, the details emerging from the whiteness of the paper. The softness of the water, the starkness of the woman, bobbing like a buoy. She looked so peaceful, and Cassie imagined the way the noise dulled under the water and how easy it was to stare up into the clouds, looking for shapes. She loved playing that game.

There would still be clouds in the future, she supposed, and she would make sure she took the time to look for them. Surely they'd still have time for the sky. The feeling clawed at her, the one that always burbled up when she thought of their forthcoming time travel and whether she was smart enough to compete with a mega-Empire. She was quite sure that she was not—and positive she didn't want to.

"Hello, beautiful."

The voice came from behind her and when she turned her head from the glare of the sky, she saw Omar, leaning against the clapboards of her beach hut like he'd always been there. If he noticed the wetness of her eyes, he didn't mention it and she hoped he'd chalk it up to the wind.

"I've missed you," he said.

Cassie blushed, then smiled, feeling downright silly at being so elated to see him, an almost complete stranger she'd waited all week for. She'd thought about him so much that she'd drawn him. And not just once; she'd sketched his face a number of times. Now he was in front of her, she realized she'd not recalled his eyebrows quite right. She would fix them in the next one.

"Hi, there," Cassie replied, and he took it as an invitation to sit beside her, this time close enough that his knee knocked into hers, a little electricity buzzing between them.

"Wow." He pointed at the floating-lady picture. "That's amazing."

She knew she'd nailed the subject matter this time and was so glad he noticed that she didn't even try to hide the drawing. A warmth crept over her. Omar looked out to the ocean, where the woman was walking back to her towel and discarded clothing. She looked serene, reminding Cassie of Joy when she'd return home, whatever having happened out there in the water making her cells buzz. It had usually worn off by about 7:30 a.m., when Joy's face would return to its slightly sharper edges, the line etched between her eyebrows as deep as ever.

"What's been happening, Sassy?"

"Oh, nothing much," Cassie replied. She didn't think there was ever a good answer to that. Telling him she was about to be hurtled twenty-seven years into the future probably wasn't the best idea. And mentioning it was almost her birthday seemed painfully childish. "What about you?" she asked instead. "I haven't seen you around." She flinched; she had just revealed she had been waiting for him. Perhaps he wouldn't notice, but the crimson burn crept up her neck in any case.

He had noticed, though, smiling in a way that suggested he was pleased with this turn of events. Cassie wanted to rewind the moment, act cooler, be more sure of herself. Talking to the opposite sex was harrowing but exciting. It was something she felt very fish-out-of-water with, although she had never agreed with that saying. A fish out of water would be flopping around, fighting for its life. She was more like a fish still in its bowl, staring with wide eyes out through the glass.

"Busy, you know. We've been working over in Werribee most of the week, which is cool, although my boss can be a bit of a dick, you know?"

She did not know. "Oh, right."

"And I just kept thinking about this fine, green-eyed lady I'd met on the beach and wanted to be back this side of town so I could see what dead animals she was drawing this time around."

Her eyes were hazel, but easily enough confused for green. "No dead animals today," she said quickly, wishing that hadn't been the thing that stuck with him.

"You should show these pictures somewhere, or at least make an Instagram page for them. People would pay for them."

It had never occurred to her that anyone might be interested in her work. "Would they?" she asked.

"For sure. This stuff is dope. Plus, look at you. It's the perfect combo." Omar grinned.

Cassie frowned. "Mum wouldn't like that. It's better I keep them to myself."

His brow furrowed. "How old are you?"

He'd opened the door to mention her birthday, so she offered it up. "Twenty-one tomorrow."

"Twenty-one," he said, whistling like it was a big deal, which only made her cheeks burn brighter. "Tomorrow. Well, happy birthday, Sassy Cassie."

She still wasn't wowed by that name, yet Omar saying it made it seem almost sweet.

"Means you're old enough to do what you want," he said.

"Whatever I want?" This was a totally foreign concept to Cassie.

Omar was staring at her. "Actually, your eyes are a bit more brown-like today. They're not just green."

She was glad he'd noticed. He drew so close she could smell the coffee on his breath, and that sandalwood scent again. And then he was kissing her.

It was unexpected, though she didn't think it was unwelcome. Perhaps this was the way it happened. She had been friendly toward him, she supposed, or at least more friendly than she usually was. Almost forward, if she thought about her behavior. Had he picked up on that? No wonder he thought she would be open to such a thing. And she was, or at least she thought she might have been, but she would've appreciated a little warning. Dismissing her reservations, she leaned into the kiss, finding the act itself quite confusing. In the books she'd read, sometimes the making-out scenes gave her a little tingle that radiated from her stomach down to her thighs. Sometimes she would save those parts of the book for when she was alone and could read them slowly, savoring every word. If it was a book Joy had deemed particularly spicy (Mum's word, not hers), Joy would black out paragraphs or glue pages together. Cassie had expected kissing to feel like some sort of explosive, amazing, romantic thing, but the reality was that Omar's tongue felt big and wet in her mouth and they bumped teeth more than once. His stubbled chin was rough and felt like sandpaper against her skin. His hand slipped up to the side of her neck, near her ear, then dropped to the open buttons on her polo shirt and lingered there, like he didn't really know what to do with his arm. And then it all ended just as abruptly as it had begun, and she had to resist the temptation to wipe the shared saliva from her mouth.

"You are amazing, Cassandra," he said.

"It's . . . um . . . it's Cassiopeia, actually."

"Is that French or something?" he whispered, still very close, closer than she felt truly comfortable with.

"Um, no. It's a constellation."

"That's so perfect for you."

She wasn't sure how to respond to that.

"Cassie!"

She was sure she heard her name, then the wind whisked it from her ears. She looked up but didn't see anyone and decided it was just her imagination.

"Cassie!" This time it was louder, and closer.

"Oh, shit," Omar said. "That lady looks pissed."

Her mother stormed toward them, her pace slowed by the sand that made it almost impossible to walk fast; she looked slightly comical. Cassie didn't dare laugh, though. Joy Moody did not take kindly to being ridiculed.

Omar leaped back, widening the distance between them.

"Cassiopeia, get yourself back to the shop this minute. What are you thinking?"

Cassie quickly got to her feet. Joy grabbed her arm as she neared and put herself between Cassie and Omar.

"How long has this been going on for?" Joy was fuming.

Cassie shook her head. "It hasn't; it's not been going on. Nothing's been going on, Mum."

"Doesn't look like nothing. What are you thinking? Who is this?"

Joy had her back to Omar, little drops of spittle flying from her mouth as she yelled.

"I'm sorry, Mum," Cassie said and looked at her mother solemnly, the way she'd defused Joy's anger many times before.

But Joy barely registered it, instead turning to Omar and throwing her hands wildly about as she chastised him for "debasing" her daughter. They'd kissed, but Cassie didn't think that constituted debasement. She decided it was not the time to correct her mother, though.

When the tirade was finished, Joy turned abruptly and started to march back up the beach. "Cassie, *come!*" she commanded.

Cassie had never been so embarrassed and looked quickly to Omar, who appeared confused. Hurriedly, she followed her mum; there was no point making her madder.

She could remember just one other time when Joy had been this mad. It had been a long time ago and was something they worked hard to avoid. The receiving end of their mother's wrath was not a place either sister wanted to be. They'd woken up to find Joy sweeping up broken glass downstairs.

"Did someone try to break in?" Cassie had asked, terrified.

"Yes, they did." Joy was on edge, her shoulders held tight and high.

Andie came quickly down the stairs behind Cassie and they both stopped and watched Joy with the little pink (because of course it was pink) dustpan and broom set as the glass tinkled into the small tray.

"Was it The People?" Andie asked.

"The who? No, I don't . . ." Joy stopped short, pushed the hair off her face, and considered them sternly. "Maybe it was."

Cassie looked to her sister, who went pale. It was terrifying to think anyone would try and get in, let alone The People. Andie burst into tears—something she did much more frequently as a thirteen-year-old than she'd ever done since. As if she ran out somewhere along the way.

"Girls, there's no need to fret. I will always keep you safe, you know that."

Andie was already dashing back upstairs, her feet pounding against the floor above them—it was always so loud when someone was up there. Then she was back, clutching three magazines that she held out, in trembling hands, to Joy.

"It's all my fault," Andie sobbed, her words hard to understand.

"I kept these, and I read them, and I entered one of the competitions with our address. I brought them here, didn't I?"

Cassie's gaze flicked desperately from Mum to Andie and back again. The word *Cosmopolitan* ran in tall, block font across the glossy front page. Cassie had seen the magazines, even flicked through them. She didn't realize that Andie had kept them all this time.

Joy took hold of the magazines and deliberated over them. It was like waiting for a firework to pop. "I don't like you reading these, Andie. They give young women the wrong idea. Life isn't like it's written in these." She sounded disappointed; this was always worse than shouting.

Andie couldn't get any words out, although Cassie was sure she was trying to say "sorry." Snot mingled with her tears, and it was all meeting on her top lip. Cassie plucked out some tissues and pushed them into her sister's hand.

"'Are you getting enough?'" Joy read from the front cover, a blonde, pouty woman staring back at them. "'Lose weight for summer,' 'Have you fallen for an older man?' Oh my goodness, Andromeda, this is the sort of thing young women get brainwashed with. They start to think these are the important things in life." Joy threw them to the ground. "How they look and what men think of them. Honestly!"

Andie wiped her face; her cheeks were red. Tears had dripped down onto her pajama top. Cassie wanted to help, but didn't know how.

"Get rid of them," Joy said calmly, firmly. "And you must be more careful. You're both far too special to be lost to this sort of nonsense."

Later that day, while the glazier fixed the window, they went to the mini mart. Sangeeta asked what had happened, and Joy explained she'd been de-cobwebbing the windows with the broom and slipped, putting it through the glass. It was the first time Cassie had really understood that Joy's life was burdened by having the twins with her. She had to lie to her friends and protect the girls against trained hunters from the future. It was becoming abundantly clear how very brave their mother was and how grateful they should be. She never wanted to make her mad like that again. Cassie had looked up to Joy ever since.

But now, as they powered away from the beach, with Omar left stunned behind them, Cassie felt less grateful. Couldn't she just have something for herself, for once? What harm was it, really? Cassie hurried across the train tracks, trying to keep up with her mother. As Joyful Suds came into sight, Cassie realized she'd left her sketchbook back on the beach. She turned and Joy grabbed her arm, not roughly, but not particularly gently either.

"What is it?"

"I forgot my drawings."

"You're not to go back there, Cassie."

"But my pictures!"

"You can draw more."

Cassie sighed. Her mother was using the voice that meant the matter was not up for debate.

"And do up your buttons." Joy pointed at her polo shirt. "I'm so disappointed in you."

It wasn't so much that Cassie would miss those particular drawings; she could always draw more. She just didn't want Omar to look through the sketchbook, because if he did, he'd realize Cassie had drawn his face a number of times. She felt a thud of mortification as she imagined him finding out just how much she'd thought about him over the past week. And to add to that, her mother's outburst and actions were beyond embarrassment.

It took most of the day for her shame to subside enough for Cassie to realize she'd just had her very first kiss.

CHAPTER 12
ANDIE

Andie was in the laundromat and had just emptied the coin drops on machines one through five. As was her usual way, she'd pocketed two coins from each. It was her savings plan, one that was being slowly thwarted by the increased use of credit cards. The machines had both options, and quite often there were too few coins for Andie to skim from.

She was careful to avoid the shop camera, not knowing how much attention Joy paid or how often she looked at the footage. Her mother had been forgetful lately, but there was no point becoming complacent. The camera was above the front door, facing the counter and the door to the in-between and it was all operated through Joy's phone and laptop, all under her sole control.

Andie often thought of Joyful Suds as a pink prison. Her idea of this, of course, was all from fiction; she had never seen or been near a jail or anything of the sort. But Joy often acted like their jailer, issuing many rules, and the twins had a distinct lack of freedom. There were days, though, when being in the laundromat felt like slipping on a warm pair of slippers: when Andie would stand opposite her sister at the folding table and they'd talk and joke and laugh so hard she couldn't fold properly. Was it possible to love and hate Joyful Suds at the same time?

Machine six was the free one, so there were no coins to be emptied from there. Andie moved on to the bank of dryers, careful to turn her back to the camera as the loose gold and silver clinked into her canvas bag.

Two other cameras covered the front sidewalk and the parking lot. Joy used these to race outside and shriek at anyone who parked illegally. It was almost like a sport; she seemed to get an adrenaline rush from it.

The CCTV system had been there since The People had tried to get in, back when they were teenagers. Joy said it would make them think twice before trying again. She had always been security conscious—how could she not be with the threat of a secret society out to get them? But now Andie wondered if it was actually just paranoia, or the need to control her daughters' every move. The more Andie thought about the break-in, when Joy had saved them from the intruders climbing in the downstairs window, the more she questioned it. To begin with, most of the glass was outside on the pavers, and it didn't take Miss Marple (her favorite Christie crime solver) to deduce that meant it had been broken from the inside. Then there was the choice of window; it was a high, small rectangle that a person would barely fit through. They had plenty of other windows that would've provided easier access should someone have really been trying to cause them harm, and that particular window had been cracked for as long as Andie could recall, something on Joy's "to-do" list of things to fix. Was it that Joy decided to kill two birds with one stone? Get the window replaced and keep the girls in line at the same time? It had scared the twins half to death. They topped and tailed in their single beds for weeks after that, needing to know the other was right there beside them.

One other thing had bothered her. When she'd put the garbage

out that afternoon long ago, tossing it into the trash can in the backyard, Andie noticed a colorful package and dug her arm in to find out
what it was. It was a packet of five lip glosses that Andie immediately
recognized as the ones she'd entered the *Cosmopolitan* competition
to win. Prize in hand, she'd marched back into the house, furious, because finding this meant that Joy had known about the magazines
before Andie had admitted to them. Back then it wasn't the whole
story, future destiny and all, that Andie doubted. She could never
have imagined how far-reaching the lies would be. The worst part
(at least to her thirteen-year-old mind) was that she had been denied
the prize she had so desired. When Andie tossed them on the table
in front of her mother, trying to articulate as best she could that she
knew her mother was lying, Joy had looked stunned.

"Why did you throw them out?" Andie demanded.

Her mother calmly picked up the package, looking between the
girls. "I didn't."

Andie was determined to find out what was going on. "Why were
they in the trash can, then?"

Joy's eyes blazed. "*They* brought these here. This confirms it, it
was The People. I was quietly hoping it was just a random burglary,
but now I see how close they came. We must be more careful."

Now Andie realized she should've pushed harder, asked more
questions. But it had never occurred to her that her mother would
be capable of something so duplicitous. The change jingled in her
pocket, ready to be added to her stock of coins in the Omo box in
the shed. She never stayed in there long; it gave her the heebie-jeebies.
It had a weird mix of scents from the fabric softeners, the bulk-buy
disinfectant, and the bags of blood-and-bone fertilizer Joy bought
for the veggie patch, which she always had in supply despite being
a woeful gardener at the best of times. She said it kept her hopeful
she'd have the time to get around to it one day soon. Too late, Andie
thought. According to Joy, they were way past "one day soon."

Cassie and Joy blustered into the laundromat with a tense air about them. Mum didn't stay long; she checked the tags on a couple of orders and opened one bag because she always thought Andie took shortcuts with the folding when she wasn't watching. Then she huffed off to the house, leaving Cassie behind. Joy was right, Andie did take shortcuts, but only with the things she put in the bottom third of the bag. The top two-thirds were always Joy-standard—Andie wasn't stupid.

A customer came in and loaded up a machine with towels that had the tell-tale bleach marks of a hairdresser's. The woman was on her phone, talking loudly and laughing a little maniacally to someone she called "babe" a lot.

Neither Cassie nor Andie said anything to each other, although it was clear that Cassie was sulking. She had always been terrible at disguising her emotions, often coming off like a petulant child.

Andie had so many questions but wanted the shop to be empty before she started in on Cassie. As if the woman knew Andie was willing her to leave, she seemed to take her time, rooting around in her handbag at a painfully slow pace before finding a handful of change to drop in the slot. Machine four eventually started humming away, the water hammering in, and the hairdresser left, still rapidly chatting to "babe."

As soon as the front door swung closed, Andie pounced. "What's going on?"

Cassie gave her what was meant to be her "back off and butt out" face, but Andie was immune to it, like all siblings become over time.

"What? Come on. You want to tell me, you know you do."

"I. Do. Not."

Andie rolled her eyes. "Don't be so dramatic. Just tell me. We have other things to discuss."

"Like what?"

"Like tomorrow."

"What about it?" Cassie still looked annoyed, but Andie knew her sister's curiosity would get the better of her.

"Tell me first."

"No, you."

Andie envisaged this verbal tennis match going on for quite some time, so she cut to the chase. "I know who our father is."

Cassie whipped a hooded sweater out in front of her, then smoothed it against the front of her body. "What do you mean?"

"I know you don't want to believe this, and you're always quick to shoot me down when I've mentioned it before, but I have evidence now."

Smugly, Andie pulled a folded sheet of paper from her back pocket and handed it over, wary that if Joy was tuning in to the camera above them, she'd see this exchange and no doubt want to know what they were discussing. Linh had printed the History Mystery results so Andie could show Cassie, who was bound to side with their mother. Joy had always been Cassie's beacon of truth; she believed everything their mum had ever said.

Now Andie knew she'd been right to dig—the DNA results proved it. Plus, she'd been reading *The Fortis Trilogy* every chance she got, skimming through a lot of the chapters, then slowing down for the parts that seemed relevant. The parallels were not just disturbing, they were almost word for word what Joy had been feeding them for years.

In book one (*Daughters of Now*), the mother gets the girls to hide in the basement because she believes The Society is in a helicopter circling overhead. Reading by the light of her lamp, Andie had felt ill with the memory it evoked. Years ago, Joy had them lie like yin and yang in their bathtub as she covered them in lengths of aluminum foil. They didn't have a basement, so presumably the bathroom was as bunker-like as it got.

"What's going on?" Cassie had whispered.

"Can you hear that?" Joy had asked, panicked.

The girls listened and beyond the rustling of the foil in their ears, they could hear a helicopter, its rotors turning rhythmically. It sounded close enough to think it might land on the roof and the twins had both been seized with fear; they had no idea what to do. What if they were taken?

Andie couldn't say how long they'd stayed in the bath, but it was long enough for her legs to cramp and for her to wonder if she was going to wet her pants. It was also long enough to notice that Cassie could afford to be a little more liberal with the underarm deodorant.

"Mum, can we come out?" Andie had asked when she couldn't hear the noise overhead anymore.

"Almost time, girls."

Joy remained nearby. Andie couldn't see her, but she could hear Joy's breathing and she knew she wasn't far away.

"What's going on, Mum? Are they coming to get us?"

"The foil stops their radars from working," Joy said. "Don't worry, girls, they'd have to get through me to get to you."

Andie worried that her mother might get hurt. And then where would they be? Although she supposed if they got past Joy, it wouldn't matter, because they'd all be destroyed. Dead. A word that didn't mean as much to a fourteen-year-old as it would later, when the permanence of that state was better understood. That's what The People did: they made you dead.

Just when Andie thought she'd risk being caught for the chance to straighten her legs, Cassie burst into tears.

Joy ripped back a corner of the foil. "What is it?"

"It's all my fault," Cassie sobbed.

With a flicker of selfishness, Andie realized she wasn't going to be the one in trouble that day.

"I went down to the beach with a couple of girls from the bus stop. I didn't tell you. I'm sorry." Cassie shuddered with sobs.

"Why would you do that?"

"They asked me to go." Cassie's words were hard to hear. "And they seemed nice."

"Anything else?" Joy's eyes narrowed, and Andie had a crystalizing thought—her mother knew something.

"They gave me some of their cigarette," Cassie all but whispered. "I didn't really have any, just pretended. I didn't want to be rude."

"Cassiopeia, I'm so disappointed in you." Joy peeled more foil back so Andie could see her too.

"Can we get out now?" Andie asked.

"Not yet," Joy said crisply.

Andie swiveled her body a bit so she could stop her knee from aching and knocked Cassie on the chin as she did so.

"Stop fidgeting," Mum said. "Cassie, it's of the utmost importance that you tell me the truth now. Did you say anything to those girls about where you're from?"

"No."

"And anything about your real parents?"

"No, Mum, I would never."

Joy looked somewhat relieved by this response; they both knew Cassie wasn't prone to lies. Although Andie would not have thought she'd be smoking with strangers either. She realized then, with a flash of disbelief, that Cassie didn't share everything with her.

The next day, they'd both been given watches to wear *at all times*: "These were designed in the future. They will keep you safe by blocking your geolocators." Joy handed Cassie a green one and Andie a yellow.

"Our what?" Andie asked.

"Your parents obviously know where to find you. But they factored in that they may not survive until the time comes to collect you. So they implanted trackers. Not like the ones the Empire mandates—different ones, safer. That way, when the time comes, you can be found."

Andie was so excited about the new watch she didn't take a moment to be horrified about the idea of being monitored. She was fourteen, after all. A new gadget was exciting.

They still always wore their watches, their Geolocation Protection Systems: GPS for short, the initials molded into the plastic watch face.

Cassie's voice brought Andie back to the present. "I don't know what this means." She threw the report from History Mystery down on the folding table.

Andie put down the socks she'd just balled together, picked up the report, and pointed at the relevant bits as she spoke. "Right here. 'Tyler, male, fifty percent shared DNA, parent.'"

"I don't know why you'd do this, and behind Mum's back."

"*Parent*, Cassie." Andie just about tore a hole through the paper with her pointing. "He's our *parent*."

"Ours?"

"Well, yes, ours. I don't care about who anyone else's parents are, do I?"

"You shouldn't have done that without asking me."

"Your DNA is my DNA, so I can do what I want with it." Andie wasn't trying to be prickly, but Cassie was missing the point. "If he is *my* parent, he's your parent. And he's not from the future."

"You don't know that."

"His results are on History Mystery. He lives here, now, in this year."

"There are plenty of reasons his DNA could be recorded."

"Like?"

"Maybe he's a baby. That makes sense, doesn't it? In twenty-fifty, he'd be, like, thirty or something, so our future dad would be a baby now." Cassie looked pleased with herself.

"And why would a baby be recorded on History Mystery?"

"Maybe all babies are on there."

"That's stupid." Andie hated to admit that Cassie's suggestion wasn't actually ridiculous. She didn't want to buy into it, though. Just moments ago she'd been so sure of herself, ready to call Joy out on a lifetime of untruths.

Cassie was blinking back tears, which Andie had no time for today. Always with the waterworks. She just wanted her sister to have a conversation like a normal person. She pushed the test results back into her pocket, then pulled out her Fruit Tingles and flicked one into her mouth, crunching it loudly. It was a losing battle, she realized, trying to flip Cassie on this. Cassie wasn't looking for a way out of going back to the future, she'd accepted it. On the nights when Andie confided in her that she didn't want to go, Cassie would sigh and tell her it didn't matter—they had to.

But Andie wanted more. She imagined planes to other countries, cocktails with fruit wedges arranged on the side, the flat, red plains of the desert, the Taj Mahal, the northern lights, Victoria Falls. There was an entire world waiting for them, where they didn't have a stupid destiny hanging above them like a guillotine. They could be selfish and make mistakes and the world would still be okay. She didn't want to go to the blasted future.

The shop door opened and Andie's gaze shot to the incoming customer. Kevin, a regular. He always sang while he was doing his washing. Sometimes it was lyrics to an actual song, but quite often he just made a tune out of putting coins into the machine or loading his basket. She had once heard him sing about scratching himself on the backside.

He nodded at Andie. "Just checking on my washing, my washing, my washing." His tongue clicked out a beat.

Andie forced a smile—her attempt at being professional—before jerking her head toward the in-between. She and Cassie moved into the space and kept their voices low.

"I'm worried about what's going to happen tomorrow. I've been reading some books Linh gave me and—"

Cassie cut her off, outraged. "You've told Linh?"

"Some things. Not everything. But that's not the point."

"It *is* the point. That's against the rules, Andie."

"It's all in the book! She's been telling us a story."

"You're not making sense. I know you're scared of what might happen, even though you pretend you're all tough."

"I'm not scared," Andie snapped.

"It's okay to be—"

"I'm not scared!"

Kevin's singing stopped; he was listening.

"We've got washing to fold." Cassie sniffed, her expression making it clear she was done with their conversation.

"We've always got washing to fold. All this *busy work* . . . Do you think that maybe there's a reason Mum doesn't like us having time up our sleeves?"

"Because she's got a business to run?" Cassie replied. "I'm done with getting into trouble today." She walked out of the in-between without a glance over her shoulder.

Cassie might be willing to follow their mum blindly, but Andie couldn't anymore.

After the chapters she'd finished reading that morning, Andie feared just how far Joy would go to make their birthday play out like it did in the books. She was quite sure her mother would go to any length. And if that was the case, she realized now that both her life and Cassie's were at stake.

CHAPTER 13
JOY

August 1, 2023
The twins turn twenty-one

5:50 a.m.

Whenever Joy Moody swam in the ocean, she imagined she was a mermaid. It was a ridiculous fantasy for a fifty-six-year-old woman, but when she was out there in the mornings, all by herself, she could be whoever she wanted to be. And that was a woman pretending her feet were a tail.

The sky was still dark, the ocean mingling with the horizon, and it was the last day she believed she would enjoy this view. It was, but not for the reasons she thought. It was the last of Joy's time in 2023, but also the last day of her life.

It didn't take long in the water for her body to become almost completely numb, and eventually she knew it was time to head in.

Wrapped in her towel, she took her hot water bottle from her bag, cuddled it to her middle, then pulled her feet in so she was curled up like an echidna. Usually she went home quickly—there were things to do, always things to do—but today she wanted a little extra time. The sand was damp and she watched the waves breaking with a flash of white squall just a little way from the shore.

The waves will continue, she thought. *It will all just go on.*

It was right around here that she had stumbled across Britney White, over two decades ago. She could keep track of how long it had been for obvious reasons.

Twenty-one years without Britney. Twenty-one years with the twins.

Joy wasn't sure if she still visited this spot to remember the teenager, or if she came here because she always had. Both things might have been true.

In the past week, Joy had been planning. At first, she thought she would take nothing material with her at all. Just her girls, which was all she'd ever needed. But then she thought in more practical terms and withdrew her entire savings. The teller had had to clear it with the boss—apparently they didn't hand over thirty-four thousand dollars just like that, even if it was her money. She would carry it with her on the off-chance cash was worth anything in the future and that her bag survived the trip. All those coins in all those washing machines over the years had added up. In hindsight she might not have had to have been so frugal. Perhaps she could've updated the furniture or been a little more generous with the girls. She'd always been the sole source of income, though, and it had seemed more important to have a little nest egg than a new couch.

Her brother had laughed when she'd opened Joyful Suds. "There's no money in laundromats," he'd said not long after her grand opening (which wasn't especially grand). Why on earth he'd come, she had no idea; to scoff, it would seem. "Did you get this paint on special or something?" he'd said, taking in the parakeet-pink walls and the blush front counter, which she'd painted herself. Joy hadn't asked for his opinion, but he thrust it at her anyway. Grant thought himself "in the know" when it came to small business, but she knew money slipped through his fingers like water through a sieve. He was always jumping on board the next scheme to make more money, faster, always faster. He didn't care how he went about it either; he was unscrupulous like that. Joy preferred honest hard work and a budget.

He was her only sibling, though, and their distant relationship was a source of disappointment to her. She'd wanted a sibling like Cassie and Andie had in each other—a pigeon pair, a dynamic duo. Three years older than her, Grant had expressed little toward her other than annoyance, especially through their teen years.

She had no idea about much of his life. He'd resurfaced a couple of times over the years for a special occasion here or a Christmas there. One time he'd hit her up for two thousand dollars. He must have caught her at a magnanimous moment, because she'd agreed, writing a check on the spot. They were family, after all. That loan turned out to be the sort that wasn't a loan at all. She'd never seen a cent of it again, and the next time he'd come, it had been for six thousand dollars. That time she said no, because all she could see were the requests increasing in value with each visit. So she'd closed the Bank of Joy and he'd been none too happy, calling her a "miserly spinster." If anything, she was a miserly divorcée, but she didn't bother to correct him. He'd dropped off the radar after that, and she'd not seen him for years until recently, when he'd had the audacity to try to stake a claim on the laundromat.

Joy squeezed her legs closer to her body, letting the rapidly diminishing heat from her hot water bottle absorb into her damp skin.

Life had been fulfilling and Joy was satisfied with all she'd done. There'd been a time when she didn't think she'd ever have the pleasure of raising children, and for a long while she thought she'd never be able to pick herself back up after Arthur and his scheming harlot, Nina. That she'd managed to do both was quite impressive, and she was pretty damn proud of herself. She'd told Grant, and anyone who she thought needed an explanation, that Cassie and Andie were foster children, placed with her from birth. Her old role as a social worker had made this especially believable; she knew the ins and outs of the system. For a big, fat lie, it sounded plausible enough.

The day she had found out about Arthur's affair was one of the hardest days of her life. She'd woken up with blood leaking through the back of her pajamas, which meant another month of not being pregnant. They'd tried for five years by that point, and every period felt like she was being punished for something she couldn't recall doing. This was when she wished her mother was still around, so she could cry to her about her failings and be reminded that she was complete just the way she was. Instead, she had Arthur telling her there was "always next month" in his perfunctory manner that implied she was being overdramatic. The wife character that Joy had created for him didn't trouble her husband with things like fertility and ovulation cycles and periods, so she would dust herself off, put a tampon in, and go to work, faking a smile. Which she did that day.

Joy hadn't counted on walking into a shitstorm. A young couple, *her* clients, had reached a melting point overnight. They had been holding on by a thread after the birth of their baby. Desperately immature, they fought constantly, had financial difficulties, and exacerbated everything with cannabis and amphetamine use. Where they found the money for that, she didn't want to think about. They ticked all the boxes to have their child removed, but Joy had engaged every support service possible to get them help to keep Shem, their son, a cherubic boy with a perpetually dirty face. They adored him, and it had seemed like they were doing okay—not great, but okay.

How wrong Joy had been. When a neighbor had heard an argument the night before, they'd called the police. Will, the father, had barricaded the door to their house by the time the police arrived. Will was impetuous like that. Joy found out when she arrived at work and raced out to the address with her regional manager, Leonie, hoping she'd be allowed to speak to Will. They'd always had a good rapport; he thought she was trying to help and she genuinely was. That was all Joy ever wanted to do. She always meant well, *always*.

The police had blocked off access to the house and most of the street in both directions, and Joy had no chance of getting close enough to speak to Will or Jedidah, his girlfriend. She just wanted Will to see a familiar face in the hope that he might realize all was not lost. She pleaded her case to get closer with the police officer standing sentry at the barricade.

"But I know them," she'd cried, to no avail. He wouldn't budge, wouldn't even consult the heavily armed police farther up the road, and he spoke to Joy with a pompous "Leave it to the boys" attitude that made her want to headbutt him.

Joy was beside herself, but the worst was to come.

When the SWAT team, or whoever they were, kicked in the door of Will and Jedidah's house, they found him barely alive after what turned out to be a deliberate drug overdose. He survived, but Jedidah and the baby were dead in the bedroom and had been for some hours. Once she knew all was lost, Joy couldn't hear another thing Leonie said to her. She fell into a pit that she'd been standing at the edge of for months.

All she'd wanted to do was help.

She'd failed them all. Joy was the one who'd left the baby in that house.

This troubled family were the straw and she was the camel, and it was all over for Joy Moody at that moment in time. She didn't think she could ever go back to that job and its endless, hopeless cases.

Leonie dropped her off at home and she walked inside in a daze. Had she been in a better state of mind, she'd have noticed Nina's car in the driveway and she might have even heard the hurried, intense grunts coming from her bedroom. All she wanted was for Arthur to hold her and comfort her and tell her it was going to be all right.

But her husband was otherwise occupied, his face buried deep between the thighs of Nina fucking Nguyen, her best friend, who immediately became her former best friend. And Joy watched what he was doing with morbid fascination. The act he was performing was something he said wasn't appropriate to perform on his wife. "That's not the sort of thing nice girls do," he'd said once, and she'd never been so offended to be referred to as nice.

For a flicker of time, before either Nina or Arthur noticed her, Joy wondered if this was it for her. She was no longer able to do her job, she was redundant as Arthur's wife, her uterus was a barren pit, and she had no close family. In the space of one morning, she had been cut adrift from everything that had ever mattered to her. She wished she was dead.

Right there in the doorway to the bedroom she'd lovingly decorated, Joy started wailing.

Once they were untangled and Arthur was dressed, he found Joy in the kitchen, sobbing into one of the tea towels she'd embroidered daisies onto. He didn't even have the good grace to apologize, but at least he didn't try to convince her she was making a fuss. He did like to tell her she was making mountains out of molehills, even when she knew she wasn't. This was most definitely a mountain and he didn't deny that he'd climbed right to the top of it. Arty pulled the tea towel away from her face and obliterated any last trace of hope she had. "It's over, Joy. Nina and I are in love and I want a divorce."

Arthur and Nina left Joy in the tainted house that night, where she lay on the single bed in the spare room (because she couldn't stand the idea of being near her marital bed) and cried until she slept, and then woke with a start and cried some more. She moved out the next day, heading to the vacant shop she'd inherited from her dad with a sleeping bag, a suitcase of clothes and toiletries, and *The Fortis Trilogy*. She would collect more over the coming weeks, including her antique wedding trunk, which it seemed ironic to have kept, in light of the circumstances. But the trunk had been her mother's and she couldn't stand the idea that Nina and Arthur would get to keep it or, God forbid, have sex on it, or anywhere near it. Joy put it straight into the shed after that thought, because everything that had come from her home—now Arthur and Nina's home—seemed to be infused with adultery.

That first morning after she woke up in the almost empty house at the back of the grubby shop on Station Street, Joy had felt lost. She'd gone out for a walk and found herself at the edge of the ocean. With hardly a second thought, Joy walked in fully clothed. In the gentle swell she had swum and cried, and dunked her head and screamed into the ocean. And she'd done it almost every day since, although she rarely felt the need to scream anymore.

On her way home from that first swim, soaking wet, she'd met Montgomery Doyle. Standing at his shop door, sipping a coffee, he'd watched her drip her way up the sidewalk and unlock the front door of what would one day be Joyful Suds. He nodded politely at her and she returned the gesture, pleased he was respecting her space. She liked him from the get-go, but tried to remain distant around him—she wasn't ready for any more heartbreak and the easiest way to avoid that was to steer clear of dashing men.

That Joy was such a different person, such a lost soul. Not at all like the determined, strong woman who was now facing forward, ready to tackle whatever came her way. In 2050, she wouldn't have to worry about the girls; they'd have their biological parents too, and they were old enough to look after themselves. She could seek medical help from doctors with almost three decades more experience with brain tumors than the ones now. Whatever happened, she and her girls would be together.

A glimmer of sun was piercing the horizon and her water bottle had gone cold. Time to head home. She would make the girls their Special Birthday Breakfast and they would all prepare themselves for the afternoon. The supermoon would rise at 4:39 p.m. and they needed to be ready.

As she approached their block of shops, which she had called home for over two decades, she stopped and stared, taking them in. They could've been any set of buildings in any suburb. But they weren't just any set of buildings, they were hers—her house, her livelihood, her pocket of the world—and she cared about their occupants deeply, even if she never really showed it. Even Linh, whom she'd been determined not to like. She imagined telling Andie that it was okay to be in love with a woman; she wasn't sure she'd ever told her that before. It was a little late now, Joy knew. If she had her time again, maybe she would change a few things.

"Joy?" Monty's voice surprised her. She was frozen in place just short of Ellen's yellow-painted frontage.

"You're up early," she replied, as if nothing at all was out of place.

"You've been standing there the better half of ten minutes and although you're a lovely sight, I did start to think something may be wrong."

"Nothing's wrong, Monty. Everything is quite good, actually."

The sight of him still warmed her.

He had been named for the actor Montgomery Clift, who appeared in *From Here to Eternity*. He'd told her this story a long time ago, explaining that his mother was so besotted by the movie she'd named him after the leading man. He'd never even watched the film, he said, just never got around to it. "You should make the time," she remembered saying, "for something your mother thought so fondly of."

Given that story, Joy had decided the stray cat Cassie had found should be named after an actress from the same movie. It was also a calculated move; Joy had hoped that naming the cat Donna, after Donna Reed, would make Monty more willing to adopt her. Whether it was the name, or just a quiet love of bedraggled animals, he'd put up little resistance.

It had been lovely living next door to Monty, and in another life, she thought they could've been something. She knew she probably loved him, although she didn't intend to dwell on that. It was too tenuous, too unpredictable. She hadn't allowed herself to enter relationship territory; it had always felt far too dangerous, and not just because of the heartache. If she'd let Monty into the twins' lives, properly let him in, then he would've been entitled to some honesty about where they were from.

Joy moved toward him, as close as publicly acceptable.

"The twins' birthday today?" he said.

"Twenty-one," she replied.

"Plans?"

"Keeping it low-key." She smiled. "But we're celebrating."

"Yes, of course. You've raised wonderful children, Joy. They're very special. As are you."

Monty Doyle's grin still displayed the mischievousness she could envisage on the twenty-year-old version of him. He didn't discuss that era of his life and she just put it down to him being private, or maybe he'd suffered a lost love like her.

"Thank you. I'm very proud of them."

"As you should be," he said. "See you tomorrow?"

"See you tomorrow, Monty," she lied.

Before she left, she took a few extra seconds to take one last look at her handsome neighbor's face.

CHAPTER 14

CASSIE

8 a.m.

"I'm going to ask her about it." Andie's voice interrupted Cassie's semi-awake state. She wasn't ready to open her eyes yet, not properly.

It was the last day in that bed, in that house, in that time. She was about to travel twenty-seven years without aging a day; never had time seemed so slippery or unsettling. The brutal reality was: time was up.

When Cassie glanced over, Andie was sitting stiffly on the edge of her own bed. She looked harried and was already dressed. On their birthday, they had always had their bacon, eggs, and pancakes in their PJs, it was tradition. It seemed there would be nothing normal about today.

Cassie licked her dry lips and sipped water from the glass on her bedside table. "Ask her about what?"

"Our real father."

"Really? Today?"

"Cass, if I'm right—and you know I am—then we will find out today one way or another. So why not ask? Aren't you just hanging to know?"

"No." Cassie rolled onto her back and used the palms of her hands to rub her eyes. "And happy birthday to you too."

"Just birthday. No happy today."

"Whatever. Can you wait until after breakfast?" Cassie asked.

"I need you to know what happens in the final chapter of the first book," Andie said. "In *Daughters of Now*."

Cassie looked at her sister, wondering why Andie couldn't let it go, accept their fate. Or at least stop talking about it. It was making her even more anxious about what the day held. "Go on then."

"They all get poisoned," Andie said.

"Who does?"

"The sisters in the book, Stellar and Lunar. They are poisoned and the only thing that saves them is being whisked to the future by their real parents."

"So they don't die?"

"Well, no, as it happens, *they* don't. But the people who raised them do. Their versions of Joy die. The parents are reprogrammed by 'The Society'—think of them as The People—and it makes them try to kill Stellar and Lunar. That's us. They poison them all."

Cassie shook her head. "Wait, why would they poison themselves?"

"Because it has to look convincing. And The Society doesn't give a hoot about what happens to the people who raised the sisters."

Cassie found her twin's persistence tiring. "Can you just leave it be?"

"No."

They stared at each other in the way that siblings do the world over. Silently daring the other to give in, break focus, storm off. Cassie would feel far more confrontation-ready if she wasn't in her cozy cartoon-dog pajamas. They were possibly a little childish for a twenty-one-year-old soon-to-be hero.

Andie broke away from the stare-off first and Cassie banked the victory quietly.

"And then this morning I found these." Andie pulled a packet of tablets out of her pillowcase.

"What are those?" Cassie leaned over to snatch the packet from Andie. She read the label. "Endone?"

Andie nodded, her eyes open wide. Too wide. The sort of look that would make Cassie think she needed to double-lock the register if she saw it on a customer.

"Where did you get these from?"

"Mum's cupboard in the in-between."

"But it's locked." Cassie immediately worried Andie had broken it open and Joy would discover it. She always felt on the verge of being in trouble when Andie was up to something, and lately her sister always seemed up to something.

"She leaves the key in her bedroom when she goes for a swim. I just borrowed it." Andie waggled her eyebrows as if Cassie should be impressed with her wiliness, but the treachery just made her feel sick. No wonder Andie seemed wide awake; she'd been up for hours.

"I'm sure there's a reason she has these."

"Yeah, to murder us. I've read the instructions—this is heavy-duty stuff. Mum does not need these."

"You've read too many Agatha Christies. Mum is not going to kill us. Why would she?"

"Everything else in this story has been played out almost to the letter."

"Okay, well, what do they eat that poisons them? We'll just avoid it."

"Champagne."

"That should be easy then, we've never had champagne." Cassie threw the pills at her sister. "You need to put those back before Mum notices."

"I don't think she'll even realize. She has more of them—like shitloads of them. As if she's stockpiling them for something." Andie shook *Daughters of Now* at her. "For *this*."

Cassie narrowed her eyes, wondering when Andie had turned into such a fearmonger. She pulled her slippers on. "Today is a big day—the biggest, in fact. And we will get through it together." She was determined to be the sensible one. "Let's just go and get some breakfast. Or do you think she's laced the pancakes too?"

"I don't know what she's capable of."

"She hasn't poisoned the pancakes, Andie. Come on."

Cassie headed downstairs and hoped Andie would follow. The smell of bacon fat frying called to her.

"Happy birthday, my beautiful stars." Joy rubbed her hands on a tea towel and flicked off the hotplate. Cassie took in the mess that was their kitchen and saw that Joy had made their table look quite festive with the good tablecloth, neatly arranged cutlery, folded pink cloth napkins, and a pickle jar stuffed full of peppercorn tree leaves as a centerpiece.

The bell rang in the shop, and Joy put the spatula down and rushed out the connecting door. Cassie was not surprised that the laundromat was still open on such an important day. Professionalism, after all, was one of their key service values and that included maintaining reliable hours of business. What would happen tomorrow? The doors would automatically unlock, but the house and shop would no longer hold the Moody family. How long would it take anyone to notice their absence? The thought of Monty realizing they were gone was unbearable, and she wondered if she could leave a note for him to explain everything. She didn't want him to feel abandoned.

Andie sat at the table, eyed the mound of Joy's homemade pancakes, and then loaded two on her plate. Cassie relaxed. Maybe she had gotten through to her sister.

"You need to be careful around her today," Andie said while Joy was out of earshot.

"Andie, she would never . . ."

"Just be careful."

Joy hurried back in. "Mrs. Hughes does love a chat, doesn't she?"

Cassie had never found Mrs. Hughes particularly chatty. In fact, she was usually quite standoffish.

"I can't believe my girls are turning twenty-one." Joy's face crinkled with happiness as she plonked a plate of crispy bacon down on the table before pulling out her own chair and joining them. She dabbed at her flushed face with a tissue. "I'm so proud of you both. Today is going to be so very special."

Cassie looked at Andie, giving her a desperate last telepathic plea to just let things be.

"What time is everything happening today, Mum?" Andie gave Joy a smile that, to Cassie's eye, gleamed with mischievousness.

"Moonrise." Joy looked pleased. "Four thirty-nine p.m. exactly."

"What if they reschedule again?" Andie asked, forking pancake dipped in syrup into her mouth.

Cassie kicked out at Andie and got her shin. Her sister grimaced, but Joy seemed none the wiser. She was buzzing with a frantic energy, but so was Andie. Cassie was the only rational one in the room.

"No, no, no. I don't think that's the case at all. The supermoon is tonight—that's significant, you know. And it falls on your birthday, which is what they've waited for. What they needed. This is definitely it." Joy looked distant. "I think."

Andie reloaded her fork. "Is their time machine powered by the moon?"

"I don't think it's a time machine so much as a hole we will be able to get through, you know. Caused by the moon being so close to the Earth." Joy waved her hand dismissively. "I'm no scientist." She picked up some bacon with her fingers and bit a chunk off the end.

Cassie watched, horrified. Joy always used cutlery, even for pizza. Who was this woman?

Andie, it seemed, was not done with provoking their mother. "You've just always been the authority on it, that's all."

Joy sniffed and her eyes darted to Andie. Cassie watched as her mother appeared to center herself, breathing deeply. She had the distinct impression Joy was trying to hold in an outburst. Cassie watched her mother, who seemed to be sitting on a precipice. And then, as casual as she'd ever been, Joy said, "Eat up. You'll need full bellies to tackle the future."

Cassie was pissed off. Special Birthday Breakfast was all but ruined. Her pancakes felt gluggy and hard to swallow. She didn't even feel like cross-thatching bacon on her stack of pancakes and drizzling maple syrup over it, sweet and savory all mushed up together, her favorite way to eat them. Had Joy or Andie been paying attention, they would've noticed Cassie was not enjoying herself, but they were both too self-absorbed to care.

Cassie had been thinking long and hard about what Andie had said about their supposed father. She knew a bit about DNA from their biology textbooks, and sharing fifty percent DNA with someone left little room for any other familial links beyond being either their mother or father. Maybe she had been onto something to think that he had been recorded on the History Mystery database as a child. But she kept thinking it was more likely that the ability to travel through time was why this had happened, whether by accident or not. Or else—and this thought only occurred to her at the breakfast table—The People had engineered this whole scenario so Andie would have reason to turn on Joy and accuse her of lying. Like how the Empire weaponized the citizens against each other by reprogramming them. Maybe they were all just pawns in a game they had no real control over.

She shuddered, the food bitter in her mouth.

The biggest problem was that either her mother was lying to her or Andie was. Neither option was great; these were the two people she loved most. If her mum was the deceitful one—which was a huge, terrible, horrible thing—then they were just average, everyday people. But it would mean they could stay put, in the comfortable here and now. Whereas if Andie was lying—or just plain wrong—then they'd all be hurtled into the future in just a few hours. Andie's reservations had really started to eat away at her. It compounded her longing not to leave, a completely traitorous wish after all the effort Joy had put in to safeguarding and preparing them.

Amid all the doom and gloom, a thought occurred to her. If Andie was right—and she still wasn't convinced she was—then it meant she would get a shot at a second kiss with Omar, who she was quite sure she was falling in love with.

Cassie considered her sister and her mother carefully. It seemed like a fifty-fifty bet as to who was right, and she had no idea who she hoped would win.

CHAPTER 15

ANDIE

12:15 p.m.

Andie was cleaning in the shop when Joy returned with their birthday lunch. This was another tradition; they each got to pick anything (within reason), but it had to be from the same place. Special day or not, Joy only intended to make one stop. It was an easy pick, McDonald's every time.

Andie was humming with energy, ready to have the conversation that Cassie had tried to stop. Someone had to have it, and what if Mum actually admitted she'd been doing the wrong thing? Andie needed Cassie there to hear it, or she'd never believe it.

She had played out the conversation with her mum a thousand times over in her head. It was quite good, the way Andie imagined it, although she had a feeling real-life Joy might be less agreeable. Despite acting like the tougher of the twins, Andie's stomach felt wrung out and she'd been a fidgety mess all morning.

To everyone else in the shop, it was just a regular Tuesday. The cold months were always a little bit busier because no one wanted to use multiple clotheslines while they waited for Melbourne's feeble winter sun to dry their washing.

Tina and her son, Tiny (they presumed it wasn't his real name, but that's what his mother called him), were in and Tiny had regaled Andie with his latest adventures in remote control car races. He'd won on the weekend, he said, and Tina beamed proudly.

Andie disappeared through the in-between, shutting the door and locking it behind her.

The hinges of the back gate squeaked, signaling her mother's return. Cassie was madly drawing something on the couch, as if it was a desperate last attempt to capture everything she could before 4:39 p.m. Andie wanted to take Cassie's anxiety from her. If only she would accept what Andie had tried to tell her. They weren't leaving; there was no need to panic.

Joy came through the back door with three brown bags of McDonald's and plonked them on the table. The smell was reliably mouth-watering. Andie loved a Filet-O-Fish, while Cassie and Joy always went for the cheeseburger. Andie lowered herself into her chair, knowing the confrontation was imminent, but unable to resist getting in at least a few bites before it started. It was her birthday, after all, and no point arguing on an empty stomach. She reached for a carton of fries. Cassie tossed her sketchpad down onto the couch and joined them.

"One sec, girls," Joy said. "Something special before we start."

Andie slowed her eating, hoping Joy didn't reprimand her for not being polite enough to wait until they were all seated. From the fridge, Joy pulled out a bottle of champagne. Andie felt her world slow down, then freeze. She looked to Cassie, who was equally shocked. It was exactly as Andie had said that morning, like Joy had listened in and was following the script.

"Oh, crap," Andie hissed under her breath.

From the top cupboard, Joy pulled out three tall glasses that they'd never before had cause to use. She had always said that indulging in alcohol was asking for trouble.

Andie's heart quickened, rattling at her ribs, seemingly loud enough for Joy and Cassie to hear.

"Oh dear, they're so grubby. They need a quick wash. You girls go ahead and start," Joy said.

"It's all right, we'll wait." Andie couldn't stop watching her mother, turning on the water, waiting while it heated, rinsing the glasses, drying them on the tea towel. Then Joy popped the champagne, which should have been a special moment, but it wasn't because all Andie could think was, *Are we about to die?* If Joy really did think they were going to the future—and she'd been quite unshakeable in that belief—then it wasn't out of the question to think that she was going to carry out other parts of *Daughters of Now.* Poisoning Cassie and Andie would mean she didn't have to tell them the truth.

Andie watched avidly, sure that if she didn't see her mum sprinkle in any crushed-up tablets or add any liquids from suspicious tiny vials into their glasses, then perhaps they'd be okay. For now at least. And maybe she was wrong. She really hoped so. Her jaw was pressed so tight, her back teeth ached. Joy couldn't—she wouldn't, would she? But one thought loomed ever present, and larger than anything that offered reason in Andie's mind: Joy had had time to plan.

"Now, I have to admit," Joy said as the bubbles fizzed over the edge after her first pour, "it's a low-alcohol sparkling wine. I know that seems a bit overly sensible, but it's a big day, and I didn't want anything to ruin it." She laughed, positively buzzing with excitement. "I'd hate the bubbles to go to our heads and for us to need a nap. Not worth the trouble, is it?" She carried the three glasses to the table. They were full to the brim and she placed them down carefully. "But this is too important a day not to celebrate, and who knows what we will face in the future. Best not to waste this moment."

The champagne suddenly felt too obvious, and Andie realized

the poison could be in anything; it might have been added to their food. She dropped her sandwich back into its packet. Her mouth felt coated in something unnatural and her stomach swirled.

"Here you go." Joy pushed Andie's fizzing glass toward her.

"You want us to drink this?" Andie asked.

"Yes, of course, silly. That's what it is for. Oh, Andromeda, you do make me laugh."

None of them were laughing.

Joy settled in her chair, quite girlishly giddy. "A toast," she said. "To the future." She indicated they both needed to pick up their glasses. They did.

Andie brought hers close enough to her face that she could hear the bubbles fizz and feel them lightly spray her nose and lips. She looked at Cassie, who was beaming at their mother, glass poised, ready to drink.

"To you both, the Daughters of the Future Revolution. Our own trilogy, together through time."

This was really happening, Andie thought. What the hell was she meant to do?

"You, Cassie and Andie, are an incredible bunch of atoms."

Joy pushed her glass forward and the twins clinked their glasses on hers. Instead of immediately sipping the drink, Joy paused and looked at the girls. That was all Andie needed. With a sweep of her arm, she ripped Cassie's glass away from her and threw it against the wall, where it shattered, spraying liquid over some of the sketches taped there. Then she hurled her own glass onto the floor, the delicate crystal fragmenting against the hard wood and skittering across the boards.

"Andromeda! What are you doing? They're the good glasses!" Joy yelled.

"Why didn't you drink?" Andie shouted back. "*Why?*"

"What do you mean?"

"You waited for us to go first. What did you put in it?"

"In it? Andie, what do you mean?"

"These are what I mean." Andie took the blister pack of tablets from her pocket and threw it onto the table.

Joy snatched the packet up and inspected it. "How did you get these?" Her eyes were wild.

"Is that what was in the champagne? Were you drugging us?"

"No," Joy said, almost solemnly. "There's nothing in the champagne. I mean, just alcohol, but not much, like I said. Look." Her mum took a sip from her own glass, but this did not calm Andie down one bit. It was just further trickery, she was sure of it.

"How are we meant to believe that? You've lied to us so often."

"I have not."

"You *have*. You think you're going to the future. You are not!"

Joy twitched. "I thought you'd be happy I was coming with you?"

"No, Mum, I mean none of us are going. We're not going *anywhere*."

"But you have to. *We* have to. The fate of the future—"

Andie cut her off. "There is no Global War, there are no people chasing us, there are no future parents. There's just the here and the now and whatever happens in twenty-seven years, then so be it. But it's not one of your goddamn fantasy novels."

"What?" Joy gulped in air, like she was struggling to fill her lungs. "What do you mean?"

Andie assessed her mother, who was not backing down. Why wasn't she backing down? Andie needed something else to show Joy she had been caught out. She raced upstairs, her feet thundering on the floor. From her bed, she grabbed the books Linh had loaned her, the History Mystery results bookmarking her place. Back downstairs, she threw them onto the table, knocking Joy's champagne over in the process.

"I've read these. I know what happens." Andie was shaking with anger.

"My books? What about them?" Joy whispered, confused.

"They go to the future just like us? A bit of a coincidence, Mum."

Joy's bottom lip shook as she considered the novels, running her hand over the smooth front covers.

Andie flipped over *Daughters of Now*, reading the blurb. "In 2042, The Validus Empire formed: a superpower intent on world domination. Scientists Tuck and Laurel know they have to protect their daughters and do the only thing that will save them: give them away. They find a tear in time, a way to get the children of these rebel forces to a safer place, decades earlier, where they can be raised away from the devastation Validus is reaping. They return to the future on their twentieth birthday. Sound familiar, Mum?"

Joy had listened without interruption. Andie couldn't tell if she was unable to speak or just caught off guard and scrambling for more lies.

"And this." Andie opened up the DNA test results. "Who is Tyler?"

Joy took the paper from Andie, read it, shook her head and kept shaking it. "I . . . I don't know."

"Andie, can you just stop?" Cassie stood and came around the table to be closer to their mum. Joy's face had paled; she wasn't reacting the way Andie had expected at all. Not defensive, but confused and bereft.

"I've got a headache," Joy said finally, quietly. Defeated.

"Mum. I know we aren't going to the future. We aren't going anywhere. We live and work in a laundromat. We're just normal girls. Your daughters. Or . . . someone's daughters." Andie felt desperate to have Joy tell her that she was right. She was as close to tears as she could recall being in a long time. Instead of relief at getting her suspicions out in the open, she just felt hollow, as if her insides had been scooped out with an ice-cream spoon.

"Have The People gotten to you?" Joy asked, then put her hand up. "No, that's not right, is it? There's no . . ." Joy sighed, rubbing her forehead, and Cassie clutched her mum's shoulders. The counter bell rang in the shop, three times in quick succession.

"Stop it, Andie, you have to stop." Cassie was crying.

But Andie was unable to slow down. She felt as if she were a rogue wave that had knocked Joy down and now was refusing to let her get to her feet. "There are no 'People,' Mum. Just everyone going about their normal, everyday, boring lives doing nothing extraordinary. No one is traveling through time and space. Except in the normal way. Day by day, twenty-four hours at a time. That's the only time traveling we're doing."

Cassie and Joy were staring at her like she was a monster, as if she'd physically reached out and hit them both. For a split second she considered doing just that, but instead she marched loudly to the back door.

She turned, stared straight at Joy, and spat words, hoping they'd inflict pain. "You've ruined our lives! I wish you were dead!"

Cassie gasped through sobs. "No. You don't mean that!"

"Where are you going?" Joy asked.

"To live my life!" Andie called back, feeling dramatic but not caring. She flung open the door to the courtyard. "Happy stupid birthday!"

Andie slammed the door behind her.

CHAPTER 16
JOY

1:15 p.m.

Joy insisted that Cassie follow Andie, who was clearly not thinking straight. Joy worried about what her daughter might do while so worked up. She could tell how torn Cassie felt about leaving her, though, so she tried to look as calm and collected as she could. Once she heard the gate creak shut, she collapsed into the mess she really was.

The Fortis Trilogy was her favorite series, but she hadn't read them for some time. And there were definitely some parts of the books that echoed the twins' circumstances; that was one of the reasons she liked them so much. Although, when she thought about it for a moment longer, she realized that she had the books first, not the girls. She pondered that, her mind flicking back and forth. Something was rattling around, like a pinball in a machine. It was as if her memories had stopped short at a red light and piled up one behind another, on and on for blocks. She felt a churning sense of something terrible coming.

Joy was willfully ignorant as to the speed at which the mass in her head was growing. She had flashes of clarity, but the times when she got it wrong felt just as clear. Sometimes when she felt her least confused, she tried to write important things down in a letter so she could read it, or hand it to her daughters. But when she went back and looked at it again, it was impossibly disjointed and made little sense. Which was exactly what it felt like to be in her head 93 percent of the time.

The story she'd told the twins had started as a lie and slowly it had merged into a truth. As if she'd melted down chocolate and it had cooled and hardened again in a shape just as convincing as the original. Had she continued to see her doctor, she might have better understood what was happening, but Joy had done what she'd always done, which was to sweep aside the worry and replace it with hard work and, sometimes, reality TV. The storyline of *The Fortis Trilogy* was practically Cassie and Andie's now. The truth of where they'd come from and what she'd done to keep them came in tiny bursts, as unpredictable as getting a Draw Four in Uno.

She realized with a jolt that she hadn't reminded Cassie to be back by 4:39. But surely the girls would return. She could always check where they were on her phone. She'd given them the GPS watches long ago, after Sangeeta had seen Cassie down on the beach with some local schoolkids. The twins were meant to stay put in the laundromat while she went to have her nails done, one of the things she liked to do for herself. She had told them the watches were gifts from the future, but she'd ordered them on eBay, even paying for an extended warranty. That had been a lie, just a little one, but all for the greater good. It was her duty as a mother to know where her children were, and with the added pressure of The People out to find them, she sometimes felt unfairly weighed down with the responsibility.

Joy thought long and hard about the day she'd heard the chopper and been sure their time was up, that Cassie had compromised them all. She'd fight for the twins, to the end of her days, through time and space and whatever else they wanted to throw at her. It was that easy and that hard.

Her shoulders felt tight and her heart hammered; she wasn't so certain of anything anymore.

The shop bell rang again. Some customers were overly persistent, even with the very clear sign: "No staff in attendance until 1:30 p.m., have a joyful day." Joy straightened up and steeled herself before charging through the in-between.

The man at the desk wasn't a regular, nor was he in possession of anything to have laundered. His skin was tanned in the way that people who were careless with SPF often were and he had an eagle tattooed across his neck, the beak moving when his Adam's apple bobbed up and down. A strange choice, she thought. He was broad-shouldered, physically imposing.

"Can I help you?" Joy forced a smile that she was sure was nearer a grimace.

"I'm looking for Britney White."

He didn't sound like he was asking for a ghost, but that was exactly what he was doing. Joy couldn't do anything other than stare, but he didn't break her gaze. He had clearly spent a lot of time staring down a variety of people in his life, and the manager of a laundromat was hardly a challenge. She stood her ground, returning the glare. Her body felt ready to dissolve into a puddle, but she wasn't about to let him know that.

"Who are you?" Joy asked, though she probably should have said she'd never heard of Britney White in her life. But she had, of course she had.

"I'm Tyler Rodriguez."

"You were Britney's boyfriend." The words left her mouth before she could stop them. It had taken Tyler two decades to come here. How had he managed to arrive on this very day, of all the days?

Britney had spoken of Tyler often. Their relationship was as on and off as the light in a refrigerator.

"So you know her?" he asked.

Joy noted Tyler's use of the present tense. "I knew her, yes. I was a social worker back then. I knew the whole family."

It was funny how Joy found her recall for long-ago memories easier to conjure than recent ones. Unless, she thought with a momentary panic, she couldn't tell the difference anymore about what was real and what wasn't; perhaps all of it was blurred to the point where it had become clear again. But Britney . . . Joy's recollection of her seemed distinct. The girl who had lived with her, who she thought she could save after all the ones she couldn't. The girl who had returned, but had changed, been corrupted by The People and intent on doing the unthinkable. Which meant, in turn, that Joy had had to do something exceptional.

"Ah, right. So, you knew the whole lot of them, then?"

"Yes. Erica and all her children."

Tyler grunted at the mention of Britney's mum. "Erica hasn't changed a bit. Don't think she even noticed Brit was gone."

"I'm sure she did in her own way."

"And sorry, I didn't catch your name," he said.

Joy wondered fleetingly if she should lie but didn't see the point. "Joy Moody."

Tyler considered her answer, as if she'd just told him a riddle, or perhaps the answer to one. "Well, her sister and I have been looking for her for a long time."

"That's very noble of you," Joy said, unsure what the correct thing was to say in these circumstances. The circumstance being that she knew exactly where Britney was.

The shop seemed like the wrong place to be having such a personal discussion. There were no customers at that moment, but Joy still felt exposed and the pink walls and glossy machines all seemed a little too bright for such a serious topic.

"Not noble at all, just trying to do the right thing. Which I shoulda done in the first place."

Joy didn't reply, wondering what Tyler would think the "right" thing was. She found it to be incredibly subjective.

"I didn't do anything to her," he said, as if that was why Joy had gone silent.

"Okay," she replied.

"Is she here?" His voice was deep, coarse.

She answered quickly. "No, I'm sorry. I haven't seen Britney for years." Joy was not lying; she hadn't seen Britney since 2002. Her heart pounded against her ribs. She knew full well she could give this man the answer he'd been seeking for the past two decades. Just like that, she could set this straight. But she wasn't going to. Not yet, anyway.

"I knew it wouldn't be quite that easy." Tyler looked discouraged.

"Can I ask what it was that brought you here?" Joy asked.

"It was History Mystery," he replied.

"What is that?" Those words had been emblazoned across the paperwork Andie had thrust at her, but the feigning of ignorance came easily.

"'Solve your past fast'? They're the ones with the annoying ads on the telly."

"We don't have a television," Joy said.

He didn't bother commenting on how unusual that was, just sighed. She felt a pang of kindness toward him. "Can I interest you in a cup of tea?" she asked, surprising herself. "And you can fill me in on the details?"

Tyler gave a shrug, which Joy took as a yes, and she beckoned him through the in-between and into the house. The number of visitors Joy brought through to this part of the property could be counted on one hand. An occasional tradesperson, Monty, very few others. She was being reckless and she wasn't sure why. It might have been because she knew what it was to miss someone for years.

It was different with Arthur, of course, but it was still love and loss, and if someone could have easily fixed the pain of losing her husband, she hoped they'd have helped her.

Joy boiled the kettle, watching Tyler as she busied herself with the mugs and teabags.

"Sugar?"

"Just black for me. Ta."

"A splash of cold water, then?"

"Thanks."

Tyler's eyes roamed the room and she wondered what he saw as he took it all in. It was such a modest space, with mostly secondhand furniture that Joy had never quite gotten around to updating. The bookshelf Tyler stood in front of now had been bought at a garage sale up the road and she'd paid the man an extra five dollars to help her lug it home. The kitchen could do with a facelift, and the floorboards were very well worn. It was home. She checked the clock. Home for another three and a bit hours, at least.

He moved his foot and it crunched over a fragment of champagne flute. "There's some broken glass down here."

"I dropped something this morning and haven't had a chance to clean it up. Do mind your feet."

Tyler tilted his head to take in the wall of Cassie's sketches. "Did you do these?"

"No, my . . ." Joy started to say "daughter," but stopped herself, feeling protective. She looked to the framed picture of the girls and her on her little side table. "My daughter. She draws." Joy knew how talented her daughter was.

"They're really good," Tyler said. "Brit loved to draw."

"I know," Joy replied and his head snapped around to her, surprised.

"She was private about that. She must have liked you to tell you about it."

"Yes, we got along."

"*Was* she here?" he asked.

Joy filled their mugs with boiling water, considering how much to share. "She stayed here for a little while. I wanted to help her. But that was a very long time ago."

"Do you remember when? What date did she leave?"

Joy focused on the teabags, dangling them in the cups and bobbing them up and down. In and out of the boiling water, exactly what she felt like right now. "It has to be . . ." She pretended to think, although she could have told him the exact day. "I'd say twenty-ish years ago, now."

"Did she tell you where she was going?"

"Not exactly."

"But she told you something?"

"Said she might head north." Joy hated the lies as they tumbled from her mouth.

The traffic congestion in her brain was stacking up again; twenty-ish years ago Britney had come to take the girls. When Joy mulled it over now, it seemed clear how un-Britney-like the teen had been back then. The People had obviously gotten to her, and Joy had been left with no options. She wanted to yell it at him: "She left me no choice!" But it felt far less clear, less altruistic now with Tyler in front of her. Joy had a harrowing feeling that she was less mother and more monster.

She inhaled deeply, realizing she had been holding her breath.

"As in north like Ringwood? Or north like Coolangatta?"

"We never really discussed it further. I'm so sorry. I didn't realize it would be important."

No one had ever asked her before. She had waited for someone to come and speak to her, the social worker who had dealt with the Whites so often, but it never happened.

Tyler raked his fingers over his head, which was shaved down to stubble. Joy noted a sprinkle of gray.

She put the tea on the coffee table and opened a packet of Scotch Fingers and gestured for Tyler to sit on the couch. She hastily turned the framed photo facedown so the three Moody women's faces weren't on display.

He moved through the small room and sat.

She remembered then that the History Mystery letter Andie had flung at her was still laid out on the dining table next to the books. Joy hurried over to them, hoping to look as if she was just straightening things up. She quickly packed the books back into their glossy little case, slipping the DNA results in with them. "Such a mess sometimes." Joy attempted a casual tone, but knew it came off as rigid. "So what were you saying about the history thing?"

"It's a DNA, family tree place. It's a way people work out if they're descendants of Genghis Khan or George the Fifth, or whatever."

"And you were curious?"

"No. Not really." He laughed. "But Brit's sister, Tiffany, was dead keen on it. She's been looking for her big sister all this time. And she believes me—that I didn't do anything to her. She'd be about the only one, of course."

"Have you been waiting for her to come back all these years?"

He smiled, looking at his hands, which were interlaced, forearms leaning on his thighs. "No. I'm not quite that romantic. I was a pretty shit boyfriend back then, but I definitely wasn't into murder." He eyed Joy seriously. "I've got two kids now and it's made me a bit softer, or something. Like, I get it more, you know. Don't know what I'd do if one of them went missing." He shrugged. "Just keep looking, I guess. Can't just give up on someone, can you?"

Joy shuffled uncomfortably.

"And, of course, if we can find her, maybe the jacks might stop knocking on my door every couple of years. I think they just figure if they ask me often enough, I'll admit to it, tell 'em where she's buried. But I can't, you know?" he asked in a way that made her think he wanted a reply, but there were no words she could think of that were suitable to fill the silence. He kept speaking, giving Joy the chance to untie her tongue. "'Cause I didn't do anything."

"I'm sorry you've gone through that." And she genuinely was.

"I keep this as a reminder of her." He rubbed his hand over a tattoo, finely drawn words that scrolled and looped up his right forearm. "I didn't want to give myself the chance to forget."

His arm was a mishmash of colors and patterns that started under his sleeve and continued down to the back of his hand. She wondered how job interviews went, given his appearance, although she realized he might not have gone for the corporate sort of employment opportunities where someone would care. "It says, 'I see the future and it's all about us.' Brit loved that song."

Joy prickled at its familiarity. She couldn't place it, not immediately, and almost reached out to grab his arm to study it further, wanting to seize the memory and tug it free from whatever it was stuck on. *I see the future and it's all about us.*

"I know this." Joy's voice came as barely a whisper. The reason she knew it felt so close she could almost reach it.

"It's from a song by Wrong Turn. You must have heard it?"

Joy shook her head, not sure that was it. Her tea was too hot and she popped it back on the table to let it cool down. She picked up a biscuit and snapped it in half, letting a fine spray of biscuit crumbs rain down over her pants.

"Anyway, I got this." He stuck his hand into his back pocket. Joy tensed, hoping Tyler didn't notice. For a fleeting second she thought he was going to produce a knife. She imagined he knew what she'd done and was seeking vengeance. It was only his phone, though, and she relaxed while he found what he was looking for and held it out.

Joy took hold of his oversized phone, which displayed "History Mystery" in a vintage-style font across the top of the screen. The information was clear enough: "Andie—female—50 percent shared DNA—relationship: parent/child."

She winced. Andie hadn't even bothered to use an alias. All these years hiding the girls and Andie had simply handed over information for anyone to find her. "It's amazing you had such luck with this one company."

He shrugged. "Seven different companies, actually. Tiff had us both profiled for them all. She was, and is, determined to figure it out. And it's not like it matters who has my DNA—the coppers got it years ago."

Joy's eyes prickled, thinking of Tiffany White and the sister-shaped hole she'd had in her life for the past two decades.

"Is your daughter's name Andie?" he asked.

Despite her tea still being too hot, Joy took long, steady sips to give her hands something solid to do. The cup rattled on its saucer. *Steady on, Joy,* she told herself. *No one knows but you.*

"It's Cassie," she said, finally. "Cassiopeia."

He nodded and clicked his fingers, then sighed. "Suppose I didn't really think it would be that easy."

Joy felt uncomfortable, like Tyler was acting, playing a part. *Does he know? How would he know?* "Top up?" she asked.

"No, thanks." He indicated his full cup.

"Don't mind me then," she said and went back to the kettle. She noticed he'd shifted over to her pink armchair, where he leaned back comfortably, taking in the room.

It was odd having a stranger in her space. Joy placed her hands on the counter, closed her eyes, and took three deep breaths. It was okay, she was okay. She filled her cup and returned to the couch.

"Do you think this Andie might be a child of yours? Is that how you interpret that information?"

"Yeah I do. Mine and Brit's, I reckon."

"Oh, yes." Joy really wasn't sure what to make of this. The

People must be behind this, manipulating this man into coming to her house. It was the link to Britney that was really confusing Joy. How had they got Tyler on board? Money, she supposed.

"Are you from the future?" she whispered, just in case she could catch him out.

He looked quizzical and held her gaze.

"Don't worry," she said quickly. "Forget I said anything. And if that's all I can do to help, and I'm really sorry I can't do more, I should be getting back to work."

The kitchen clock read 1:36 p.m.; the day was getting away from her. This wasn't how she wanted to spend the time she had left. She still had to clear out the perishables from the fridge and give the windowsills another quick wipe-down. She might be leaving permanently, but there was no need to leave squalor behind.

On her way to collect lunch that morning, she'd mailed the new version of her will to Monty. She wanted it to arrive after they were gone. Ellen would be furious if she found out that Joy had gone ahead and used a basic DIY kit. Joy hadn't even gotten it from the post office, just downloaded one online and had Hal witness her signature when he'd been in the previous day. It had been remarkably simple.

"Before you go," Joy said, suddenly curious, "how did all this bring you here? There must be a million girls called Andie."

"I've met some interesting people over the years," Tyler said. "They come with the sort of work I do. *Had* to do, you know, after being questioned for murder a couple of times. Anyway, the people I know can find out all sorts of information. Like the address linked to an email account."

"Oh, right then. That is handy."

"Yeah," he said.

"And that email address was linked to here?" Joy attempted surprise.

"No," Tyler said and took a healthy gulp from his own mug.

"It took me to the tattoo joint next door. And the bird in that shop is definitely not my daughter."

"Do you think Britney is with your child somewhere?" Joy was careful not to say Andie's name, in case it rolled too easily off her tongue.

He laughed, longer than was probably appropriate for the circumstances. It startled her. She checked over her shoulder again, looking for Andie or Cassie.

"I don't think Britney is doing anything at all. I think she's long gone. But I *do* think our kid is out there somewhere. Or, more like it, *here* somewhere."

Joy placed her cup on the coffee table and looked at Tyler firmly; now was not the time for her to falter. "What are you suggesting?"

"Was there a baby?" His eyes burned into her with something more intense than just curiosity.

"No," she said, as calmly as she could.

"Know anyone called Andie?" he asked.

All she could manage was to shake her head. A silent no.

Tyler drank the rest of his tea in one go. Joy looked nervously at the little frame she'd tipped over on the table, just beside him. Her two girls in easy reach of him. She pursed her lips, felt how dry they were.

Tyler stood. He seemed taller suddenly; the room barely contained him. "I will find her, Joy."

"Britney?"

"No. Andie."

Joy couldn't help but gulp, then tried to disguise it with a cough. She had no idea why she had let this stranger into her house.

"Make sure she gets the message, yeah?"

For no logical reason, Joy found herself nodding, as if it were an automated bodily function, like sneezing. It wouldn't matter after today, anyway. As long as he left, everything was still on track.

He opened the door to the in-between and Joy felt her shoulders relax. He was going. Then Tyler turned back, as if he'd just remembered something. "There *was* something Brit told Tiff," he said. "Didn't make sense at the time, but she always thought it was just because she was young and not paying much attention."

"It happens. Memory can be fickle."

"Yeah, but now I think she was bang on. The last time Tiff saw her, Brit said, 'Joy is gonna help me get my family back together.'"

Tyler watched Joy closely, and she tried desperately to keep her expression neutral, feeling very small sitting on the couch. She was quite sure her jaw was quivering.

"Oh yes." Her voice betrayed her and sounded shaky.

"Tiff thought she meant 'joy' as in being happy. Right? But maybe she didn't."

"You think she meant . . ."

"You. I think she meant you, Joy."

She couldn't read his face then, but she felt like he could probably read hers. Like her guilt was worn plain as day across her forehead.

"So, I'll speak to you soon," he said, finally.

Joy couldn't meet his gaze, looking instead to the door to the in-between and willing him to go through it. He finally shifted, moving through the door, and left.

She went straight to her desk, opened the jar, and pulled out her mobile phone. She needed to see where the girls were. Hopefully nowhere near the laundromat.

In the monitoring app, she could see Cassie's and Andie's little avatars together, giving her a moment of relief. She knew they were safe if they were together and the twins were far enough away to avoid Tyler. Their location was the little park near the beach where the three of them used to watch the clouds on their picnic rug.

Joy brought up the CCTV. Joyful Suds looked empty, only two dryers flickering with motion. She looked at the sidewalk camera, hoping to find him gone, but he was still outside the shop, looking as if he was assessing the front of her little pink laundromat before tilting his head up and looking straight down the barrel of the camera.

He raised a hand and pointed. It felt like a dart aimed right at her.

Joy felt winded despite him being completely out of reach. Without consideration for how inconvenient it would be to customers, she used the automated system to remotely lock the front door. Monty had installed it for her long ago. Andie and Cassie could use the back.

With shaking hands, Joy checked the Missing Persons website. She hadn't looked at it in years, not since she'd seen Britney on the TV special. She scrolled through the many faces, some pictures older than others. There were just so many lost people. Tiffany White came to mind, one sister desperately searching for another. It made her physically ache.

And then she got to her. Britney. Such a familiar face, her eyes remarkably similar to Cassie's and Andie's. How could that be? Britney was not their mother. She wasn't from the future. She was just a troubled girl who had stayed with Joy for a while.

Joy thumbed through the information on Britney's profile: age at disappearance, age now, hair color, last seen location, and a reward, which hadn't been there previously. One hundred thousand dollars seemed like a lot, but then it was a pittance, really, for a life.

It was 2 p.m. Joy had just under two hours and forty minutes. This was something she should've put right years ago, but she could do it now—not so much for Tyler, who scared the daylights out of her, but for Tiffany and for Britney. Joy clicked the link at the bottom of the page.

CHAPTER 17

CASSIE

4 p.m.

Andie hadn't gone far. It was one of those times Cassie thought they must have a secret way of communicating, a sixth sense for each other. It didn't happen often, but she got a kick out of it when it did. One time Andie sprained her ankle and Cassie had limped home from Monty's, not knowing why until she found her sister with her foot up and an ice pack. Once she'd found her, they sat at the park for a long time, in a semi-silent state, before finally agreeing it was probably time to go home. They both knew they had to be there for the supermoon.

"What will you do when you realize I'm right?" Andie asked as they walked home. Their feet fell into easy sync.

"Let's discuss it at 5 p.m."

"Okay." Andie just nodded. A lot of the fight had drained from her over the course of the afternoon.

When they got to the train tracks, the crossing bells sounded and they waited at the gate for the city-bound train to pass.

"I was scared. I *am* scared. About today and what might happen," Andie said, surprising Cassie with her candidness. "I don't want to leave. If we stay here and we are just normal girls, I am really okay with that. I would actually prefer it."

Me too, Cassie wanted to reply, but wasn't sure it was the right thing to say. She waited too long and the moment was gone, the crossing gate opening. Andie's face dropped and she knew she had let her down. But there had never been a suggestion that their destiny was optional. Could she select option B—stay home? And would she?

It was 4:12 p.m. when they arrived back at Joyful Suds to find the laundromat door locked, an extremely odd occurrence. They weren't late. Perhaps Mum had decided it was best not to have customers arriving while they were attempting to skip through time. The sign wasn't turned, still reading "Open" in the front window, but the "No Service" sign was front and center on the counter. Cassie rattled the door once more—still locked. They moved through the parking lot toward the back gate. They could use the spare key to let themselves in. Maybe Joy had gone out. But it would be risky of her, this close to the deadline.

A Jeep was idling in the Joyful Suds parking lot, nose against the brick wall of the laundromat. They had just passed it when they were called by name.

"Cassie? Andie?"

They watched a man climb out of the driver's seat. Cassie noticed how his shoulders rounded, as if he were uncomfortable with his height. Neither sister spoke; they knew to be wary of strangers, especially seemingly friendly ones.

The man shook his head, as if admonishing himself. "I'm so sorry, you probably don't remember me. I'm your uncle Grant. Your mum's brother."

They had met Uncle Grant, but a long time ago. He barely got a mention from Joy nowadays, as good as a stranger. It had always seemed odd to Cassie, to have a sibling but not ever speak to or hear from them.

"The shop's shut, I thought you might've all been out. It's a big day today, isn't it?"

For a moment, Cassie assumed Grant meant their 4:39 p.m. plans. And that made her think that Joy was closer with him than she knew. But he corrected that quickly enough.

"The big birthday? Twenty-one, isn't it?" Grant smiled and Cassie felt herself relax, but only a little. "I remember turning twenty-one, although I don't remember the actual event. I blame sambuca. I've never drunk it again." He chuckled. He didn't seem unpleasant, almost endearing.

"Yes. It is today." Andie nudged her. "We need to get inside."

Cassie wondered if the right thing to do would be to invite him in. There was no telling what state their mother would be in, though. She'd been barely keeping it together when Cassie had left. Now, with the laundromat locked, and the supermoon less than half an hour away, they could find absolutely anything waiting for them. Definitely not a time for visitors.

"Look, I've gotta get going," Grant said. "I just wanted to drop these off for you." He reached into the front seat of the car, leaning over to the passenger side, and pulled out two colorful gift bags. He thrust one at Cassie, the other at Andie.

"I'm sorry, worst uncle ever. I can't tell you apart."

"That's okay," Cassie said, realizing this was the only birthday present they'd gotten that day. Peering in, she could see the shiny silver top of a bottle and guessed it was probably alcohol. She immediately thought of Joy's reaction. "We can't take these."

"You have to—they're for you. It's a special occasion."

It felt like a very adult sort of gift to receive.

"Thank you," Andie said, not attempting to hand hers back.

"I'm really hoping to get to know you two a bit. I've been MIA from your lives and you're the only nieces I have." Grant put his hand up to his mouth, a conspiratorial stage whisper. "Plus, I grew up with Joy. I know what she can be like." He laughed, but Cassie wasn't about to join in.

"We really should go," Cassie said. "I'm sorry to be rude."

"No, no, it's all good. Like I said, I would love to see you gals soon. Here's my business card. If you ever need me, I'll be there. Just let me know. I'll be like the genie in the bottle."

Cassie took the card. *Grant Moody CEO, Moody Investments.*

"Say hi to Joy for me." He clicked his fingers and then pointed them both like pistols. "Happy birthday now; don't do anything I wouldn't do."

As he climbed back into his Jeep and slammed the door, Cassie realized they were now running really late and hurried for their gate. The back door to the house was unlocked, and Joy jumped when they entered, apparently shocked to see them.

She was standing at the kitchen counter, sniffing loudly as if she'd been crying. "You're back!"

Cassie donned her best reassuring smile, for herself as much as for their mum. "We are. We're ready to go."

Joy tapped her chest, as if checking for something, but then she looked down, realized nothing was there and started scanning the room.

"What is it?" Cassie asked.

"My bag . . . have you seen it?"

"Which one?"

"The pink one, the one with the . . ." Joy looked around.

"It's right here, Mum." Cassie picked up the bag from the counter, almost right in front of Joy. The zip wasn't done up all the way and she tugged it closed, the teeth of the zipper struggling to meet, given the overstuffed contents. She couldn't help but notice it was jam-packed full of fifty- and hundred-dollar bills.

"Mum? What is this? Have you stolen money?"

"Stolen? Cassiopeia, how could you even think that? It's my money. We're taking it with us."

"I didn't think we could take anything."

"We have to try. I don't want to show up empty-handed." Joy took the bag and slung it diagonally over her shoulder. She tapped it for reassurance and then looked at the girls.

Joy was changing the rules at the last minute. "Well, can I take my drawings then?"

"No. There's no time." Her mum looked at her as if she was silly to even suggest it. "We don't want to be late."

Cassie sighed but knew she wouldn't disobey.

"What are these?" Joy asked, snatching the gift bag from Cassie's hands and inspecting the contents. "Where did these come from?"

"Uncle Grant," Andie said.

"*Grant?* Was he here? Is he here now? Where?" Joy scanned the room as if he might be hidden in the kitchen cupboards.

Cassie hurried to reassure her. "No, he was outside. Just wanted to wish us a happy birthday. He's gone now."

"You're sure he's gone?"

"Yes," Cassie said. "Should we be worried about him?"

Joy waved her hands around in front of her in a "it's silly, doesn't matter now" sort of motion, then slid the bottle out of the bag. "What was he thinking?" she muttered. "But never mind, leave them here. It's time to go."

"Yup." Andie's fingertips thrummed the kitchen counter, her expression impassive.

Her mother clapped her hands. "Let's get moving."

At 4:29 p.m., Cassie, Joy, and Andie sat together on the wooden bench in their backyard. The same place they'd apparently arrived at all those years ago as newborns.

Joy linked arms with them, like they used to do when they'd wade out in the water, before they knew how to swim, their elbows interlocking so tightly that it would be near impossible to prize them apart.

Cassie breathed deeply, slowly. She wasn't sure she was ready for this, but hoped the sheer panic and dread she felt would be left behind. The Cassie of 2050 would be so much stronger than this current version. Wouldn't she? She had to be.

At 4:39 p.m., she squeezed her eyes shut and waited to see whether it was her mum or her sister who had been telling the truth.

PART TWO
DEATH IN A LAUNDROMAT

I shall know you, secrets
by the litter you have left
and by your bloody foot-prints.
Lola Ridge, "Secrets"

CHAPTER 18

JOY

June 2002

At first she'd thought it was a bag of garbage left behind, partially obscured by dunes and scrub. Now and then parties were held down on the foreshore, the debris evident the next morning. Usually she'd collect a few errant bottles and chip wrappers and throw them in the trash can, not wanting them to wash out to sea or for her beach to look like a dumping ground.

Joy approached the beach box. The gold numbers read 149, tarnished around the edges from the relentless salt air and rain. As she neared, she realized what she'd seen wasn't garbage at all, but a person in a black sleeping bag. A hooded sweater was pulled tight around their face, a drink bottle lying next to the sleeping bag. Joy worried she might have just stumbled across a dead body—had they been out in the blistering winter cold all night? She stared, waiting to see some movement—even a twitch would do—but none came.

Joy had swum, as was her way in the mornings since Arthur ousted her from their marital home. There was nothing else like the feeling of being submerged in the ocean. Its sheer size reminded her of her place in the scheme of things: nothing, just a speck. Like

Arthur. Like Nina. Her blood still boiled every time she thought of that traitorous whore and her fertile womb.

Joy tamped down the thoughts of her husband and his new fiancée. ("Please, Joy," he'd said as if she owed him something, "let's finalize the divorce. We can move forward, move on, be better people.") Arthur asked her to lie on official documents and say they'd been separated for a full twelve months so the divorce could be settled and he could marry his now-pregnant girlfriend. Funny, Joy thought, the number of times she'd discussed men and failed dates with her former very good friend Nina Nguyen—who was often in tears about the futility of it all—only to help her find love in the most unexpected of ways.

Nina could keep her good-for-nothing husband. Joy had signed the paperwork, confirming the lie, but not before getting him to agree to give her sixty percent of their combined assets. She'd worked hard their whole married life—it wasn't like she'd needed to take maternity leave—and if he wanted to expedite her leaving, he would have to pay for it. And he did. She suspected these were the sort of moments and scenarios in which husbands killed their wives, or vice versa, to avoid all the divorce drama and payouts. How big a hole would she have had to dig to bury Arthur Tennant? She never would, of course; she just wasn't capable. And she was doing okay. She'd surprised herself by returning to work for the department, thinking of all the other families waiting to be helped—the ones she hadn't failed yet. There was always a chance that she could save the next ones. Besides, she was at a bit of a loss about what else to do with her time. She really had had her hopes pinned on spending much of her thirties occupied with Little Joys and Artie Juniors.

A tiny movement near the sleeping bag caught her eye. With the wind whipping briskly off the water, Joy couldn't tell if it was the soundly sleeping breath of its occupant, or the air on the outside. "Are you okay in there?" she asked.

Nothing.

"Excuse me." A little louder now. "Just wanted to see if you needed anything."

A hand shot up to loosen the hood. Good—not dead, which was a relief. As soon as the hood whipped back, Joy saw it was a young woman, hair a mass of unbrushed tresses around her face.

"What the fuck?" the girl said, pulling her hair back to eyeball whoever it was who had the audacity to disturb her.

She was immediately recognizable.

"Britney? What on earth are you doing out here?"

"Um, sleeping, obvs." The girl took a swig from her water bottle.

"Why aren't you at home?"

"Oh, I know you. You're one of them workers." Britney's face changed as she recognized Joy and the role she'd played in her family's lives. Then she laughed. "You've been to my house. This ain't so bad."

Britney was right. The probably uncomfortable, definitely cold, and maybe unsafe spot she'd chosen on the beach might still have been a better option than Britney's house. Her situation was almost too stereotypical to bother with the details: Britney's family was like a dozen—or more—of those Joy had in her never-ending files. Britney had younger siblings who were regularly removed from their mother's care, only to be returned later. Britney hadn't been subject to any such order for some time because she was seventeen and had almost aged out of the system. Which was to say that the overloaded social workers had to focus on the more vulnerable children and leave the older teenagers to fend for themselves. It wasn't right, but stomping around demanding things change would be a waste of energy that was desperately needed in other places.

"Did you really just go swimming?" Britney asked, taking in Joy's towel and wet hair.

"It's good for the immunities." Joy felt incredibly frivolous to have the luxury of morning beach jaunts when this teen didn't have a safe place to sleep. She took in the mottled, fading state of Britney's bruised face; her cheek, jaw, and eye all looked like she'd taken up a career in boxing.

"Come on, I'll make you a hot breakfast. See what we can do about accommodation."

Britney recognized a good offer when she heard one. "Orright then, I'm pretty hungry."

Joy picked up the girl's bag. It was heavy—either she wasn't expecting to go home anytime soon, or she was used to keeping her valuables stored in a grab bag close by. If the girl's mother, Erica, was on a bender, she would hock anything and everything to scratch together enough cash to keep the party going.

The two women made their way from the sandy dunes to the weathered, boarded path and headed toward Station Street. They crossed the train tracks and Joy nodded at the empty shopfront. "Here we are."

"You live here? In an empty shop?"

"In the house behind, actually."

"Cool."

"It's modest, but it's home."

"It's pretty sick. I'd love my own place near the beach."

"One day maybe you'll have one."

Britney rolled her eyes. "Yeah, right. I don't wanna stick round here anyway. I'll head north, find somewhere away from all this . . . bullshit."

"Anything you want to talk about?" Joy slipped easily into her social worker role.

"Nope," Britney said.

They went inside through the shop door, Joy using the front mat to try to get the remnants of sand off her bare feet.

Doyle's Locksmiths wasn't open yet—it was far too early—but the mini mart was. Joy liked the owner, Sangeeta, who seemed friendly without being intrusive. The shop on the end of the row, Scott Family Law, was home to a couple: a man who always dressed in a shirt and tie, even when gardening, and a dour-looking woman. Joy had not approached either of them yet and was in no rush to do so. Friendly, not familiar, were her thoughts on her neighbors.

They went through the shop and into the house.

Joy put on her slippers and checked the fridge. Eggs, bacon, tomatoes. She grabbed the loaf of bread from the pantry. It felt nice to be able to look after someone, and she was glad it wasn't Arthur.

Britney tossed her sleeping bag on the couch and Joy noticed a spray of sand as it landed. "Is that bacon? I fucking love bacon. Oh, shit, sorry."

Joy laughed, far from worried about the swearing. "Did you want a quick shower—warm yourself up?" she asked. "Bathroom is through there."

"Oh yeah, that'd be good." Britney pulled her jumper out so she could sniff close to her armpit. "Yeah, that's a bit hectic."

Joy took a towel from the linen cupboard. "There you go, take your time."

"Thanks." Britney paused, her expression changing to apologetic. "I know you're one of them social workers, I just can't exactly remember your name, sorry."

"It's Joy, and that's okay, it's been a while since I've visited your family. I'm the one who found your mum that drug program to complete, so she could get your little brother and sister back."

"Yeah, yeah, that's right. You shouldn't have bothered, hey? They came home and she was right back on it. Those kids need to be away from her for good."

Joy wasn't shocked by this news. The treatment programs didn't tend to stick once the patients were discharged. It was a Band-Aid solution to a much bigger problem.

"What about you?" she asked Britney.

"It's too late for me, but they're still little. They could, like, actually have some nice childhood memories and stuff."

"I'm sorry it's not better for you."

Britney shrugged. "She's mean when she drinks, and she's out of it when she's high."

"And what about when she's sober?"

"She's never sober. Or at least, not for long. The last time—after wherever you sent her—she came home and was angry for days. Threw shit, belted us. It was, like, fucked up. Sorry, but it was. And then a couple of days later I was kinda glad when I got home from school and saw Robbo—that's the guy who brings her gear over—his car in the drive, right. But then I go inside and Tiff and Koa are just, like, hungry and in their rooms with the doors shut and you can tell Koa'd been crying heaps."

Britney looked miserable. Joy popped the kettle on, not wanting to hurry her.

"I think she's pregnant again—Mum, that is," Britney said. "She looks pregnant."

"Oh, wow." Joy was thinking of her many years of trying and failing to have a child. There were a lot of new notes she'd have to make in the Whites' file, including a notation about Erica's possible pregnancy. Definitely one about neglect, the allegation of Erica hitting the children, and possible substance abuse. Joy wondered if Fay Marks, her favorite carer by far, would be open to a short-term foster placement. Maybe Britney could stay there awhile, even just for some respite.

Joy would have to call her area manager as soon as possible to tell her about the morning's events. That was policy—if it occurred outside of work hours, first make them safe and then do the notifications. Although, as far as Joy was concerned, Britney wasn't safe just yet. She'd let her get cleaned up, have breakfast, and then Joy would reassess.

"You're shivering. Go jump in the shower. I'll get some food together."

Joy felt very motherly as she instructed the seventeen-year-old. She was only thirty-five but felt positively ancient in comparison.

Britney pushed the folded towel against her face and breathed it in. "This is the nicest towel I've ever seen."

Joy felt tears needle at Britney's wonderment. Arthur had never so much as said a pleasant word to Joy in all their years together about the linens or towels, which she kept in a meticulous fashion.

Minutes later, the shower was thundering and the pipes were thumping. Joy had never realized just how loud they were from the other side of the wall.

She wondered if she had any clean clothes that would fit the teenager. Joy was, and always had been, tall and lean—"like a witch's broomstick," her father used to remark, although she was never sure why it needed to be a witch's broom specifically. Britney was much curvier than Joy, but she could probably rustle up something to do the job.

The shower was still hammering when Joy went to the bathroom door and opened it a peep. "Some clothes just here for you, Brit, if you want them."

Britney's head shot out of the shower, one of her breasts barely contained behind the pink-and-orange-checked curtain Joy had picked up for half price at Spotlight. The bruising continued down Britney's shoulder and arm, and Joy could see it was going to take a lot more than a hot breakfast to help the teen.

"Thank you—this shower is fucking awesome. Save me some bacon, yeah?"

Britney's voice and demeanor seemed positively girlish, as if she'd not had a chance to relax and let her guard down in some time. Joy thought of it like being in a game of tag and Joy's house was base. Britney was safe while she was here, didn't need to be on high alert. Joy backed out of the bathroom and heard Britney break out in song. It wasn't one she knew, but the girl was certainly trying to hit the high notes.

Joy cracked eggs and dropped them into the hot pan, glad Britney was in such good spirits. She could see a way she could finally make a positive impact on at least one person's life. Doing things exactly by the book hadn't exactly had the best results. Maybe it was time to try something different.

She never made that phone call to her area manager.

CHAPTER 19
JOY

August 2002

It was a shock when the twins were born on an otherwise run-of-the-mill winter evening. One girl slipped into the world and another shortly after, the second child even more surprising because Joy had not expected a single baby, let alone two.

They were perfect, if tiny, and started crying almost the moment they'd fallen into Joy's arms. Two girls, warm and slippery. And as soon as Joy inhaled the scent from each of their newborn heads, she was entirely consumed. She wrapped them tightly in her fluffiest towels and cuddled them while their skin pinkened and their little lungs tested out their capacity.

By then, Britney had been staying with her on and off for two months. She would show up with her heavy bag, or with nothing at all, and was usually ravenous, tired, and occasionally erratic. Sometimes she was there for two hours; once it was four days. In hindsight Joy saw what she should've seen earlier. For someone who considered herself observant of human behavior, Joy never guessed Britney was pregnant. At the same time, Britney seemed to have been willfully ignorant of her condition, or else she really had no idea. It helped that she favored loose sweaters and slouchy tracksuit pants, which billowed around her increasingly curvy frame. Even so, Joy should've noticed.

They'd become an odd couple of roommates. Joy kept a toothbrush for Britney next to her own, and stocked up on Cheetos Cheese & Bacon Balls, the teen's favorite snack. She delighted in making Britney feel special and welcome; it was nice not to feel so alone all the time.

The night the babies were born, Britney had gone to bed just after dinner, citing a stomachache. Joy found her some Panadol and decided to turn in early as well, as it was a work night and she hadn't been sleeping all that well. Sometimes sleep eluded her; there was simply too much on her mind. She had dozed off while reading, *Rebecca* still open on her chest, when she heard Britney's cries. Fearing Brit was being attacked, she raced out of her bedroom to find the girl on her hands and knees in the hallway, begging for help. Joy barely registered what was happening, let alone had time to call for an ambulance, before the first baby arrived. Joy put the newborn, slickened with a layer of white, creamy fluid, into Britney's arms. The teenager was red-faced and confused but took the baby and held her close, her naked body writhing as a tiny cry came from her, the most beautiful noise Joy had ever heard. Joy ran downstairs, almost going head over heels in her haste, grabbed a stack of towels, and returned as quickly as she could.

"It still hurts," Britney panted, her body arching in pain. Joy couldn't reassure her; she'd never been through childbirth and didn't know what it was meant to feel like. But she had read just about every book on the subject in preparation for the children she wanted to have. None of the books captured quite how simultaneously terrifying and wonderful it could be. All she could do was her best, grasping Brit's hand and speaking to her like she knew what she was doing. She cursed herself for not grabbing her mobile phone while she was downstairs, where it charged in the kitchen overnight. Britney didn't have a phone, or at least not that week. In the past month, Joy had seen Britney with at least three different mobiles; she was adept at losing them, plus she never had any credit on them when she managed to retain one.

"I'll be right back. I just need to get my phone."

"No, don't leave me!" Britney needed her.

Joy lifted the baby and wrapped her in a towel, trying to keep her warm. Britney was thrashing around so much Joy was worried she'd drop the baby if she handed her back, so she kept the child tightly clasped to her own chest. With her free hand she held Britney's, the teen squeezing it so tightly she was sure she felt a bone snap. She wondered if the pain was the placenta delivering; she hadn't thought it would be so dramatic upon its arrival.

Within minutes, and after a few short grunts, there came a second baby, screaming at the loss of her warm confines. Shocked but trying to remain a calming presence, Joy carefully put down the firstborn near the doorway of her room. She picked up the second girl, who let out a yowl, and settled her in the crook of Britney's arm, then she packed towels tightly around both baby and mother to keep them warm. Britney let Joy put the other tiny girl on her chest, helping them find their way to Britney's breasts to feed. They seemed to know what to do, their cries subsiding as they settled into the warmth of their very surprised young mother. Joy raced backward and forward from her room, collecting pillows and blankets and propping them around the trio, making them as comfortable as she could.

Britney looked exhausted and confused, somewhat in shock at the evening's events. As was Joy, of course, but she was also mesmerized by the sight of the little, bleary-eyed pink beings. The idea of calling for help became a distant, irrelevant memory.

After that first night, Britney wouldn't feed the babies again. She was adamant that she didn't want to hold them and she didn't even consider naming them. Once the adrenaline of birth had worn off, she wanted nothing more to do with the tiny twins, seeming almost repulsed by them and what her body had done. She wanted to be left alone to sleep.

Joy put the girls in with her, leaving Britney to the spare room, which she'd grown to think of as the teen's. She tried but couldn't get Brit to get up to shower, though she was allowed to change the sheets, put a nightdress on her, and ply her with sanitary napkins.

It was wildly irresponsible of her not to call for help, Joy knew, but she pushed the thought further and further from her mind until she convinced herself this was her calling. Britney had birthed the girls there, in her house, in front of her, after all Joy's fertility problems—there had to be a reason for that. And calling an ambulance would trigger a sequence of events that Joy knew would not bode well for Britney: a homeless teenager, from a family well known to the department, with no income and no support. Britney and the twins were safer where they were. Joy managed to convince herself that there was nothing wrong with letting things lie for a little while longer, but she vowed to do the right thing once she'd organized formula, diapers, a sterilizer, bottles, and something to dress the babies in.

She practically sprinted to Woolworths and back to get everything she needed, hating to leave the sleeping newborns for even that half an hour, knowing Britney wouldn't go to them if they cried and knowing there was nothing worse than those babies calling out and no one being there. When she got back and fed them,

Joy promised herself that she would call someone soon—her area manager, or an ambulance, or even just a home doctor service—but first she wanted to make sure the babies' bellies were full and they were wrapped and settled.

She broke that promise, and then quickly made another one: once the twins had a decent sleep, she would make the call. Every stupid pledge she invented she found a way to get around, busy with burping, feeding, cuddling, cooing, and changing. And then the day was over. The next day came and went, and the next, and the hundred times she swore to put everything right started to peter out because it all became too late at some point. Contacting anyone would mean admitting she should've done it days earlier. So she simply did nothing.

The only call she made was to tell Leonie at work she couldn't come in for the week, citing a family emergency, which was not entirely untrue.

Britney slept, ate what Joy brought her, and took the heat packs to press against her aching breasts, but refused to let the twins near her. If she had been in denial about being pregnant, she chose to be completely ignorant about the twins' birth. Fate could be a furious mistress, yet also a cunning one, and Joy wondered if this was part of the Universe's plan all along, from the moment she'd woken Britney on the beach.

The only thing Joy saw Britney doing, other than sleeping, was frantically drawing in a small, battered spiral notebook. When she delivered food to her bedside on a pink melamine tray, Joy noticed pencil shavings on the floor. She wanted to look inside the notebook but didn't want to invade Britney's privacy. Though they'd shared so much, that seemed a step too far.

Out loud, Joy had been calling the babies "pickle" and "possum," but quietly, when she knew Britney wouldn't hear her, she called them Cassiopeia and Andromeda, inspired by the heroines of her favorite books, who also bore celestial names. These babies needed names that inferred strength and greatness. They were so tiny, Joy wanted them to know they could be anything they wanted. She wouldn't allow them to be called something inane like "Joy." "Joy" implied that she was positive and delightful. It inspired people to say stupid things to her like "Always a joy to see you" or "En-*joy* yourself." Or Arthur's go-to, "Don't be such a kill-joy." She'd even laughed when he said it, like a good, obedient wife should. The thought roiled her.

Two weeks after the babies were born, they had a particularly rough night—one in which Joy seemed to be holding one or other of the girls at all times. The hours stretched infinitely and her body thrummed with pure exhaustion. Seeing the first rays of light appear through the edges of the curtain felt like the end of a race she had never asked to run. Something about the daytime made everything seem somewhat easier, made her feel a lot less alone. But she was more alone than she realized; Britney had disappeared in the night, leaving a note by the kettle. Joy's groggy eyes and heavy head could hardly process it.

> *To Joy. I think we both know that the babys should stay with you. I am not ment to be a mum. Can you pls look after them and make sure their not like me. Thanx 4 everything, Brit xox*

The note broke Joy's heart, not just for the grammatical inaccuracies, but for the lack of faith Britney had in herself. She was so young, but she was kind-hearted and had simply not been dealt an easy life.

Joy would do this for Britney, and she'd make sure she did it well.

CHAPTER 20

JOY

November 6, 2002

Joy was pacing the lounge room, baby Cassie pressed against her chest, when someone knocked. This was a rarity. Almost no one visited Joy. She carefully laid her three-month-old daughter in the rocker beside her sister and cautiously went to the back door.

She was wary of intruders, given she was a single mother and sole protector of two precious babies.

"Who is it?" she called.

"It's me, Britney."

Joy couldn't get the door unlocked fast enough. The two hugged like long-lost friends and Joy could tell immediately that Britney wasn't looking after herself. She was about half the size she'd been when Joy had last seen her, and although she was newly postpartum then, this was an unhealthy amount of weight to lose in such a brief period of time. Her hair was unwashed and the waft from her clothes was concerning, a combination of cigarettes, body odor, and a cover-up attempt with a sickly sweet body spray. The perfume did not have a chance against the depth of Britney's BO; the girl had clearly not showered in some time.

"Come in." Joy beckoned Britney inside, genuinely glad to see her.

"Are they here?" Britney asked.

"Who? The girls?"

"Yes, my babies."

Joy paused, feeling instantaneously sick where the lovely feeling of seeing a familiar face had just been. Had she misheard? Perhaps this was what Britney needed to do to ensure she'd made the right decision—drop in and see the twins from time to time. Of course, as the person who had birthed them—Joy didn't think "mother" was quite the right term—Britney could visit the girls. But that was all. Just a visit.

Joy breathed deeply, steeling herself. "The girls are in here. Come and meet them properly."

Britney breezed into the house as if she'd never left, kicking her shoes off and dropping her shoulder bag on the floor, like she always used to. Joy picked them up, put the shoes neatly against the wall and hung the bag on a hook.

"Can I get you something? Water? Juice?"

"No, thanks." Britney was staring at the babies, Andie dozing and Cassie still a little grizzly. "Oh, look at them. They're beautiful."

"Aren't they?" Joy swelled with pride. In the three months she'd been a mum—and that was definitely what she thought of herself as—the twins had been with her almost every moment. She'd had a pram delivered and would walk everywhere with them. In the supermarket, she beamed as people cooed over her sweet little bundles, the elderly ladies in particular finding twin girls such a gorgeous novelty. She was always mindful of people's hands, though; if they reached in to touch one of her babies, she would stop them, not caring about the looks she received. Many an old woman had tsked at her for her overprotectiveness, but she didn't care.

Once she had squeezed the last ounce out of her paid leave, Joy unceremoniously quit her job. She cited burnout as the reason for leaving, although no one had bothered to ask, her manager more focused on the unenviable task she now had of reallocating Joy's work. She wasn't the only one resigning; the job was hard and all-consuming. One of her colleagues had left to work night shift at Coles Supermarkets; the hourly rate was less, but he didn't have to decide which kids to try to save. It felt like they were all screaming into a void. They were leaving in droves.

Joy happily handed back her files—including the one on Britney's family—returned her security pass, then went to Centrelink. After filing her unemployment claim, Joy realized she had a major problem. The girls didn't have any paperwork. It had not occurred to her at the time of their birth, but the moment she went to see about getting a parenting payment, she realized that, other than to her, the twins did not exist.

"How have you been keeping? Are you okay?" Joy asked as Britney lifted Cassiopeia from her rocker and breathed her in.

Britney was singing something quietly to the baby and ignored Joy. Cassie's cry amped up; she wasn't being jiggled the way she liked. She preferred to be held upright, against Joy's shoulder. Her grizzling picked up to a proper whine, and Joy resisted the urge to reach out for her. Britney bounced the baby, her hips dancing forward and back to try to soothe the child. But she just didn't have the knack. *Joy* had the knack. She'd been perfecting it for the past three months.

"Down by the bay . . ." Britney sang so quietly the words were almost inaudible. "For if I do, my mother will say, did you ever see a froggy chasing a doggy, down by the bay."

Cassie continued to howl.

"Here, I'll take her." Joy reached for Cassie, but Britney turned away.

Joy's hackles shot up. She breathed out hard and convinced herself it was okay. The girls weren't going anywhere; this was Britney. She'd left the girls to Joy. This was *only* a visit.

"You've looked after them so good, Joy. Thanks heaps."

"Of course. I love them. I am so grateful that you gave them to me."

"Temporarily."

Joy gulped and moved instinctively in front of Andie, who was still in the other rocker.

"Did you name them?" Britney asked.

Cassie's cries had eased now but still, Joy's throat felt dry and her heart was hammering.

"You're holding Cassiopeia—Cassie. And that's Andie, short for Andromeda."

Britney's face screwed up like she'd tasted something sour. Joy noticed tears had pooled in the girl's eyes and she had a moment of panic about how unstable the teen was. Jedidah and baby Shem came to mind, and the thought made her gasp like the air had been knocked out of her.

"I wanted to call them Aaliyah and Shakira."

Joy was horrified, could not think of names less suited to the twins.

A hush fell over the women. Even the babies had quieted, and Joy saw that Cassie had heavy, milk-drunk eyelids. She was falling asleep, clutched against Britney.

"You've come back to take them, haven't you?" Joy asked.

Britney looked somewhat ashamed but managed to meet Joy's gaze.

"I'm sorry—I really am. I thought about it heaps and, like, I didn't think I was ready. But I am now. I'd regret it if I didn't try."

"Regret what?" Joy said. "This is damn hard work. You won't get a chance to enjoy what's left of your teens. Or your twenties. You could travel. Study. Sleep in."

Britney started shaking her head, hugging Cassie closer.

"You could go to university . . . or . . ."

"I don't want to do any of those things. Tyler and I are back together. We're engaged, and we're gonna get our own place."

"That's very positive of you." Joy tried not to put Britney down, but she had never heard anything so poorly thought out. "But I'm not sure you know quite how exhausting it is to raise children. Or how expensive."

"We'll get Centrelink," Britney said.

Joy was having trouble tamping down her anger. "You smell like you haven't even washed yourself since I last saw you. How on earth are you going to juggle two children? You're not ready to be a mother. You will, in time, but not now, Britney. Not now. Not these girls."

Britney erupted into tears. "I want to do better than my mum did."

"And you will." Joy's voice softened. She had to think quickly, she felt on incredibly shaky ground. "You left them with me because you knew they needed something you couldn't provide. You'll sort yourself out, and you'll have a beautiful family all of your own."

Britney struggled to speak through her tears. "It's all I've ever wanted, my own family."

Those words hit Joy like a cricket ball at full speed off the bat. She pushed it aside; it wasn't the time to let her emotions take over. "Right. Now, does Tyler know where you are? Is he waiting out front?" she asked.

"No. I actually didn't think you'd still have them here. I thought you woulda had to hand them in or, like, whatever sort of thing you're meant to do with them. I came to find out where they'd gone. Then I was gonna tell Ty."

Hand them in? Britney really had no idea. And if she knew anything about the bond between Joy and these girls, she'd know that thought had never entered Joy's mind. She had not let the twins go when they were born, and she certainly wasn't letting them go now.

She thought for a moment, wondering how to spin this to her advantage. "I did. That's exactly what I did. And they were left with me as their carer. The department could see the twins were in excellent hands."

"Oh." Britney's tears started up again and Joy saw her eye twitching.

"So, ah, whereabouts is he? Tyler?"

"He's at his mum's. I'm gonna surprise him."

"Surprise him?" You surprised people with flowers or balloons, not identical twin newborns.

"Yes." Britney beamed at Cassiopeia—certainly not Shakira. "Can you think of anything better?"

"It would be quite the shock. How old is he, Brit?"

"He's nineteen. He's almost finished his apprenticeship. We'll be able to get a house together."

"Where will you live now, though?"

"At his mum's. She's got room for us, and she needs the extra cash for the rent anyway. At least till his stepdad gets parole."

Joy just about passed out. "Right, well here's what we are going to do." She collected herself as best she could. "I will make a call to social services and tell them you've come to collect the girls. They'll have some paperwork probably, that sort of thing, and then you and Tyler can get on with being a happy little foursome."

Britney smiled, her face streaked with tears. The path they'd traveled showed that she didn't just smell terrible, she was also incredibly dirty.

"So, let me take Cassie . . . ah, Shakira." Joy struggled to say the name. "And you go freshen up. You know where everything is, and I'll get the ball rolling."

Britney handed Cassiopeia back to Joy.

When the bathroom door clicked closed and the faucet made the pipes shudder in their usual way, Joy gathered Andie in one arm and Cassie in her other and took them upstairs to her bedroom. She put them in their cot where they slept side by side, and kissed each of their soft little heads. "Mumma won't be long." They were still so small that their whole bodies seemed to move with every inhalation of air. She adored watching them sleep and loved the sweet, milk smell of their breath. They were her everything.

Joy moved back downstairs and heard the bathroom tap turn off.

Britney yelled through the wall. "Do you have deodorant, Joy?"

"Top drawer," she called back.

Minutes later Britney emerged in a cloud of steam from the bathroom. "How'd you go?"

For a moment, Joy had forgotten she was meant to be making calls to organize the transfer of Britney's babies back to her. "Oh, I couldn't get hold of anyone that could help."

"Did you leave a message?"

"Yep," Joy lied.

Britney peered around Joy. "Where are they?"

The empty bouncers were glaringly obvious, and Joy felt ashamed of herself, but what option did she have?

"Are they upstairs?" Britney's face had curled into an expression Joy hadn't seen on the young woman before.

Joy felt very vulnerable all of a sudden. "I just wanted to talk to you a bit more before we did anything rash, and the girls were due a sleep, so I've just popped them in bed. Perhaps we can have something to eat and a chat about the logistics . . . I mean, have you thought about how you'll even get them home if you take them now?"

"I'll take the pram," Britney snapped.

"But it's my pram."

"You don't need it. It's not like you can go and have more babies or anything."

The comment was especially cutting, considering Joy had spoken candidly with Britney about the trouble she and Arthur had had conceiving.

The girl was winding herself up, clearly agitated, and Joy sensed something else at play, something new. Was it drugs?

"Sit down, Britney. Let's talk. It's just me, Joy. I'm your friend." Joy swept her hand toward the couch, where they'd spent many an evening with a movie on. She could see Britney considering her, wondering if it was okay to trust her. "What's one more night? Let them sleep here, and in the morning everything will seem easier."

Joy was trying to convince herself as much as trying to talk Britney around. It seemed to be working, though; Britney went to the couch and lowered herself down. Her breathing was heavy, almost ragged, like she'd just completed a marathon. It was fair to say Joy felt much the same, adrenaline coursing through her system. She knew she had very limited options. She couldn't very well call the police for help. What would she do? Explain that the birth mother of the children she had kept, without making any of the appropriate reports, had now returned for them?

"And you'll let me take the pram?"

Joy didn't want to lie. There was no way Britney would be leaving with the pram or the babies. It was impossible to think those two precious souls wouldn't be with her anymore. It was simply not an option. Lying was about to be the least of her problems.

Britney had asked her to keep the girls safe, and she would. From anyone at any time, whatever lengths she had to go to.

The girls were hers.

CHAPTER 21

JOY

November 7, 2002

Joy paused beneath the peppercorn tree, thinking she'd heard someone in the rear lane. Her heart raced. How she had gotten herself into this mess was beyond her. She was not a bad person—only now she wasn't so sure that was entirely true.

"That you, Joy?" Montgomery Doyle called.

She'd been expecting a horde of police to slingshot into her backyard at any second, but it was just her neighbor. Her body relaxed, but only slightly.

"Joy?"

"Yes, Monty, it's me." She realized she sounded terse, but it was her house. Who else did he expect it would be?

"Can you smell that over there?"

Joy's stomach clenched; her entire being seized. Everything she'd done was for nothing if Monty caught her red-handed. "Um, no. What are you talking about?" She looked at the shed, the padlock on it glinting at her as if it were winking. *I'll keep your secrets.* Surely there would be no smell yet. It wasn't possible. Was it?

He laughed. "It's the time of the month I feed my orchids is all.

I've not had a neighbor for so long that I haven't had to be considerate of where I keep the fertilizer."

"Oh, that's all," she said, shoulders dropping. "It's no problem, don't even worry about it."

All she could do was hope he wouldn't decide to look over the fence while she held Britney's belongings in her hands. She had stuffed them in a garbage bag, but she still felt they were as obvious as a neon sign.

She'd noticed Brit's bag on the hook that morning, after the longest night in the history of nights. It had only been a few hours since Britney had knocked on her door, but everything had changed.

The sight of the teen's belongings had made her feel physically sick. Joy upended the bag onto the table, finding very little inside. A coin purse with thirteen dollars—more than Joy expected Brit to have—a train ticket, her sketchbook with a stubby pencil wedged into the spiral, and some cigarette butts. It was her chance to peek inside the notebook and she did, a necklace falling from its pages, almost soundless as it hit the floorboards. As Joy scooped it up, she noticed the clasp was broken. From the chain hung a heart-shaped pendant with tiny words engraved: "I see the future and it's all about us." The A5 pages of the sketchbook were almost completely full of drawings of people and scenes and objects, mostly in pencil, some in pen, no color on any of them. The teen was talented, that much was clear.

The illustrations toward the end momentarily stole Joy's breath as she processed what she was seeing. They were drawings of Joy and the babies; her feeding them, dressing them, smiling at them. And then she came to one where Britney had drawn her sleeping next to the tiny babes, who were wrapped in their swaddles and had the most beautiful resting faces. She didn't know Britney had seen any of these moments, or that she cared. Joy imagined the teenager sneaking around the house, stealing glances at Joy and the twins, keeping to the edges. Many pictures were dated, but only the sleeping one had a signature. Or at least, she thought it was a signature, but when she looked closer, she realized it was a word: "Family." That one was dated the same day Britney had left them the first time.

Joy's throat felt constricted, and she truly despised herself in that moment. Britney had believed Joy was the base in her life's relentless game of tag. And she'd turned out to be as big a letdown as everyone else in the troubled girl's life. Joy had slammed the sketchbook shut, not wanting to see any more.

And now the book was wedged into a garbage bag, clenched within Joy's whitened knuckles as she silently hoped Monty would *fuck off* and leave her alone while she got rid of the evidence. An internal scream made her head ache as she considered that word. *Evidence.*

"Any luck with getting the shop rented out?"

"No," she called back. Her body felt taut and wired. "Okay, bye then."

Joy reached the shed and tugged at the door, immediately realizing she'd forgotten the key to the padlock she'd fastened not even half an hour before. She'd left it in the kitchen. She boiled with rage, cursed and stomped her feet in the manner of a three-year-old in the supermarket who had just been denied a Kinder Surprise.

"Is everything all right?"

His voice coming over their shared fence again gave her cause to panic, thinking Monty might pop his head over. She shoved the tightly wrapped items into the hollow in the trunk of the peppercorn tree, where it split in two.

Joy tried to compose herself. "Just having a moment." She squeezed her eyes shut and slapped herself on the face. Now was not the time to melt down. "Sorry, I can't talk right now, I'm not feeling well." This, at least, wasn't a lie. She didn't wait for a response from her neighbor, going back into the house and locking the door behind her. On the kitchen counter, she saw Britney's other things: her bag, her coin purse, her train ticket. Joy's thoughts were scattered—why hadn't she just gotten rid of them altogether? She swept them from the counter straight into the trash can and slammed the lid down. From the first floor, she heard the babies stirring and made a determined effort to push Britney and her belongings from her mind.

It was time to feed Cassie and Andie and Joy hurried upstairs to check on them, their waking noises turning to hungry cries. She picked up Andie in one arm and then scooped tiny Cassie into her other. They were so dependent on her; she had to be strong for them now. Both babies quieted as soon as they'd nestled against her chest. Joy sang quietly to them as she made her way downstairs, taking a moment to realize the song was "Down by the Bay," just like Britney had sung the night before. She shuddered and switched tunes immediately.

Who was she? She remembered the wild expression on Britney's face. Joy breathed deeply and gazed down at the two perfect faces she was forever bound to.

She was their mother. That was all that mattered.

PART THREE

DEAR CUSTOMER, WE APOLOGIZE FOR ANY INCONVENIENCE

Out of SPACE—Out of TIME
Edgar Allan Poe, "Dream-Land"

CHAPTER 22

DETECTIVE SERGEANT HOLLIDAY BETTS

August 2, 2023
One day after Joy's death

9:15 a.m.

Joy Moody appeared peaceful in death.

In Detective Sergeant Holliday Betts' experience (eight years general duties, seven years Divisional Crime Investigation, one month Homicide Squad), the dead often did. But that wasn't a reliable indicator of how they might have met their untimely end. Or timely, depending on the person in question. Not all death was unexpected, and not all unexpected death was unwarranted. It didn't matter who the person was in life, it was Holliday's job to ensure they were treated fairly afterward.

Holliday knew some people were better off dead, although she wasn't yet sure if Joy Moody was one of them. And as this was the first job she'd been called out to since being promoted to detective sergeant, Homicide Squad, she didn't intend to make any assumptions. Fucking up was not an option.

The call Holliday had taken at 8:05 that morning piqued her interest for many reasons, all of which she had dutifully written into her daybook. She was now staring at her notes as she waited to go into Joyful Suds. Sergeant Sam Poole, who had called her and described what he'd found, made her think there was cause for further investigation, for the Homicide Squad to attend. Which she still had to remind herself was her now.

Holliday didn't rely on a sixth-sense sort of instinct, but she was thorough and knowledgeable. If anyone wanted to know the section number and wording of a particular offense in the Crimes Act, she could recite most of them verbatim, save for some of the obscure ones they never had cause to use. This wasn't due to a photographic memory; she just felt like she had to work extra hard to earn her spot in the way women often did.

An ex-boyfriend had described her as a duck on water, legs working maniacally underneath, invisible to all who saw her calmly gliding over the surface. She preferred to think of it like ballet: bloody hard work made to look easy. That boyfriend hadn't understood the hours she worked and hated when she canceled plans. He'd broken up with her about a month after she should've ended things herself.

Joyful Suds was just thirteen minutes from her house, meaning she was the first of her crew to arrive. Although she drove past it daily, she had never set foot inside the laundromat before, never had cause to, having a decent washing machine of her own. But, even in passing, she had noticed the owner's incredibly liberal use of pink.

Holliday centered herself before getting out of her car. She was in charge and wouldn't let the fact that it was her first time betray her. It wasn't like it was her first day on the job; she'd been doing this shit for almost sixteen years. She glanced in the rearview mirror and told herself to get the fuck on with it. That was always her mother's advice, although the colorful language was Holliday's own addition.

"Sam Poole." A uniformed man with sergeant epaulettes on his shoulders proffered a hand and she shook it firmly. Sometimes she went a little overboard just to make sure there was no weakness inferred by her handshake. He smiled politely. "You must be Holly? We spoke on the phone."

"Holliday, actually. Holliday Betts."

He shrugged. "Sure thing."

She checked her phone; her team were probably still at least half an hour away and she wanted to get started. "Can you walk me through?"

Sam nodded and made a grand hand gesture toward the door, as if he were a game show attendant displaying a new prize. She followed him past the constable standing guard and into the laundromat.

Her first thought was how spotless it was; should her washing machine ever be on the fritz, she'd drive out of her way to use this place. It was much nicer than the one near her, Spiffy Clean. Even though Joyful Suds was dated, it was incredibly well kept. The walls were a very deliberate shade of pink, a color that would no doubt be called guava princess or salmon dream or some such nonsense. Her eye was drawn to the bulletin board, which Sergeant Poole had mentioned when he called. She looked, without touching anything, wondering how it could be anything other than a threat.

"Time's up, Joy."

Holliday supposed that could mean plenty of things. Possibly "I'm coming to kill you now." But maybe just someone sick of waiting for their washing? "Time's up, where's my shirts?"

A photograph of a woman—Joy, she supposed—and two identical girls was above it, a pin driven right through Joy's forehead. The placement of this and the message itself—written directly onto the corkboard and not on a piece of card like the other notices—coupled with the deceased owner, seemed ominous.

"We've asked the twin daughters about that—they have no idea," the sergeant said. "And just quietly, they might be a couple of sandwiches short, if you get my drift."

Holliday nodded but dismissed his comments. Sam Poole might be right about the twins, but she'd make up her own mind. It wasn't fair to judge someone based on their reaction to police in their house directly following the death of a loved one. People did strange things in those sorts of circumstances.

Holliday and Sam moved on, through a passage separating the laundromat and the house. She'd always wondered about living behind or above a shop; there was something kind of cozy about it. And the Moodys' house was just that, aside from the newly departed Joy Moody occupying the armchair in the lounge.

Holliday's eyes scanned the room. She remained quiet as she made notes, drawing a quick floorplan as she stood, not wanting to disturb anything yet.

"The neighbor rang triple zero just past seven a.m. A man called Montgomery Doyle. One of the daughters had gone to get him when they found her here this morning."

"Has she been moved?"

"I don't believe so. No CPR performed. She was clearly . . . ah . . . past it."

"But someone found a note in her pocket?"

Sam pursed his lips. "Ah, yes. That was me. I was trying to figure out what might have happened. There was Endone too, but it's a full packet, so not really helpful, is it? They're over there, just on the kitchen counter."

Holliday walked to where Sam Poole pointed and looked at the note. It was torn neatly, as if it had been folded over, then ripped along the length of a ruler.

P.S. If I stay here I'll die.

"This is part of something more," she said. "You wouldn't use a 'P.S.' if there wasn't more to it."

"We've had a hunt around but no luck so far. It does match her handwriting, though, by the looks of some of the stuff on her desk."

Holliday noted what the sergeant said, although she would still have it forensically matched. It was amazing how clever a forgery could be if someone was trying to get away with something sinister.

"Anything on our system for her?"

"No. This place has been in business for just over twenty years and not had any trouble. The old bloke next door has some form, but we're talking almost forty years ago—a prison stint for an armed rob, but nothing since."

"And the daughters?"

"Nothing."

"How old?"

"Twenty-one. But what I mean is *nothing*. They're not even in the system. No license, no ID—not even Medicare."

"There are a lot of people who aren't on our system, though," she said.

"I know that. But not recorded anywhere? They should have something to verify they are who they say they are. But . . . nada."

It was a bit weird. "Let's get back to that in a minute. What about the message out there?" Holliday lifted her chin in the direction of the laundromat. "The 'time's up' one."

Poole opened his hands in a gesture of "fucked if I know." "There is a security camera in the shop, a couple on the outside, all run through a mobile app, but the girls don't know the password. We've sent the info back to the station. There's a guy there who'll know what to do with it."

"There're people in town who can look into that."

"Pfft, trust me, if this guy can't do it, no one can."

She'd have preferred they'd left it to a qualified analyst, but she also wanted to see what it showed as soon as possible. "And the injuries to her face?"

"The neighbor said it happened last night—she walked into a tree. But he wasn't there to see it."

"The daughters did, though?"

"Yeah, but like I said, they're . . . a little quiet at the moment."

Holliday leaned down next to Joy Moody, whose face was the color that people get when the blood really drains from it, and not just in the literary sense when someone at a Victorian tea party made a faux pas. It was a very unusual pallor, hard to describe, but unmistakable. The scratch on Joy's cheek did look reasonably fresh; the wound hadn't crusted over properly and the skin around it hadn't started puckering the way it did when it had time to begin knitting back together. Holliday couldn't immediately say this wasn't a defensive wound; she would have to wait for the experts to look at it.

"I think I'll go speak to the daughters now," Holliday said.

"Now, these girls. They're a bit . . . I mean . . ."

"What is it?"

"A bit *weird*."

"How so?"

"I don't know. They seem scared of us. One of them held up her hands like she was shielding herself from my phone. They've barely said a word. They look the spit of each other. It all screams *The Shining* to me."

Holliday frowned. "That's a bit of a leap."

"You're right. But there's another thing about them."

"Yeah?"

"They're from the future."

"Excuse me?"

"They've given us a birthday of the first of August, twenty-fifty."

Holliday blinked long and hard. "Are they just in shock?"

Poole gave her the "no idea" shrug again.

In the rear courtyard, two young women sat beneath a peppercorn tree. A senior constable lounged in a chair that was part of a set, one of those green cast-iron ones that seemed to pop up at houses everywhere, although she'd never seen them for sale in Bunnings even one time. The tree was too large for the small area and in need of a decent prune. Holliday could tell gardening wasn't particularly high on the agenda in this household, although the overgrown vegetable garden and three bags of fertilizer stacked in front of the shed made her think someone may have wanted to give it a try. Weeds sprouted between the pavers, many of which had shifted with time and what was probably the peppercorn's root system moving beneath it like a writhing bed of snakes. She was quite a fan of how mother nature always claimed things back, no matter how solid they seemed.

During the initial phone call with Sam, Holliday had been told the twins' names were Cassiopeia and Andromeda, but she wasn't sure who was who. They *were* remarkably alike, the sergeant was right, although horror movies didn't come to her mind; they were far too striking for that. The twin on the right was twitching in a manner that seemed nervous and uncontrolled at first, but when Holliday watched her a little longer, she realized the woman was drawing something in the air. Had she paper and a pencil to slip underneath, she was quite sure she would see a picture appear.

She didn't give Sam Poole time to make any introductions; she liked to do that herself. "Hello there. My name is Detective Sergeant Holliday Betts. Do you mind if I sit with you?"

Neither objected, and she dragged one of the heavy, green chairs closer to the bench the women occupied. The senior constable barely moved, certainly not offering to help, nor putting his phone away. She'd address his unprofessionalism at a more appropriate time.

The girls were wearing pajamas—cartoon dogs on one and cats on the other—both with loose sweaters pulled over the top. They looked incredibly young; if she hadn't known their age, she would have guessed they were fifteen.

Holliday sat. "I'm very sorry about the loss of your mum. I'm here to help find out exactly what happened." She knew not to mention Homicide; it tended to discombobulate people. And when they were confused, they clammed up, which was difficult before there'd been a chance to establish who was a suspect and who was not.

One sister reached over and put her hand on the invisible pencil her twin held. It didn't stop its incessant movement; it continued to twitch even beneath her sister's grasp.

"Can I ask your names? I'm not actually sure who is Cassiopeia and who is Andromeda. I hope I've said them right?"

A zingy, chirpy sound effect was emanating from whatever game the officer nearby was playing. Holliday turned and stared at him, sure he would take notice. He didn't, but Sam did and he moved forward, nudged him, and muttered, "Shut it off for a bit, mate."

"I'm Andie," the one in cat pajamas said.

"And I'm Cassie," the one whose hand wouldn't still added.

"I'm sorry to meet you in such circumstances. And I am sorry to have to keep asking questions, but it's all to find out what happened to your mum. Okay?"

Two nods, almost simultaneously.

"And the birth date you've provided is the first of August, is that right?"

"Yes," Andie replied, her voice crackling the way Holliday's did when she was overtired.

"But the year—I think we've got that mixed up. Can I just confirm it's . . ."

"Twenty-fifty," Cassie replied quickly. "We've always been told it was the first of August, twenty-fifty."

Holliday pursed her lips and leaned forward. "That's twenty-seven years from now."

Cassie looked adamant. "That's right."

In her many years in policing, Holliday had spoken to numerous eccentric people. Once, she'd met a man who walked an invisible dog, a West Highland terrier called Randall. Another time she'd attended a house where a woman was convinced her husband was an alien. But she had never before spoken to someone who claimed to be a time traveler.

"Are you saying you're from the future?"

"That is what *she* told us," Andie said flatly, pointing toward the house, toward Joy Moody. "But we know now it wasn't true."

Cassie made a noise like she had something lodged in her throat, but it was simply a precursor to sobbing. "You don't know that for sure."

As much as Holliday didn't want to agree with Sam Poole, there was something a little bit *The Shining* in the way Andie addressed her, and the way the two sat so straight and still. Their eyes seemed empty, and she wasn't sure what to make of them. Andie seemed to be lacking in grief entirely. This wasn't as unusual as it sounded; many people couldn't understand the complexity and finality of a deceased relative for days. But it was more than that.

"It's a bit of a story," Andie said. "A long one."

"I'm partial to a story. I would love to hear it."

"Detective, can I have a word?" Sam Poole asked.

She was annoyed to be disturbed, but answered politely. "Of course."

They walked to the end of the yard and out through the gate into the lane where they were almost certainly out of earshot.

Sam thrust his phone at her, an image—obviously from a security camera—on his screen. "You need to see this."

There was a man standing in front of the laundromat, pointing directly down the barrel of the camera.

"He doesn't look happy."

"That," Sam said with a lip-smack of satisfaction, "is Tyler Rodriguez. He is all sorts of trouble. This was pulled from the cameras, time-stamped 1:56 p.m. yesterday."

"What 'sorts of trouble'?" she asked.

"All of them."

"Can you be more specific?"

"He's one of our regulars, this bloke. He hasn't done much for a while, admittedly, or at least, he's not been *caught*. But ten years ago, this guy was top of our tasking for drug trafficking and run-throughs on other crooks' houses. I think he's softened a bit over the years, had some kids, that sort of thing. But he's well known to us. Not to mention, he's been in the gun for the murder of his girl-friend back when he was a teenager. She went missing, never seen again. Missing Persons are sure he's involved."

Holliday stared at the image. "So why would a guy like that come here?"

"I don't know. Maybe this Moody lady was into drugs, maybe the daughters are?" Sam held his hands out in a non-committal way. "All I'm saying is, the fact Rodriguez has been here stinks like hell to me."

Holliday had never been reliant on gut feelings or Spidey-type senses; she worked her butt off to solve crimes and charge the right people. But Sam Poole was right. There was something very odd about Joyful Suds and its occupants, and she really wanted to know what it was.

CHAPTER 23

ANDIE

The detective, Holliday Betts, was smiling at Andie in a way that made her wary. They were sitting in the back seat of a police car, another officer in the driver's seat, both sets of eyes on her. She got the impression they thought she and Cassie were stupid, which was a fair presumption, given Cassie's declaration that they were from the future. She thought that had been settled, given the supermoon had come and gone and nothing had changed. Of course, everything had changed now, just not in the way they expected.

Andie recalled the previous night, standing next to her mum, her hand trembling as she looked at the empty syringe resting in her palm. She'd panicked, thinking she heard Cassie's feet moving about upstairs, and slid it into the gap between the ceramic planter and the plastic inner pot of the pink orchid on Joy's desk. She wondered why she hadn't just left it beside Joy. In hindsight, it would've looked far less suspicious, like Joy was responsible for her own death. Quite simply, Andie had panicked; she had a lot to learn from Miss Marple. She knew now that questions would be asked, ones she didn't want to answer, because how could she explain being downstairs in the first place, and how would she ensure Cassie wouldn't end up losing someone else she loved? Joy's face was imprinted on Andie's mind. She wished she hadn't looked; she hadn't expected Joy in death to be so different from Joy in life.

It was better, at least for now, to keep her mouth shut. She'd told Cassie to do the same.

They'd been fourteen, maybe a little older, when Andie realized how important it was that she look after Cassie. Her sister didn't think sensibly in a crisis. They'd heard a commotion in the laundromat and she and Cassie had stepped through the in-between to see a man violently shaking the vending machine. He punched it once, twice, his knuckles splitting like the skin of a ripe plum. The pain must have been incredible, although he didn't appear to register it. Andie ran to get Joy, not realizing her sister wasn't hot on her heels. Cassie later told her she felt compelled to approach the ranting, spitting man who was growling at the snack machine like it had personally aggrieved him. What possessed her sister to think he was someone she should talk to? Andie had sensed a threat and knew to run the other way. She had just assumed Cassie would follow, because she always had.

When Joy and Andie stepped back through the in-between, breathless and worried, Cassie was gone. They found her sitting with the man—who was swigging from a can of Coke—and talking calmly, almost like they were friends from way-back-when. Sangeeta had called the police, who showed up quickly and hurried the man away from Cassie before any harm could befall her. Joy told her off, and rightly so—that man could've been anyone. Cassie was far too unworldly; she needed Andie to tether her to reality. If they stayed together, they'd be fine.

Only now they weren't together. The twins had been separated, told they needed to make individual statements, and Andie had the stomach-tightening feeling that when the police asked you to do something, you had to do it or be arrested.

"Can I call you Andie?" Detective Betts paused.

Andie nodded her consent.

"Do you know if anyone visited your mum yesterday?"

"No, I don't think so." Andie stared at Holliday Betts, wanting to get out of the car, go upstairs, and get into bed. Unsurprisingly, she had not slept well, knowing what they'd wake up to find. She was exhausted. "I mean, customers come in all the time. But that's not what you mean, is it?"

"Hard to say what's important at the moment. Anyone in particular spring to mind?"

"No. Oh, my Uncle Grant came and dropped off presents, but I don't think he even saw Joy. That's not to say he did anything. Just that he was there, which is only unusual because we never see him, not because . . ." Andie stopped to breathe. So much for keeping her trap shut.

"Because?"

Andie could only shrug, looking over at the car her sister had been moved to, wondering if she was okay. Holliday made some notes, her pen moving quickly. Andie tried to see what she was writing but couldn't make it out from the angle she was at.

"Do you know anyone called Tyler?"

Andie wondered if Detective Betts noticed her reaction to that name. Until those History Mystery results, she'd not known a Tyler and, technically, she still didn't. So she shook her head, confident it wasn't a proper lie.

"Was the business in any trouble, or had Joy borrowed money off anyone recently?"

Andie thought of the bag of cash Joy had been determined to keep close. They knew not to ask questions about their financial situation; that was Joy's business.

Before the police came that morning, Monty had told them to hide the pink bag away; he said he didn't trust cops around cash, that they had sticky fingers, whatever that meant.

"Those are adult things. We didn't get involved in adult things."

"*Adult* things? What does that mean?"

"Handling money, making decisions. They weren't for us to do." That was oversimplifying things, Andie thought, and perhaps made Joy sound quite dictatorial. But then again, a spade was a spade, no point calling it a spoon.

"Did your mother have a lot of rules?"

Andie shrugged. She had nothing to compare it to, other than mothers in fiction like Margaret March or Mrs. Bennet. "I don't really know."

"Did you get along with your mother?"

"I didn't know my mother."

The detective frowned. "Was she a hard woman to know?"

"No, I mean she wasn't my mother."

At that the detective's eyebrows lifted. It was a spiteful comment, and Andie instantly realized she should've kept that to herself, Joy would've hated having her dirty laundry aired. It had been their secret for so long, and now Andie was announcing it mere hours after Joy's death. She felt a prickle of regret. Over Holliday's shoulder, she could see Monty and Linh speaking with an officer in the parking lot, which had been blocked off. They didn't look happy, maybe upset by the spectacle being created on Station Street. Bad for business, she supposed.

Holliday leaned forward, blocking her view. "Do you mean you were adopted?"

"I don't think so."

"Then what makes you think she wasn't your biological mother?"

"She told us. We've always known."

"Do you know who your mother is?"

Andie sighed, closed her eyes, and told herself it was time to be quiet—a little too late, but better now than after any other slip-ups. She shook her head. *No.*

"Is there anything you want to tell me about yesterday? It would really help us to establish what happened to your mum." Holliday paused, before clarifying, "To Joy."

Andie bit her bottom lip hard. If there was ever a time for her to cry, perhaps this was the moment. It might soften the detective's intense stare. But she couldn't will any tears into existence, so she instead resolved to keep her mouth shut.

CHAPTER 24
CASSIE

Cassie didn't have a problem keeping quiet, but she disliked Andie assuming she wasn't smart enough to do so without instruction. She wasn't about to tell the police she thought her sister had done something, but that didn't mean she couldn't *think* it.

She'd woken up just before midnight and realized Andie's bed was empty. Bleary-eyed, she'd tiptoed to the top of the stairs and seen Andie near Mum's desk, doing something with the orchid. Cassie hustled back to bed, threw the duvet over herself, and pretended to sleep. Andie had snuck back in a short time later. Never in her wildest dreams had Cassie imagined going downstairs the next morning to find her mother so still and so cold, despite the heater being left on all night. She had never looked death in the face before, never had any experience with losing a loved one. But when she'd looked at her mum, she'd known. It was as if what she was looking at was just the empty chrysalis her mother had left behind, unable to take it wherever she'd gone.

Cassie knew if she called out to Andie or ran next door for Monty, if she did anything at all, then it would all be confirmed. Mum would really be gone. So instead she had sat on one of the dining chairs as if she were the sentry for her mother, keeping watch on the back of the armchair until someone came to relieve her. Her focus was the crochet blanket, still draped over the back, the different-colored squares forming an ombré of pinks.

Now, from the back of the comfortably warm police car, Cassie wondered if the color pink would always bring to mind that moment. The radio hummed quietly. Detective Leo Collins had sat with her in the car and asked her some questions. They weren't hard questions: how long have you lived here for, does anyone else work in the laundromat, that sort of thing. Her whole body ached with loss; she hadn't known how physically painful it felt to lose someone. She didn't answer his questions, both because she didn't think she could and because her sister had told her to keep quiet.

Her sister. Who had yelled "I wish you were dead" at their mother the day before. And then their mum had died. Cassie knew not to tell the police that.

The stern woman detective came over to the car, and Detective Collins climbed out so she could take his seat.

"Hi Cassie, how are you feeling?"

Cassie almost answered, but then decided against it. She didn't want to be tricked into saying anything that would be misinterpreted. And the fear still loomed large about the police, who had always worked hand in hand with The People. Neither were to be trusted. Or had Andie been right? On top of her mother dying, Cassie was trying to navigate her way to the truth. If they weren't from the future, were The People real? Or was this all part of the elaborate scheme to hunt down the Daughters of the Future Revolution?

"I understand what this morning must have been like for you, I really do."

Cassie couldn't see how that was true.

"It's just, right now, we have a whole lot of things we can't quite work out, and we're hoping you might be able to help us."

Instead of holding eye contact, Cassie stared at the seat in front of her. She wished she weren't still in her PJs, but they hadn't let the twins go back inside the house.

There was a long pause before Detective Betts spoke again. "Can you tell me about the future?"

Suddenly tears were rolling down Cassie's cheeks. She felt so stupid and confused. It was like she'd been cheated out of a future she wasn't even sure she wanted anymore.

"Do you know who your mother is, Cassie?"

Cassie's head snapped around. "Mum is. I mean, Joy Moody is. She's our mother."

"Okay, I understand that. But we believe you have different, ah, biological parents? Are you able to tell me who they might be?"

The weight of that sentence was like a slap. She looked at the car her sister was in. The windows were too glary to make her out. What had she said? Internally Cassie was bursting, wanting to rip out of her skin and howl, or scream, or something. She was suddenly furious at her mother, who had lied to them for years upon years about everything that had ever mattered. And then she'd up and died, which made Cassie even angrier at her. How could she do that to them?

Using the sleeve of her jacket, Cassie wiped her face. Holliday Betts pressed her lips together and moved them about wordlessly while she flicked through pages of her notes. A woman knocking at the window made them both jump. It was yet another person in a dark blue police uniform.

The detective cracked the door open.

"Um, I hate to bother you, but . . ."

"What is it?" Holliday Betts was brusque, but not impolite. It was very Joy-like, Cassie thought.

"There's a lady on the phone insisting she speak to you."

"Can it wait?"

"She's the lawyer for these two, um, witnesses. Um . . . what should I tell her?"

Cassie looked around and saw Monty standing close to Station Street, feet shuffling and arms crossed over his signature flannelette. He stood behind a plastic length of blue-and-white tape. Linh was beside him and they were both staring in Cassie's direction, formidable gazes on both faces.

Detective Betts hopped out of the car to take the call out of reach of Cassie's hearing. Minutes later, the detective marched back looking uncomfortable, or maybe just annoyed. "Do you understand you can leave at any time?" she asked. "That you're not under arrest?"

Cassie wondered why she was being asked this; it felt like a trick question. When she cast her gaze back to her neighbors, she saw the police officer who had brought the phone returning it to Monty. What was going on? She could only assume if Monty was involved, it was probably okay.

"Am I in trouble?" Cassie asked.

Holliday Betts sighed. "No, you're not. We are hoping to get as much information as we can to establish what has happened to Joy. And we will need to revisit this at another time. But it's important you know that you are free to leave."

Cassie bit at her dry lips. "I can go?" She had no idea where she'd go, but getting out of the stuffy car seemed like a good start. She was terrified if she sat there for too long, then she would accidentally mention Andie being downstairs the night before, very possibly the last person to see their mum alive. Maybe even being the reason their mum was no longer with them. The thought sent a jolt of cold energy through her, causing her to shudder.

"Cassie, we are worried someone might have done something to Joy that caused her death. I would very much appreciate it if you could stick around and answer some more questions."

Cassie looked at Monty, who wore a despondent smile, like he was trying to be reassuring. She turned back to Detective Betts. "I want to leave."

Holliday Betts gave a resigned sigh and opened the door wide so Cassie could slide across and hop out. She saw Andie making her way toward their friends on the sidewalk.

"What happened to her, to Mum?" Cassie asked the detective quietly.

"I don't know, but I will find out." The detective's expression was firm, although not unkind. Maybe she was working for The People.

"Cassie!" Andie yelled across the parking lot, and Cassie stepped unsurely over the gravel toward the only people she had left in the world. Andie wrapped her arms around her and squeezed her tight.

Holliday approached them, holding out a business card. "Here's my number and details. I will be back to see how you're going in the next day or so."

Linh took the card, calm as always, although it seemed clear she'd been crying. "Any requests can be made through their legal representative, Ellen Scott."

Cassie registered shock. How had Ellen become involved?

Monty's face looked drawn and he sniffed hard, wiping his nose with his handkerchief. She'd been so selfish in thinking that the loss of Joy was hers and Andie's alone.

Cassie felt Monty's hand press between her shoulder blades, encouraging her to walk away from the police. Outside the shop window, she paused and stared in at the uncharacteristically quiet interior of Joyful Suds. No customers, no machines whirling, the sign on the door turned to "Closed." She expected to see Joy come through the "Staff Only" door at any moment, but she wouldn't. Not today and not ever. The silent, breathless lips of her mother came to mind and her hand twitched with the need to commit that image to paper, purge it from her memory.

Monty gave her a gentle nudge. "Come on, Cassie-love, I'll make the coffee today."

She let him move her along the sidewalk, through the door of his shop, and into his house, the others following quietly.

"Let's get some food into you," Linh said, although Cassie knew she wouldn't be able to stomach anything.

In her neighbor's lounge room, Cassie found herself standing in the exact spot she knew Joy was occupying in the house next door; Monty didn't have an armchair there, just empty space. She noticed Andie shifting uncomfortably about, not knowing where to sit or what to do.

It had all become too much. Cassie stepped forward and dropped onto the sofa, curling herself into a ball. She caught sight of Monty's face and his expression was heartbreaking; she didn't know if it was for her, or Joy, or the whole miserable situation. She cried then, not trying to disguise it like she sometimes felt she should. Cassie hugged her arms around herself and felt the sobs roll through her like waves.

Cassie bawled until sleep took over, and in a half-awake, half-asleep state, she felt Monty drape a heavy, soft blanket over her while the others ate a solemn lunch.

CHAPTER 25
ANDIE

August 4, 2023
Three days after Joy's death

The girls returned home, but the laundromat remained closed. Neither Andie nor Cassie could bring themselves to flip the sign and open the door. However, they found comfort being in the shop; Cassie had even started the free machine just to break the silence.

The twins sat on the yellow stools against the back wall, partially obscured by the front counter. Joy would be horrified at this lack of professionalism, but that in itself made Andie okay with it. They had both donned their pink Joyful Suds polo shirts that morning for a reason neither could explain, knowing full well that they weren't going to open the shop.

Brett Carmichael, whom they knew Joy had never liked, rattled the door, found it wouldn't open, and jiggled it a little more aggressively. He peered in the window to get a good look inside and gave them a "what are you doing?" sort of gesticulation.

Andie just stared back, not caring what he thought or if he came back once they reopened—*if* they reopened. Cassie, however, always loath to be outright rude, pointed at the spot where they'd taped a sign. If Joy knew they'd handwritten something and put it on display, she would die all over again, and Andie found a tiny delight in the rebellion. She'd even made a deliberate mistake in Joy's slogan, just because she could. "Closed due to death. Have a Joyous Day."

After slowly reading the sign, Brett shrugged, appearing nonplussed about the death reference and more miffed at the inconvenience of having to cart his basket of dirty washing back home.

"He offered me fifty dollars to see my breasts once," Andie announced, something she'd never told anyone before.

Cassie reeled around, forehead crinkled. "That's disgusting!"

Andie shrugged. "Well, I did it."

"What? Why would you?"

"It was fifty dollars."

"What did you need the money for?"

Andie sighed. "Just in case. And I wanted to see what it felt like to be looked at like that."

Cassie made a noise that indicated her distaste at the whole thing, which was why Andie had never mentioned it before.

They sat in silence.

"So was it nice? To be looked at?"

"Hmm, nice would be the wrong word. It was nice to get fifty dollars. It was very . . ." Andie scratched her head, trying to think of something to say. "Transactional."

"Ew," Cassie said. "Actually, I've been meaning to tell you something . . ."

Andie's head whipped around. Cassie's voice dropped low, almost inaudible as she said, "I kissed someone. I think I'm in love with him."

"What?! Who?" Andie was equally intrigued and jealous. She had never kissed anyone before, not even been close.

"His name is Omar. I met him down at the beach." Cassie's cheeks pinkened and she stared at her feet. "He's very special."

"Was this what Joy was so mad at you about the day before . . . ?"

Andie didn't want to say the day before she died, but she was also a bit miffed that her own sister hadn't shared this story with her.

"Yeah." Cassie tensed her jaw.

"Well, you can see him now, whenever you want. You don't have to worry about what Joy says."

"Maybe."

"Not maybe, *definitely*. We don't have to work here anymore, and we can go wherever we want. There're no gamma rays, there's no secret society. Cass, we can leave."

"But where would we go?"

Andie laughed. "Anywhere!"

"What if I don't want to leave?" Cassie's voice sounded like someone had turned the volume all the way down.

"It's been like a prison here. I thought you'd be excited to leave. You can see Omar, you can draw pictures of places you've never been to before. Which is, like, everywhere else in the world." Andie pulled her Fruit Tingles from her pocket, flicked one into her mouth, and waved the packet at Cassie.

Cassie shook her head. "I don't know what I want to do."

"Would you prefer to be in 2050 right now? Saving the world?"

Cassie looked to the ceiling. "I just wanted to do what Mum expected of us. I didn't want to let her down."

"Did you even *want* to go?" Andie asked.

Her twin leaned back against the wall, then rolled her head to face Andie. "I was terrified," she said quietly.

Silence took over then. Andie didn't know what to say, but she knew a diatribe about Joy wouldn't go down well. Their mother, who wasn't their mother—more like their jailer—had wielded such control over them. She'd told them what to do and what to think for so long that now Cassie didn't seem to know the way forward without Joy's guidance. Andie felt furious, but tamped it down; it wasn't what they needed. Not that she had any idea what they *did* need. Realizing Cassie was crying, she leaned over to the front counter and grabbed the tissues.

"I miss Mum," Cassie murmured.

Andie winced at the word "mum," but didn't think Cassie's fragile emotions would take kindly to her fact-checking their parentage in that moment. She didn't miss Joy, and wasn't sure she would. Instead, she was thinking about whether or not they could afford a television. She wondered if they could use the money from the bag; surely it belonged to them now. After Monty suggested hiding it, Andie had squirrelled it away into the corner of their wardrobe upstairs.

The door rattled again, another customer who now stood back to read the sign. It was Lori-Jayne and her French bulldog, Winston. Andie liked her; she was always friendly and let Andie feed Donna's treats to her dog. Lori-Jayne clasped her hand to her chest, as if a great pain had shot through her. She hadn't seemed to notice the twins sitting in the back of the laundromat, watching her.

Andie wondered why a customer would have such an emotional reaction at the news, when she hadn't felt anything of the sort.

Lori-Jayne nudged Winston forward. He didn't want to go, dropping his rump firmly on the pavement, meaning Lori-Jayne had to pick him up and carry him away. Presumably Winston was feeling ripped off for not getting his usual handful of salmon-flavored biscuits.

It was as she watched them go that Andie noticed the red-and-blue van next door, too big and obvious to be anything but an ambulance. Cassie had already seen it and was frantically unlocking the front door. Andie followed Cassie out onto the sidewalk and into Monty's store; she couldn't have stopped her sister even if she'd wanted to. Doyle's Locksmiths was empty, but the in-between was wide open and Cassie darted straight through.

"Monty!" Cassie's voice was edged with physical pain as they saw him being moved onto the carry chair the EMT had wheeled in.

"I'm all right, Cass, it's okay." Monty tried to sound calm, but Andie noticed him wince. He put a green tube in his mouth and sucked in deeply; it looked like he was about to play it like a recorder. His face loosened as he breathed deeply. "It's just my knee. It'll be all right."

One of the paramedics helping Monty addressed them. "We're going to take him to Frankston Hospital. You can get an update from there. But we need to get going."

"Is it really just his knee?" Andie asked, thinking the worst, that they were sugar-coating the news.

"Yeah, looks to be. It's going to have to be assessed by an orthopedic surgeon. He'll need some scans."

"It's okay, girls. I will be right back. Sorry for the fuss. Can you take the keys and lock up? Maybe put something up in the window to tell my customers?"

Andie put her arm around Cassie, who was softly shaking as she sobbed, watching as the EMTs gathered their things. Cassie went to speak but choked on her words.

Donna wove between Cassie's legs and mewed loudly until she was picked up. Her sister buried her face in the cat's soft white pelt. That cat had always hated Andie for some reason; she knew Donna would never accept this sort of closeness from her. It had always made her dislike Donna in return, both for her standoffishness and because she picked Cassie over her.

"Can you please feed her?" Monty asked and Andie nodded quickly.

The twins followed him out to the waiting ambulance and watched Monty be loaded in. Andie tried to guide her sister back into Joyful Suds, but she wouldn't budge, not until the ambulance had pulled away. Only then did it occur to Andie that they had no way to check in on their neighbor once he got to the hospital. They might have just as well been taking him to the moon.

Once the ambulance was a pinprick in the distance, Cassie was finally okay with going inside. She kept Donna clutched to her chest, although the cat was getting a little testy at the excessive attention, so Cassie took her inside to get her something to eat.

Andie found some paper behind Monty's work bench and scrawled a note about the shop being shut until further notice. She didn't bother with any snide inaccuracies for the handwritten sign for Doyle's Locksmiths. She was walking back to the front door to paste it across the window when she noticed Uncle Grant striding down the sidewalk from the direction of the parking lot. He caught sight of Andie and made a beeline for her. She hadn't locked the shop door yet, and he pulled it open and let himself in. He stood closer to her than she'd have liked.

"I came as soon as I heard," he said, reaching out and putting his hands on her shoulders in what she assumed was meant to be a comforting gesture. "I'm so sorry, Cassie."

"I'm Andie."

"Oh, of course you are." Grant gave her a look of pity. "I've come to help."

She knew nothing about Joy's brother; they'd had so little to do with their extended family. Joy had never let him get close to them, but then she'd never allowed anyone to do that. Joy had isolated them, lied to them. She would only refer to her as Joy from then on, Andie decided. She hadn't earned being called Mum.

Maybe Grant had some of the same thoughts about Joy as Andie did. It might be nice to have an ally. She shrugged, unsure yet what to make of him but deciding it couldn't hurt to see what he could do for them.

CHAPTER 26
CASSIE

Cassie's memories of Uncle Grant were vague. She knew he was three years older than her mother and that the siblings had never been particularly close growing up. That didn't seem all that unusual, based on her limited knowledge of family dynamics. It wasn't as if they were twins, inextricably intertwined right from the beginning.

She recalled meeting him when they were much younger, maybe a handful of times. Once, he'd dropped off Christmas presents, which was a novelty; they never got anything other than what Joy picked out for them, and she tended to be practical, so they'd get something new to wear and maybe a puzzle or a game. Uncle Grant had bought them a variety of things that Joy said weren't suitable: DVDs, a makeup set, and once he bought them a Tamagotchi each. The twins had managed to pester Joy into being allowed to keep the virtual pets, which had provided hours of entertainment. Cassie had proved to be much more diligent about keeping her little pet alive, which was not really a surprise to any of them.

Cassie didn't think it was that Mum didn't *like* Grant, more that she simply didn't see anyone outside of their little trio, besides the occasional visit from Monty or a chat on the sidewalk with San-geeta before she and her husband had moved away.

It actually gave Cassie a sense of relief to have Grant in the house. She felt like she could relax now that he had arrived, because he was a proper adult and there to help them.

"I was devastated when I heard the news, girls. I am so sorry about your mum."

Cassie made tea and took it over to the coffee table. It was strange having a visitor. Grant sat down in Joy's armchair, and nei-ther Andie nor Cassie told him that was the exact spot where Joy had taken her last breath. It occurred to Cassie that Mum would never sit there again. The thought made her throat constrict.

"So you're probably wondering why I'm here," Grant said, al-though it hadn't occurred to Cassie until he mentioned it.

"Yeah, I'd like to know," Andie said, somewhat warily.

"The police got in touch with me, let me know about Joy," he said, and then gulped. "That was a shock, I'll give you the tip."

"What tip?" Andie asked.

"It's a saying," he said, shaking his hand dismissively. "I always thought Joy and I had time to make up our differences, you know. She was my little sister and I . . ." Grant succumbed to sobs, and Cassie handed him the tissues. He blew his nose noisily, then pushed the damp tissues behind the cushion on the chair. "I guess, in some ways, I lost my sister a long time ago. But for you two, what a hole she must leave." He rubbed his nose again with another tissue. "It's just like I said the other day, we're family and family's gotta stick together." He smiled at them, his eyes rimmed red.

Joy, Andie, and Cassie had always stuck together, but now it felt like they were divided, as if an axe had been taken to their family. It would never go back together again properly without Joy.

"There're a few things we have to organize, like the funeral. I mean, when the body is ready . . . I mean, when they release Joy from the . . . Anyway. Have you given any thought to burial or cre-mation?"

"No," Cassie said, and they hadn't; they didn't know a thing about death or what was meant to happen next.

"Let's have a think about it then. You two decide on some songs she might like played, or any photos you'd like displayed."

They had very little in the way of photographs, and Cassie had no idea what songs her mum would want played at her funeral. Often Joy would break out into song or pull them into a dance around the kitchen if she heard something she liked on the radio. Sometimes she'd spin the girls in pirouettes faster and faster while they laughed and tried to stay upright. They'd grown up listening to Taylor Swift and Lady Gaga, although Cassie had a feeling that wasn't the sort of music people played at funerals. She couldn't be sure what might be appropriate. Sadder songs, she supposed.

"Can we think about it? The music, that is?" Cassie asked, sud-denly grateful Grant was there. "I don't know what we'd do if you weren't here. We don't even know where to start."

"Of course you don't, how would you? Girls, I am here for you. Anything you need, you just let me know and I will do what I can."

He leaned over and put his hand over Cassie's. He couldn't reach Andie from where he was sitting, nor did she try to join in. Instead, Andie sat back and glowered at him, maybe regretting her decision to invite him in. Cassie thought her sister could've been a little better mannered. He was a guest in their home, after all.

"We have to do some things that are a bit delicate. Do you know where she kept her will?" Grant asked.

Cassie shook her head. She knew about wills; they were of-ten a contentious plot point in novels. She looked over to the desk where Joy did all her paperwork, not knowing if her mum would've thought to make one.

"It would be in her desk, I guess," she said.

"You can't go through her things." Andie crossed her arms.

"It's all right, Andie," Cassie said, squeezing her sister's forearm, hoping she'd unfold them at the very least. "He's trying to help."

Grant put his hands up as if surrendering. "I'm not trying to get in the middle of anything, little ladies. I just want to make this as easy as I can for you. I lost my mum when I was young, you know—younger than you two—and I understand grief. I organized everything for my dad's funeral, so I know my way around these things. Honestly, Uncle Grant just wants to help." He started rifling through the envelopes and documents in Joy's desk, then tugged at the bottom drawer; that one was always locked. "Where's the key for this?" he asked.

"I don't know," Cassie replied. They'd never had cause to open it and knew to respect their mother's things.

"If I was a key, where would I be?" Grant lifted the pens out of a cup and inspected the inside. He moved on to the orchid, lifting it out of the planter to see if anything was under it.

Cassie heard Andie inhale a deep, hard breath and she stared at her, wanting her to notice. She knew what Andie thought was about to be uncovered, but Cassie had already moved the empty syringe to the spot under the loose floorboard in their bedroom. Andie sensed her hard gaze and looked back, her eyes wide, pupils perfect orbs of black. If anyone knew to look for it, their eyes were one of the easiest ways to tell them apart. Cassie's right eye contained three dark brown flecks in it, like a smattering of freckles that had spread to her iris.

"Nothing." He dropped the pot back into place, some dirt falling out and onto the clean surface of the desk. He rattled the drawer again, hoping maybe it would open with a bit of pressure. The desk was old, but sturdy, and it didn't budge.

Grant moved on to the filing cabinet next, flicking through the folders that their mother used to keep track of all her important business correspondence. Cassie couldn't help but feel uncomfortable seeing him rat through Joy's private things. She reminded herself he was there to help.

"How about another cuppa, girls? Would you mind?" Grant asked, bent over the files.

"Of course." Cassie picked up their cups and took them to the sink, flicking on the kettle. There could have been many things in that syringe she'd seen Andie hiding, but none of them made her sister seem any less guilty. The memory of the vivid blue of Joy's lips returned.

Had Andie and Joy been keeping their own secrets from her? Maybe Andie had the right intentions, but something had gone seriously wrong. It could be completely explainable and not related to Joy's death. Cassie desperately wanted to ask her sister, but once she did, she would never be able to unhear the answer and she wasn't sure she was ready for that.

The kettle switch popped up noisily, jolting Cassie back to the room. She cast her gaze around and watched as Uncle Grant slid an envelope into the pocket of his puffer vest. He wouldn't know she'd seen it, and for a split second she opened her mouth to demand to know what he'd found. She didn't, though; she couldn't find the words and was worried how impolite it would seem. These were the times she wished she had Andie's confidence. She shot a look at her sister, but she hadn't been paying attention.

Cassie felt her neck prickle with heat and worry, trying to convince herself that there was no need to doubt their uncle; he was just taking care of things so they didn't have to.

"I should really get your phone numbers, girls. It'll be easier to sort out things for Joy."

"You'll have to ring the shop phone," Andie said.

"Don't you have a mobile?"

"No." Andie didn't elaborate.

He looked surprised. It was similar to the reaction they got when anyone heard they didn't have a television. "You two do know how to use a phone, don't you?"

"Yep." Andie's tone was pithy.

"And you've still got my number?" he asked as if they were children.

"We do."

He checked his watch. "I have an important meeting to get to—time is money and money is time. Now, you call me if you need anything. Day or night. I will be here, you got that?"

Cassie nodded.

"I'm sorry again for your loss." Grant placed his hand on his heart as he spoke, before surprising Cassie by rounding the kitchen counter and drawing her into a generous, warm hug. She couldn't manage to relax enough to find any real comfort in it, although she was surprised by how much she appreciated the gesture. He moved over to Andie and drew her toward him in a similar manner. Her sister adopted an expression much like the one Donna wore when she didn't want to be held.

"Goodbye, girls," he said, and Andie showed him out through the in-between.

When she returned, she was incensed. "You're too trusting."

Cassie hadn't expected this, wasn't sure why she was in trouble. "What did I do?"

"He appears out of nowhere and you're all 'Thank you so much for coming' and 'What would we do without you?' Do you think maybe there's a reason Joy kept him at arm's length?"

"She kept everyone at a distance."

"You're incredibly naïve, Cass."

"And you sound just like Mum," Cassie replied, knowing exactly how to get to her sister. She'd had twenty-one years' practice, after all.

Andie scowled before storming off up the stairs, her steps loud and purposeful on the upstairs landing, her displeasure clear.

It had been a mean thing to say, but Cassie was sick of her kindness being treated as a weakness. She was always being underestimated, and she was fed up with it.

When they were younger, a man had been in the laundromat, trying to smash his way into the vending machine. She'd been scared at first, but when Andie immediately ran through to the house to get Joy, she stayed behind. The machine was shifting a little with the force he was using, the glass front of it becoming spattered with blood from his fist, but it refused to yield to him. This seemed to make him angrier, but it was a short-lived burst of energy and he tired out: panting, hot, agitated. She took a couple of the coins from the tip jar behind the counter and stepped around him, dropping them in the coin slot and looking at him, eyes wide, hoping he took her gesture in the manner it was offered. She couldn't fix everything for him, but she could help him get a drink.

He looked stuck, not sure how to proceed, but his anger was subsiding.

"Coke?" she asked and he nodded. She pressed the buttons, not fearing him at all. His anger wasn't at her, and she just sensed it would be okay.

He took the Coke gratefully, quickly pulling the top open and chugging most of it in one go.

"Is your hand all right?" she asked, and he looked at the split skin and bloodied mess across his knuckles as if it was how they always looked.

"Yeah, it's okay."

Cassie reached behind the front counter and grabbed a cleaning cloth, handing it over, careful to mind his personal space.

Someone had called the police, but by the time the officers arrived, the man—Stephen—was sitting with Cassie on the laundromat stools, facing out the front window. As he walked out of Joyful Suds with the police, he called out to her, "Thanks for seeing me." And she'd instantly known what he meant, because she was often the one people didn't see, the other girl, the second twin, the quieter, underestimated one. She knew about being mistaken for something less than you really were.

Joy had been furious and Andie had treated her like she was an idiot. But Stephen had seen her that day, and she'd come to understand her kindness might be a very mild superpower.

CHAPTER 27
ANDIE

1 p.m.

Upstairs, Andie was fuming. She didn't want Grant taking over their lives. If he had come to act as a proxy for Joy, then he could disappear right back to wherever he'd come from. Andie was reluctant to admit that she might agree with Joy on this; Grant needed to keep his distance. She'd gone from being curious about him to doubting him completely. Something about him was off, she just couldn't put her finger on what it was.

Andie pulled off her Joyful Suds polo and vowed never to wear it again. She hated the stupid color, she hated the stupid "Joyful day" embroidery, and she hated that Joy wasn't there to tell her to put it back on and stop being a brat. Her wardrobe was full of stuff she felt childish in, and she didn't want to be mistaken for a kid anymore. She and Cassie were in charge of Joyful Suds now, and she had to look after Cassie, and she didn't want to be told what to do by anyone, especially Uncle Grant. His showing up now that Joy wasn't there didn't sit well with Andie. She might not have been particularly worldly, but she'd read enough to know that family weren't always good to one another just because they had to be.

They weren't living in the pages of *Little Women*. Although if she had been, she would definitely choose to be Amy so she could travel to Paris; she'd prefer to skip marrying Laurie, though.

In just her underwear, Andie charged across the hall and into Joy's bedroom. It had always been strictly off limits, although Joy had stopped locking it a long way back. Perhaps Joy knew she'd trained the girls well enough to not enter her little sanctuary, and for the most part that was true. Every now and again, though, Andie had ventured in there, just to see if she could get away with it. She always had, and it gave her a smug, superior sort of feeling she quite enjoyed.

Even knowing Joy wasn't there to tell her off, Andie still stepped into the room tentatively. The police had been through it and disturbed the good order of the room. Joy would never have left her bedside table drawer slightly open or knocked over the perfume bottles on the dresser without straightening them up.

Andie righted the little glass bottles, arranging them neatly. She sniffed one with a large number five printed on the bottle, found it quite pleasant, and then sprayed it liberally on her neck. The smell of the fine mist was intoxicating. It didn't remind her of Joy in the least; her fragrance was softly scented washing powders (especially the Omo Floral Indulgence, which she would stockpile when it was on sale) and the apple shampoo from Woolies. Andie realized that Joy rarely, if ever, would have used any of these perfumes, making her wonder why she'd even bought them. But perhaps they were gifts—although who would have given such things to Joy Moody? She would probably never know.

Andie moved over to the wardrobe and slid the door open. It was incredibly tidy, the hanging items neatly spaced with a pedantic sense of order. All the clothing on the shelves was carefully folded and stacked as if on display in a store. Most days of the week, Joy had worn her Joyful Suds polos, and at night she would get straight into her pajamas. The wardrobe contained many clothes that Andie had never seen her mother wear, clothes that were intended to be worn to places that Joy and the girls never went. A black top with shiny black sequins dancing across the front dared her to pick it up. It was beautiful and slinky, and she slid it over her head hoping it would fit. It was a little snug around her bust, but the mirror suggested she could get away with it. Andie pulled her shoulders back, enjoying the sensation of the different fabric on her skin and the idea that wearing something of Joy's would have really pissed her off.

She tugged at a green sweater, yanking it from its neat stack. As it came free, so did a small black rectangle, which dropped to the floor. It was just like Linh's iPad. Andie picked it up, a shot of anger rising through her as she thought of all the times Joy had gone on about gamma rays and geolocators and how dangerous electronic devices were. It made her want to hurl the iPad at the wall. Andie knew not to destroy it, though, holding it tight in her hands instead and imagining Joy tucked away at night, using the device and laughing at the gullibility of her daughters. Her hands trembled with fury.

"What are you doing?" Cassie was standing in the doorway. "This is Mum's stuff."

"Look what she had all this time." Andie waved the tablet.

"So what? Isn't it just like her phone? She probably kept it there to keep us safe."

"She was busy keeping us away from everyone and everything while she was doing all the things she told us were bad."

"No, I don't think she'd do that."

"Then explain why she would need to hide it."

Cassie looked weary but didn't reply. She'd run out of defenses for Joy eventually, Andie supposed, but she'd keep trying to wear her down in any case.

"She was basically keeping us prisoner."

"No, she wasn't," Cassie snapped.

"Oh, really?" Andie replied. "She made us work here for years, she controlled who we saw and when, and we were fed a bunch of lies to keep us quiet. What else would you call that?"

Cassie shrugged. "Isn't that just what growing up is?"

Andie scoffed and tossed the iPad onto Joy's bed. "I'm going out." She lifted her chin in a show of confidence she didn't necessarily feel.

"What? Where?"

"Don't you worry about that. I am going to go and *do stuff.*" Andie was sick and tired of erring on the side of caution.

"Like what? I don't want to be alone."

"Come with me then."

Cassie looked conflicted; the scary world with her sister, or alone in the safety of the laundromat. "I can't," she said finally.

"Fine then. I'll be back later." Andie marched down the stairs, followed closely by her sister.

"Please don't leave, Andie. We can play Uno and open the good biscuits. Please, I don't want to be by myself."

"Grow up, Cassie." It was a mean thing to say, but so was comparing her to Joy. She was *nothing* like the woman who had raised them.

Andie had no plan or destination; she was flying by the seat of her pants and it was a thrill. She picked up one of their shopping bags by the back door and grabbed the shed keys. A thought occurred to her, and she strode purposefully back into the kitchen. From the gift bag Uncle Grant had given her, she slid out the bottle of wine and inspected the label. Andie mouthed the word "moscato," which meant nothing to her, but rolled nicely off her tongue.

"What are you doing with that?" Cassie asked.

"Are you about to tell me it's a 'quick path to calamity'?" Andie did a poor impersonation of Joy, but she'd made her point and Cassie's lip curled up in disapproval.

Andie went outside to retrieve the coins she'd been saving up in the empty Omo box in the shed. Donna followed her out there, but stopped at the door. The cat never crossed into that shed. For whatever reason she just seemed to hate it; maybe it was the smell of all the laundry products. It could be quite overwhelming, especially on a hot day.

At the back of the bottom shelf was Andie's makeshift money box, holding all the coins she'd been skimming from the machines for the past few years. It was hidden from Joy in fairly plain sight as the job of lugging the washing powder boxes to and from the shed always fell to the twins; their mother rarely went out there herself. Andie went to scoop out some of the gold coins, but decided she didn't know how much she'd need, so she picked up the whole box and dropped it into her makeshift handbag. It jangled as she moved, and she liked the heaviness of having her own money and choosing her own adventure.

"Be careful, Andie." Cassie's voice from the back door was small and desperate.

Andie reattached the padlock, threw the keys to her sister, and headed for the lane.

"Now who sounds like Joy?" Andie said, not sure why she felt the need to cut her sister so deeply. She opened the back gate, realizing it didn't squeak and wondering when that had been fixed.

As she strode down the back lane, unsure where her feet and bag of money might lead her, Andie wished she felt as confident as she sounded. She was absolutely terrified, but she couldn't very well turn back now.

CHAPTER 28

CASSIE

2:30 p.m.

The gate slammed shut, and Cassie went to it, listening to her sister's footsteps as they crunched down the back lane, growing ever quieter the farther she went. It was not a trick; Andie was actually leaving her by herself. Cassie put her hand on the handle, deciding if she should run after her and beg her to stay or swear at her—or both. Her stomach hurt and crying was inevitable.

She let go of the handle and noticed a can of WD-40 on the fence rail but couldn't think why it would be there. If the police had left it, they'd probably come back for it, she thought, not touching it.

Donna was walking along the low branch of the peppercorn tree, and Cassie called to her, desperate for company. The cat eyed her before leaping for the fence, then onto the roof of Monty's greenhouse, out of sight. Even Donna wasn't interested in being her friend.

There had been times when Cassie enjoyed being by herself, but now that she was properly alone, she felt lost and unfocused. She didn't want to read, and there was no washing to fold. She wasn't even sure she had the concentration to draw anything, which was unusual. She hadn't drawn a thing since their mum had passed. Her worry was that if she put pencil to paper, she'd draw the thing that was on her mind, which was her mother, in her chair, breathless, lifeless.

Agitated, Cassie walked through to the laundromat and considered opening it, just so there was a chance someone might fill a tiny part of the abyss she found herself in. She needed someone to tell her what to do. Her fate had been to travel through time and fight. It may not have been her choice, but it was all she knew and she had worked fervently toward that goal her entire life. Now she was motherless and directionless.

Upstairs in her mum's bedroom, she picked up the little computer that Andie had become so incensed over. Cassie held it somewhat gingerly, because she couldn't be sure all her mum's stories weren't true. If the technology really was dangerous, she should stay away from it. She stuffed it in the bedside table drawer. The bed was soft and smelled like her mum. She fell back against it and felt the bone-aching tiredness in her limbs that had been hounding her for the past three days.

From where she lay, she could see into the wardrobe. Andie hadn't bothered to close the doors, no doubt an attempt to irritate their mother on the off-chance she knew about it in the afterlife. Cassie's twin always seemed to revel in butting heads with Joy. Cassie eyed a line of thinly spined books on the top shelf. She got up, curious, and pulled one down. It was a scrapbook with writing on the front in broad but neat marker: "*Andromeda 2010.*" She flicked through and found childlike drawings, Andie's name written in the corner or sometimes just "A" or "AM." The drawings were glued in neatly, some folded in half so they could be contained within the scrapbook. There were other things too: a math test from Suds Secondary, a license to use a proper pen in grade 1, something Joy invented so they could graduate from just pencils. Every now and again Joy's distinctive handwriting detailed something brief but important enough that she'd deemed it worthy of recording.

June 2—first crochet square completed solo.
Sept 28—beat me fair and square at Rummikub.

Cassie found herself smiling because she recalled getting the pen license certificates, along with a beautiful, blue pen with a gold casing and "*Cassiopeia*" engraved down the side.

She pulled more scrapbooks down: "*Andromeda 2011*," then "*Andromeda 2012*."

Farther along the shelf was a row of books marked with her own name and the relevant years. Drawings, paintings, tests, memories scrawled in the margins. She blushed when she saw the date of her first period recorded. Even the odd photo was in there. They'd never really taken many photos; Joy used to say that if it was important enough for the camera, then they would remember it. "Record it with your mind, girls," she would say, so they'd learned to pay very close attention.

Cassie realized the books were piling up around her, all the memories of her and Andie's lives kept meticulously by their mum. Cassie had always assumed these sorts of things had been thrown away. She had never considered her mum to be overly sentimental, and yet it was all there. It made her feel less alone somehow, but also sadder. Why hadn't Joy just shared these things with them? Cassie had no idea why her mum had been so afraid to show them this level of endearment. She could count on one hand the times Mum had said, "I love you," although she didn't doubt Joy did. Maybe it was that she wanted to save it for big moments, times when it would matter the most. Instead she would say, "You're an incredible bunch of atoms," which seemed like the best she could do.

Even though it was only late afternoon, Cassie curled up on her mum's duvet and closed her eyes. The scrapbooks remained spread haphazardly in front of the wardrobe. She hoped Andie was okay, that she'd return home soon. Andie had been almost absent of emotion since they'd found Joy, and Cassie couldn't help but think it was all a bit of an act to safeguard herself from realizing she was actually heartbroken.

CHAPTER 29

DETECTIVE SERGEANT HOLLIDAY BETTS

5:10 p.m.

Holliday should have wished long and hard for a stabbing. Or a shooting, or something that was hands-down, no-questions-asked *murder*. Not just a suspicious death that might very well be from natural causes or, even worse than that . . . a murder she would never be able to solve.

She didn't need her first case at Homicide to be marked the dreaded "Unsolved."

Their crew had worked hard in the past couple of days; she couldn't have asked for more from any of them, other than an arrest and full admissions to whatever had happened to Joy Moody. Tracking down the laundromat customers was painstaking, but one by one they were ticking them off the list. The CCTV was as helpful as it was infuriating. It showed nothing, or at least nothing of interest in a murder inquiry. There was a very good chance someone appearing in the footage had something to do with Joy's death but, at the same time, there was an almost equal possibility that they didn't. The clientele was varied and some had no real memory of being in Joyful Suds on the first of August, or at least that's what they told the police. To them, doing their washing was as routine as getting gas, driving to work, or grocery shopping; they barely gave it a second thought.

Holliday was staring out the window at the Melbourne skyline. Seventeen floors up, the Docklands building had a view worth the fifty-minute drive to the city. It was early evening, one of her favorite times, when the sun made the myriad of windows around her glow orange and pink and yellow, reminding her of a Klimt painting. Her desk faced inward, so she had to swivel her chair to look, but she did so often. She never wanted things to move so fast that she forgot to appreciate this simple thing.

A vibration on her desk drew her eyes to her phone. *Her* phone, not the work one—two entirely different beasts. When her own phone beeped or buzzed, she didn't have to spring to action or wonder if she needed to bring her overnight bag, and her first thought wasn't "Who died?" She'd kept a pillow (because motel ones were always shit) and carry-on luggage in her car trunk ever since getting the Homicide spot.

It was her mum messaging, whom Holliday honestly did mean to make more time for, although the days kept slipping through her fingers. Bernadette "BeBe" Betts, whose sing-song name was entirely in keeping with her upbeat personality, had a much better social life than her daughter. Most of the time, Holliday was the one turning down her seventy-two-year-old mother while marveling at her energy. BeBe, for the most part, was fairly good spirited about it, but she was persistent. This was a trait mother and daughter shared, although they applied it in entirely different ways.

Mum: *Saturday night—I need you to come to Pilates with me.*

Holliday: *Why?*

Mum: *I think the instructor is flirting with me, but I need a second opinion.*

Holliday: *Do you want him to be flirting with you?*

Mum: *It's a she, darling. And yes, I think I do.*

Holliday's parents had divorced just after she finished high school. She assumed—although never asked—they'd waited to let her get through her final exams without too much disruption. They were about as well suited as when Cher and Tom Cruise had gotten together for a blip of time. To that end, there was no shock when her mum and dad finally sat her down and announced they'd split. Separately, they became almost normal. Her mum had had a series of partners since, though no one BeBe deemed serious; "Been there, done that," she'd say as if commitment was a one-time-only sort of thing. Holliday thought of relationships much like her mum did, although her own reasoning had more to do with not having the time rather than the interest. She'd probably be better off starting with a pet. Or maybe just a nice houseplant.

Mum: *And it's good for you. You need to spend some time on your chakras.*

Holliday: *Wouldn't that be a yoga thing?*

Mum: *Don't sass your mother. Pick me up at 7, wear stretchy clothes. We will get pho after and you can remind me how to pronounce it.*

Holliday: *Fuh.*

Mum: *Am I meant to know what that means?*

Holliday: *Yes. It's how you say it. Like "fuh."*

Mum: *See you tomorrow, Daisy xx*

Holliday: *Ok xx*

Her mum was the one person who called her Daisy and probably the only person she'd let get away with it. She liked how presumptuous her mum was, and it was a good tactic by BeBe, because if she put her request out there as a question, Holliday would likely say no. She imagined by tomorrow she'd be wanting to mix a strong vodka soda and binge-watch season two of *The White Lotus*. Although the way things were going, she would still be working.

The office was open plan, each crew seated together. It reminded Holliday of high school, where they'd compete across the year for points to see whose house would finish on top. The title was meaningless, attached to nothing except ego and kudos and teaching them that life was a competition. Sure, now she and her colleagues were one squad and weren't exactly vying against each other, but they kind of were. Nick Tan's team had solved fifteen cases in a row, and she knew this because they told everyone. She also knew the sort of things they'd say if she didn't solve what happened to Joy Moody. She'd beaten other applicants for the detective sergeant job and one of them worked in the office, still a rank beneath her. Holliday was an outsider, having never worked Homicide before, and the other sergeants had made it pretty clear that if they'd had a say, she wouldn't be there. Someone even made the quip that she'd only gotten the spot to fill their necessary quota of women. She knew that wasn't the case, or at least she hoped it wasn't. Either way, it still made her feel like she needed to win the race.

She hadn't realized Leo Collins was standing at her desk, and she spun around to face him, the golden light outside reflecting around the office and making it look a little church-like. "You've found Tyler?" she asked, because something in his expression suggested he was poised to give her good news.

Getting hold of Rodriguez, sooner rather than later, would be beneficial, although there was a good chance he'd go "no comment" and had disposed of any evidence, if anything existed to begin with. Despite what the local police thought of him, he might not be responsible.

"No, not him. Something very interesting just came through from one of the Missing Persons sites."

"To do with what?"

"This whole thing."

"What? About who killed Joy Moody?"

Leo was enjoying dragging it out, the theatrics. "No, it appears to be from Joy herself."

A message from the beyond, Holliday thought, taking the printed sheet from Leo. She read it quickly, then reread it to make sure she'd gotten it right.

"What do you think?" Leo asked.

Holliday wasn't sure what to think. The whole job had been peculiar, but this message—whoever it was from—was more than just a bit unusual. She checked her watch, not that it mattered. Knocking off on time was only for days when they didn't have murders to solve.

Holliday looked at Leo. "Start typing a warrant. We need to go back."

CHAPTER 30

ANDIE

7 p.m.

"Cassiopeeeeeeeia, whatcha doing?" Andie called to her sister. Her words slurred and her back was damp from the uneven pavers she was lying on in their backyard. She didn't know how long Cassie had been standing at the back door watching her. By rolling her head to the side she could see her sister, backlit by the glow from the house, but she couldn't sit all the way up because every time she did, she got a whirling, swirling sort of feeling that she attributed to the bottle of wine, now almost completely empty.

Once she'd marched off down the lane, coins ringing like little bells and the warm moscato nestled beside them, Andie headed to the railway station. She hadn't decided which way she was heading and thought she'd just board whichever train arrived first, and she was pleased to find one was arriving in just eight minutes. It was all part of the adventure, she told herself. A sign reminded her that it was an offense to travel without a ticket and this panicked her. She hurried over to the ticket machine but couldn't figure it out. An impatient man was waiting behind her, so Andie stepped back and let him go first. She breathed deeply and decided a bus might be a better option. Except the bus was just as confusing, because the driver spoke too quickly and she was none the wiser about how to be allowed on or why he wouldn't take her detergent-dusted coins.

Andie sat in the sheltered bus stop, opened her wine, and sipped straight from the bottle.

"You can't do that here," a man said from behind her. Andie turned to find two police officers, waists laden with equipment. The sight of the uniforms made her pulse quicken; she'd seen more than enough of them lately. Her eyes prickled and she willed the tears away. *She* wasn't the crier.

"I was just . . ."

"No alcohol at the train station."

"But I'm at the bus stop."

"Don't be a smart-arse. You can't drink here." The man rested his hands on his equipment belt as if he were ready for Andie to challenge him. She certainly wasn't planning on any such thing.

"It's a bit early in the day, isn't it?" the second policeman said.

She checked her watch before replying, "It's four p.m."

"Oh wow, we got a live one here, Hawkey."

Andie felt herself flush with panic, unsure what was going on. She tightened the cap on the wine and pushed it back into her bag.

"Where do you live?" Hawkey asked her, relatively politely, but it was very personal information to share with someone she'd never met.

"I can't tell you that."

He furrowed his brow. "Why not?"

"You're a stranger."

"We're the police, young lady. And you are obliged to give us your name and address if we believe you are committing offenses on public transport property." He sounded rather robotic.

"I-I'm not . . ." Andie stammered, deciding that running away seemed like a really good option. Her body felt shaky.

"How old are you?" Hawkey asked.

She pulled her bag in tight to her side, saying nothing.

"What have you got in there, miss?" He pointed at her bag.

Andie wasn't about to risk having him help himself to her money. Monty had warned her about the authorities being thieves. She looked at their hands, considering what "sticky fingers" would actually look like. "Nothing," she said.

"Well, it looks very heavy for nothing. Open it up."

One of their radios crackled and they both tilted their heads to listen. Thinking it was about her, that she was in more trouble than she knew, Andie wrapped her arm through the jingling bag of change, leaped to her feet, and took off.

"Oi!"

"Hey!"

Both policemen called after her. She didn't slow down, even though the noise of the coins sounded like the little bell attached to Donna's collar.

She heard them start to run after her, but she didn't look back, racing out onto Nepean Highway and narrowly avoiding a car, which honked at her as she skimmed past it. Andie ran to the beach and walked in the direction of home, knowing to turn when she got to her sister's favorite beach box. She drank from the bottle as she walked, a lovely, calming feeling extending through her body with every sip and step she took. It made her tingle with delight.

Once through the back gate of 225 Station Street, Andie collapsed in a heap on the pavers and swallowed another generous gulp of warm wine. She felt she deserved it for making her way home in one piece.

Now, Cassie came and sat down beside her in the courtyard, leaning her back up against the fence. "What are you doing out here?"

"I wanted to see the sky. I've missed it."

"It's been here all along, you know."

Andie thought for a moment before pointing into the dark, cloudless sky. "I see a fox with a chicken in its mouth."

"No, you don't," Cassie replied. "Why are you being like this?"

"And a chicken with a fox in its mouth." Andie started laughing and then realized she couldn't stop. Cassie didn't join in, so Andie knew she was still mad. Her laughter slowed and she lifted her heels and laid her legs across her twin's thigh. The word "sorry" danced about in her mind, but she didn't know how to phrase it.

"You can miss her *and* hate her, you know," Cassie said softly, resting one of her hands on Andie's shin. When Andie looked at her sister, she was staring into the sky, perhaps trying to find the chicken or the fox.

"I don't miss her," Andie lied.

"Do you hate her?"

Andie breathed deeply, looked at the glut of darkness above her, and wondered if Joy was still keeping an eye on them. "No, I don't hate her," she said finally. "Do you?"

Cassie shook her head. "No, I don't either. Can I ask you something? It's about the other night."

Andie propped herself up on her elbows so she could look at Cassie properly. If she was going to ask her about what happened to Joy, she was ready to tell her the truth. "Okay, what is it?"

Cassie sniffed loudly. Andie wiggled herself up a little straighter. The movement gave her a weird feeling, a rush of blood, and a sudden need to . . .

"I'm gonna be sick," Andie groaned before turning her head and vomiting.

CHAPTER 31
CASSIE

August 5, 2023
Four days after Joy's death

The police knocked hard on the back door. They couldn't know they'd arrived on the morning of Andie's first-ever hangover, or that Cassie had practically had to carry her sister to the bath the night before to rinse the vomit from her hair.

The back door rattled and the sound echoed around them as if they were surrounded. Cassie made it downstairs before Andie had managed to lift herself from the couch. As soon as she opened the door, four men wearing ties and shirts, all sporting neatly cropped hair, barreled past her from the courtyard. There was a moment of panic that something terrible was happening, a smartly dressed gang invading their home or some such thing. Then one said "Police" so she came to understand who they were, even though she didn't relax with this information.

People were coming through the in-between too, and she found herself racing to Andie on the couch, who looked rightfully confused. Cassie recognized Detective Holliday Betts in the group and her heart thundered. Why was she there?

"Andie, Cassie, we're here with a search warrant." Holliday put a sheet of paper down on the coffee table in reach of them both, just as Andie picked up the bucket and vomited loudly. There was really nothing left for her to throw up, so it was more noise than anything else. The detective's expression dropped and she looked as if she might need a bucket of her own.

"What's going on?" Cassie asked.

"You're here for me, aren't you?" Andie wiped her mouth with the back of her hand. She seemed ready to confess to something, and Cassie panicked that it was about the night Joy had died, that Andie was about to finish the conversation they'd only just started the night before. Andie suddenly seemed delicate, like she needed protecting. "Is it because of yesterday?"

Detective Betts looked curiously at Andie before speaking. "No, that's not why." She formed each word carefully. "But let's get back to that. We have reason to believe there may be remains on the premises."

"Remains?" Cassie asked.

"Human remains. And I know that sounds confronting, but let's let these guys do what they do best"—Detective Betts indicated the men and women who had come along with her—"while we have a chat."

Cassie felt as if the room were closing in around her. A "chat" implied it was a nice sort of visit, with biscuits and tea, but nothing about this felt nice. "Can we go out the back for some air?"

"Ahh, no, not for now. That area is actually the focus of the search."

Andie picked up the document on the table and scrutinized it. "Remains of Britney White," she read. "Who is that?"

"Britney was a seventeen-year-old who went missing. That was about twenty-one years ago."

The detective began to lower herself into Joy's armchair, then she reconsidered and brought over a chair from the dining table. Another woman, taller and with dark features, sat at the table watching them intently.

"Let me try and explain. Some of the items we recovered from here the other day have been DNA tested and matched in our database to a long-term missing person." Holliday pressed her lips together and slid a photograph out of her folder. "This is Britney White."

A round-faced teenager with messy bleached hair and dark eyebrows stared back at her. She wasn't smiling, nor was she entirely serious either; it was a playful expression that suggested she was fond of whoever was behind the camera. She had an air of familiarity about her, Cassie thought, but she couldn't work out why.

"I don't know who this is," Andie said.

Holliday nodded. "The percentage match from the items we tested wasn't high enough for it to be her, you see. But the results suggest a child or sibling of hers has been here. Which was interesting, of course. That's why Detective Sergeant Rania Crew has come along—she's from Missing Persons. It's been her investigation."

The other woman, silent until that point, nodded in greeting. "We've been looking for Britney for a long time."

Detective Betts put the photo of the woman back in her folder. Cassie wanted to reach out and take it; she felt like it was important to keep.

"What's this got to do with us?" Andie was still clutching her plastic bucket.

Detective Crew dragged her chair closer to them, the legs scraping across the floor. "Britney's sister has long maintained the belief that her sister was pregnant when she left home. A couple of things made her think this. And now a possible familial match to her DNA has been found right here." Crew waved her hand around the room.

Holliday Betts continued. "There are no records of you two anywhere. Births, Deaths, Marriages have nothing about twins with any version of your name or approximate date of birth. There are no school records, and nothing online whatsoever. We are waiting to hear back from hospitals about any twin births in the right time frame, but that means going back through some archives."

Cassie's pulse slowed to a deliberate, deafening thud. It was the feeling she had when she knew she was in trouble, like her body was trying to fold in on itself and disappear.

"It really is as if you two don't exist." Holliday paused. "Except, quite clearly, you do."

Cassie knew their names weren't on anything official, for obvious reasons. It would give them away, make them easy targets for The People. Any time they visited a doctor, it was with a Medicare card in someone else's name, and never the same doctor more than once. Joy pocketed things from the lost property in the laundromat, knowing what use they could be. "It's not theft if it's necessity," she said once, when Cassie caught her rifling through a lost purse. She knew her mother would never dream of taking cash or something of real value, like a wedding ring or laptop, but no one would notice if something like a Medicare card was missing until they next needed it, and then they could easily replace it. The rules were allowed to be bent when Joy wanted them to be. In fact, *only* when she wanted them to be.

Andie wasn't getting it either. "You're saying you think there's a pregnant teenager here somewhere . . ."—she lowered her voice to barely a whisper—"*dead*?"

"Not quite," Detective Crew said, looking at pains to elaborate. "We think she had the baby before she died."

Holliday chewed at her bottom lip. "Babies, actually." She paused. "We believe you two are the children of Britney White and that Joy never registered your births for that reason."

Andie swallowed hard and appeared on the verge of vomiting again. Cassie thought she might join her.

"I would like a DNA sample from each of you to determine that for sure," Rania Crew said.

"But what makes you think that Britney's here?" Andie asked. "Surely we would know if there was a . . . ah . . . um . . . a *body* . . . somewhere in the house."

Holliday shrugged and looked genuinely contrite. "I think that Joy was quite good at keeping secrets." She handed a sheet of paper to the girls. "This was sent via our Missing Persons site. It was time-stamped just before 4 p.m. on your birthday."

They read it together.

> *To Whom It May Concern,*
>
> *Britney White is in the shed at the rear of 225 Station Street, Bonbeach. Her death was an accident and no fault of her boyfriend at the time. I apologize for not bringing this to your attention earlier, but I had concerns that the police weren't to be trusted and there were some important things I needed to take care of. I am not in a position to answer further questions regarding this until 1 August 2050.*
>
> *I sincerely apologize for any inconvenience.*
> *Kind regards, Joy Moody*

Cassie looked to Andie to gauge her reaction, but her sister's face had barely shifted. Her mouth remained in a sullen line, and Cassie wondered if they were even reading the same words. Why would their mother know anything about a death? And why would she suggest that there was a person in their shed? Cassie's head spun. It felt like an elaborate hoax or a test of some sort. But for what, she had no idea.

"That took a couple of days to filter through to the right department, and now here we are," Rania Crew said. Her face was harder than Holliday Betts', although she still looked kind beneath the stern exterior.

The twins did as asked, pushing cotton swabs around their cheeks and dropping them into plastic bags to be sealed and sent off for testing. Was it possible they might find out who their birth mother was, but also that she was dead? What a cruel blow that would be. And what would be the point of knowing if they had no chance to meet her? Besides, Joy Moody was their mother, and she always would be.

Cassie picked up the note again. The formality of it felt especially Joy-like, although maybe this was another trick—of the police, or of The People. They wouldn't leave Joy alone even after death. Or was it all lies, just as Andie said? She clenched her jaw, wondering how much pressure it would take to crack one of her teeth.

A great deal of noise was being made in the backyard: voices, the sound of hammering, a thumping of some sort. Cassie thought of all the neatly stacked boxes in the shed and how often she'd been in and out of it over the years. The idea of there being a body out there unsettled her.

Holliday was looking from one twin to another. "Why didn't Joy trust the police?"

Cassie eyed her sister, who looked about as washed out as she felt. "It won't make sense to you."

"Try me. I've heard a lot of strange things over the years."

Cassie took umbrage to this. "We're not strange."

"I didn't say *you* were strange," Holliday said quickly. "I phrased that wrong." The detective held up her palms, in a conciliatory manner. "I'm sorry. Will you tell me why?"

Andie shrugged, as if it no longer mattered. Even so, Cassie spoke tentatively, still not sure which side of the truth they fell on.

Pulling secrets out of their hiding spots was hard work, but she told the two detectives about The People infiltrating the police and how careful they'd had to be their whole lives.

To her credit, Holliday Betts didn't laugh. "I can see why our presence might upset you so much."

Despite the circumstances, and the possibility that Detective Betts was working for The People, Cassie appreciated her understanding.

An overall-clad officer wearing a large camera around her neck came bustling through the back door, an energy of excitement about her. "Holliday, Rania," the officer said with a thick and quite lovely accent, "we've found something."

"You've found her?" Rania Crew asked.

The woman said nothing in reply, but her face made it clear that Britney White had been found exactly where Joy had said she would be.

A month ago, Cassie would've been adamant that her mother would not be capable of playing any part in hiding a body. But so much had changed in such a short time, and it was becoming abundantly clear that she didn't know as much as she thought about the two people she was the closest to. If their mother could do something so heinous, then was it also possible that Andie could too? They'd not finished their conversation from the previous evening, and now Cassie wasn't sure she ever wanted to.

CHAPTER 32
DETECTIVE SERGEANT HOLLIDAY BETTS

Gray mottled skies watched them outside the laundromat. The sun had barely appeared and the wind was biting in the way that made your bones feel like the marrow had turned to ice. Holliday couldn't see the end to her shift happening anytime soon and could only hope it wouldn't rain. They'd still have to do the work, but it was harder in the mud, and she didn't think her shoes were up for it. She really needed to get herself a decent pair of gumboots, or a different job. That thought occurred to her about every six months or so, when she felt overworked and underappreciated and that buying a coffee van seemed like a pretty good option. Every time she thought of getting out, though, she knew she'd miss it: the ever-changing landscape of work, the chase, the catch—not to mention the nine weeks of paid holiday each year.

They would need lights in the yard before long, but that meant calling in the State Emergency Service and it already felt like a bit of a circus. She'd give it another hour.

She was really struggling to get a handle on the twins. They answered her questions, but there was something quite unconventional about them. It was almost impossible to believe that these

two women, twenty-one years of age, had grown up in relative iso-
lation while being in the middle of a well-populated suburb. If it
were Macquarie Island or Moggs Creek, she'd understand it better. Those places had plenty of space for secluded properties and no
neighbors for miles. But these two had come face to face with customers every day of their lives, and yet no one really knew anything
about them. Most people who knew them couldn't even tell them
apart, she'd discovered. One customer, Brett Carmichael, hadn't
even known there were two of them. If she hadn't known better,
she'd think they'd been raised in a cloistered, religious cult.

They remained high on the list of persons of interest.

So did the brother of the deceased, Grant Moody. His had been
an interesting statement to take, Holliday immediately getting the
vibe that he was an absolute turd. By his own account, he'd only
seen Joy and the twins less than a handful of times in the past ten
years, had a barely existent relationship with his sister, but had co-
incidentally visited on the day of his sister's death. Coincidences,
Holliday liked to think, were usually because someone hadn't asked
the right questions. Grant was also quick to cast suspicion on the
twins. "If you ask me, those girls are trying to fast-track their inheritance," he'd suggested, unprompted. Yet he was the one with the
mountain of debt, giving him an excellent motive to get rid of his
sister. And they still hadn't been able to find Joy's will.

Joy's death was her crew's investigation, but this new arm of
it—the Britney White angle—meant Missing Persons were now on
board in a collaboration of sorts. Holliday Betts was not the best at
sharing; it came with being an only child and a single woman who
liked things a certain way. Two bodies within a week in one little
laundromat was highly unusual. Which raised the question, how
many more were hidden? They were going to have to take a thorough look at the entire property, including turning over the whole
courtyard, ripping up pavers, and making sure they didn't have to

come back a third time. After nightfall, they'd use luminol inside the property to try to establish if Britney's death had occurred in the house; that was an important part of the puzzle.

And what did Cassie and Andie know? She wanted to pepper them with questions, but she knew it was best to make sure her ducks were in a row first. Currently, Holliday Betts felt like there was no row whatsoever and that one of the ducks might very well be a pigeon.

Once the toxicology results on Joy were back, and they'd tracked down Tyler Rodriguez, perhaps she'd be ready to properly speak with Joy's daughters. It was possible the interview would end in the arrest of one of them, maybe both. Holliday was annoyed with herself for not having a clear suspect yet.

They were having trouble finding Rodriguez, although she was confident he would turn up; his sort always did. Then they could ask him why he was at Joyful Suds on the day a woman died and why he wrote a threatening message on the bulletin board. Holliday had read his dossier in detail. He'd had his fair share of trouble, but Sam Poole might have gone a bit overboard with the rundown on him. Rodriguez was a crook, but he wasn't about to be featured in an *Underbelly* series. He probably had it in him to kill Joy Moody, but Holliday firmly believed that most people, pushed hard and far enough, were capable of murder. If Tyler had found a way to break in and kill her, he had been incredibly subtle about it.

The link between Britney White and Rodriguez did trouble her, though. He was White's ex-boyfriend and the only suspect in her disappearance. In what Holliday found pretty woeful police work, no one had investigated Britney's whereabouts for eighteen months, writing her off as just another troubled runaway. Not only had the teenager deserved better, but the delay meant they'd lost crucial evidence. Witnesses struggled to remember things that had happened the same day, let alone almost two years later.

Britney had a nice smile, Holliday had thought, looking at her picture. Her upbringing had been shit, and she'd died before she got a chance to see things come good. It might turn out that Joy Moody had died of natural causes, but it was unlikely that Britney had, not in the least because wrapping herself in plastic and stuffing herself into a locked trunk wasn't particularly easy to do.

The CCTV had been helpful and not at the same time. It didn't cover enough of the premises to conclusively rule out anyone entering the house from the rear. If someone had come through the shop, they'd have been seen, but that still left the back lane and courtyard. They knew Tyler had been in the laundromat, but the girls had said Joy was still alive after he left. The neighbor had confirmed it too; he'd seen her, agitated and face scratched that evening, long after Rodriguez had scrawled his message and gone. Even more troubling was that less than a week prior to Joy's death, she'd taken all her savings out of her account. They'd confirmed with the bank that Joy Moody had gone there in person and withdrawn the entire thirty-four thousand dollars. So where was it now? Had she taken it out to give to Rodriguez for a loan she'd struggled to repay? Or was it money to keep him quiet about something she'd done?

More than anything, Holliday would have loved an explanation for the note in Joy's pocket. "*P.S. If I stay here I'll die*" danced through her head at least every ten minutes. She wanted to find the rest of that letter, needing the context to even begin to make sense of it. Holliday struggled to see how it pointed to anything other than Joy fearing for her life.

She suddenly remembered her plans to do Pilates and have pho that night with her mum. Work was always a legitimate reason to cancel, but it never made her feel any less of a disappointment. She also had to go and tell *The Shining* twins that they needed to stay out of the crime scene, which just so happened to be their house, while they finished carrying out forensic testing.

Holliday: *Gotta cancel tonight, sorry. At a job. H xx*

Mum: *Is it the one on the news? I think I saw you xx*

Holliday cursed, then checked the website of one of the news channels she thought was usually reputable. There it was: "Dirty Laundry Uncovered in Melbourne Suburban Laundromat." It hadn't taken them long to get hold of the story, even if it had been inevitable.

Holliday: *Yeah. Thanks for the heads up.*

Mum: *Be careful, Daisy* 🌼

Holliday: *You too . . . Pilates instructors are known to be pretty wild.*

Mum: 🖕

Holliday: *Love you xx*

She knew the media would be beating down their door shortly, if they weren't already there. She'd better start thinking about what to say to the reporters.

CHAPTER 33
ANDIE

August 6, 2023
Five days after Joy's death

They woke up at Monty's house, a construction-like noise thumping from next door—their house. Cassie had taken the couch and Andie the floor. They didn't venture upstairs to investigate the spare bed situation; it seemed too much of a breach of their neighbor's privacy. It was enough that they'd let themselves in to sleep there. That wasn't why he'd left the keys with them, but they'd not had much of a choice; the police had turned them out. Andie was quite sure Monty wouldn't mind.

She'd have knocked on Linh's door, but her friend was away for the week at a conference in Sydney. As soon as Andie saw the sign on the door at Lotus—"Closed until 10 August"—she remembered Linh telling her. Andie was frustrated, and she wished she had a way to speak to her.

The police had brought in some sort of machinery to turn up the pavers. Andie wasn't entirely sure what they were expecting to find. Although if she'd been asked two days ago if the body of a young woman would be found in their shed, she'd have said no, so what did she really know about the house next door? It was feeling less and less like home.

Had *she* started this? Caused this unraveling with her nosiness and DNA testing?

Cassie was still sleeping when Andie got up and boiled the kettle. Being in Monty's house was like stepping into a parallel universe, where the layout was the same as their home but everything was in different places.

With a cup of tea in hand, she went through to Monty's shop and tried to make out what was happening next door. The shopfronts all ran in a straight line, so she couldn't see inside Joyful Suds without going outside. A police car was parked out the front, two wheels mounting the nature strip; Joy would not have been impressed. Blue-and-white-checked tape still formed a barrier between the laundromat and everywhere else. It fluttered gently in the wind, unaware of its role in the week's life-changing events, as inanimate objects so often are.

For all Andie knew, this was exactly what happened every time a body was discovered in someone's backyard. But she didn't know, and couldn't guess, and had no one to ask. It was very frustrating not having all the answers. Where had Joy gotten them all from? She'd made life seem so straightforward with her no-nonsense decisiveness.

Andie wondered what sort of mother Britney White would have been to the twins. Given she knew absolutely nothing about Britney, it was easy to imagine her as someone who liked to give hugs, laugh gregariously, show the twins how to apply makeup, and let them paint their nails as bright as they liked.

At the other end of the shops, just near Ellen's, she spied a white van with some sort of satellite dish on top. Andie shook the idea of gamma rays from her mind; that sort of nonsense was just that—nonsense. But a man was standing beside the van, setting up a tripod. Andie pressed her face farther into the glass, trying to see more.

Uncle Grant's face appeared in the window, making her shriek and jump back. He put his hands up, animatedly apologizing.

Andie unlocked the door and let her uncle in.

"Hop back from the window. I don't think they realized who you are, but it's only a matter of time. Probably because they didn't see you with the other one, so they didn't know it was you."

"The other one?"

"Andie."

"I'm Andie."

"Well, you know what I mean."

"Are you talking about the man outside with the tripod? What does he want?"

"To know everything, of course, about the body in the shed. He's from the media—you know, the TV news."

It hadn't really occurred to Andie that the man was there for them and Joyful Suds and the salacious secrets spilling from the innocuous-looking building. She swallowed hard.

Uncle Grant held up a brown paper bag and coffee tray. "I've got breakfast. Where's your sister?"

In the house behind Doyle's Locksmiths, Cassie was stirring. When she saw Grant come through the door with Andie, she sat up, pulled the blanket around herself, and rubbed her still sleep-heavy eyes. "What is it? What's happened?"

"Good question," Grant said. "Why didn't you call me?"

Andie shrugged. "The police came."

"I can see that, but what I mean is, why did I have to hear about it on the radio this morning rather than find it out from the pair of you, my own nieces?"

She didn't love the way Grant addressed them, but he'd brought them coffee and pastries. Perhaps she just needed to be a little less prickly—a little less Joy-like. "Um, we didn't really think about it is all."

"Okay, well, next time, have me on speed dial, hey?"

Andie hoped there would be no next time, and she wasn't sure he'd be their first call if there was.

"So is it true?" Grant's question presented as morbid fascination. "Who was it?"

"We don't really know."

"Come on, girls. Who the hell is under the shed?"

"No, not under." Cassie sat up straighter. "*In* the shed. In an antique trunk."

Grant clasped his hand over his mouth dramatically. "Mama's wedding trunk?"

All Andie could do was shrug. "I guess. It's been in there forever."

"Hells flippin' bells," Grant said. "What a scandal."

Cassie burst into tears and Grant's face dropped.

"I'm sorry. Here." He thrust coffee at them as if it were a cure-all. "This makes what I've come to talk to you about even worse," he said.

"What is it?" Andie asked, unable to shake the wariness she felt around her uncle.

"Maybe we'll talk another time, yeah? I was just trying to get things in order to help you both out. There's a lot to do behind the scenes, and I didn't want you two to feel like you had to go it alone."

"Thank you, that's very kind of you," Cassie said, wiping her nose with a tissue.

"Tell us, please," Andie asked.

Grant opened the brown paper bag and pulled out a golden-colored croissant. He ripped a chunk off the end, scattering pastry flakes all over himself and the floor. He pointed the bag at the two of them, motioning for them to help themselves. "The laundromat is in a lot of debt," he said. "It's barely keeping afloat."

"No, that can't be right." Andie knew Joy was many things, but a bad businesswoman was surely not one of them.

Cassie dabbed her eyes. "Mum never mentioned anything."

Grant shrugged. "She probably didn't want to worry you both. She had to take out a second mortgage. It's not far from being fore-closed by the bank."

The mention of the bank made Andie remember the bag of money they'd hidden in their wardrobe. She hoped the police hadn't found it; she should have taken it to Monty's with them, but they hadn't been let in, not even for their toothbrushes. "So what do we need to do?" she asked.

"I'm looking into some options, but I think the best bet is to cut your losses and sell."

"Sell our home?" Cassie spluttered the words out, fresh tears starting up.

Grant creased his forehead, looking at them both solemnly. "Is it somewhere you think you still want to be? After all she's done?"

"What do you mean?"

"Well, that body didn't put itself in the trunk, you know."

Andie shot a look toward Cassie, who was unlikely to concede Joy was involved.

"There has to be an explanation." Cassie fumbled about for a reason. "She just couldn't, she loved us."

"Of course she did," Grant said. "In her own special way, she did."

Silence fell as the twins considered his words.

"What do we do now?" Andie asked finally. "Joy wouldn't want us to sell."

Cassie grabbed at the tissues and shook her head.

"I understand that, I do. But if there's no money, there's no money. Right? Life is expensive, girls. And there's a lot of interest from developers. This land is worth a lot."

"The land?" Cassie said. "They'd knock Joyful Suds down?"

"It's old, Andie."

"That's Cassie," Andie corrected him, wondering how to explain the differences so he'd remember, or care.

"It might be time to move on," Grant said. "And we could get you set up somewhere else, somewhere nice. Both of you." He paused again, biting into his pastry. "And there's the other thing."

"What thing?" Andie said, breathing deeply, bracing for yet more bad news—she knew there was no way it was good.

He sighed and took a large slurp of his coffee.

"Are you going to tell us what's going on?" she asked, disliking his drawn-out, dramatic manner.

"The building here, the laundromat, was *my* father's. And he left it to Joy, his daughter, in his will, but there were conditions on that. It is a family property, you see, and legally, you two aren't related. Not officially, by all accounts. There was no adoption. So the house and laundromat, I'm sorry to say, are actually mine."

Andie stared at him in disbelief. She had not seen this coming. Not only that, but he didn't look sorry in the least.

CHAPTER 34

CASSIE

"But of course I'm not going to throw you out on the street," Uncle Grant said.

It was unfathomable to think the twins wouldn't be able to live at 225 Station Street. The idea of leaving, after their last-minute reprieve from going to the future, felt like they'd been helped up off the ground only to be pushed straight back down again.

Cassie understood that living wasn't free, although for the past twenty-one years the logistics had been sorted on her behalf. She'd certainly never had reason to consider the ownership of their home.

"So we can keep living here?" Andie asked.

"Ah . . . for now. Yeah, but I don't have the money to keep the place indefinitely. Not to mention, no one is going to want to touch it once whatever Joy has been up to hits the news."

Andie looked at Cassie then, her forehead creased in deep, worried lines. Cassie knew Andie had craved freedom, but she didn't think homelessness was what she'd had in mind.

"I have been workshopping a bit of a plan," Grant said, popping the top off his coffee cup and using his tongue to remove every last bit of froth and chocolate from the plastic lid. "I'll find you both a new place—somewhere around here if I can—otherwise, maybe it's time for a fresh start. I'm gonna put up the first month's rent and the bond—that's a fair whack, girls, out of my own pocket—and then I can offload this place for whatever I can get. Once I've paid out what Joy owed on it"—he paused to sigh loudly—"I'll hopefully not be too far in the red. But that's what family does, hey?"

"In the red?" Cassie asked.

"In debt. That's what I'm saying—there's no money, nothing left. Joy has gone and left you a steaming pile of shit to deal with, but I just won't let you shoulder that burden alone, or together alone, you know, since there's two of you and all." Grant tossed his cup and lid toward the trash can. The dregs of coffee splashed on the floor, but he didn't get up to wipe it. "You have my word."

A silence fell over them all. They had to leave Joyful Suds.

"Can we use your phone?" Cassie asked.

"What for?" Grant asked.

"To speak to Monty, our neighbor." She wanted to hear his calming voice and measured advice. He'd know what to do.

Andie nodded enthusiastically. "And Linh too?"

Grant sighed. "Sure thing, gals. But there's not great news on those fronts either."

Cassie's thoughts immediately flew to the idea that Monty must have died. What else would Grant possibly have to tell them? She clutched her hand over her mouth.

"Settle down, Andie." Seeing her face, Grant put his hands up in front of him. "The old bloke's not dead."

"That's Cassie," Andie said sharply. "Is Monty okay?"

Grant waved his hand far too casually for the circumstances. "Yes, he is. He's blown out his knee, had problems for years apparently, but it's gonna need surgery. He'll be in hospital till next week, earliest."

"But he's really okay?" Andie looked at Cassie reassuringly. "That's great. Did you speak to him?"

"Yeah I did. I rang the hospital. That's not actually the bad news. It's hard to say, is all, girls . . . You see, he's a bit done with you both. Wants you to leave him be."

"What?" Andie snapped, and Cassie was breathless all over again.

"He said you can stay here a couple more days, keep an eye on the cat and stuff, but then that's it. He's done with the drama."

"We're not drama!" Cassie shouted.

Grant rolled his eyes, then shook his hand at the wall, indicating their house next door. "Hardly good fun living next to the house of horrors at the moment, is it?"

"He wants nothing to do with us?" Cassie felt sick repeating the words.

"He's washed his hands of you." Grant shrugged. "Said 'They can hitch their wagon to someone else.' Pretty brutal, hey?"

Andie wrapped an arm around Cassie's shoulders.

"And the tattooist girl—I'd be careful around her. I saw her speaking to a journo."

"Who was she speaking to?" Andie asked. "Is she home?"

Cassie knew how it would hurt her sister to know Linh was back and hadn't come to see them.

"A journo, like, a journalist—someone who scrounges for news-worthy stories." Grant paused. "You need to stay away from her. She'll be giving them the inside scoop for a bit of fast cash."

Cassie felt their tiny world shrinking even further.

"I did bring you this though." Uncle Grant pulled a mobile phone out of his pocket. "It's impossible to get hold of you two, so I've got you this. But it's on the proviso that you only speak to me."

Cassie could tell Andie was bristling at that.

"Just while we work out the lay of the land, yeah?" he clarified quickly. "Once we know who we can trust, then you can go ahead and do whatever you like. But for now, Uncle Grant is just trying to keep you safe."

Those words echoed in Cassie's mind. Joy had said the same thing many times over. Every time she'd warned them about The People or the perils of having a television, or explained why they were being homeschooled, she'd cited *safety*. The twins might have been old enough age-wise to be considered adults, but they fell short in every other way. They needed him. They weren't worldly; he was. He would make sure they didn't get taken advantage of now Joy was gone.

"Now I've gotta get along. I've got some places to go look at for the two of you." His smile was wide and warm, but it was missing something, as if he was trying to reassure himself. Maybe he'd change his mind too, like Monty had. He was doing so much for them, and he didn't have to. Would he realize it was drama he didn't need, too?

Grant stood and dusted the croissant crumbs from his clothes onto the floor. "You can go where you like, of course. But make sure you take that." He pointed at the phone. "You need to remember, there are reporters waiting to pounce on you, so it's wise you stay put. They're after a story, and you two looking like you do is exactly what they want. A photo of the two of you together would be worth a mint! If you need me to bring you anything—food or whatever—just ring me, yeah?" He looked from sister to sister. "You do know how to use a mobile phone?"

Cassie had no idea, never having had reason to use one previously, but Andie was quick to assure him.

"I've programmed my number in. So if you see my name on the screen, you'll know to pick up. If you don't see my name, *don't* answer. It could be anyone." He paused, sniffed noisily, and looked at them intently. "Got it?"

"Yes, Uncle Grant," they chorused.

Cassie was comforted by her uncle's presence, even though she got the impression Andie was just being agreeable so he'd hurry up and leave. Of course she would have preferred her mum to be there, but she was grateful to Grant for coming to see them when he could've kept his distance, like everyone else. She would do everything within her power to make sure having the twins in his life was as uncomplicated as possible.

CHAPTER 35
ANDIE

August 7, 2023

Things had finally gone quiet in the house behind the laundromat, making Andie think the police must have found what they were looking for. Or else they'd turned up every floorboard and paving stone and dug through every drawer and found nothing other than what they'd discovered in the shed two days earlier.

Just as Andie was readying herself to sneak down the fence line and listen in, Detective Betts came through Monty's back gate to confirm they were done. The twins were welcome to return home. The diminutive detective looked tired, her clothes crumpled, and a just-as-exhausted Detective Leo Collins stood behind her.

"Your shop and house are secured. I know it's been a really hard few days for the two of you, and I am truly sorry for the inconvenience."

Andie found the apology genuine, although she wasn't sure the detective really had anything to apologize for. This was on Joy. "Can you tell us what happened to her—to the woman you found?"

Holliday Betts took a deep breath and considered Andie with an expression that said she'd had more than enough of the Moody family. "It will take some time to find out what exactly caused her death. We can only speculate at this stage."

"Did Joy do it, though? Did she . . ." Andie couldn't even say it. It was one thing to think of the woman who'd raised her as a rigid disciplinarian, another to think of her as a murderer.

Holliday shuffled, staring at her feet and then at the man standing just behind her. She wore her exhaustion like a heavy coat. "I don't know. We may never know for sure with Joy gone, but we did find traces of blood in your house, enough of it to paint a bit of a picture that something occurred inside. It will need to undergo forensic testing, of course, to confirm our suspicions that it's Britney's."

Andie met Detective Betts' gaze, hoping she would tell her more. Andie wanted to know everything, but she also wanted to pretend none of it was happening and go back to their home, blissfully unaware.

"You don't seem shocked."

"I don't really know what to be." Andie hoped Cassie couldn't hear their conversation. If Andie was anything less than resoundingly supportive of their mother, Cassie would be upset. Her sister wasn't coping well—she'd taken to sitting at the table in Monty's shop and moving pieces around the chess board. Not playing the game, just making a pattern with the pawns and then sweeping them off and starting again, like she was stuck in some sort of loop.

Andie wanted to know if the police had found the money in her wardrobe or the syringe. She didn't actually know where the latter was anymore, but she certainly wouldn't draw attention to it by asking.

Holliday Betts handed the house keys to Andie and straightened. "We'll speak again soon."

The ominous undercurrent of that statement felt like a gut punch. Andie walked back into Monty's and found Cassie awake in the lounge. Andie assumed she'd heard the entire exchange. "The detective said we can go home now," Andie told her, "if we want."

She was quite sure she saw her sister's face visibly lose color at the thought of returning to 225 Station Street.

"There's no rush though," Andie said, feigning nonchalance she didn't feel. "Why don't we stay here and maybe watch some TV?"

Cassie shot a cautious look over her shoulder at Monty's large television, the blank screen reflecting both their faces. Andie knew it unsettled her; Cassie still thought it was sending them subliminal messages, while Andie was quite sure this was more of Joy's bluff and bullshit. Maybe she should've asked the detectives, although Holliday Betts already looked at her like she'd landed from another planet.

"Are you sure we should?" Cassie gazed anxiously at her.

"I really think it will be okay."

Despite her reluctance, Andie could tell Cassie was curious to see what all the fuss was about. She confidently pressed the biggest button on the remote. The TV lit up, and Cassie hunkered down behind the couch. Andie presumed it was so her body wasn't exposed to the harmful electro-magnetic waves. She didn't laugh; it was going to take some time to get used to all the changes.

Judge Judy spoke to them from the screen, telling someone off in a tone that echoed Joy somewhat. Andie flicked to another channel—*Flip or Flop*—and was intrigued by the accents, as well as the glimpses into other people's homes and lives. Life would slowly expand, she hoped, and these things would seem less foreign.

It wasn't long before Andie's stomach growled. On inspection of Monty's cupboards, she realized they'd picked them almost clean. "Do you want a cheeseburger?" she asked Cassie, knowing that her sister would never be able to refuse.

Cassie remained shielded from the full view of Monty's television but had leaned her arms up on the back of the couch, watching the demolition of a newly purchased home with avid curiosity. "It's not a special occasion," she said.

Andie shook her head smugly. "Well, we can start a new tradition; eat what we like, when we like."

"How will you find the McDonald's?"

"I'll ask someone." Andie sounded more sure than she actually was, but it couldn't be that hard.

"Take the phone? Just in case?" Cassie pushed the mobile Grant had left in her direction and Andie shrugged, sliding it into her pocket.

"I won't be long, okay?"

Cassie nodded, not completely convinced, but Andie was determined to make this trip better than her last. People went to new places all day, every day. She and Cassie weren't going to be kept prisoners forever.

A quick look out the front confirmed that the news cameras weren't there. The police had packed up too, although they'd left traces of their presence outside Joyful Suds. A torn section of crime scene tape was tied to the "No Standing" sign on the sidewalk, waving about in the wind, marking the laundromat like balloons would mark the house of a kid's party. When they'd been younger, she'd seen balloons like that on a mailbox and, ever curious, asked Joy why they were there. She had said the balloons were to celebrate the mailman's birthday. Andie had felt terrible; they'd never done that for their mail carrier before and she sought to rectify it as soon as possible, asking Rob—their postman—when his birthday was and explaining why. He had laughed and said it was lovely she'd thought of him, but that those balloons were for the kids having parties inside their own houses, to mark it for the guests. She understood, even back then, that Joy had constructed that lie to spare them the truth of being friendless. They hadn't ever tied balloons outside their house to show their birthday party guests where to go, because they'd never had a party, at least not a proper one like she'd read about in books, with hot dogs and party hats and a table especially for presents. Joy had been furious with Rob, and Andie's ears had burned with embarrassment, knowing it was her fault. As far as she could tell, Rob's only wrongdoing had been telling them the truth.

Andie stepped out the front door and locked it behind her. Her confidence was ebbing, but her determination overruled it. She stopped at Linh's door, where the sign was still up—"Closed until 10 August." She frowned, wondering if Linh would really betray them, but she realized she knew very little about what motivated people. She had a lot to learn.

CHAPTER 36

DETECTIVE SERGEANT HOLLIDAY BETTS

Holliday had barely let herself relax into the couch when her phone rang. A *Murder, She Wrote* rerun had just begun. It was no coincidence that she'd sat down in time for an episode; she owned the box set and loved to wind down with Jessica Fletcher.

"Should we ignore it, Jess?" Holliday asked the television sleuth, although there was little chance she would ignore the call. Much to the frustration of her mother and pretty much every boyfriend she'd ever had, Holliday almost always put work first. Becoming a detective sergeant with the Homicide Squad came with sacrifices, including relationships. Keeping friends like Jessica Fletcher was sometimes just easier than letting real-life ones down.

The Moody twins were weighing on her mind. She might have clocked out, but her brain hadn't gotten the memo. There was no way they could have been involved in Britney's death—presuming it was Britney White in that trunk. The body had been there far longer than the twins could have been capable of carrying out such a crime. Combined with Joy's confession about the location of the body and the last time the teenager was seen alive, it made sense to think they were looking at a twenty-year-old cadaver. In any case, it was remarkably well preserved. Holliday had not seen the likes of it before. The pathologist had remarked that the tight plastic wrap, the low body weight of the victim, and the conditions in the shed had caused her to dry out and become a sort of human jerky. The thought of it could have turned Holliday vegetarian if she didn't enjoy bacon and KFC so much.

But her investigation of Joy's death was pointing more and more squarely at one of the Moody sisters. The problem she faced was if it was only one twin involved, which one? They were barely distinguishable physically, their DNA was identical, and neither of them had all that much to say. Not yet anyway.

Finding the exact quantity of cash Joy had withdrawn in the twins' wardrobe had bumped Cassie and Andie up the persons-of-interest list. Holliday had been almost positive the money had been handed over to Tyler at some point prior to Joy's death, but clearly that was not the case.

Her ringtone deafening, Holliday finally answered the call. The volume was essential to ensure she would answer it, because when she slept, it was sometimes so deep a hurricane wouldn't stir her.

"Hey Sarge, it's Linc." Lincoln George was her team's analyst.

She couldn't stifle a yawn as she replied, "Everything okay?"

Lincoln was very good, but he had a problem with knowing when to knock off. But then again, they all did. Just after 2 p.m., Holliday had practically escorted her entire team out of Morningside Police Station to make sure they left and got some rest. They'd been working almost nonstop since Joy Moody had died, and they needed the break. And so did she, but she couldn't knock off unless her crew did. Her couch and her *Murder, She Wrote* collection were calling to her. She would've manhandled them out of the station if she'd had to.

"Yeah, yeah. No worries here."

"Do you have anyone waiting at home for you?" Holliday hadn't gotten to know her crew on that sort of personal level just yet.

"Is that an offer?"

She blushed. She hadn't meant to come across as forward. "No, I just thought you may have better things to do." She hoped her voice didn't betray her embarrassment.

He laughed, making her wonder if he had been the one attempting to be sleazy. It wouldn't be the first time a colleague had made a pass. "Yeah, well, I wanted to tell you what I found on the iPad we seized."

Her curiosity was piqued. Jessica Fletcher typed noisily on her heavy, black typewriter, her auburn bob bouncing along. Holliday turned the volume down. "What did you find?"

The device had been found in a bedside drawer in Joy's room. The Moody house had been quite pleasant to search; it was meticulously clean, although the tests they'd done to check for traces of blood showed it wasn't as spotless as Joy Moody may have thought. It was clear that something had happened at the bottom of the stairs; the luminescence from the chemical reaction to blood was hard to dispute.

"There were some pretty interesting searches done."

"Like what?" Holliday asked. Linc seemed to be enjoying dragging this out. She was not.

"Right, so . . . 'insulin overdose' . . . 'is an insulin overdose painful' . . . 'insulin in blood tests.'"

"Wow. Do you think Joy was just checking out options for how to off herself then?"

"No, no way. Joy's been dead for, what, a week? These searches were done three days ago. And one of them was 'penalty for covering up death.'"

Holliday heard herself gasp, an image of the twins filling her mind. What had they done? Or was it what they felt they had to do in order to escape the control of their mother? It was time to go back and get the story from them, whether they liked it or not.

She made Lincoln promise he was done for the night before hanging up. Within seconds of tossing her phone on the coffee table, it rang again and she cursed her analyst's persistence before answering tersely. "I told you I'd see you tomorrow."

An unfamiliar voice replied. "Ah, sorry, have I got the right number? Is this Detective Holly Betts?"

"Holliday. Yes." She snapped into professional mode.

"Constable Dylan Percy here. I'm on the Morningside van." She remembered her days working general duties, making calls to detectives and hoping like hell that they didn't berate her for mistakes she hadn't realized she'd made.

"How can I help you?

"We've just, um, arrested Tyler Rodriguez." In the background, the distinct crackle of a police radio and the whoosh of traffic were audible.

Holliday cracked her neck from left to right, noises she was quite sure her body shouldn't make. She slid to the end of the couch and got up. Her shins ached at the thought of putting her work shoes back on. She'd wear her sneakers instead. "I'll be at the station in twenty."

CHAPTER 37
CASSIE

Eventually Cassie moved from behind the couch to sitting on it. With Andie gone, the television made her feel less alone. She kept wondering how she could go about explaining to Monty that they hadn't meant to cause so much hassle, that they *were* worth the effort. She thought of Monty as family. Maybe he'd forgive them if Cassie got a chance to defend her position, in person.

She looked for Donna, but she wasn't in one of her usual spots, and Cassie was pissed off that everyone, cat included, had somewhere better to be. She desperately missed her mum, but it wasn't an easy emotion. She'd never lost someone she loved and had gone from nothing to what felt like the top of that mountain so quickly her head was spinning. Andie was still ignoring her emotions, or was actually devoid of any. Cassie felt like it was only a matter of time before Joy's death hit her sister like one of the morning express trains.

"It might look like every other suburban laundromat, but this one has more than its fair share of dirty laundry to air out. Joyful Suds, in Melbourne's Bonbeach, has been the subject of a police investigation this week, as not one but two deceased women have been found on the property."

Cassie's jaw dropped. The woman on television, dressed in a stiff red blazer that was surely dry-clean only, spoke as if she was talking directly to Cassie, although she knew this was not how TV worked.

"Andie!" she called, before remembering her sister wasn't there. No one was there.

The woman continued. "The laundromat has been subject to intense scrutiny after the owner of the shop, Joy Moody, was found dead on Wednesday morning. Sources have told us this is being treated as suspicious, with the Homicide Squad in attendance. Three days later, detectives from the Missing Persons Squad returned and spent almost two days conducting a thorough search of the premises. There, they solved a mystery that has haunted a local family for over twenty years. The remains of Britney White, who was seventeen when she went missing in 2002, were found behind the house.

"But that's not all. In what sounds more likely to be the storyline in an episode of *Stranger Things*, the surviving occupants of the house, identical twin sisters, have claimed to be time travelers from the year 2050. Sources have told us that detectives are working under the belief that the twins were kidnapped at birth by Joy Moody. The sisters, Cassiopeia and Andromeda, are reported to share a unique telepathy and were only allowed to leave the premises under the strict supervision of the woman they called mother."

The screen showed a photograph of the twins sitting on Monty's couch, the exact spot Cassie was occupying that very moment. She was leaning against her sister's shoulder. She closed her eyes, wondering at the impossibility of such a picture being on the television, and when she opened them again, the photo was gone.

Next, the street frontage of Joyful Suds appeared, which gave her a pang of homesickness so intense she went to the screen and touched it. It was only next door, but she felt like it was on the other side of the planet. The electric static feel of the screen was off-putting and she pulled her hand back, only to see Linh onscreen, unlocking the front door of Lotus Tattoos. Questions were fired at her: "How did you not know what was happening next door?" "Were you surprised to find out your neighbor was a kidnapper?" Cassie watched as Linh disappeared into her shop. "Oh, I forgot something," Linh said, smiling as she stuck her head back out. She raised her middle finger at the camera and yelled, "Đụ má mày!" Cassie didn't know what that meant, but she felt a pang of solidar-ity with Linh and wished Andie had been there to see it.

The woman in red reappeared; her hair was styled impeccably. "As the police removed numerous bags of evidence from the scene, the tragic tale started to emerge." It took a moment to recognize their own backyard, it was such a mess. Pavers stacked and broken, soil in piles, police in overalls with shovels and wearing masks. The peppercorn tree loomed large and Cassie caught a flash of white cat. If she didn't know that yard so intimately, she would never have known it was theirs. She felt the need to cry, but nothing came.

And then there was Omar. Omar from the beach, Omar of her first kiss. Her heart leaped and dropped all at once. He was sitting in a room that looked homely, and Cassie presumed it was his own house. A smile twitched across her lips, thinking she might get to see him again. Maybe something good would come from all this.

"Omar Farouk is a local tradesman who was working on the train line in Bonbeach when he met Cassiopeia Moody. He is one of the few people who have actually spoken to the enigmatic twins."

Seeing his face again was wonderful. She was quite sure this was what love felt like.

Omar spoke. "I used to take my coffee breaks down on the beach, and I think she must have followed me there or something like that. I thought she was just a young girl with a bit of a crush, you know, and I was nice and said hello and stuff."

"And then things started to change?" the reporter asked. The woman in red was now in blue, a different, straight-shouldered jacket, almost identical to the other. Cassie was surprised she could get changed so quickly. Omar looked handsome in a neat white shirt with the top button undone, black hair visible on his chest. She remembered how he smelled, the way it broke through the sea air.

"Yeah, it just got weird. I mean, this was a really different chick, you know. She was not normal."

"Why are you saying this?" Cassie cried out.

"And she started leaving these for me"—Television Omar held up one of her sketches of him and her stomach sank—"on my car, or sending them to my house."

"That's not how it happened," Cassie said. "I don't even know where you live."

"And I thought, harmless young girl, yeah. Until we got this one with a dead possum on it and my wife freaked out, thinking it was a threat. We have our kids to think of, you know. Who knows what someone is capable of?"

Cassie felt sick. He had a wife and kids, but he had come to the beach, he had sought her out. He was the one who kissed her. And yes, she had kissed him back, but now he was lying about everything and he had her drawings, which did make it look like she'd been watching him, but that wasn't how it was. How was he allowed to lie like that?

"So I went to find her and tell her to stop. She was back at the beach, where I first met her. It was my lunch spot, you know—get some fresh air and that. I think she was waiting for me. And then she tried to kiss me. Which of course, I was like"—Omar crossed his forearms over one another—"no way."

"And then this lady came down the beach and she was wild. I had no idea who she was until I saw the story on the news."

"And you realized it was Joy Moody."

"Yeah, it was Joy Moody. And she threatened me. She said if I ever came near her daughters again, she'd kill me and no one would ever find the body. She said she'd done it before and she could do it again."

"She never said that!" Cassie cried out at Omar, horrified. She thought of what Uncle Grant had said about not being able to trust anyone. Confused and feeling almost winded, she got to her feet, held up the remote, and pressed numerous buttons without finding a way to make it stop. She got down onto her knees and scrambled about behind the cabinet, finding the power cord and yanking it free. The television finally went quiet.

She sat on the floor and tried to rid Omar's face from her mind. "She was not normal." Something pounded inside her chest, but it felt far too loud to be her heart. Even without the voices from the television, her ears rang as if there were something electronic surrounding her, and she struggled to catch her breath. The room was both too big and too small all at once. Cassie cuddled her knees into her chest and tried to find some sort of equilibrium. She longed for tears so she could at least feel like herself, but even those had abandoned her.

CHAPTER 38

ANDIE

4:30 p.m.

When Andie proudly returned from her successful mission, sweaty McDonald's bags in her hands, she found Monty's house deserted. She raced home to Joyful Suds, taking in the mess that was now their little courtyard, but not stopping to dwell on it. She needed to find Cassie, wondering if she was okay.

Whether her sister was okay or not wasn't immediately clear. Andie watched her twin from the door at the in-between. They hadn't been back home in two days, but it may as well have been two years. The place felt so different. Cassie was at the folding table, the pink walls appearing even pinker in the late afternoon light. Andie recognized the time and the significance of it. It was 4:39 p.m.—would she ever not think of that time as the end of life as she'd known it?

Cassie was surrounded by towels and sheets and clothing, muttering and frantic, not registering that her sister had returned. She smoothed out a T-shirt, folding it in the precise way they'd always done it. For a moment, Andie thought Cassie must have opened the shop, taken in some serviced wash orders. But then she recognized the T-shirt her sister was pulling taut as her own. Then a towel, un-mistakably one of theirs—monogrammed with either a J, C, or A in three different shades of pink. Blush for Joy, salmon for Cassie, and dusty pink for Andie. It was like peak hour at Joyful Suds, Cassie's folding swift and focused. As if she were automated, Cassie reached for another item to fold, but found none in the basket at her feet. She looked around, still not noticing Andie had returned, then picked up an already folded stack, dropped them back in the basket, and started again.

Andie realized she should never have left her alone.

It took Andie almost an hour to coax Cassie away from her folding and help her into her pajamas. Cassie had stripped their twin singles and folded the sheets. Andie located the linen in the laundromat and remade their beds. Cassie didn't fight her, letting her sister lead her, look after her.

The way she was acting scared Andie, even more so because Cassie was devoid of tears. Cassie was always crying; it was her default. She cried when she saw Monty's orchids in bloom or when Donna nuzzled into her neck. Not crying was so much worse.

Their McDonald's had gone cold, and Andie didn't care. She threw it straight in the trash, the brown bags shiny with grease. She'd lost her appetite anyway.

She lay down on her own bed and watched her sister, who fell asleep almost immediately. Andie reached across the space between their beds and held Cassie's hand, glad to find it as warm and familiar as she remembered.

Andie slept in fits and bursts, waking with a start now and again to make sure she hadn't let go of Cassie's hand. She hadn't, nor did she intend to.

CHAPTER 39

CASSIE

August 8, 2023

Cassie hadn't recalled getting into bed, but that was where she found herself. She had a vague memory of coming home and of an aching pit in her stomach that might have been hunger, loneliness, unhappiness, or exhaustion. It wasn't gone when she woke, but at least Andie was there. Given the chance, she thought she could've curled back up and slept for at least the next thirteen days, maybe more. Her mum was gone, she wasn't a time traveler, her sister wanted to leave her, Omar was married and accusing her of being a deranged stalker, and she was scared of *everything*. If she could time travel, though she now knew that was not the case, she would go back a month and make everything stay exactly the same. There would be no DNA tests, there would be no wasted first kiss, no dead person in their shed, and most importantly, her mum would still be there.

Andie tried to convince her to get out of bed, but Cassie didn't feel physically able to move. She could see and hear everything, but her body seemed to have forgotten how to function, like the atoms had stopped talking to one another. Her sister brought a plate of toast to her bedside, but the idea of eating was beyond her. She didn't feel hungry and couldn't recall the last time she ate.

"What about Uno?" Andie went and grabbed the cards. "You love Uno."

Andie's voice had a quiet, worried tone and her brow crumpled when Cassie shook her head. Uno reminded her of their mum; she had taught them how to play and keep score. She was the one who told them it was okay to put a Draw Four on a Draw Four. Cassie didn't want to play without her mother.

Lying in her bed, staring at the ceiling that had been peeling in the same three places for years, she realized her hand hadn't twitched with the need to draw for days. That should've evoked a sadness, but it didn't. She felt nothing, just hollow.

Cassie heard footsteps and closed her eyes, hoping that Andie would think she was sleeping and leave her alone.

Andie moved loudly down the hallway. "Cassie, you need to wake up."

She didn't want to.

"*Cass.*" Andie's voice was so desperate she couldn't ignore it.

Holliday Betts was standing in her bedroom beside her sister. The detective looked fresh, an air of excitement about her.

"What now?" Cassie asked, her eyelids impossible to keep open. She would have sat up, but she didn't have the strength.

"Cassiopeia Moody, I'm arresting you on suspicion of involvement in the death of Joy Moody."

Cassie breathed out deeply as the detective's words flowed through her like the wind straight off the ocean. Only then did she realize her sister's wrists were in handcuffs.

Detective Betts continued. "You're both coming to the station."

CHAPTER 40

ANDIE

At Morningside Police Station, Andie nibbled on a piece of Vegemite toast and sipped from a polystyrene cup of tea.

The building that housed the police was a hulking, beige monolith. She and Cassie were driven there, huddled together in the back seat of a police car. Having her sister next to her was a comfort, even though neither of them spoke a word. This was not the sort of adventure Andie was looking for with their newfound freedom. She realized they should have told Ellen Scott where they were going, but it was too late for that once they were being sped away from home.

Now they were separated and they were *under arrest*. The words resonated in her mind, although she knew very little about what that actually meant. Andie had no idea if they'd be leaving the police station that day, or ever again. She supposed the jail was underneath the building, windowless and full of angry, pacing men and women who had been denied their freedom for committing heinous acts.

Her stomach roiled at the thought of joining them. Cassie definitely shouldn't be there; she'd done absolutely nothing wrong. Maybe if Andie came clean, owned up to what she'd done, they'd let Cassie go. But how could she be sure? Suddenly the tea tasted too bitter and the toast felt too dry.

There was a moment while she waited that she thought she could hear Cassie crying through the wall. Andie pressed her face up against the grubby plaster and listened carefully, but she couldn't hear anything and decided she'd probably just imagined it. Of course, there could be innumerable people crying in the building. And why wouldn't they be? It was a miserable sort of place. Everyone there should be in tears.

But just in case it was her sister, she put both her palms on the off-white wall and imagined Cassie was on the other side doing the same thing. She hoped that maybe if she willed hard enough, she could send Cassie a message and tell her that she wasn't far away. Andie wished their telepathy into existence, but she had no way of knowing if Cassie felt anything in return.

Before long, Holliday Betts bustled in, bulging binder in hand. Detective Collins entered behind her. Andie was getting the impression he just followed her everywhere. She sat down, hoping they hadn't seen her pressed up against the wall trying to communicate with her sister. They already thought she was weird.

"Is Cassie all right?"

Holliday eyed her and nodded. "Of course. No harm will come to her here."

Andie didn't believe her. She remembered Joy talking about the police the day they'd come and arrested the man who'd been smashing up the snack machine. Her mum's lip had curled in disgust. "Never mistake that they care, this is just a job to them." Joy told so many lies, but that one felt like it was rooted in truth. "Can I see her?" she asked.

"No. Not for now." Detective Betts was flicking through the paperwork she'd brought into the room. "Is there anyone you want to contact before we start?" Holliday looked up at Andie and then clarified. "Do you want to make any phone calls before we formally interview you? A friend or relative, a legal practitioner? You have the right to do so."

Andie had no phone and no one's numbers. Should she call Ellen now? She dismissed the idea. What could Ellen do to help? She was better off trying to sort this out on her own. Andie shook her head in reply.

"Let's get started then," the detective said.

Andie looked at the machine beside her as Holliday Betts pressed "record." The detective then reeled off a great deal of information, prompting Andie to give her name and address, before opening her binder and taking a deep breath.

"I want to talk to you about the night of your birthday, the night your mum died."

"She's not my mum."

"Let's call her Joy, then?"

Andie gave a halfhearted shrug of agreement.

"I want to know about the night Joy died."

Andie stared at the face of the detective who sought the truth, which sounded simple, but it really wasn't. Not in the least. And certainly not before she'd had a chance to speak properly to Cassie about it. Finally, Andie replied, "What do you want to know?"

"Everything."

"Everything?" The story started years earlier, long before their twenty-first birthday.

"Start with Joy. Tell me about who she was," Holliday said. "What you thought of her."

"She was a liar."

Leo Collins scribbled notes, off to the side, while Andie and Holliday sat directly opposite each other. They'd be perfectly positioned to play a game of chess, she thought, although she wasn't sure why chess was coming to mind.

"Tell me about that," Holliday Betts said.

Perhaps it was the right question at the right time, or maybe Andie was just sick of holding an unsteady stack of lies, waiting for them to topple. She would tell these detectives the truth, at least almost all of it.

Andie told them about their life, even the things that felt silly or too small to bother about. They wanted to know how much she earned working at the laundromat (nothing), if Joy ever hit them (just the once on their birthday), if they were allowed to leave the house (sometimes, sort of), what they'd been told about their real parents (scientists from the year 2050). Andie told them about the History Mystery DNA test and why she knew the name Tyler. She reluctantly admitted to asking Linh to help her with the computer stuff. She'd hoped to leave her friend out of it but had no way of explaining how she'd made the online purchase without revealing Linh's involvement.

Andie started to unwind. It wasn't so bad, being asked all these questions. There was almost something cathartic about cataloguing the past twenty-one years. Until it started to get harder—so gradually that she barely noticed them closing in on her.

"What did you know about Joy's health?"

"Nothing, really. She was private about those things."

"But you lived so closely."

Andie shrugged. "We knew what she wanted us to know."

"Did she take any medication?"

"Yes, painkillers."

"What for?"

"Her back."

"Did she injure it?"

"She said she did."

"You didn't believe her?"

Andie shrugged again. "It didn't seem to hurt, but it wasn't my place to ask."

"Would it shock you to know that Joy had a brain tumor?"

It was far more than just a shock; that sentence took her breath away. "She was sick?" Andie asked.

"Yes." The detective shuffled through her papers and pulled out a printed sheet. "The pathologist we spoke to said it was an advanced glioblastoma, and he would've thought the effects would be rather noticeable."

"Effects like what?"

"Hallucinations, delusions, aggression, confusion, headaches, fatigue. Maybe not all of them, but those are the common symptoms."

Andie could associate almost all of them with Joy over the past few months, especially the recent weeks. What did that mean, though? That Joy wasn't to blame for anything that had happened? Maybe that's what the detective was getting at. "How long had she had it?"

"She saw an oncologist in February, so at least since then."

"She'd been to a doctor?" Andie said, to herself more than anything. "But she didn't have it when we were babies? She knew what she was doing back then?"

The detective shrugged, shooting her a look tinged with pity. "I guess so."

"And was it something that would have eventually . . . I mean . . . would it have . . . would it have made it happen anyway?"

"What do you mean?"

"Would she have eventually died from it?"

Holliday leaned forward, cocked her head, and looked at her strangely. Perhaps it was sympathy, but Andie couldn't be sure. "Eventually, yes."

Andie scrunched her eyes closed, thinking of Joy, thinking of the night of their birthday. "So that's why it was time," she muttered.

"What was that?"

When Andie looked again, both police officers were watching her intently. Their stares were harder than they needed to be, as if the power of their gaze might make a confession inadvertently spring from her. "Nothing."

"It's interesting." Holliday swallowed, kneading her fingers together. "When we told your sister about the brain tumor, she asked if that was *why* Joy died. But you asked if it was something she *might* have died from in the future. As if you already know what caused her death."

Andie stammered through her words, which were meant to be "That's not what I said" but sounded nothing like it.

"And Cassie was really concerned—and interested—to know *why* Joy died. You haven't asked once."

Why hadn't she asked?

"Do you know how she died, Andromeda?"

Andie shook her head, feeling her cheeks flushing.

"Do you know what this is?" Holliday put a photo in front of her of a computer tablet. It looked the same as Joy's.

"I think so."

"Have you ever used it?"

Andie breathed deeply. "Yes."

"What did you search on it?"

"I didn't search, I just looked at the movies on it."

"So you know the password?"

"Yes." Cassie had worked it out: 2-0-5-0. She didn't want to mention Cassie using it, wanting to leave her out of this completely. She'd done nothing wrong.

"And what about Cassie? Did she use it?"

"I don't know." Andie did know, though; she'd seen Cassie with it, just days earlier. She thought her sister would've been too worried to even touch it, having seen her reaction to the television. But she'd watched her twin for a good five minutes, wondering how she'd learned to use the iPad and what she was doing.

"'Insulin overdose, is an insulin overdose painful, insulin in blood tests, penalty for covering up death,'" Holliday read from her folder. She stared at Andie. "Are these things you've searched recently?"

Andie's underarms sprang hot and prickly with sweat. "No. I didn't look that up."

"Did Cassie?"

"No. No, she wouldn't. She's scared of the internet."

"Are you sure about that?" Holliday's eyes bored into her.

She wasn't sure.

Holliday put the photo down. "Now, tell me what you really think of Joy Moody."

"I don't know."

"You must think something—she was your mother, as far as you knew."

"I don't really know what to think."

Holliday pressed further. "Joy Moody might have murdered your birth mother to steal you and your sister. She then raised you on lies and kept you hidden. You must feel something."

Andie shook her head defiantly and leaned back in her seat. Her cheeks were still burning.

"You were mad at her that day—you'd found out the truth. You knew about Tyler and you knew you weren't going anywhere."

The detective's voice had risen. Andie watched her cautiously.

"You knew she was sick."

"No, I didn't."

"You fought with her."

"I did, but . . . I just wanted her to be honest."

Holliday's eyes were brimming with energy. "You fought."

"No. We didn't fight, not like that."

"You scratched her face."

Andie felt her chest constrict, her voice struggling to form perfect words. "No! No, that's not right. That was outside. F-f-from the tree. I didn't do that."

"And you saw the cash she had—you wanted it. You took your opportunity, and you killed her."

"No, that's not true." Andie slammed both hands on the table.

"But you hated her? Right?"

Andie felt as near to tears as she'd been in a long time.

"You're allowed to hate her, Andie, after what she did to you."

"But I don't," Andie said, biting her bottom lip and refusing to cry. "I want to hate her, you're right. But I don't and I have no idea why." She wiped her nose with her sleeve.

It was possible she hated parts of Joy, but she didn't feel outright disgust. Joy had kept them safe, and fed and clothed them. For the most part they'd been happy. Although she was furious with the mess Joy had left behind, Andie knew it hadn't always been terrible. But Joy hadn't equipped the twins for life without her, and Andie was mad at her for that. Joy should've made them less dependent on her. She should've shown them how to be more like she was.

"I want to go home. Can I leave?" Andie stood and pressed her hands together as if begging.

Holliday sat back in her chair and shook her head.

Andie repeated herself. "Can I go home?"

"We found thirty-four thousand dollars in your wardrobe. Thirty-four thousand dollars had been taken out of Joy's bank account the week before she died. What were you doing with that money, Andie?"

"Joy was taking it with her to 2050."

"But you weren't going to the future." Holliday looked at her notes, then back to Andie. Her stare was earnest.

"I know." Andie spoke louder than she meant to when she added, "I'm not sure that Joy knew that, though."

"You really think that Joy believed that?"

Andie considered this long and hard. It hit her with an uncomfortable sadness. She did think Joy believed it. Maybe not always—maybe she had lied at first—but by the end, she had bought into the bullshit she was peddling. Joy had read *The Fortis Trilogy* so many times she had made it come to life under her own roof. If Andie hadn't been so damn furious, she would have felt some pity for the woman who'd raised them.

Andie laid her arms on the table and put her head down on them, watching her feet and wishing that they all bloody well *had* gone to the future.

CHAPTER 41

DETECTIVE SERGEANT HOLLIDAY BETTS

Holliday wasn't buying Andie's act. Some might accuse her of being heartless, but she was immune to the dramatics that she had seen so many times, especially from women. As a young, green constable she'd fallen for it on more than one occasion but she was not planning to be sucked in again. One look at Leo Collins told her he didn't have the same immunity as she did, though. He almost looked sorry for the girl.

One of the twins might have committed murder, but Holliday wasn't sure she could prove it. She hadn't counted on these two rather naïve women being quite so wily. And there was another problem she faced, which her boss had grilled her about before she'd gone out to arrest the Moody sisters. The toxicology showed nothing of note in Joy's system, and the coroner's report detailed the cause of death as being consistent with a malignant brain tumor. The pathologist had since remarked that if they'd been advised of the possibility of insulin being involved, they'd have tested for it, but it wasn't done routinely and now that ship had sailed. While insulin could not be ruled out as the cause, they could never prove that it was, either.

Unless Cassie and Andie admitted to the murder, the file was being sent back to the local Crime Investigation Unit to prepare a brief for the coroner, as they would for any unexpected death that wasn't a crime. Holliday's boss's words were still ringing in her ears: "We're not the natural death squad." She couldn't refute him, but that didn't mean it sat right with her. The office had received notice of a fatal shooting and a potential triple poisoning over the preceding days, and the detectives were being stretched to their limits. There had been some very odd occurrences at 225 Station Street, but how could they continue to throw time and money at something that had been deemed non-suspicious by a medical expert? Rania Crew was still in charge of the investigation into Britney White, so there wasn't much left for Holliday's team to do. She'd finish interviewing the Time Traveling Twins and then have to move the hell on.

The night before, she'd let Leo Collins take the lead on interviewing Tyler Rodriguez. She could've done the same with the twins but felt oddly possessive about them. She wanted to do it herself, *had* to do it herself.

Tyler had been surprisingly forthcoming, and it became almost immediately apparent that he hadn't done anything to Joy Moody. He had been at the laundromat, and he had admitted to writing the note telling her that time was up. But his alibi was pretty solid. He had intended to intimidate her with his withering stare at the sidewalk cameras, but when he'd left, Joy was very much alive. And there was no criminal charge to be laid for pointing at a CCTV camera.

After visiting Joyful Suds, Tyler had taken himself to Crown Casino and spent the next six hours there playing roulette, before adjourning to one of the bars. They were able to track down footage and establish he'd finally left the casino around 4 a.m. with a couple of associates he didn't want to name. He didn't have to;

they were easily identifiable to any cop who had ever worked on a task force involving gangs. But it was clear Tyler Rodriguez had not been directly involved in Joy's death. He was pretty pissed off at her, though, and happy to tell them why he believed Joy was responsible for Britney's disappearance.

"Have you seen her daughters?" he'd asked. "They look just like Brit."

And he'd seemed sad, because it had taken him twenty years to work it out and because he knew he should've looked after that seventeen-year-old girl much better than he had.

Now, Andie Moody had sat back down, but Holliday was running out of questions. She was meant to have full admissions by this point; she wanted to be able to mark her first case at Homicide as "Solved." The pathologist's findings could be ignored if she could get one of these twins to just spill the beans.

"There was no way out and you couldn't go without Cassie, could you?" Holliday wanted to give it one last go. "And she wouldn't listen to you while Joy was such a huge presence in the house. So you did what you had to. You injected her with insulin. You wanted to kill her, rid your life of her. Then you could take the money and start again. Is that what happened, Andie?"

Andie's mouth opened. Holliday hadn't seen this one cry but thought she was close to it now. She didn't want a confession to get lost in a flood of tears, and she hoped Leo knew to keep his mouth shut. She counted on this girl needing to fill the silence.

"That's not how it happened."

Holliday noticed the phrasing. Andie hadn't said she didn't do it.

Someone knocked on the door to the interview room. It was such incredibly inconvenient timing, she wanted to scream.

Leo got up, opened the door, and a man bustled in.

"Andromeda Moody?"

Andie nodded.

"I'm Patrick Chen, your legal counsel. Don't say another word." Patrick looked straight at Holliday while pointing toward Andie. "This woman is not capable of being interviewed without an independent third person. It doesn't matter what she's said to you, she doesn't have the capacity to understand her caution and rights."

"Hello, Mr. Chen." Holliday had recognized the lawyer before he'd said his name. He was a brash, experienced solicitor who knew his stuff. How he came to be there and how these young women could afford him was a mystery.

Patrick smirked at her, although not unkindly. "You should know better, detective."

Holliday wasn't giving up that easily; this was all part of the game lawyers and detectives played daily. "This is a twenty-one-year-old, educated woman. She understands just fine."

Patrick sighed and pointed his finger at Andie. "Did you know you don't have to answer these questions?"

Andie shook her head. "They said that I should just tell the truth."

Patrick screwed up his nose in a "told you so" face that made Holliday want to throw her binder at him. The recording was still running; there was no getting around it.

"I'll need to speak to my client alone now, please."

Holliday took a deep breath to calm herself down. They wouldn't be signing any murder charges that night. She got up and left the room.

CHAPTER 42

CASSIE

Seven days after the death of the woman they had always considered to be their mother, the twins found themselves on the front steps of the Morningside Police Station. It was midafternoon and the skies were ominous and it was breathtakingly cold, but the wind that smacked them in the face tasted like freedom. Rain threatened to burst from the sky but hadn't yet, and Cassie hoped they could get to the train station well before they needed umbrellas they didn't have.

Patrick Chen had walked them out of the station and advised them to stay put while he went to speak to the detectives. When he'd burst into the little holding room Cassie was in, Patrick winked and told her Ellen Scott had sent him. Never did Cassie think hearing their curmudgeonly neighbor's name would bring such an overwhelming wave of relief.

The twins leaned against the wall, trying to shelter themselves from the wind. Lightning split the sky and Cassie looked heavenward, counting as she always did to see how long it was between a bolt of lightning and a clap of thunder. Joy had said it was meant to tell them how far away the storm was, but Cassie now suspected this was a way to distract scared children. Today, though, the counting soothed her. Six . . . seven . . . eight . . . Thunder sounded violently, a reminder that they were all just specks; everything was bigger than them.

The lightning lit up again and the sound of rain spattering the pavement surrounded them. The twins were just out of reach of the fast-falling drops, beneath a small awning.

It was only then that she noticed the way Andie was breathing. It was labored, her hand rubbing at her sternum as if she had pain in her chest. She appeared to be searching for an answer to a question Cassie hadn't heard. She'd never seen Andie like that before.

"Something's wrong. I can't breathe properly," Andie whispered, her voice scared and her hands clenched tight.

Not knowing what to do, Cassie looked in the door to the police station, but she couldn't see Patrick in the brightly lit foyer. There was no way she was walking back into that building again. She returned to stand in front of her twin, closer than comfortable, staring into the face that was almost identical to her own. "We will get through this," Cassie said in her soft, soothing voice.

Andie shook her head, looking confused and worried. "It's all too much. I don't know what to do anymore. I wanted it to be different, I wished for it. And now, everything is . . . is . . . wrong. What have I done?" She began shuddering, which soon turned to sobbing.

Cassie realized that every tear she had failed to cry in the past few days was now right there, raining from her sister. She wished she could take them from her. The rain hammered now and thunder roared overhead. Water was dripping slowly but surely from the awning onto Cassie's back but she ignored it and held both her sister's hands—which were icy cold—and channeled all the strength she could through herself. She leaned her forehead against Andie's and spoke the words Joy had said so many times before: "You are an incredible bunch of atoms."

Andie laughed through her tears and wiped her dripping nose with her palm. "That's such a stupid saying."

"No, it's not."

"Mum stole it from the books."

"So what?" Cassie said. "She meant it. She lived for us, Andie."

Andie's sobs were petering out, her breathing slowing down.

"And you know you just called her Mum?"

"No, I didn't," Andie snapped, but not angrily.

It occurred to Cassie in that moment, amid the tears and rain and despair, that things would actually be fine. She couldn't say why, but she just knew it would. She'd be okay if Andie was. "She's not the worst person in the world to be like, you know."

"I don't think Britney White would think that was true."

"We weren't there, we don't know what happened." Cassie realized she was defending her mother again. It was like a bad habit she couldn't kick. "But there is something I've been wanting to tell you."

"Yeah?"

The sky lit up again, illuminating everything around them for a flash of time.

"I woke up the night of our birthday and you were gone. So I went looking for you."

Andie's eyes widened.

"I saw you downstairs putting something in the flowerpot."

"You found the syringe?"

Cassie nodded. "Did you . . . Was it . . . ?"

"Oh, Cass." Andie rubbed her hands over her wet face. "I did nothing to Joy. You have my absolute word on that."

"Pinky promise?" Cassie held out her little finger. They had not done this since they were children, but it had always been an all-powerful truth reckoner.

"Pinky promise."

They linked little fingers and shook them up and down.

Cassie watched a woman walk past the front of the building.

She was drenched but seemingly unfazed, still yapping on her mobile phone.

"Did you move it?" Andie asked and Cassie knew she meant the syringe.

She nodded. "It's under the floorboard. I don't think they found it."

"Did you tell the detective?"

"No. Did you?" Cassie asked.

Andie shook her head.

Cassie was terrified to know the truth, but she had to ask, even if the answer changed everything. "So what did happen then?"

Andie wouldn't meet her gaze. Up, down, to the street, to the gutter, everywhere but at Cassie herself. "I can't explain it just yet. I'm not exactly sure how to. But I will. Can you just give me a little more time?"

"It's been a week. How much more time do you need?"

Andie looked skyward and bit her lip. "I will tell you but please, just not right now."

"Okay, I guess." Cassie was now bursting to know, but she knew if she pushed it, Andie might clam up for good. She would just have to wait.

The sky shook again with an almighty clap of thunder. Cassie stared upward, watching the raindrops as they hurtled to earth. "Do you think there's any chance she could have gone to the future without us?"

Andie replied quickly, "No, I don't. Absolutely not."

"But it's nice to think that maybe—"

"Cassie, there's no such thing as time travel."

The automated doors of the police station slid open and Patrick Chen, handsome in his well-tailored suit, stepped out. He looked unimpressed with the turn in weather and reached into his briefcase, producing an umbrella. He opened it above the three of them and shot them a reassuring look. "Right. It's time to get you two home."

"Are you taking us?" Cassie asked.

He smiled politely. "No. Your ride should be here shortly." He looked up and down the street, then checked his phone.

A short way from where they were standing, a car horn sounded. The woman who had been on her phone, now in the middle of the street, threw her hands up at a silver car, shouting, "Piss off, idiot!"

"That's not a crossing!" someone in the car yelled.

"Jerk!" chimed in a woman's voice from the driver's side of the car, followed by a barrage of something foreign.

"Linh," Andie whispered. Cassie had thought the same thing. As the car drew closer, she could see it was Joy's car, the old VW with dull silver, weathered paint, faded from years of saltwater winds and being parked in a lane with no garage. Monty and Linh sat in the front seats, beaming at them. Linh pulled up abruptly, causing the car behind her to slam on its brakes and honk long and hard to show the driver's displeasure.

Linh was unperturbed. "Go around, fuckers!"

Joy's VW mounted the curb and Monty's door swung open. "Cassie! Andie!" His voice was as excited as Cassie had ever heard him.

She felt like they'd been underground for days, starved of light and air. Seeing her friends was like emerging into the bright sun. She was overwhelmed with gratitude, despite the honking cars and angry pedestrians. It really would be okay.

"Come on, get in!" Monty yelled. "Let's get out of this goddamn place and out of this goddamn weather."

Cassie turned back to Patrick, who appeared amused beneath his wide umbrella.

"Ellen sent them too," he said. "We will reconvene tomorrow and discuss what to do from here. For now, get going, you two."

Neither Cassie nor Andie had to be told twice.

CHAPTER 43

ANDIE

It was warm inside the car and Andie felt better the moment the door slammed shut.

"You two are a sight for sore eyes," Monty said, then laughed. "And sore knees."

Cassie looked worried. "Are you okay? Should you be out?"

"I'll be fine. Just a bit achy. But don't worry about me. Are you two in one piece? I promised Joy I'd keep an eye on you, and look at this mess."

"You did?" Cassie asked.

"Of course I did. You think you're getting rid of us that easily?" Monty swiveled around as far as he could from the front passenger seat.

"But Grant said you were happy to wash your hands of us."

Linh banged her hand down on the center console and ranted in Vietnamese, before reverting to English. "I knew he said something to them. I told you, Big M."

"I've told you not to call me that," Monty said. "It sounds inappropriate."

Andie hadn't even realized Monty and Linh were friends, let alone using nicknames.

"I've seen him slinking around the laundromat, looking like a shifty, shithouse rat," Linh said. "He had people in today and I followed one of them, made them tell me what was going on by pretending I was ready to sell too. He was a developer and he told me that 225 Station Street is for sale! Your piece-of-crap uncle has been taking offers."

Andie sighed. "It's his, though. Turns out the laundromat belongs to him."

Monty scoffed. "Who told you that?"

"He did."

Linh again reeled off something angry Andie didn't understand.

"That's a load of fertilizer," Monty said.

"Listen to this." Linh pulled her phone out of her pocket and used her non-steering hand to scroll through. The car veered and Monty reached over, placed a calm hand on the wheel, and held it steady while Linh found the recording. "Amazing the things you hear over the fence. Or over two fences and pressed up against Big M's greenhouse, hoping your piece-of-shit uncle would be kind enough to speak into the microphone."

They listened closely, leaning in to Linh's phone. "I've got a decent offer, but I think I can get him to up it. The interest has been huge." Grant's voice was distinctive. "No one even cares to see it. They're gonna knock it down anyway."

"He was on the phone," Linh said. "Bit scratchy, but keep listening."

"No, mate, they've got no idea. They're a couple of mushrooms." Grant paused, then laughed. "I reckon I can get them to sign pretty much whatever I want. They'll believe anything."

Andie felt her jaw clench as she realized he was talking about them. There was a lull in the recording; he must have been listening down the line.

"There won't be a will to contest, I've got it. She woulda never filed it anywhere." After a moment of silence, he spoke again. "They don't exist on paper. They're fuckin' ghosts, Baz. Plus, I've pretty much tipped off the jacks that they've done something to her." Grant guffawed, sounding incredibly proud of himself.

"That asshole," Monty said.

Linh shushed him and Grant's voice began again. "Get the paperwork together, mate, and I'll sort you for the usual. What, twenty percent?" Silence. "Thirty? You greedy bastard." A considerable pause this time. "Okay, okay, I do value you, mate, but this is highway bloody robbery."

The scratchy recording stopped and Linh dropped the phone back into the center console.

"I saw him take something from Mum's desk," Cassie said. "But I didn't say anything. Why didn't I say anything?"

Andie rubbed her arm. "It doesn't matter."

"It does, though. He took Mum's will. And we aren't actually related, so what if he's right?"

"That place is not his," Linh said, her face showing she meant business. "We will get to the bottom of it, don't you worry about that. The traders association is taking on a new role."

"I don't think it's within the agreed guidelines," Andie said. "Ellen won't like it."

"Ellen *suggested* it." Monty caught Andie's eye and, surprisingly, wasn't joking. "You know, she had quite a soft spot for Joy."

"Really?" Andie was genuinely shocked by this. She didn't think Ellen had a soft spot to give anyone.

"Ever since her husband died, maybe even before. But your mum used to drop off food for her."

"To Ellen? Really?"

"Yep, for a good few weeks after Wes died."

"She told us those were for Hal, the guy who came in to use the free washing machine."

"Oh, she made things for him too. But Ellen wasn't in a great state after Wes went. She put on a good front, but Joy was onto her. Ellen can be a bit Jekyll and Hyde, but she's a good enough sort."

Linh changed lanes, the car hydroplaning through a puddle.

"How do you know she did that?" Andie asked. "Mum . . . I mean, Joy."

Monty grinned and tapped his finger on his temple. "I pay attention." His grin widened. "Oh, and is now the time to mention I have Joy's will?"

"You do?" Andie was shocked.

"Yeah. Joy was very careful about her financials. She posted it to me, must've been just before . . . just before she went. Just in case we needed it. And turns out we needed Justin after all."

"Justin? What?" Linh asked.

"It's a joke, don't worry." Monty waved his hand dismissively.

"Does it leave it all to Grant?" Cassie asked.

"Hell, no," Monty said. "The new one leaves me as the sole benefactor."

The twins gasped.

"New one?" Andie asked.

Monty cleared his throat and clapped his hands. "I should explain properly. I only got them when I got home from the hospital. Your mother sent me two wills, the first one dated the year you were born. It left everything to you two, with old Grant the Greedy as the fallback. She clearly had second thoughts about that and updated it about a month ago. In the new one, she leaves it all to me." He hurried to clarify. "But that's only because Joy expected you all to be in 2050. The one your uncle nicked gives everything to you, which I know because I have a certified copy of it. Joy sent me everything we need. She was a smart lady, that one. And it's all yours, girls, plain and simple. The laundromat is *yours*. Ellen will make sure of it."

Linh shot them a grin from the driver's seat. "You should've seen Ellen. She was so furious that Joy used one of those DYI kits to do it."

"DIY," Monty corrected.

"Whatever, you know what I meant," Linh snapped. "Khùng."

Andie leaned back against the seat, listening to her friends bicker, feeling the creak of the vinyl and the warmth of her sister's shoulder wedged against her own. Through the rivulets on the window, Andie saw the train tracks, recognized it as Station Street, and knew they were almost home.

Home. She'd never been so glad to be heading back to Joyful Suds.

CHAPTER 44
CASSIE

"Come in for a cuppa? Or straight home?" Monty asked.

"Straight home," Cassie said. "Definitely."

Their little party of four crunched to the gate at the rear of 225 Station Street. The gravel beneath their feet was checkered with little puddles but the rain had almost ceased, at least for now. Cassie's clothes felt damp and she looked forward to the heater going on and a hot shower and fresh pajamas and being foot to foot with her big sister on their couch.

The last time she'd seen the courtyard it had been a muddy mess, pavers stacked everywhere. But now it was complete chaos. The peppercorn tree that had grown along with them was now split almost in two. One of the big branches had broken off, blocking their way to the back door. Cassie felt pained at seeing their tree destroyed.

"Holy shitballs!" Linh looked up at the sky, as if it might give her an answer. "I wonder if it got hit by lightning."

Monty picked up the can of WD-40 from the back fence and gave it a shake. "I wondered where this was."

Cassie eyed him curiously, remembering exactly when that can had appeared. Questions popped into her mind. His kind eyes met hers and she wondered about Monty and Joy as she had done on many occasions before. Her mum had left *everything* to Monty, but was that why she was dead? Had he known, had he been involved? Cassie hated that she was even considering that deceitful thought. Monty would never—or at least she hoped he would never—do something so underhanded and horrible. Though, of late, she realized she didn't have all that great a grasp on the true character of people.

Donna distracted her, rattling the fence as she landed on it from the greenhouse roof, looking her usual smug self. From there she launched herself over to the fallen branch, seemingly unbothered by the destruction that surrounded her. She padded the length of it before settling in the hollow where the limbs of the tree used to meet.

Andie moved toward Donna. "Look. Something's here."

Donna hissed as she approached.

"Get the cat, would you, Cassie? She still hates me."

"I don't know how she can tell the difference between you two," Linh said.

"Cats are smarter than people," Monty said, as Cassie plucked Donna from her spot. She loved that the cat favored her.

From the joint of the tree, now torn apart like a chicken wishbone, Andie retrieved a little square parcel about the size of a novel, covered in black plastic.

"Is it a book?" Cassie reached her hand forward to touch it, but Andie pulled it away.

"Careful."

"I *was* being careful," Cassie snapped. The cat nuzzled into her neck and purred softly. She had missed her.

Andie peeled off the plastic to expose a notebook, very much like the ones Cassie liked to draw in. Cassie's hand twitched as if expecting to pick up a pencil for the first time in days. Andie opened it carefully, mindful of how delicate it might be.

The tree, it appeared, was ready to give up its secrets.

A tarnished gold chain slipped from between the pages as Andie turned them. Cassie scooped it up. A little heart hung from the links.

The sketchbook in her sister's hands was almost full, illustrations bursting from every page. Andie had paused on a drawing of a woman and two babies, all of whom looked to be asleep.

"Is that Joy?" Linh asked, inspecting the woman whose hair was messily tied back and whose features had faded slightly, but were still strikingly familiar.

Monty nodded and looked almost pained by the image. "That's our Joy, all right."

"Mum." Cassie ran her hand down the page and then pulled it back, worried her fingertips would take something away from the drawing, or erase it completely. She studied the pendant in her hand. "This has something engraved on it." She pulled it in closer; the dim light wasn't making it easy to read the tiny words. Linh flicked on her mobile phone light, the bright burst startling Cassie for a moment before she squinted closely at the necklace. "I see the future and it's all about us."

"The future?" Andie whispered.

Cassie felt a realization dawn. It was a message from their mum. "She sent this to us, Andie."

"No one sent it, Cass. There will be a perfectly good explanation for it."

The sisters locked eyes. Cassie wasn't stupid; she knew Joy had gone somewhere permanent, somewhere they could not follow. The afterlife, though, was filled with possibility. No one knew for sure what happened once you departed one life for the next. Beneath the broken branches of their tree, Cassie just wanted something to ease the pain.

Then Andie nodded, her forehead creasing. "Maybe she did."

CHAPTER 45

ANDIE

August 9, 2023

Joyful Suds remained closed, but a sign on the door instructed customers to ring the doorbell should they need to collect any serviced washes that had been locked in since Joy's death. Cassie had taken charge of the counter for most of the morning because Andie was still prone to fits of emotion, with no control switch. She wasn't sure how she'd fare if Tina, Lori-Jayne, Kevin, or any of the other regulars asked after Joy. If they offered their condolences, she knew she'd turn to water. It was as if the twins had switched roles. Andie thought perhaps that was how it was with twins; when one of their defenses fell, the other rose and vice versa. Like a seesaw that never evened out.

When the bell rang, Cassie was eating lunch in the house and Andie told her to stay put, that she'd go. But it was not a customer she was greeted by at the front desk of Joyful Suds.

"Why haven't you been answering your phone?" Uncle Grant asked, his displeasure clear.

"We turned it off."

He looked at the ceiling and shook his head as if it were the most ludicrous thing anyone had ever said. "Doesn't matter. I've got great news. I've found you a place just down the train line. I think it's the fresh start you both need." He smiled, and Andie wondered how it was ever possible she'd considered trusting him.

"We live here, and we're not leaving," Andie replied. She did not feel as brave as she sounded.

He tilted his head and watched her. "We've discussed this—that's not possible. Where's your sister?"

Andie stood firm. "We just want to be left alone."

"Not really an option, though, is it? I've been charitable enough to let you stay, rent-free. Don't throw it back in my face, missy."

Andie's teeth clenched and her hands pressed against the counter, steadying herself. "You're lying."

"Is everything okay? Has something happened?" he asked, as if he were a paragon of kindness.

She wasn't falling for it. "You lied to us about Monty and Linh."

He shrugged, unmoved. "I cannot be responsible for any misunderstandings. You two have been very emotionally wound up, perhaps that's what it was."

"You sold a photo of us to the news. Cassie saw it. No one else would have been able to take it."

He visibly prickled, turning his head first left, then right, making cracking noises. It was as if Grant was limbering up for a bout of boxing. He spoke through gritted teeth—she knew she'd gotten to him. "That doesn't sound like something I'd do."

If he wanted a fight, he'd get one. Andie held his gaze. "And you stole Joy's will."

Grant sniffed in a way that sounded like he needed to blow his nose, but he didn't, just wiped it with the back of his hand. He looked around at the empty shop, then leaned in over the counter, so close Andie could smell the mint of his toothpaste, and said in a quiet, savage tone, "Good luck proving it."

She just glared at him and he stood straighter, dusted some invisible lint from his jacket, and then returned to his normal voice. "I've found a buyer for this." He waved his hand around the pink laundromat. "I've paid the first month on a cabin for you both. It's beachside, so you'll be able to hear the ocean from your doorstep. Don't go forgetting what I'm doing to help you both. You should be incredibly grateful."

Andie felt very small in front of him, her confidence evaporating, until she remembered the recording Linh had made. "We're not mushrooms." Her voice shook, but it was clear.

He eyed her suspiciously. "What did you say?"

"We heard you say it. You called us mushrooms. Said we'll believe anything you tell us."

"Cassie!" Grant shouted through the in-between. "I'm going to try speaking to the other one, since you're not making any sense."

Andie was right behind Grant as he strode into their house. Cassie was at the dining table, chewing on a cheese-and-lettuce sandwich. Her demeanor changed at the sight of their uncle and her face turned furious. "What's going on?"

"I've come to give you the good news about your new place, but your sister is treating me like a leper."

Cassie stood up, brushing breadcrumbs from her mouth. "You told the police we did something to Mum."

"I did nothing of the sort." Grant scoffed. "And do you two have any idea how much debt this shop is in? Joy wanted to sell it—she was trying to dig herself out of a hole. No wonder she killed herself."

Andie crossed the room to stand beside her sister, which seemed to buoy Cassie. She stepped forward defiantly. "The shop is *not* in trouble. We know what you're trying to do. Joyful Suds isn't yours to sell."

"Well, it sure as heck ain't yours. You're not even a real Moody.

This was my father's shop, and he should never have given it to Joy."

"It's our home."

"It's soon to be your nothing." Grant wiped his nose again, and Andie wondered how it would feel to punch him right in his snotty face.

She thought of Joy. She knew her mum wouldn't be taking this sort of nonsense from anyone, and she imagined what Joy would say. "We have a lawyer now, to keep what's rightfully ours. You won't take advantage of us," she said.

"Me? Take advantage of you? That's all Joy ever did. She used you as free labor in her sweatshop here. She didn't want daughters, she wanted servants."

"You don't know anything about our lives," Cassie snapped back.

"I know *plenty*." Grant put his hands on his hips and glowered. "I'll tell you what, you can pack your shit up and be out by the end of the day if this is how you're going to act. I was just trying to do the right thing by you both."

"No, you weren't." Linh walked through the in-between. Andie had never been so glad to see her. The tattooist held out her mobile phone and Grant's voice crackled through the recording. "I reckon I can get them to sign pretty much whatever I want. They'll believe anything."

"How dare you record a private conversation. That's illegal."

"You'd know all about being above the law, wouldn't you?" Linh scowled. She looked more beautiful in that moment than Andie could ever recall.

"Don't you have someone to tattoo?" Grant flicked his hand at Linh like he was swatting away a fly.

"Sure. How about I tattoo a big cock on your forehead so at least what you see is what you get?"

Grant frowned at Linh. "Go away, little girl."

"And you should know"—Andie was relieved to hear Monty's voice as he came through the back door, leaning heavily on his walking stick—"the traders association can call an extraordinary meeting if they think the need arises. It's section 49, subsection 4. And Ellen has gone ahead and called one."

Then the most surprising visitor of all entered, Ellen Scott herself. She gave a calm nod to Andie, as if this was no big deal. As far as she knew, this was the farthest Ellen had been from home in almost six years.

Monty continued. "The meeting is to decide whether or not we evict you from the premises. And in the absence of the registered owner of this property, the association can vote. So, can I see a show of hands as to who thinks this man needs to get the hell out?"

Monty and Ellen raised their hands in unison, and Linh thrust hers in the air with her middle finger up. Andie swelled with gratitude.

"And another thing," Ellen said, "you should know the people in this area are very good at keeping secrets, as well as bodies, hidden for years. So I'd suggest you run along now."

"Are you threatening me?" Grant asked.

"Yes," Ellen replied.

Grant rubbed his hands together. "I'll have you charged."

Ellen put her hands on her hips; Andie thought she'd make a great character in an Agatha Christie novel. "By all means, report this to police. It would really expedite the process of having you kept as far away from these two young women as possible."

"And besides, we heard nothing. Right, Big M?" Linh crossed her arms and stared Grant down.

"What's that? I'm a bit hard of hearing these days," Monty replied.

Grant glared at them all, his body tensed as if he was going to lunge forward at any second. "You're a piece of work."

"Thank you," Ellen said and nodded her head at the in-between. "I'd suggest you make tracks while you can."

Grant grunted and mumbled all manner of horrible names under his breath. "See you in court." He scowled from the doorway, then turned and stormed off through the laundromat.

"Have a Joyful Day!" Cassie called after him and Andie laughed, both at her sister's timing and for keeping such a cool head.

"Good old section 49, hey?" Ellen said.

Monty chuckled. "I think we should definitely add section 49 going forward. In fact, I'll add it to the agenda for the next meeting. The power to do whatever the hell we want."

Ellen made a short burst of noise that Andie thought was perhaps a laugh, something she hadn't heard the woman do before. "I think you already do that, Monty."

Andie felt herself choking up. The tears were back, something she'd happily return to Cassie.

"No need to get emotional." Ellen gave Andie a wink. "It's quite unprofessional, you know. Now, I think we should schedule a meeting in my office at 9 a.m. tomorrow. I have the will—thank you, Monty—but I think it prudent that you know exactly what it is we are putting together."

"Okay." The sisters nodded.

"This will be a gratis service, do you understand?"

"Not really."

"It means it's free, Andromeda. I do not wish to be remunerated by you or your sister. Is that clear?"

"Yes, very."

Cassie suddenly lurched forward and threw her arms around Ellen. The lawyer looked like she was about to shake her off, but instead she dropped her arms to her sides, then hugged her back.

"Now," Monty said when the silence became a little awkward, "if everyone could accompany me, I have something I think you should all see."

At Monty's, the five of them huddled around the door to his greenhouse, none the wiser as to why they were there. Andie never would have picked Monty for revelling in a theatrical reveal, but he seemed to be enjoying himself.

"I've been quite slack with the orchids lately—there's been a little bit going on, you understand. Usually I try to get out here a good three to four times a week."

"Montgomery Doyle," Linh prompted, "the point would be a good place to get to."

He dropped his head but smiled. "You're right." He opened the door to the greenhouse. "It appears our Donna has been busy."

In a black plastic tub that would've once housed seedlings, Donna lay with a squirming, writhing pile of colored fur. Cassie gasped, rushing forward, and Andie felt a jolt of excitement.

"Donna, you right little tart," Linh said, leaning over Andie, holding on to her to stop from tipping over. "What have you been up to?"

"Well, I think that's abundantly clear," Ellen replied.

"How many are there?" Cassie asked, kneeling down in front of the makeshift cat bed to examine the tiny, adorable kittens.

"Five," Monty said. "I think they're about four days old. But I'll take them to the vet this afternoon just to check they're okay."

"You're going to keep them, aren't you?" Cassie asked. "You can't get rid of them."

"I don't need five more cats, Cass. We will find good homes for them, don't you worry. But there was something else." Monty held up his finger, reached onto a shelf, and pulled some papers out from

under an empty pot. "When I found the kittens this morning, I noticed something a little odd about where Don had decided to have
them. I think she's been out stealing, making a cozy little nest for
her family."

"What do you mean?" Andie tried to get a look at what Monty
was holding.

"I think I can solve the mystery of the note the police found
in Joy's pocket. I do believe the rest of it is right here." He handed
Andie a piece of paper. "Donna has been collecting the mail."

Andie recognized Joy's handwriting immediately. It was penned
to their future-parents. She read out loud: "I hope this letter finds
you well. I have kept the twins safe, as you asked, and now I have
a request. I hope to accompany them. I am optimistic that in the
future there will be medical treatment not yet available here. I
hope you give due consideration to my request. Kind regards, Joy
Moody."

Cassie was watching her closely.

"You can see where she ripped off the bottom," Andie said. "Do
you think she thought she was a little over the top with the 'P.S. I'm
going to die' bit?"

Monty sighed. "Joy didn't like to sensationalize things."

"Well, that's not strictly true, now, is it?" Ellen said, although
her tone was kind. "Quite the conundrum, our Joy. Right, we will
give that to the police tomorrow. I'll organize it with the woman
detective." She patted Monty on the shoulder, pointing at the mess
of kittens in front of them all. "I'll have the little black-and-white
one, when it's ready."

CHAPTER 46
CASSIE

August 14, 2023

Detective Sergeant Holliday Betts, coffee in hand, strolled into Joyful Suds at 11 a.m. Detective Leo Collins followed her, sporting a white shirt and a salmon-colored tie. Joy would've approved of the color choice, and Cassie noticed his whites were very white; this was someone who took pride in his laundry.

Cassie had been wiping down the bank of Speed Queens and enjoying the fabric softener scent that lingered in the air. She'd missed it. Kevin had been one of the first customers to return to the laundromat and was on his second load for the morning. He had loyally decided not to do his washing while Joyful Suds was shut, and was now perched at the front bench with the newspaper splayed out before him, whistling as he read, which was almost more annoying than his singing.

"Good morning," Detective Betts said. "Cassie, is it?"

She nodded. "Good guess."

"Is there somewhere private we can talk to you and your sister?"

Cassie appreciated they weren't just bursting through the doors this visit.

"Leo and I just wanted to follow up on a couple of things after our conversation on Thursday."

It wasn't lost on Cassie that this detective, Leo, was also named for a constellation. It seemed like a good omen.

The previous Thursday, Ellen Scott, Patrick Chen, and the twins had met with the detectives in Scott's Family Law office and handed over the torn note. They explained Donna's involvement and took them to Monty's to show them the kittens, now relocated to inside his shop where they slept near an oil heater. A vet check had showed them to be in top health, and Donna seemed to be thriving as a mother.

Patrick had helped them draft their witness statements detailing their lives, Joy, and everything in between.

The empty syringe and its current location remained omitted from these written testimonials. Andie assured Cassie it wouldn't change anything, and that it would all become clear soon enough.

With the two police officers now in front of her, Cassie found it remarkable how calm she felt. It would seem the police didn't rattle her in quite the same way they had before. So much had changed since that first time.

She directed the detectives into the house and invited them to sit at the dining table.

"Andie's next door with Linh. I'll go and get her."

"We'll wait." Holliday smiled and sipped her coffee.

A few minutes later, the two officers and the two sisters were seated around the dining table at the back of the laundromat.

"Ellen knows we're here, but you are welcome to check in with her." Holliday's demeanor was different to how she'd seemed at the police station. That was a side of her Cassie didn't want to have to encounter again. It wasn't so much the detective, she realized now, but the room, the handcuffs, the questions. On the girls' own turf, the police seemed far less intimidating.

Andie shrugged. "I think we're okay."

"Tea? Water? Anything?" Cassie asked.

"No, thank you." Holliday indicated her coffee cup and Leo shook his head. Cassie liked Detective Collins' long, blond eyelashes. She blushed as he caught her eye and gave her a fleeting grin.

"There are a few things I wanted to discuss with you. Our meeting the other day was certainly helpful in putting a few pieces of the puzzle together. Thanks for that."

Cassie knew they'd been honest, but only to a point, and she wondered if Holliday could see right through them.

"Firstly, we are handing the investigation into Joy's death back to the local Crime Investigation Unit—they'll prepare the brief for the coroner. It has been determined not to be suspicious. Officially, the cause of death is due to her tumor."

It was a relief, but still a sobering moment and all they could do was nod. Regardless of the reason, they had still lost Joy.

"I am not a fan of chalking things up to coincidence—I prefer to deal in facts—but it would appear quite a number of things happened incidentally on the first of August to lead us to the original conclusion that Joy had come to harm."

"We understand," Andie said and Cassie agreed; it had been a very peculiar birthday.

Holliday scratched the back of her neck, and Cassie got the sense she was nervous. "I am sorry to tell you that the funeral home went ahead and followed Grant Moody's instructions. They cremated Joy, which unfortunately was done before anyone could intervene. He was listed as the next of kin, you see, and so the decision was handed to him. I really am very sorry."

Cassie felt winded by that news. She had held a flicker of hope that she would get to see their mum just one last time. Now that so much had changed, she really wanted to hold Joy's hand and tell her she forgave her. That they'd be all right.

"Now that we understand more about Grant's intentions—
which appear to be to defraud you both—we have arranged the
collection of Joy's ashes with Ellen Scott. She will discuss that with
you. Grant will not be able to claim them."

"Thank you," Cassie said, not sure what else was appropriate in
the circumstances. She didn't want to believe that Joy was in a con-
tainer somewhere. She was quite sure there was a place their mother
still existed.

"Did you arrest him?" Andie asked. "Grant?"

Holliday shook her head and studied her hands. "We have
handed the information to the Morningside police about the theft
of Joy's will and his attempt to illegally transfer the property. It will
all be followed up thoroughly, you have my word."

"We just want him to stay away from us," Cassie said, not caring
what happened to Grant as long as she never had to see him again.

"I understand. Now, he has put a caveat on this property—that
means he will make a claim for it, and he is allowed to do that. But
I believe Ellen Scott has it well in hand. I get the impression she is
not a woman you'd want to have a showdown with."

Cassie was inclined to agree. "Do you think Joy really believed
it?" she asked both detectives, looking from one to the other. "That
she might go to the future? At the end, at least?"

Holliday twisted her mouth around and shot them a look of
commiseration. "I think she did. The calendar over there on the wall
counted down to the first of August. She canceled her regular appointments, she withdrew her savings, plus the note and the information she sent to Missing Persons . . . So, yeah, I really don't think
she expected to be here after your birthday. We think that's the reason she told us where Britney was—she wanted to put it right."

"She wasn't terrible." Even now that Joy was gone, it seemed
more important than ever to speak up for her.

"I don't think anyone is all bad, but that doesn't mean she did the right thing," Holliday said. "And speaking of Britney, I'm sure you have both reached the conclusion that she was your biological mother and Tyler Rodriguez is your biological father. The DNA you supplied to us confirms that. He and Britney's sister, Tiffany White, are very keen to meet you. I have contact details for them for when you're ready."

Cassie liked the idea; she couldn't imagine losing her sister. She wanted to meet her aunt, ask her about her real mother. Learning of Britney's love of drawing had made Cassie start sketching again. They had quickly figured out that the sketchbook from the tree had been Britney's, although how it came to be there was a mystery they presumed would never be solved.

"Tiffany is really lovely. She's been pretty desperate to find her missing sister all these years. I think she'd give Jessica Fletcher a run for her money." Holliday looked at Cassie's blank face. "Sorry, that's a reference from . . ."

"*Murder, She Wrote*," Andie finished. "I watch it now." She nodded toward the new flat-screen television that had been delivered two days earlier. After the legitimacy of Joy's savings was established, Patrick Chen had the money returned to the twins within twenty-four hours. It turned out the police weren't quite as prone to thievery as Monty had suggested. The TV was their first purchase, and then Andie treated herself to a whole box of Fruit Tingles.

"Did Joy murder her?" Andie asked, the coarseness of the word *murder* really hitting Cassie hard.

"That is not my investigation, but I have spoken to Detective Crew about it. You met her—she was here for the search warrant."

"We remember," Cassie said. The feeling of that day remained raw.

"She was happy for me to pass on the initial findings from the coroner. It shows blunt force trauma to the back of Britney's head. The blood on the stairs would tend to indicate she had fallen down them. We may never know the full story about the death—that's something I believe Joy has taken with her—but the working theory is that it might have been an accident that Joy felt she had to conceal, for fear of losing both of you."

"Did she steal us?" Cassie asked.

Holliday considered this question carefully. "The pictures in the notebook you found were dated up to November of the year you were born. Other family members recalled seeing Britney between August and November, and she never mentioned a baby, let alone two, to anyone. It was as if she'd birthed you and then pretended she hadn't. I'm sorry—that might be hard to hear. We think she felt safe coming here, maybe visiting regularly. Tiffany told us Britney had started using drugs and was behaving quite erratically. In hindsight, it would seem she hadn't coped at all well after abandoning you both. Britney's story—your mother's story—is heartbreaking."

Cassie felt for Britney, young and lost. But she felt for Joy too, who had been raising the twins as her own and then stood to lose it all. It was an impossible situation, where winning and losing seemed interchangeable.

"Are you open to the possibility that Mum has traveled through time?" Cassie asked, fiddling with the pendant around her neck. It was the one from the tree; she'd polished it until it shone and hung it on a different, unbroken chain and didn't plan on taking it off. She liked having it close; it felt important.

Leo shifted awkwardly in his chair and Holliday answered carefully. "Well, no. We are not thinking of that as a viable alternative."

"Why not?" Cassie didn't shift her gaze from the detectives.

"Ah, it's . . . I guess it's more that we have no proof that is what happened. It's never happened before, you see."

"To the best of your knowledge."

Holliday inhaled deeply and looked at her colleague.

Cassie knew how she sounded. She wasn't entirely sure she believed that was where Joy had gone, but it was nice to think she might have. She had a sudden, burning feeling that they'd never really know everything that happened, just a version of it. The truth cobbled together from the fragments left behind. If Mum had covered up a tragic accident, surely that was forgivable. And, of course, it was easier to forgive someone in death than it was in life.

The detectives stood to leave. They all walked through the laundromat, Kevin no longer in the shop, and Holliday stopped at the front door. "Can you let Monty know I'll take the tortoiseshell kitten when it's ready?" Holliday pinkened a little as she spoke, Cassie noticed.

"Of course." Cassie smiled, pleased another cat would be heading to a good home. She'd been working on getting Lori-Jayne to take one too; she thought Winston would love a feline friend.

From the front window of Joyful Suds, the twins watched the police car pull out from the curb and slip into the traffic.

"She thinks you're out of your mind," Andie said. "Talking about time travel like that."

"It's not something she can really disprove, though, is it? Not for another twenty-seven years."

"But you don't really . . . Do you think it? Really?"

"Sometimes." Cassie looked skyward. She noticed a cloud that looked like a baby chick in a rattan basket but didn't point it out. "It doesn't hurt to, does it?"

Andie sighed, then shrugged.

"Do you think we did the right thing, not mentioning the insulin or the syringe?"

Andie was quick to answer. "Yes, I do. And I'm ready to talk about it now."

"Okay then . . ." Cassie had a troubling feeling she might not want to hear the story, but she also knew she had to.

"About six months ago, around the time Mum started having all her appointments and acting differently, I saw her and Monty together." Andie paused. "Don't even mention I called her Mum then, just let me tell the story."

Cassie hadn't even considered interrupting her.

"They were in the courtyard and I saw them kiss. I think she'd been drinking."

"She never drank!"

"I know. But she was upset. And he helped her inside and I heard them. He said, 'Don't worry, I'll look after you, whatever happens.' And she was crying, but he kissed her and then she sort of came to her senses and told him she was making a fuss and to leave her be. So he did.

"And you know what she said when he left and the door was closed? She said 'I love you, Montgomery Doyle.' But he was long gone, he didn't hear her. She never wanted him to know."

"I think he knew."

"I think so too. And then on our birthday, Cass, I was there. I was in the in-between when it happened. When Mum died."

"*What?*" Cassie was amazed that Andie had been able to keep this to herself. "What happened?"

Andie stepped out of the shop, walked out onto the sidewalk, and looked toward the key-shaped shingle above the locksmith's.

"It was Monty," Andie said calmly.

PART FOUR
UNDER NEW MANAGEMENT

Our only true life is in the future.
George Orwell, *1984*

CHAPTER 47
MONTY

August 1, 2023
The day of Joy's death

5:25 p.m.

Andie came into the shop, just as Monty was closing up. He knew immediately it wasn't Cassie; they were night and day to him. This was Andie and she was in a flap.

"You okay there?"

She shook her head, looking quite upset. Andie was the stoic one with the stern gaze who would ask questions; she had no idea how much like Joy she was. Cassie was the one he felt a fatherly attachment to, but in truth, he'd do anything for any of the Moody women. Being neighbors with Joy and her daughters all these years had been good for him. Knowing them earlier in life would've served him well, he often thought. In fact, if he'd met Joy Moody as a young man, it might have derailed his Tough Guy act, which meant he'd probably have said no to doing the robbery that got him three years locked up in that hellhole Pentridge.

"Is it Cassie?" he asked.

"It's Mum."

Monty was out the door and following her back to the laundromat without a second thought, his knee aching from the speed at which he moved. Joy was pacing about the lounge room when they got there, Cassie watching her carefully, clearly worried. And rightfully so. Joy was speaking into the bookshelves as though they might very well reply to her. The three of them watched Joy as she moved her hands frantically, her voice low and insistent. He noticed the smooth skin of her cheek was scratched deeply. He didn't bother asking why. That was the least of their problems.

Joy turned. "We didn't go anywhere? We were meant to go," she told him, her face strained with distress.

"Where were you going?" he asked gently.

"To the future. I was taking the girls to the future. But it's a secret, Monty, I can't tell you about it."

"It's okay, Joy, I won't tell anyone."

From his armchair research, he knew her tumor would affect her personality as it grew. Forgetfulness, hallucinations, memory loss, mood swings. He should have been much more intrusive, paid much more attention. The times he'd found her asleep in her car, he'd wanted to start the conversation with her, but it was like she'd forgotten the intimacy they'd once shared. Joy had always been hard to get close to, but she had let him in before, and he hoped it would happen again. They'd been together physically on a number of memorable occasions when the girls were younger, but it was more than that. He loved her.

"She thinks we were going to 2050. That's where she's told us we're from," Cassie said quietly.

Joy tsked. "Careful, Cassiopeia, you never know if he's The People."

"It's Monty, Mum. He's not part of them," Cassie replied.

Monty was catching up as quickly as he could. Snippets of information over the years were drawing together, things he'd heard over the fence, from the twins or Joy. Should he have asked questions

earlier? He knew doing that would have just made Joy hold her secrets even closer. "I think we should head up to the hospital." He
tried to sound calm, but his entire being was surging with worry.

Joy immediately became more agitated. "No hospitals!" she
snapped. "We need to stay here, in case the timing was wrong. Or
they're late. Maybe they're just late." Joy's eyes brightened as if
she'd just realized something significant. "They're late!" she cried
out. "We need to go back to the tree and wait. Give them more
time. We have to be there when they come." She went to the hook
on the back door and pulled down her cardigan, the one he'd seen
her wear to the beach on more occasions than he could count. She
tugged it on and pulled it tight across her body.

This woman, with whom he'd lived side by side for over two decades, suddenly seemed more frail than she'd been the day before.
He had been seeing her through such hopeful eyes all this time and
had failed to admit, even to himself, just how unwell she was.

He heard the in-between door open and turned to see Andie slip
out quietly. He didn't have time to wonder where she was going. He
turned back to Joy. "Maybe we do. But how about we send Cass
out to check?" He looked at Cassie, who shot out the back door,
not needing to be asked twice.

Joy came close. She still smelled the same, clean linen and a distinct sweetness that was purely her. Her face was glossy with sweat
and her cheeks burned a bright pink. "You understand. I knew
you'd understand, Monty, that's why I love you."

Even though he knew she was not herself, he took her words
and banked them where all the wonderful things about Joy were
kept. He'd never heard her say that before. Not in those simple
words. They would remain seared onto him, like a tattoo. Although
not like the one of Ned Kelly he regretted having started (and never
finished) on his shoulder blade when he was twenty-five and not

long out of prison. Back then he thought he was as badass as they came, and it was his "fuck you" to the police. He'd been tempted to sandpaper it off but didn't have the nerve.

Andie was back, whispering to him. "We should give her these— they might calm her down. She used to give them to us sometimes. We'd always go straight to sleep." She held out a packet of medication to him, Phenergan. It wasn't a bad plan if they could get Joy to take them, but he wasn't about to pin her down and forcibly medicate her.

"No secrets," Joy wailed, seeing him and Andie whispering.

"No secrets," he agreed, "but you need to be thinking straight."

"I suppose." Joy looked frazzled. Her hair was always pinned back so tidily, but today tendrils were loose about her face.

"A couple of these, with a cuppa, then we sit and wait a bit."

He felt his heart slowing down as he saw Joy's face slacken. She was listening to him. It was all he could do to stop himself from lurching forward to wrap his arms around her. He wanted to imprint himself upon her, make sure she knew it was him—Monty— and that he would take care of her forever.

Andie went to make some tea. Monty popped out two pills and handed them to Joy, who promptly swallowed them. The phone rang in the shop and Andie looked at Monty. "Just ignore it," she said.

"No. You can't do that, that's unprofessional," Joy tutted.

"You get it, Andie," Monty said. "I'll wait here."

He already felt Joy calming down, and he lured her over to her armchair. She sat down, on the edge at first, and then she slowly sank back into the chair's soft embrace.

"Maybe there's no daylight saving in the future. Maybe the time was wrong." Joy was talking to herself. "But then it was meant to be moonrise, and the moon is up. The supermoon, Monty, *don't you see*? They happen so infrequently and it was happening *today*.

It was the sign! It meant everything was right and it would happen and they would come for us. They would come if they could. Yes, yes, they'd come if they could."

"Maybe it wasn't about the moonrise specifically," Monty said.

Joy's eyes rested on him; she needed his reassurance. How he loved those eyes.

"Maybe just anytime tonight?" he asked. He knew he shouldn't be encouraging her delusions—it felt cruel to call them that, even in his own head—but he just wanted to ease her angst.

"Anytime tonight?" She thought about this long and hard, resting her face in her hands. "Yes, that would still work." Her breathing slowed as she dropped her hands into her lap. The calmness washed over them both. "Monty," Joy said, her voice different somehow, more lucid now. "I've done something that can't be undone."

"What do you mean?"

"I sent something today, on the computer. About something that will get me in a lot of trouble. I mean, I did it for the right reasons, but it wouldn't be looked at in that manner. Not unless they know the girls are the Daughters of the Future Revolution. And of course," she bent forward, whispering now, "I can't tell them that. Too risky. And you know, the police are with *them*. They've been infiltrated." Her head swiveled from left to right, as if someone could be listening in.

"What did you tell them?"

"Where to find Britney."

"Who's Britney?" Monty asked, but he thought maybe he knew. He wasn't sure of her name, but there was a girl who would visit his neighbor in the early days, before they really knew each other.

"She came to get them, but I'd sworn to keep them safe," Joy said. "But what I did. That wasn't right. I know that."

What had she done? He'd done questionable things for considerably less than protecting the ones he loved; he didn't want to judge.

"And the man who came looking for her, he deserves to know where she went. Where she's been all these years. He got the blame, you see." Joy closed her eyes and Monty knew she was remembering those tiny babies. He could picture it all so clearly himself: two sweet faces, their small bodies wrapped tightly, side by side in the pram as Joy proudly walked her girls around the neighborhood. Her voice sounded weak with tiredness and the medication taking hold. "She wasn't getting them. They weren't hers."

Joy's face started to relax and he thought she was falling asleep. He was startled when she sat forward again, eyes open, so close her breath was on him. "She tried to get them, so we fought, Monty, and she fell. It was an accident. I didn't mean for it to happen the way it did, I just couldn't let her take them."

"I think I understand."

"I'm not a monster. I've only ever wanted what was best for Andie and Cassie. But the way she fell, she was very badly hurt. I should've gone for help, but I knew they'd take them from me. I wouldn't have coped." Joy shook her head sadly. "I was so selfish."

"Was Britney their mother?" He thought of the young girl, thought he remembered her face, although it had been a long time.

"No," Joy said quickly, but then paused. "I don't know how that's possible." Her whole face dropped, the deep creases softening and the corners of her mouth tilting downward. "But I think that *is* right. I'm afraid I'm really not myself today."

"It's the tumor, Joy. It's affecting your thoughts."

"Yes, I suppose it probably is."

"Where is she? The girl?" He couldn't bring himself to use Britney's name; he didn't want to make her seem real.

The look she gave him seemed to come from someone else, from somewhere different than the Joy who had just been speaking to him. It was her. Really her. Old Joy. "She's in my mother's wedding trunk in the shed. I lost the key years ago. I meant to move her, but I couldn't. I didn't."

Monty was shocked, but he tried to keep his face as neutral as he could. That he'd been in such close quarters to a—for want of a better term—coffin all this time was almost unthinkable. He thought of how Donna had hated that little tin outhouse for as long as he could recall. It was where she'd been found by the girls, trapped, all those years ago and he'd just assumed that was why she steered clear. But perhaps she'd known all along. Cats were smarter than people, after all.

Joy was still talking. "You know it's time. I know things have changed. I'm not the same. It will never be the same. And you promised you'd help me." Her eyes closed.

The door to the in-between clicked open and Andie came in, flustered. "Okay, now what was I doing?" The kettle flicked off, as if in answer. "Tea. I will make some tea."

Joy's breathing became gentle and even, the moment between them gone.

"Let's skip the tea. She's resting now," Monty said. "We should let her sleep."

While Joy slept, the twins told him everything, or at least what they had known to be the truth: all about the future and The People. When Monty looked at them dumbfounded, Andie pressed *The Fortis Trilogy* into his hands. He wondered how he could live next door and be none the wiser to the drama unfolding daily. Perhaps he was just willfully ignorant to it all, like he'd been to the extent of Joy's illness.

What the twins didn't know about was the body Joy had hidden, or how desperate things had become for her. The situation was not about to get any better, that much was clear.

"Let's leave her be and see how everything looks in the morning," Monty said. "I think we should take Joy to the doctor."

"She wouldn't like that," Andie said.

"It's a bit out of her hands now." He already knew Joy would hate it and he had no intention of taking her. He just needed some time. "Come and get me if you need me, okay?"

The twins agreed readily, both looking exhausted.

"And I think it'd be okay to shut up shop a bit early tonight, don't you? We could all do with some rest."

Montgomery Doyle walked back to his shop, considering life and how he had mistakenly believed that they'd had more time. He had dated women in the years since he was last with Joy, but there had been no one who captivated him like the woman next door.

In 2002, when Joy had moved into the house, she was not noticeably pregnant. But then Joy's twins arrived and the teen who'd visited often stopped coming by. They lived so closely together it was impossible not to notice these things, and he was an observant man; he'd learned to be in prison, a place where a slip in concentration could be very dangerous. He hadn't given any thought as to whether the twins were meant to be with Joy. She was a social worker, and he assumed they were placed with her because they couldn't be with their birth parents. Whatever way the babies had come to be with his neighbor, it seemed the right place for them.

Monty didn't think much of the police, and that wasn't just because of his period of incarceration. It had been the longest thirty-six months of his life and he'd barely gotten out with his sanity intact. The cops back then believed in beating a confession out of you, and they'd gotten one from him. He had, after all, been guilty of what they accused him of, although he'd thought himself tough enough to lie and get away with it. It was the sort of ignorance that afflicts the young. He didn't know the other guys had brought real guns along, not until he heard the shots ring out, and that's when he knew they were in dire straits. He was only the driver and was lucky, in a way, that he didn't cop a longer sentence. What's more, he never gave up the other two guys and they got away with it scot-free. Did that bother him? No, not at all. That was the gamble with the business they were in. Big rewards, high risks, and above all, keep your mouth shut.

So Joy's business was Joy's business, until he fell in love with her. He wasn't simply holding a candle for her, she *was* the candle. It was Joy or nothing, and it seemed nothing would have to do. But he'd known something was seriously wrong with her lately. There had been days when he'd seen her pace the sidewalk in front of their shops three or four times in a row. She looked like a woman on a mission but then she marched back seconds later, confused, as if she'd forgotten something. More than once he'd seen her staring at Joyful Suds as if she were stuck in some sort of suspended animation.

It was a wonder no one else had noticed Joy's decline. In place of her slim but sturdy frame was a new fragility, and even her hair (always the color of autumn) had lost something of its shine. He knew something was taking Joy from them piece by piece. And the hardest thing of it all was that she didn't look at him the same. For so long she would give him a smile that was for him alone. A lift of the corner of her mouth, a tilt of the head, and a sparkle in her soft, brown eyes that made him recall the feeling of her hands and the scent of her skin, even when she was meters from him. But he hadn't seen that smile in months. The last time had been in February that year, when he heard her over the fence, while he was enjoying the summer evening, drinking his cup of tea outside. He heard her crying, an unusual thing, and he peeked through the weathered palings and saw Joy beneath that big tree whose roots weren't only lifting her pavers, but had crept through next door and cracked his concrete. A silly tree for such a small area. A bottle sat beside her and she held a thin book. She sipped, screwed her face up at the burn of the spirit as it slid down her throat, and then wiped her face with the palms of her hands. He had to go to her.

Donna followed him as he walked out his gate and through the lane to Joy's as he had on every one of those long-ago occasions where he'd had Joy all to himself. Just as he'd thought they were on the cusp of becoming a serious, permanent arrangement, she had pulled the rug from beneath him. Andie had almost caught them, and Joy didn't want anything to distract from her most important role. He knew she was protecting herself, but he'd struggled to accept her decision.

The gate gave its tell-tale creak as he opened it; it had always been more effective than a doorbell, and Joy spun around. It was dark, the stars blanketed the sky above them, and apart from the gentle whoosh of passing cars, it was relatively quiet.

"Monty, you scared me."

"I'm sorry. Can I join you?"

She swigged from her bottle, grimaced, then held it out to him. He shook his head; he hadn't had a drink in over thirty years.

"You okay?"

"It would appear I am not." She laughed, but it was a sobbing type of laugh.

"What do you mean?"

"I am . . ." She searched his face, as if the rest of her sentence was there. "I am up shit creek." She pushed the pamphlet she'd been holding over to him: *Living with Cancer*. "Funny title, really," she said, "given I cannot actually *live* with it."

His chest felt like it was being compressed. "Is there treatment?"

"No." She wiped her tears with her sleeve. "I mean, yes, but I don't want it. The odds are . . . crap, and I just can't . . . I just don't want to go down that path."

He reached for the bottle and took a slug from it, needing to dull the pain. "We can do this together. I'll drive you to appointments, support you, look after you, whatever you need."

"I know you would." She took his hand and held it tight, then just as suddenly, dropped it again. "What I need, Monty, is for you to promise me that when the time comes, you won't let me become . . . someone else. You'll make sure I go while I'm still *me* and before I am just a vessel for this tumor." Joy tapped her head. "I'll do it myself if I can. But it terrifies me I won't be able to when the time comes. I can't do it yet. I just need a bit more time." She looked up at the windows of the top floor of her house. "I have some things to put straight."

He knew what she was asking. But surely she didn't think he would be able to do such a thing, even for her. "I couldn't . . ."

"You are my oldest friend. In another time, in another life, you and I were . . ." She trailed off and he thought of a million ways to finish that sentence.

You and I were perfect.

You and I were meant to be.

You and I were in love.

You and I. She didn't finish the sentence, just left it hanging between them.

He reached for her hand and held it tight. "I promise, Joy," Monty told her, although he hoped with every fiber of his being that he'd never be put in the position to test his resolve.

Then she kissed him, long and hard on the lips like she used to, and his heart exploded into a million tiny fragments, each one of them screaming her name.

He thought they'd had longer, but that had been wishful thinking.

Now, as he stepped back through the front door of his shop and locked it behind him, he knew the time had come.

On his way out of Joyful Suds, he'd pocketed Joy's mobile phone. He had her passcode, since he'd helped her set it up. He moved through his shop, into the house, and boiled the kettle for a coffee. He'd need it; it was going to be a long night. He'd made a promise after all.

At 11:22 p.m., way past his usual bedtime, Monty checked the CCTV at Joyful Suds using Joy's phone. He considered turning off the cameras but thought better of it, knowing that would be hard to explain. Instead, he checked the angles they covered so he knew how to get in without being seen. The shop was dark, and there was no movement on the cameras. He couldn't see into the house, so he could only hope he'd waited long enough for Cassie and Andie to be asleep. If they disturbed him, he'd just have to pretend he'd popped in to check on Joy.

He slipped out the back door and down the lane, moving slowly to avoid making the gravel crunch. Having remembered the creak of Joy's gate, he had brought along his trusty WD-40. He gave the hinges a quick spray, waited a minute, and eased it open. The creak was gone, and he put the can on the crossbeam of the fence as he clicked the gate shut, barely making a sound. There was no light on upstairs at 225 Station Street—good. He needed a little luck on his side.

He nimbly picked the lock on the back door, his hands steady, his focus strong, and listened for sounds that would indicate anyone was awake. Hearing nothing, he stepped through the door, closing it gently. The warm air from inside swirled around him and he immediately felt his face start to thaw.

Joy was in the same spot as when he'd left hours earlier, a cold cup of tea and a glass of water beside her, a quilt draped over her lap. A pink crocheted throw over the back of the chair framed her face, her cheek bones sharp, her face as beautiful as the first time he'd seen her, dripping wet and sparkling with an energy he'd wanted to get close to.

Monty had come prepared to act quickly, drawing the capped syringe from his shirt pocket where he'd made up a dose of insulin too big for even a very high blood sugar day. She could slip out of the world peacefully before the police came or before she was sent to the hospital. He was simply doing as she'd asked, although that was cold comfort.

Her chest rose and fell and she snored ever so delicately. For a moment he was tempted to wake her up, just so he could tell her he was keeping his promise. There was no way he'd let her go to jail, which she surely would even though the girl's death had been an accident. Hiding a body and keeping it in a makeshift tomb for twenty years didn't come without penalty, but his Joy did not belong in prison, not if he had anything to do with it. He would wear this decision like an anchor, but he was not unfamiliar with the weight of regret.

He had to act. Pulling her arm from beneath the quilt, he rolled up her cardigan sleeve, staring at the smooth, soft skin that he'd once been allowed to kiss and touch and hold. He was going to inject her with the insulin and leave the needle beside her, to give the impression she'd taken her own life. It felt underhanded, but he wasn't above admitting that he feared going back to prison. He'd draw up an even bigger dose just as quickly, if he thought that was on the cards for him. His always-steady hands trembled.

Sighing, he put the fine-tipped needle on the little table, noticing the frame that usually held a photo of Joy and the twins now stood empty. He dropped his head into his hands. This was going to be harder than he'd thought.

Joy stirred and Monty tilted his head, waiting to hear any movement on the top floor. There was nothing, but in front of him, Joy moved again and he turned back to her. She was looking right at him.

"Monty," she mumbled, her voice heavy with sleep. "Is it time for me to go?"

He grabbed her hand and leaned in so he could speak as quietly as possible. He breathed her in; he'd bottle that smell if he could.

"I heard something. Check the stairs," Joy said. Her face was calm and he did as she asked. Monty listened hard, but it was just branches scraping the walls and other noises old buildings tended to make.

"It was nothing," he said, kneeling in front of her, wincing at the pain that shot into his hip.

Joy's eyes were the brown of acorns; autumn would never not remind him of this woman.

"I don't know if I can do it," he said. "I don't want you to go."

"I know. But it's okay, it's done."

He looked over to the table and saw the syringe had disappeared. "Joy, where is it?" he asked, louder than he intended.

She moved the blanket back and showed it to him, the plunger down, the liquid gone.

"Why did you do that?" It came out harsher than he meant.

"So you didn't have to."

The reality hit Monty harder than he expected. It was, after all, what he'd gone there to do.

"Tell the girls I love them and that I'll see them when they get there."

"Joy, there is no . . ." He tried to explain, but she shushed him.

"I know, Monty, I know. You'll make sure my girls are okay?"

"Always."

He felt her squeeze his hand and he clung on tight. Her last thoughts might have been of Cassie and Andie, but he selfishly wanted to be the last person in Joy Moody's life.

"See you on the other side," Joy said, barely a whisper.

Monty couldn't say how long he sat there for. Ten minutes or an hour, it felt like the blink of an eye and he would have sat there for another hour if he could. But he was sure he heard footsteps creaking upstairs and his legs were aching from the way he was sitting, and he knew he had to leave before his bad knee gave out and made it impossible.

He held his fingers to the pulse point on Joy's wrist and felt nothing. It was 11:57 p.m., still the twins' birthday, and Joy had gone, just as she'd hoped to.

It may have seemed like a very mundane place to die—in a little house, behind a pink laundromat—but that would suggest it had been a mundane place to live. And there was nothing dull about this woman, or her life, of that he was quite sure.

The back door locked behind him as Monty let himself out of 225 Station Street, with no idea Andie had been listening from the in-between the whole time.

CHAPTER 48
ANDIE

October 2023

On October 12, 2023, Cassiopeia and Andromeda were officially born, twenty-one years after the actual event. They had no interest in rebranding themselves and kept the names Joy had given them all that time ago, with a small addition.

Andromeda Joy Moody-White and Cassiopeia Joy Moody-White collected their birth certificates at the registry office in Melbourne. Linh had driven them in, just as erratically as she had spirited them away from Morningside Police Station weeks earlier. But despite a close shave or two, they'd made it, and a soft-faced, kind-eyed woman obligingly posed for a photo with the oldest newborn twins on record.

In the box beside "mother," Britney White was listed, and Tyler Rodriguez was recorded as "father." Just as it should've been had they been registered properly at birth. It might have been the norm to be named for their father, but there was nothing traditional about this family dynamic, and changing their surname was a simple way to honor Britney's legacy.

A week prior, the twins had been invited to the burial service of their biological mother. They went, standing shoulder to shoulder in the small crowd, between their aunt Tiffany and Tyler Rodriguez. They'd never had a dad, and they were only just getting to know him. It would be a slow process, and maybe they'd never apply the term *father* to Tyler. He was heavily tattooed and weathered, with a nose that had been broken more than once, yet there was something familiar about him, right from the get-go. Perhaps shared DNA meant there would always be an intrinsic bond.

All her life Andie had lived with a family tree that didn't extend beyond their small house, and now she had a half sister, a half brother, and aunts and uncles. She also had a grandmother, although Erica White was another story entirely. If there was meant to be a soft, maternal kindness about grandmothers, Erica had not gotten that memo. She had gone out of her way to speak to any media outlet with money to offer and sold a story that was never hers to tell, even inviting a journalist to the funeral, part of a *Newsline* exposé that neither Cassie nor Andie wanted anything to do with. The journalist asked repeatedly in saccharine tones for an interview, offering the twins a large sum to participate and pitching it as their opportunity to "set the record straight." They didn't need the money and they preferred their privacy, so had declined the offer and hoped the whole spectacle would fade to nothingness.

On their way home from the registry office, they met Tyler at McDonald's. For all their options, the twins still had trouble going past their favorite sandwiches.

"Here you go." Linh dropped the bags of food down on the laminated table. They'd chosen a booth, the red vinyl seats creaking every time they moved.

Tyler reached in for his fries and Andie stopped him, grabbing hold of his arm. "What does that say?" she asked, pointing at a tattoo. It was one of many that covered his arm, but it was the words that struck her.

"That's for Brit, actually," Tyler said. "It's a song we both loved."

Cassie sat forward and pulled the necklace out from under her top. "It matches. 'I see the future and it's all about us.'"

Tyler looked surprised, maybe that the necklace still existed after all the years that had passed. "I got that for her. For your mum."

It still didn't sound right, that term being used in relation to someone other than Joy. Andie contended with that daily, since there were reminders of her everywhere, especially at the laundromat. But it wasn't all bad; it had never been all bad. She was slowly coming to grips with the idea that she could have two mothers, and that those mothers didn't have to be perfect.

Cassie clutched the heart pendant in her hand and Andie saw just how much it meant to her to have something that had once been Britney's. They knew so little about the woman who was the very reason for their existence. But they were learning slowly and they wanted to know more. It was amazing to find out that Britney had been such a talented, avid drawer like Cassie. Andie couldn't help but wish there was something she shared with her other mother in a similar fashion. They couldn't get to know her properly, but there was comfort in having something in common.

Andie let Tyler continue reaching for his fries before taking her own. She shoved the loose ones from the bottom of the bag into her mouth and felt the oil seep out of them as she bit down, the salt making her taste buds ping.

"I haven't seen someone eat one of those for years," Linh said, pointing at Andie's Filet-O-Fish. "I think they had to go dig it out of the deep freeze."

Tyler laughed, watching Andie flip open the top of her burger and layer fries into it. She squished the top back on and took a bite. He was staring right at her.

"What?" she asked, mouth full.

"That's exactly how Brit used to eat them," he said.

Andie looked at the man who formed the basis of her existence. His eyes were bright, the corners of his mouth turned up. He laughed and she did too. A shared love of Filet-O-Fish might have been small, but it was still something. She looked forward to finding out more.

CHAPTER 49
CASSIE

November 2023

By November the pink walls of Joyful Suds were painted white, though the checkerboard floor and the yellow vinyl-covered stools remained. The twins wanted to refresh the shop, not wipe its personality completely. They kept the sign that had been installed way back when as it was, other than getting a sign-writer in to restore it to its original flamingo-pink charm. Andie and Cassie toyed with changing the name but decided Joyful Suds had quite a nice ring to it. Besides, rebranding wouldn't erase history. It might disguise it slightly, or lead people to believe it wasn't the one they'd seen on the news, dubbed the "Little Laundromat of Lies," but they didn't want to appear ashamed or embarrassed of the place where they'd grown up. Because they weren't. The news stories died down after the police officially declared Britney's death an accident and Joy's as a result of the glioblastoma. It ended up being a tragic tale that inspired sadness more than morbid curiosity.

The twins understood the police had made an educated guess about what had happened to their birth mother. No one still alive knew exactly what had taken place the night Britney died. Cassie wanted to believe the official police ruling; it was far better than thinking that Joy had done the unspeakable.

The laundromat, despite Uncle Grant's assertions, was not in debt. The mortgage had been paid off before Joy even inherited the shop. As they'd thought, Joy had been more than capable as a businesswoman and had run a watertight ship. The twins engaged an accountant—a friend of Linh's—and he thoroughly checked and balanced the books. An easy job, he told them. Everything was already in perfect order, the ledgers kept in the locked drawer in the bottom of Joy's desk. Alongside those, they'd found the beginnings of many letters to the twins that Joy hadn't been able to finish. Dated in the months around her tumor diagnosis, the letters showed that Joy was trying to put things straight, but she wasn't able to define the edges of her own truth and lies. There, in the letters, the twins had found the words Joy always struggled to say outright, for reasons they'd never know. In Joy's own handwriting, she detailed how much she loved them and how she'd only ever wanted to keep them safe.

Cassie stuck the letters into one of Joy's scrapbooks, page by page, filling almost the whole thing. The half-written letters told a miserable tale of a woman who feared being alone. But that was only a small part. That didn't take into account all the things that hadn't made the pages: the Uno games, the dancing, the cloud spotting, Special Birthday Breakfasts, the endless stories Joy read them at bedtimes, the way she always made sure Cassie had sketchbooks on hand and Andie had Fruit Tingles. She hadn't needed to make note of them, because they all knew. It was easy to lose sight of the good things when the bad ones weighed so much.

Once she'd gotten her head around the way the accounting was done, Cassie started applying her math knowledge to the business and quickly picked up what was meant to go where, how to file quarterly tax returns, and how to bargain with the wholesalers.

Ellen was knee-deep in proceedings to have Joy's estate turned over to the twins, and Grant, true to his word, had lodged his claim. They had nothing to do with him. An intervention order prohibited him from approaching them, and if that hadn't kept him away, a visit from Tyler Rodriguez certainly had. Ellen had a renewed sense of vigor about her; she had been leaving her house regularly and conveyed updates to the twins with such delight they couldn't help but share her excitement.

Outside of Cassie and Andie, no one knew that Monty Doyle had been at Joy's side when she'd passed from one life to the next. They'd discussed it in detail with him, and he'd broken down in tears, glad to be relieved of holding on to her final moments alone. It broke Cassie's heart to see Monty so bereft, not because he feared being caught or turned in to the police, but because he missed her. Monty wished Joy had known how he felt before she died, but Cassie was quite sure she had.

They knew Joy Moody had not been someone who was deterred easily; had he not brought the insulin to her, she would've found another way. Cassie had been the one who searched online for answers, worried Joy might have suffered, still thinking it was possible her sister was involved. She'd also wanted to see what would happen if Andie had gotten caught. She regretted it now, realizing how sinister it looked from the outside.

A glimmer of light peeked over the horizon on the morning they scattered Joy's ashes. It was only fitting that they sent her off in this manner. Beach box 149 stood behind them, bathed in cold blue light from the pre-dawn sun. They would never know the significance of it standing watch, that it had been the place where Joy Moody's life had veered in a whole new direction.

The sand was cold beneath their bare feet and the gentle lapping waves moved perpetually ahead of them. They were a small group, no fuss, just as Joy would've liked it: Monty, Linh, Ellen, and the twins.

Andie was holding the tube Joy had been put in for just this purpose. She was about to release their mother when Cassie stopped her, pointing into the water. "Not here. We need to go out there."

Andie laughed, not thinking her sister was serious, but Cassie was resolute.

She moved toward the water, calling over her shoulder for them all to follow along. She had planned this, wearing her bathing suit under her jacket and pants. She'd packed them all hot water bottles too, knowing they'd need them for what the morning would hold.

"That's not fair," Linh called, her voice rising higher as the biting waves lapped her ankles. Even in November the water was like ice.

"I didn't think you'd come if you knew," Cassie replied.

The five of them walked out until they were waist-deep. It was the right place to be.

"Does anyone want to say anything?" Ellen asked. "Because I would."

Cassie nodded, blinking back her tears. She had been able to cry again of late, and she appreciated having the full gamut of emotions back.

"You and I were two of a kind, Joy Moody. A couple of old battle-axes." Ellen stopped and stared out at the orange streaks across the sky. "Rest easy, old girl. We've got everything under control."

Cassie started toward Ellen, wanting to hug her, but Ellen held up a steadfast hand. "No, young lady. I will not be hugging anyone today."

Cassie felt stung, but then Andie sniggered and so she giggled too. Ellen—like Joy—would do things her own way, in her own time.

"Joy," Linh said, looking to the heavens, "I'm taking your damn parking lot signs down."

They all laughed in the sad sort of way happiness tended to co-exist with grief. "And you are missed." Linh blew a kiss to the sky.

"Nothing from me," Monty said, the bottom of his flannelette shirt soaking up water. "Joy knows what I think."

The looks on Linh's and Ellen's faces made Cassie think they all knew what Monty thought. It was perhaps the worst-kept secret on Station Street.

Andie took a deep breath. "Joy. Ah . . . Mum, you were like no one else. I wish I had appreciated you more when you were here. I was so busy trying to be nothing like you but maybe being like you is not so bad. Not *entirely* like you, but I think you know what I mean." Andie looked at her sister. "I hope you find Britney, wher-ever you are, and I hope the two of you make peace. We may never know what happened, not really. But I think she knew when she left us that we were in good hands. Joy Moody, *you* are an incredible bunch of atoms."

Cassie was sobbing. "Let's let her go."

"Don't you want to say anything?" Andie asked.

"Yeah, I do, but I don't know if I can." Cassie licked her lips, tasting salt and snot, but she didn't care. She wiped her nose with her hand and washed it off in the water. "See you on the other side, Mum." She looked to her sister; tears were flowing from her too. Andie and Cassie held the ashes together and upended them into the water.

In the shop later that morning, Cassie stared out the front win-dows. The sun beamed through them in a way that made her think of everything she had to look forward to. And not just the coming summer days, but the plans for the future—the real one. Andie had been narrowing down destinations. Paris, Auckland, and Vancouver had all made the final list, and Cassie enjoyed listening to her sister deliberating over pros and cons. Andie was determined to see the world, while Cassie would keep the shop running, the home fires laundering; she didn't have the same desire as her sister to be thousands of miles away. She did fancy a couple of smaller adventures, though, the National Gallery for one, and she really wanted to try her hand at archery again. She still fancied herself as a Katniss in the making.

The dryer beside her stopped and she popped open the door and pulled the clothes out, piling the washing onto the folding table.

Andie was in the back, binge-watching *The Real Housewives of Orange County*. Before that it had been *Selling Sunset* and before that it was *Hell's Kitchen*. The gamma rays didn't inspire fear anymore; Cassie could watch television on the couch now too, not hiding behind it. She liked shows that made her laugh.

A familiar face walked through the door: Shawn. Cassie couldn't stop herself from smiling broadly. He was pushing his cart with boxes of snacks and plastic-wrapped cans of drinks stacked high and wore his Vin's Vending shirt, stretched tighter across his stomach than last time she'd seen him. It had been months.

"Shawn," she said, "it's been so long. I thought you'd quit!"

"I know, right? But, nah. I did two months in Peru. Bali gave me this out-of-body experience, and I realized I needed to see Machu Picchu." He held his hands out, like he was being bathed in ethereal light. "So I went."

"How amazing. How was it?"

"Peru was incredible." He looked up to the ceiling, as if he were dreaming about it right there in the laundromat. "But I blew through all my savings, so I'm back to save for the next trip."

"Sounds like a solid plan," she said.

"What's with the sign? Are you guys leaving?"

She looked at the banner they'd hung in the front window announcing they were "Under new management." "No, we're not. We're here to stay."

"Good. I'm glad." He grinned in a slightly lopsided way.

Cassie's hands were moving fast, sorting the pile of washing before her. Shawn was watching her closely and she didn't mind.

His hand pointed toward her, slowing her movement. "What's that you've got there? I didn't know you had a tatt."

"Oh, it's new." Cassie blushed while extending her arm toward him.

The drawing sat just above the crease of her elbow, something Linh had helped her design. They'd struck up a friendship over their shared love of art. Linh had even shown Cassie the painting she'd won the Artemis Prize for, something she generally didn't show anyone. It hung innocuously on the wall in her lounge room, Linh almost ashamed of it. The whole experience had sent her running from the art world, she said, intimidated by the "real" talent she decided she didn't have. Apparently winning one of the country's biggest art prizes wasn't enough to convince her she'd earned her spot. It hadn't helped that some of the art critics had been brutal in their judgment of the youngest person to ever take the prize, accusing the judges of making the controversial choice to appeal to a younger audience and garner plenty of attention.

They'd helped each other, really. Cassie's interest and incessant sketching had inspired Linh to start creating again, more than just inventing tattoos for customers. Linh hadn't painted anything for the love of it for a long time, but now she'd set up her easels and paints in her second bedroom, the one that watched over Station Street. Cassie joined her a couple of days a week, and Linh let her use the makeshift studio anytime she liked. Cassie knew her sister had bristled about this at first, feeling jealousy over the budding friendship and shared love of the arts. But it was very different to the way Andie and Linh spent time together. Linh and Andie were something else entirely, leaving Cassie to wonder if maybe they did share a twin telepathy. Or maybe it was just obvious to everyone that love was blossoming on Station Street.

It had been on one of the days they'd worked together in the up-stairs art room at Lotus that Cassie had asked if Linh would tattoo her. She'd been thinking about it for a while, and Linh was more than happy to oblige. Across the soft skin on the inside of her el-bow, Linh tattooed the outline of two washing machines, with a cat—Donna, of course—perched on top, sitting haughtily, as she did. The whole design was made to look like it was one continuous, black line. Linh had laughed, said she'd never thought she'd tattoo a washing machine on anyone. Andie had been impressed but still hadn't worked up the courage to get one done herself.

"It's really cool," Shawn said.

"Thank you. It's a bit silly, I guess."

"Nah, I'll tell you what's silly." He yanked up his pants leg, showing off his ankle where a small colorful ball was imprinted on his sun-tanned skin. "I lost a bet when I was eighteen, and my friend got to pick anything he wanted to tattoo on me."

"What is it? A planet?"

"Yes. Specifically, though, it's Uranus."

"Oh." Cassie burst into giggles.

"Childish, hey? But seriously, he could've done so much worse to me. I would've if he'd lost the bet. But whatever—I can just say it's Mars, or Jupiter or something else."

"No, it's definitely got to be Uranus."

Shawn chuckled and opened the front of the snacks machine. "So hey, what do you think about getting that drink? Now you've had some thinking time?"

Cassie thought about what her mum would say, but then real-ized she didn't have to consider that anymore. It was a slow learning curve, one she loved and hated in almost equal measure. The twins were free to make their own decisions, which was as exciting as it was harrowing. Their lives involved no set destiny, no journey to the future, just laundry and beach boxes and salted potato chips. And whatever else they collected along the way.

"Yeah, I would actually really like that."

"Cool. Shall I get your number then?"

She nodded and pulled her phone out of her pocket. The smartphone was something she finally felt comfortable with now that Linh had given her a crash course in using it, but she still occasionally put it in the foil-wrapped jar overnight, just in case.

Once they'd exchanged numbers, Shawn got back to the business of stocking the vending machine. He looked around. "You guys have painted. It's good, although I was kind of fond of the pink." He shrugged. "So, what else is new?"

Everything and nothing, she thought. How on earth could she sum up the last few months? All that they'd been through: learning how to navigate life without Joy at the helm, getting birth certificates, meeting Tiffany and Tyler and her new brother and sister, finding out about Netflix and Candy Crush. Not going to the future. Just being with her sister, in a laundromat near the sea.

The world was huge and magnificent, and it was right there in front of them.

"Nothing much," she told Shawn, then smiled and neatly folded a pair of jeans.

EPILOGUE
JOY

November 6, 2002

Joy thought she'd gotten through to Britney, that she was seeing the logic in Joy's words and that she was going to leave Cassie and Andie with her. Joy had put the TV on, hoping it would let Britney unwind and zone out. She thought she had the situation under control. But when she had gone to make them a pot of tea, Britney shot straight up the stairs. The teenager was enraged to find the bedroom door locked and tried to force it open by crashing her body against it.

This level of aggression wasn't something Joy had seen in the teen before. Her mind went straight to baby Shem and his angry father, how she'd been too late to save him. Britney shoved Joy, slapped her, pulled her hair, and shook her violently by the shoulders.

Joy had no choice but to defend herself.

She hadn't realized how very close to the top step Britney was when she pushed her, or how hard she'd fall.

At the bottom of the stairs, Britney lay splayed, face-up, on the hardwood floor. As Joy reached her, she made a tremendous groaning sound. Her face was a mess, blood seeping from the back of her head, pooling around her at a disturbing pace. It was as if she had spilled a giant tub of paint.

Joy was horrified. What had she done?

"Are you okay?" she asked, breathless. She could hear the babies had woken from all the ruckus, and she hated not being able to go straight to them.

"What did you do?" Britney said, but it was garbled; her front tooth had cracked across the center, a jagged stump remaining. Blood flowed from a cut on her lip.

"I'm so sorry, Brit. It was an accident."

And *it was*. This wasn't the way things were meant to happen. But Britney's anger had not subsided. She pushed Joy's hands away.

"They're my babies!" Spit and blood spattered from the teen's lips as she shouted.

Joy grabbed a pillow to slip under Britney's head, thinking of how to make her more comfortable. She knew she couldn't move her in case she had a spinal injury. That was basic first aid, as was calling an ambulance.

Call for help, her brain screamed at her. Joy couldn't fix this on her own.

A disturbing clarity came over her. Everything she had worked hard to create for herself was about to be ruined. Britney had to understand the girls were hers now; she couldn't part with them. No mother would.

"You're so *fucked*," Britney hissed.

"I am really sorry." Joy dropped straight down onto Britney, the pillow covering her face, and she pushed against it with the entire weight of her body. Joy was strong and Britney hadn't seen it coming; she had the advantage.

"I *will* look after them," Joy said through tears, tightening her grip on the pillow. "I'm sorry, I'm sorry." She hadn't realized this monster lurked within her.

Perhaps, though, this was exactly how it was with mothers everywhere. The line between monster and mother blurred until either side was almost indistinguishable. The right things for the wrong reasons, and the wrong things for the right reasons.

She repeated her apology again and again until any resistance in the teenager's body was gone and she lay completely still on the floor. The pillow remained over her face; Joy couldn't bear to look at what she'd done.

She heard her daughters crying, rousing her from her spot on the floor. She inspected her hands for blood, knowing they'd need to be scrubbed before she went upstairs, but also knowing they'd never really be clean again.

ACKNOWLEDGMENTS

When I pitched this book to my publisher, Beverley Cousins, I half expected her to send someone to do a welfare check on me, rather than agree to publish my book. I told her I was writing about a strung-out mother in the suburbs with identical twin girls, which was almost autobiographical at that particular moment in time. But she told me to go ahead and write it. Thank you, Bev, for believing in me (and Joy) and pointing me in the right direction. I'm a very lucky author to have landed you.

Thank you to Amanda Martin for making *Joy Moody* so much better and making me laugh with your comments in the margins. Bella Arnott-Hoare, thank you for hooking me up with the places I need to be and making everything so easy. And to the rest of the Penguin team whom I've met or emailed with, or who have championed my books. You've all made this so much fun.

My amazing agent, Elaine Spencer at the Knight Agency: Thank you for taking me on and for making my publishing dreams come true.

Thank you to the team at St. Martin's Press: Sallie Lotz, Jill Schuck, Dori Weintraub, and everyone else who has made this happen.

Not to mention for bringing me the cover I dreamed about when I invented a little laundromat called Joyful Suds in my head. It's perfect! Thank you.

Joyful Suds was inspired by a photograph titled *Dear Customer* by Mrs. White (aka Abbie Davis). It was the beginning of my love of laundromats.

Thanks to the laundromat owners who probably never knew I was there, but never kicked me out if they did. I love that you open so early. Laundromats are a great place to people-watch and type. Also probably handy if you want to do your laundry.

I thought writing the first book was hard . . . Well, this one was no walk in the park. I appreciate the calming words of a number of people. In particular: my mum, Heather; Wifey for Lifey Dee; fellow authors Kate Solly and Emma Grey; *New York Times* best-selling author and all-around awesome person Sally Hepworth; my good friend Brendan Nolan; and author/mentor Lisa Ireland. Essentially this part of my acknowledgments is just to name drop how many authors I know.

To my first readers: Heather Merrett, Megan MacInnes, Alice Campbell, Andria Richardson, Dee Burton, and Aidan Prewett. I appreciate your insights, feedback, and encouragement. Thank goodness for the encouragement.

For their professional advice: Kylie Ladd, who is not just a great author, but a clever woman who is very interested in brains (largely because it's her job). She is also a hoot on the wine. Dr. Kara Donchi, who steered me in the direction of Bill Donchi, who was able to offer some very personal insights into how Joy might be feeling and acting. Thank you, Bill and Kara.

Professor Roger Byard, who speaks of forensics with an exuberance one wouldn't usually attribute to the field. Thank you for agreeing to talk to me about concealed homicides and other mysteries of death. I loved our chat and hopefully can bother you again in the future. (That is to say I will most definitely bother you.) And Dr. Kush Stevens for your doctorly advice.

I would like to acknowledge that any factual/medical/time travel mistakes made are mine and not a reflection on their advice.

Jen "first female detective at Homicide" Wiltshire, thanks for allowing me to pepper you with hypothetical murder questions. I was so lucky to get to work with you and do not forgive you for retiring.

Bich-Tram Maxwell for allowing me to distill your language skills down into a couple of Vietnamese swear words. They were really good swear words, if that helps.

If you know me and see your name in this book somewhere, chances are it's because of you. UNLESS you dislike the character, in which case it's a complete coincidence.

Mum and Dad, as always, huge thanks. You started all this. I mean this in all the ways. We miss you, Dad.

This book is ultimately about family but, in particular, sisters. I am most grateful for mine, Jessica, and I have no doubt she can't believe her luck for landing a sister like me.

This book is dedicated to my husband, Gary, who makes it very easy for me to step away to write or edit a chapter, or go to a book event.

To the fab four: my kids. In particular, numbers three and four, who have given me a front-row seat in life with twins. To the parents out there nursing babies into the night, fraying at the edges, loving those babies desperately, but wanting sleep even more, I can assure you that it won't last forever. Look after yourselves. And please don't tell them they're from the future.

Hearing from readers has been one of the joys (pun intended) of getting a book out there. So please, hit me up on the socials. I'd love to hear from you.

© Kelly Dwyer Portraiture

Kerryn Mayne is an author, former wedding photographer, and current police officer. When not at work attempting to solve crime, she is writing about it or preparing an endless stream of snacks for her four children. Kerryn lives in the bayside suburbs of Melbourne with her husband, children, and a highly suspect lovebird. She is the author of two novels: *Lenny Marks Gets Away with Murder* and *Joy Moody Is Out of Time*.